OXFORD ROAD

DEREK WALSH

Contents

Chapter 1 1
Chapter 2 23
Chapter 3 42
Chapter 4 55
Chapter 5 64
Chapter 6 68
Chapter 7 74
Chapter 8 84
Chapter 9 94
Chapter 10 100
Chapter 11 112
Chapter 12 120
Chapter 13 127
Chapter 14 135
Chapter 15 143
Chapter 16 149
Chapter 17 152
Chapter 18 158
Chapter 19 164
Chapter 20 172
Chapter 21 175
Chapter 22 181
Chapter 23 186
Chapter 24 193

Chapter 25	199
Chapter 26	205
Chapter 27	211
Chapter 28	222
Chapter 29	230
Chapter 30	237
Chapter 31	245
Chapter 32	254
Chapter 33	260
Chapter 34	267
Chapter 35	275
Chapter 36	281
Chapter 37	291
Chapter 38	296
Chapter 39	305
Chapter 40	315
Chapter 41	320
Chapter 42	330
Chapter 43	335
Chapter 44	340
Chapter 45	350
Chapter 46	357
Chapter 47	365
Chapter 48	375
Chapter 49	382
Chapter 50	389
Chapter 51	396
Chapter 52	406
Chapter 53	414
Chapter 54	421
Chapter 55	431
Chapter 56	438
Chapter 57	443
Chapter 58	452

Chapter 1

Why can't I just fall back into a deep sleep? Please, I need to. Please, just one more hour. Is that really too much to ask? I can't handle this. This is too fucking hard. What am I going to do? This is too much. Please, just let me go, God. Would it really be that bad for your plan, just to let me go? Why are you keeping me alive? What for? Am I really that important to you? In this state? I'm no use to myself, and if I'm no use to myself, then how I can be of any use to others? Why couldn't you just take me away, like I had asked? Like I prayed to you for?

And I had prayed. Last night, full on a whole box of Bin 67 and four Nytol, I had dropped to my knees, both in despair and in hope. I had never prayed like this before. In fact, I hadn't prayed for years. I was agnostic, but last night I was desperate. As an agnostic, I hadn't ruled out completely the existence of God, so I had prayed in sheer hope that if he did exist, then he would answer my prayers. If I could see that there was no point in continuing to battle my despair, then surely the one who made me could see this too, and perhaps he could, but refused to help me, because I questioned his existence. Perhaps the prayers of agnostics have far less potency than those of believers. That would make sense. Anyway, I was still here. *Fuck it.*

It was a bleak morning. Sheets of rain lashed ferociously against my bedroom window. The wind whistled and shrieked, muffling the distant tweeting of bird song. Usually I found the sound of rain lashing against my window and the screeching wind comforting. I loved the contrast of feeling warm and protected inside, against the rugged and striking forces of nature outside, whilst they rattled on my widow, trying to break in. But right now, these outside forces of nature were a thing of fear. They seemed like a warning, a bad omen perhaps. I was shivering, cowering, and short of breath. My heart was racing at what seemed like a dangerous pace. But I was angry too, really bloody angry.

Why had she done this? We had a bond – a strong bond. We had stood solemnly in front of a rather frumpy registrar, professing our deep love and a lifelong commitment to each other. We had professed this also, in front of our friends, cousins, and strangers – well at least to me they seemed rather strange – and with a solemn significance, we had professed this deep, unconditional love, in front of our parents. Then one day, a little over three months ago, it all changed.

A short while after her drunken admission of lost love, I had moved in to where I now was, and today, not only would I be leaving this place, but the town also.

I liked Guildford. What bound me to the place wasn't really the town, but the friendships that I had forged over my three years here. It seemed like a great injustice, that she had made the decision to break what we had, and that it was me who had to leave. I was struggling to understand this paradox of unconditional love, against what was now at best, a casual indifference.

Shivering in my pit, I wasn't ready to move. But I had to. I had too much to do. I'd had a whole week to perform a basic task, of simply picking up items, going over to a box, and then dropping items in. But no; instead, I had spent my evenings getting wasted on Bin, and listening obsessively to Vivaldi and Radiohead.

I pushed my creased, purple duvet to the side, exposing myself to the cold winter chill, and then stepped out onto the wooden-panelled floor. Suddenly I felt nauseous and ran to the toilet. I made it just in time. I wiped the chunks and slime from my mouth and looked in the mirror. My eyes were tiny dots of wine red, and my usual ghost-like complexion was peppered with blotches of faded rouge. I could almost imagine the capillaries, pleading with me to slow down.

Jodie, my boss at "Fastend Telefonic", had revealed himself to be the decent man that I didn't think he was. He had arranged with HR to give me a week off, fully paid. They had filed it under "bereavement leave", which meant that it wouldn't affect my statutory holiday pay. It wasn't as if I could afford to go anywhere. Still, I appreciated the gesture.

Through the slightly opened door, I peered with a sense of fear into the main room. It was a messy collection of shirts, T-shits, underwear, jeans, trousers, books, DVDs, CDs, pots and pans, and my gold-plated cheese toasty maker. It didn't seem so bad now. All I had to do was put things into boxes.

This was the least of my concerns. Looking at the boxes and my cluttered life, scattered all around the floor, the table and the sofa, I was suddenly struck with the finality of it all. I still loved her and was struggling to imagine how I was going to be able to ever live without her. I hated the fact that I loved her. It was far more than she deserved. I could feel my throat muscles tighten. I knew that I had far too much to do, but I needed to cry. So, that's what I did. Tears began to trickle down slowly, and then before long, I was sobbing uncontrollably. I didn't care if I was being self-indulgent, or if any of my neighbours heard me, through the paper-thin walls. I knew they were paper-thin, because I had received a few complaints about my music being too loud. It wasn't loud. It was just that the walls were thin. So, if my music disturbed them, then they were in for a real treat. Right now, I couldn't stop. I walked over to the table, pushed the mound of clothes off my CD player, and pressed play. It was loud - very loud. Antonio Vivaldi was still in from the night before. I was relieved that it wasn't "Radiohead". His homage to the much-maligned season of winter soared high, and around the room. It was beautifully overwhelming. "How do you like that now, neighbours?! Vivaldi and unashamed wailing! Enjoy it! It won't be a combination that you'll ever hear again! Enjoy it, you lucky bastards! Enjoy!"

My eyes were stinging from the tears. I wiped them away, but they seemed to come back, each sting increasing in sharpness. I had no choice. I had to at least try to compose myself. Right now, I didn't have the painful luxury of tears. There was too much to do. Although Greg wasn't due for at least seven hours, I knew that I'd have to do this now. Otherwise, I'd spend the next few hours immersed in despair, and then it would be too late. I couldn't do this to the big man.

The carpet on the whole, had actually looked cleaner than when I first moved in. There was however, one blemish – a rather significant one, both in size and colour – a large, red wine stain. I had tried absolutely everything to remove it. Salt, vinegar and a whole tub of Jiff lemon had been applied with haste. When none of these had worked, I had on the basis of "sound advice", poured half a bottle of white wine onto it, in the belief that it would somehow cancel out the red. I was sure this would work. Greg had told me that he had read somewhere that this was the best course of action to take, "when all else has failed". It was one which I was only prepared to take as a very last resort. Over the previous months, I had developed an enhanced fondness for white wine. So, by pouring out what was a little over half a bottle of my favourite wine – Bin Chardonnay 64, I was going strongly against my nature. Then, to see it not work, was an extremely difficult outcome to bear. In the end, I had no other option but to call a professional carpet-cleaning company, to send one of their people around to assess the damage.

Having been furnished with the full extent of my mishap, it was decided that given its severity, there was nothing else for it than to send in, "The Diamond." The smoky-voiced lady at the other end assured me, that while all their people were experts in the area of carpet-care, Daryl "The Diamond", had a particular knack at vanquishing the big splatters. Two days later, "The Diamond" arrived.

Upon consideration at what lay ahead of him, his conclusion was that he would have the rest of the carpet cleaner than ever, and with a citrusy scent of pine lingering, for a while after. This was provided that I limit smoking to the balcony, and banned red wine from my flat completely. "For red wine," he said, "has been the big player in the creation of this stain." I had feigned absolute surprise when informed of this. I wasn't sure if he was insane or pretending to be. I had then told him of my attempt at removal. I had included Greg's flawed wine removal theory, and my sheer surprise at its failure. He in turn had remarked that I was a fool for having wasted such a decent bottle of white.

"Well, can you remove it?" I had asked.

"I'll be honest, mate. I can't say for definite if I'll be able to remove it completely, but I can certainly do a job on it," had been his rather vague analysis.

Compared with my earlier despair, this response was good enough for me. So, we set about the task of dragging his hulking silver beast of a cleaning machine up three flights of wide marble stairs.

Despite his best efforts, and a stubborn resolve to not accept defeat, he had conceded reluctantly, that it wasn't the result he had hoped for. Every fibre of my being was urging me to tell him that this was a view we absolutely shared; however, that would have been unnecessary and mean-spirited. In not being able to achieve what he truly believed himself capable of, his spirit was more than sufficiently crushed. He had exhausted everything in his vast arsenal of industrial strength cleaning products.

It was apparent from the outset, when gliding back and forth on the carpet, over the crossed foam lines created by him and his "Numy", that here was a man who took absolute pride in his work. They had indeed sent the very best there was. This infectious enthusiasm had in turn instilled in me, a confidence that his earlier analysis, of merely just "doing a job" on it, was a rather poor attempt at modesty. This confidence, sadly, was to be misguided.

Apart from on television, in newspapers and looking in the mirror three months earlier, I had never witnessed such a look of abject defeat on anyone. There was poetry in his despair, in which he poured and massaged in six different types of concentrated cleaning fluid, to that stubborn spot. I felt for him. He had tried his best, refusing to yield in the face of such overwhelming odds.

He had offered to charge me only half of what we had agreed upon. This was not an option. It was wholly inconceivable. I had witnessed his entire heroic effort, willing him not just for my financial well-being, but for his own sense of worth, to vanquish this stubborn foe. The worry of losing my deposit faded willingly into insignificance.

Not only had I been adamant that he accepted the full agreed amount, I was insistent that he join me in a newly opened bottle of Bin. Mine was his final stop, and as I didn't have a car, I offered him my allocated parking spot. He lived close by, and said that if walking home proved tricky, then he could always jump in a taxi.

He explained how it had all started for him – getting into the cleaning game. He'd been in it for twenty-two years and had his own business for two of those. He spoke with great pride at being the owner of a second-hand Mercedes-Benz Sprinter. He gave me a riveting insight into what it is like to be behind the wheel of such a giant. He explained that with such power came a great responsibility, in how its driver should always show due consideration towards lesser vehicles. I got the strong impression that this man - Daryl Micklewhite - had little time for those in his position who use their might to lord it over more modest vehicles. He had certainly made me question all my previous pronouncements on "WHITE VAN MAN". His ultimate expression of pride though was reserved for his "Numy" – official name TT3035S Numatic 780417. He had told me of the many sacrifices he had made in order to acquire "her". If he was to ever amount to anything in the cleaning game, he said, then he'd have to have a Numatic. Every sacrifice – the lads' annual Benidorm bash, going to watch his beloved Chelsea, and even missing out on his father's stag do, had all been a price worth paying. He had recounted the quite varied jobs that he and his "Numy" had been on. He had enthused that when grabbing hold of her arms, "it's as if we become one and can take on the whole world." There wasn't a challenge at which they couldn't prevail.

Well, not quite. He again had looked at "that stain", with utter disbelief and bemusement. "It really must have been some party!" he had exclaimed. He was right.

It had started off well enough but had ended in disaster. I was three weeks into my tenancy, and was impatient to show everyone, including Tanya, especially Tanya, my new bachelor pad, and its accompanying lifestyle. It was very important for me to show all our mutual friends that not only had I prevailed, but had discovered an unparalleled sense of joy. To achieve this end, it was vital to underpin this statement with precision. There could be no lazy slip-ups. I would have to go to great effort and pain. It would all be worth it in the end.

Over the years of living with Tanya, I had often sat watching with sheer admiration as she with skilful efficiency, banished dust and general uncleanliness from the various homes in which we had lived. Watching her work was a privilege. From time to time, the suggestion was voiced that perhaps I should take the reins, even just occasionally. But each time, I respectfully and with regret declined, reasoning that as I lacked her finesse and deft touch, it would be nothing more than a hollow gesture.

As I glided effortlessly, cleaning utensils in hand, banishing all traces of dust and general uncleanliness from my own home, I felt vindicated in the knowledge that I had indeed observed and learned from the very best.

I had even prepared food. Few among our group of friends would ever consider going to the trouble of providing food. Such gatherings usually only constituted somewhere to go back to when the pubs had closed. I was particularly proud of my vol-au-vents and my Chicken Tikka Masala – both of which I had purchased, and without a trace of shame, had passed off as my own culinary masterpieces.

With the food "prepared", I had then set about transforming my front room, to reflect that of a man liberated from the constraints of marital bliss. A great array of "lads' mags" were scattered strategically throughout. My PlayStation and the accompanying discs were tidied, but remained in prominent view in front of my 48-inch plasma television. In the bathroom, my collection of various bottles of cologne were arranged in a neat, uniform line, alongside my exfoliating face wash for men, and my recently purchased straight-edge cut-throat razor.

With the stage set, I had then retired to the balcony of my period 70s block of flats, to ponder what lay ahead, wondering if my dear friends would see through this façade.

As the nicotine coursed through my bloodstream, I had looked up towards the top of the leafy Edwardian and Victorian streetscape which framed my block, wondering if all, one day, would once again be still.

Attendance had begun with a trickle at first. I was questioning the wisdom or lack thereof, of this showboating, suddenly wondering if it would all back-fire on me in spectacular fashion. Perhaps it was churlish, to think that my friends would attach even the slightest significance to the day, other than it being a party. I was wrong. Practically everyone had brought some form of flat warming present, and expressed how happy they were to see me in such good shape, and in such great spirits. By now, with the consumption of very generous amounts of Bin to the good, I was gradually coming into my own. I was proving to be the consummate host. The food had been very well received. Amazement at my ability to cook so well had been expressed all round. They were very much impressed with how well I kept the place, and envy had been voiced when admiring my almost cinema standard, centrally placed, "screen of dreams."

As the sound of laughter and general cordiality filtered around, with the film of cigarette smoke, the bell rang. I looked around. Everyone I invited had arrived, except two. When liberally dishing out the invites, I hadn't really given much thought to how I might feel seeing her, so soon after moving out. I had been operating on a wave of heightened optimism.

I believed it to be a non-issue – not worthy of even a second thought. I made my way to my front door, forgetting that I'd left it ajar, and there she stood. She appeared to be sporting a smug self-satisfied grin. She wasn't. She was happy with her lot and it showed. I resented her for that. Suddenly, any trace of confidence in my ability to project carefree nonchalance, evaporated. I was still very much in love with her. I just hoped that it hadn't showed.

I suddenly felt transported all the way back to that day, once again, the pitiful feeble soul, confronted with her life-shattering herald of liberation.

"No Nigel then today?" I had enquired.

"Err, well, I didn't think it would be fair to bring him, to be honest," she had replied.

This reply had seemed somewhat glib and fortified with arrogance. So, plunging me into despair wasn't enough? She had now felt the need to attack my pride? The one thing I had left? What exactly was she saying here? That her Nigel had something that I couldn't have? That I even wanted? Of course, I wanted her, but she wasn't meant to know this. Of course, the very thought of her new man, holding her like I used to, upset me greatly. I had to draw upon all reserves of strength, in order to keep hold of my dignity. I focussed, waiting to voice a response worthy of such a statement. After an uneasy protracted silence, I found that voice.

"Honestly, Tanya, that would have been no problem at all. I mean why would it be? After all, I did invite both of you. If I wasn't cool with the situation, then I wouldn't have invited you both. I'm actually really happy that you've moved on. It's all good".

Her response this time had been to shrug slightly, while forcing a polite smile, which resembled a slightly clipped grimace.

I was pleased with my counter punch, and at the clam manner in which it had been dispensed. It was perfect. I couldn't have hoped for a better one. More importantly, it had in no uncertain terms demonstrated, that I couldn't care less if her precious Nigel had come or not. The fact that his coming would have troubled me greatly, was wholly irrelevant.

Like the estranged former couple we now were, we embraced somewhat awkwardly.

Seeing her there, wearing that beige suede jacket that I had bought her on our day trip to Brighton, had given me a brief glimpse into happier times. It spoke of times when we had the world in all its beauty, in all its sadness, and in all its blessings, to face together. I could feel my disguise slowly slipping. I had to act quickly.

"Anyway Tan, you go ahead, I'll follow you in later. Help yourself to the vast array of drinks and get some of my homemade Tikka Masala down ya, before it's gone."

"Homemade Tikka Masala?!" she gasped. "But you can't even get toast right!"

I countered with a rather lame attempt at laughter.

"I AM impressed," she continued.

I made it into the bathroom just in time. I was on the verge of collapse. I looked in the mirror to see if there were any obvious signs that may have signified a slip in disguise. None seemed apparent. I was sure that my eyes at the very least, would have revealed the truth.

Although my place was warmly populated with many dear friends, I was now nonetheless struck with an acute sense of loneliness. Although only a little over two hours into my showboating, the party for me was now over. It was very much apparent that this whole party stunt had been a mistake. It was ill-judged and wholly ill-conceived. I had been very naïve to think that I was ready for such a challenge. I had wanted to have a party, but having one without inviting her and indeed Nigel was inconceivable. The invite had nothing to do with their sense of worth, but a strong affirmation of mine. If I had a party and didn't invite them, then it would be obvious that I was still finding the breakup difficult. On the other hand, inviting them was always going to be the ultimate in challenges. It was a challenge that on the outside I had risen gallantly to, but on the inside was one that had crushed me.

I continued with purpose over towards the main table, with the aim of replenishing my empty glass with yet another generous serving of Bin. As I entered the room, some of those assembled looked up acknowledging me. I returned a somewhat relaxed, cool, upside-down smile. I could feel a sharp jet of confidence enter me. Sadly, this was to be only a brief respite. With the table within a few short steps, I could suddenly feel control of my right foot abandon me, and over I went, knocking over a carelessly placed, opened bottle of merlot. Some of the contents emptied on to Tanya's suede ankle boots, with the rest depositing at the foot of the sofa, on to my bright, neutral-coloured carpet.

I had tripped over my carelessly positioned PlayStation. An object of personal pride had now played a large part in my downfall. I arched my neck upwards, as some of the assembled nervously tried to avoid eye contact. I couldn't help feeling that such irony was not lost on them.

On one level, Mr Micklewhite had, it seems, been spot on. It really had been some party.

Five months later, with the deposit safely and very graciously returned, I now sat alongside a great many shape of packed box, awaiting the arrival of Greg.

To my surprise, upon reaching the conclusion of the long-dreaded inventory, the landlord had smiled, gently bowed, and then handed over an envelope containing my full deposit. Considering that his once neutral-coloured, fine deep-wool deluxe Axminster carpet, now sported an unsightly off-red blemish, this was indeed an act of fine generosity.

Had I been of a mind to, there would have been nothing to prevent me from positioning myself strategically, thereby shielding him from it, and myself from awkward questions, which I knew I wouldn't have the mental resilience to endure. There was always the risk, that just like my friends eventually seeing through my proud façade all those months ago, I'd let something slip, compounding a potentially distressing scenario.

So I took the pragmatic decision to point it out to him, as soon as he came through the door. Before he had a chance to settle, I had furnished him with every detail I had on the subject. All throughout however, he had appeared curiously disinterested.

In the early days of separation, I had once in mid-sentence broken down in his presence. It hadn't been planned, but something perhaps in my subconscious, had told me that it was safe to let go in front of this man – this stranger. He had a type of face and voice that somehow exuded familiarity. His response had been to tell me in his kind, calm, gentle and reassuring manner, that none of this "matters one bit". With these words being replayed, I could feel myself about to implode yet again. This time however, drawing on whatever paltry resolve I could muster, I held firm.

Standing in the autumn twilight, I again wondered what would become of me. I wondered if I would prevail. I wasn't even sure if I wanted to. With a marked anxiety taking hold, I was finding it difficult to breathe. "Get a grip man!!" I exclaimed loudly. "Get a fucking grip!" I managed to compose myself sufficiently enough to answer my mobile. It was Greg.

"Hi Pudders," he said. "Are ya all set for your wee adventure?"

I was slowly dying inside, but I had to conceal this from him.

"Yeah, of course man. Bring it on! New chapter and all that! Reading here we come!"

"By the way, Pudders," he continued, "you'll owe me a massive drink after all this. You do realise that, don't you?"

Before I could answer in the affirmative, he continued…

"Just to let you know, I'm running about an hour late. That fucking network Nazi nabbed me just as I was leaving. He got me to help him patch some ports. Sorry 'bout that. I know how desperate you are to get this done. But look, we'll have a few beers tonight, when all this is behind us. Keep the faith old bean! Yeah?"

"Defo," I replied, "I'll be fine".

I was far from fine, but I was happy that I had managed to conceal this from him. This wasn't going to be easy on him either. He had worked ten hours that day, in a demanding job. He'd then have to drive one hour to get to me, fill his car with my crap, and then drive another hour to Reading. That was a lot of concentration for one day.

I rolled up a cigarette, and mindful of Daryl's advice, walked back towards my balcony to smoke it. I was suddenly struck with a bleak realisation, that this was the last time I would set foot on this three-foot-wide, by four-foot-long, slab of concrete. In an hour's time, with Greg's arrival, and his car packed, this place would no longer be my home. Officially of course, this was already the case. Once I was gone through, a giant punctuation mark would be struck. I was struggling. I knew that moving away made absolute sense. I had blown practically my entire, "starting up all over again" fund. I had been living well beyond my means for a couple of months now. I knew that it made sense, to move to a place in which I could afford to live within my means.

I was now being gripped by an almost overwhelming sense of finality, but this move had been planned for weeks. It wasn't as if it had all been foisted upon me at the last minute.

I was moving in to a two-up two-down Victorian townhouse, close to the centre of Reading. I would be sharing this house with a good-natured couple of Afrikaners, namely, Jacques and Adri. I knew Jacques relatively well, as I worked with him. I had met Adri on a few occasions. She seemed pleasant, and of a generous spirit. I was fond of both. In the midst of all this gloom was a dim, flickering hope, that perhaps the very action that may well destroy me, may on the other hand prove to be my redemption.

With far too much analytical intensity having taken place, time seemed to have passed by much too quickly, and with my life packed into Greg's 1987 model Sierra, we were ready.

As journeys go, this one hour seemed more like ten. Tanya and I made the same journey many times before. Tonight's journey was littered with reminders of these shared travels.

Long before we had reached the A329, punctuation marks were being struck with painful accuracy. This was it. This really was the end of my chapter with Tanya – the final piece. It now seemed that even if I had done the sensible thing, and attempted to prepare myself mentally for this night, the impact wouldn't have been any less acute. I took whatever solace I could from this, acknowledging that there was no right or wrong way that I could have handled it.

As we ambled slowly on past the Guildford Spectrum, its hulking presence striking high into the twilight seemed to be bidding me a not-so-fond farewell. It was as if the whole town in various physical embodiments had gathered in a festival of celebration, willing a swift conclusion of my tenure there.

After a long tense journey, the green fluorescent "Star" kebab house sign finally came into view, punctuating the end of an exhausting day. We pulled up just outside number 8 Ayrshire Street, Reading – my new home.

An hour later, with my life packed away into my room, we both made our way downstairs to greet my new housemates. They were watching "Coming to America". This rather twee, clichéd, and utterly hilarious film was the perfect tonic. As I had just spent an entire day submerged in a deep state of analysis, the last thing I would wish to do, would be to engage with anything that required yet more of the same. For the first time that day, a sense of calm began to descend upon my troubled mind. From the sofa at the back of this high-ceilinged front room, I began to drift off into this absolute drug of a film.

I had honoured my end of the deal, and had furnished not just myself and Greg, but the four of us, with a great many bottles of Bin. I had a feeling that perhaps salvation wouldn't be as out of reach as I thought. Still, I knew full recovery would be a long way off. Something was telling me that it wasn't a question of would I prevail, but when. Moreover, this time I knew that I wanted to.

After the film, at the insistence of Jacques, we didn't leave the room until we had "totally drilled" every last bottle of "piss" we could find! The conversation between us all had been effortless and warm. Nicely insulated from the perils of sobriety, we awkwardly made our way upstairs – Greg to the large double bedroom, and me, to my rather cluttered, slightly claustrophobic, box room.

After what seemed like one of the briefest escapes into semi-consciousness, we were wishing each other well for the day ahead.

"Hey Pudders, old bean," said Greg, in that faux aristocratic accent of his. "It'll be fine mate," he continued, in his calming Ulster burr. "Seriously mate. You'll be alright".

I wasn't convinced.

Chapter 2

Right now, I had two choices – return to my cluttered box room in an attempt to fall back into a state of semi-consciousness or investigate my new environs. Considering my cluttered little room, with its sickly sea-green-coloured walls and black borders, was relentlessly attacking my senses, the latter seemed by far the better option. Besides, curiosity was urging me onwards. I was intrigued to know where exactly it was that I had moved to.

With my decision made, I began with a certain degree of trepidation to journey down my street, towards the Oxford Road. Every Readingite I knew, when referring to Oxford Road, always insisted upon using the preposition of "the", thus implying a sense of notoriety.

I reached the corner of Argyle Street and Oxford Road and began to survey this unfamiliar streetscape. It was early still, and the reddish mid-morning sky illuminated this wide urban thoroughfare. From what I could gather, it appeared to contain the usual mix of buildings associated with such a place. It was raining slightly, and the wind was building, providing an apt haunting soundtrack to a place I really knew nothing about.

Traffic too was building, and a few lost souls wandered its rain-drenched pavements, whilst a kit of pigeons close by, competed for the best purchase on a discarded fried chicken container. Intrigued with what may lie beyond a rather bulky iron bridge, I preceded. The fall of rain had now increased but I didn't care.

In the near distance, the clattering of various shutters being lifted, provided a rhythmic symphony, marking the beginning of another day for the shop keepers. The road was gradually waking from its slumber, with more and more people of differing shades making their way with purpose towards their places of work.

Here I now was, standing alone in my brave new world. Mistakes of the past were again beginning to bear down heavily, illustrating with an acute rawness precisely why it was that I was now standing here. With my curiosity satisfied for now, I decided to make my way back towards my new little room, to prepare myself for what was sure to be a challenging day.

Today was my quarterly evaluation at Fastend Telefonic. The slippery Daniel Witterington would be the one providing this evaluation. Taking everything into account, this couldn't be happening at a worse time.

Usually, this would be nothing more than a minor irritation. I had enough sarcasm in my armoury to deal with Daniel's nonsense, and enough resolve to see me through it safely. Today would be an entirely different proposition, however. I couldn't imagine how I was going to be able to absorb platitude upon platitude, buzzword upon buzzword, and then have to listen whilst feigning interest, as he regaled me with all the gory details of his latest conquest.

Daniel was a walking corporate cliché. He was also quite probably the best-dressed man in Reading and, by extension, the whole of Berkshire. He had an unfathomable success with the fairer sex, or the "bints", as he liked to call his conquests.

I turned and made my way back under this imposing iron bridge. The rain had subsided, and a haze of mist lifted from the pavement. A cocktail of noise and petrol fumes accompanied the sense of urgency, with the static lines of traffic populating the road.

There was a certain type of essence about this place. I couldn't quite work out what this was.

The much-needed excesses of the night before, were now introducing their delayed impact robustly. I had no idea how I was going to be able to cope today.

I was in a trance-like state. I had to process it, but I couldn't. I wanted to cry but I was too numb. I wanted to vomit but I didn't feel ill enough.

Once back inside the house, I made my way upstairs quickly, whilst mindful to not wake Jacques and Adri. I quietly entered the bathroom, and gently shut the door. The door was of a thick balsam. This would ensure absolute privacy of sound. I then lifted the toilet seat, shoved two fingers down my throat, gagged, and then waited, both in fear and in hope, but nothing came.

Can't even get that right!

I looked in the mirror and observed this stranger looking back at me.

Well, Pudkin old chap. Here it is now. There ya are. Welcome to your new life. How does it feel to be pushing forty, living in a shared house, and with a failed marriage to your name? You really are such a sorry fat bastard!

But I actually wasn't fat anymore. In the early stages of separation, when getting back to my flat, I subsisted largely on a diet of dry white wine and fish finger sandwiches, whilst watching Rocky Balboa pit his wit against more polished opponents. This would in no way have been deemed acceptable behaviour when married – and rightly so. So, it seemed after all, that there were some advantages to being exiled.

Pound upon pound of lazy excess, had seemed to melt away as seamlessly as my marriage dissolved. In a very short space of time, I had shed roughly a quarter of my body weight. Some of my friends had commented that I had lost a worrying amount of weight, and too soon – others that they had never seen me look so healthy and so good.

The physical transformation which gave the impression of an outward confidence, masked my inner turmoil.

I couldn't vomit and I couldn't even cry. If I couldn't perform these basic tasks, how then was I meant to function, even in a most modest sense?

It suddenly struck me, that the world would keep turning whether I was in it or not. After all, we all have to die sometime. No one is immortal. Surely it was better to check out while I still had my health. I had never looked so good in my life. Die (reasonably) young, and leave a beautiful body or some other such trite sound bite. If we're all going to die one day, it seemed illogical to spend my life getting to this point, in a deep sense of despair. I decided that I would explore this option in more detail. A rather eerie sense of calm began to descend upon me, with the realisation that I now had the means to finally bring about closure to my despair. Right now though, I would have to put all this to the back of my mind. I had an evaluation to attend.

An hour later, and mindful of the time, I walked briskly along the leafier Bath Road. I hadn't really noticed how majestic it was up until now. The stretch between the town centre and beyond my place of work at 45-47, didn't contain a single retail outlet. It was purely residential, thereby lacking the sense of pace of Oxford Road. It was a road rather than a street-road, which I had decided Oxford Road was. The mixture of Doric granite-columned mansions, and Bath-stone-rendered houses, illustrated its majesty.

I crossed the road, almost slipping in a mulch of congealed leaves. I really was dreading this day.

With the main entrance in view, I walked over, slid my ID card down the slot, and walked in through the spacious mezzanine reception area. I noticed a few familiar faces, but none that I really knew well. I was glad of this, as I couldn't stomach being asked yet again, how I was bearing up. Everyone in the office knew that I had moved to Reading, and why. It was embarrassing.

Aside for a few nodding glances from people I recognised, but didn't know, I arrived largely undetected at *Kennet side me*eeting room. I was ten minutes late, but Daniel wasn't around. On one hand, I was relieved, as I was in no mood to endure the smug dressing down, which I knew he would revel in. On the other however, with no distractions to occupy my mind, this left me at the mercy of a sadness that I didn't feel fully equipped to deal with.

I looked around in an attempt to occupy my mind.

It was no good. The reality of my situation was now pressing down hard. The option to simply end it all, now was becoming more attractive by the second. *That's it!* I thought. *I'm doing this.* I tore off a piece of A4 from my pad and began to write. It couldn't involve violence. What if it went wrong? What if it didn't work? What if I survived, only to have to lead a more miserable, more restricted life?

It would have to be achieved as seamlessly as possible, and with little or no pain having been sustained. Based on this plan, the best way to achieve this, I decided, was to simply fall into a deep sleep and never wake up.

It would involve sleeping pills and wine. This seemed the perfect way to go. Why bring pain into the equation if it isn't necessary? But where would I do it? Straight away, I ruled out my room. I couldn't check out in such depressing surroundings. Thinking about it now, somewhere along the river could be a good spot to do it. In fact, it would be perfect. I have always felt at peace by rivers. Whenever I felt stressed, or just generally troubled in any way, I would head straight to the river. It seemed to offer such strong healing qualities.

Living for a brief period in West London, before coming to University, I liked to stroll along the Thames towpath, visiting along the way some great riverside pubs. From the wooden decking area, I loved to gaze out on to the wide expanse of the river, simply just drinking in the various forms of activity that accompanied it. It was my perfect place to be.

Among the various experiences amassed here, one in particular stood out. It really was quite profound.

Bored and restless one day, I had decided to take the short tube journey from my home in Putney to Richmond. It was a crisp sunny day, and a light drizzle deposited refreshing spray, as I kicked up mounds of congealed leaves along the towpath. I had noticed patterns developing lately, in which my mood could change at just the slightest provocation. There weren't always obvious triggers either, which was confusing. When I was bored, that was when I was at my most vulnerable. Boredom usually opened the gates to those dark elements, which seemed to attack me at will.

A solitary red kite glided gracefully above me, scanning the surroundings for discarded scraps of food. The sunshine glistened on the river vessels of varying sizes, whilst the river fowl competed for pieces of stale bread and other leftovers, from the foot of the wooden decking of the Albert pub.

There was a decent enough-sized crowd in – not too many – not too few. There were enough in, to provide me with a chance to people-watch, but not enough to induce a sense of claustrophobia.

I had noticed them almost straight away. They were a very handsome couple, with a certain timeless quality about them. Of a similar age – mid to late sixties, their animation and a perceived eccentricity seemed to set them apart from the groups of families enjoying their Sunday roast, and of friends mostly attired in Rugby shirts. I wanted to be in the midst of what was obviously an enthralling conversation. I wasn't ready to intervene and invite myself in just yet. I decided to sit back and wait to be asked to join them. I wasn't one for butting in.

Her long slim fingers seemed to act like a wand, as her hands gently swayed, directing the conversation. It was clear who was dictating the pace, but it was a gentle, unhurried pace. It all seemed entirely in harmony, with the soft refreshing breeze fanning us down. He seemed absolutely at ease, playing the role of listener. There was rhythm in the way he nodded in affirmation. I had known many strong, loyal and caring couples in my life, but none that seemed so at ease and in complete harmony with each other, as this one. I was becoming increasingly moved with the passing of each second. Perhaps it mightn't be such a good idea to introduce myself after all. They were perfect as they were. They didn't need anyone extra polluting their air space.

After a while though, curiosity won out, and I introduced myself. "Hi, I hope you don't mind my imposing on your time, but I'm a bit bored sitting by myself. Is it OK if I join you? Oh, my name's Alastair, but my friends call me Pudkin."

"Well then, as we don't know you," replied the man, "we shall call you Alastair, and of course, we would be delighted if you join us. Wouldn't we, Dolly?"

Dolly nodded in the affirmative. She had an air of effortless sophistication about her – as did he. She had the look of classic 1950s Hollywood glamour – a bit of a Garbo, albeit one in her sixties. He had the look of a mature Cary Grant. Curiously though, neither seemed as animated as they had initially appeared.

I pulled out one of the two vacant heavy wooden chairs and sat. I suddenly felt nervous and slightly awkward, as if I was imposing. Initially, when introducing myself, I had felt at ease, but not now. The previously enthralling conversation that I had witnessed was no more. They had a look which politely told me that I had put them in an impossible position. Appearing polite, they couldn't have possibly spurned my courteous introduction, but it was clearly an interruption, and that had irritated them. I felt terrible. I wanted to leave, but I had no idea how to voice this with care and diplomacy. I decided that the best thing would be to remain silent and wait for them to start things off. However, both remained sullen and stoic.

With the passing of every silent minute now, a strong feeling of irritation was taking hold. Finally, after a long-drawn-out protracted silence, I stood and politely excused myself.

"Errm, I'm really sorry, but I think I've obviously misread the situation. I'm sorry for imposing. I'll leave you to it."

"Please no," said the man. "But you mustn't go." His deep furrowed brow was fixed, and his expression intense. This unnerved me.

"You see," he said, "within our joy, there lurks a deep sorrow. For us, it is but a fleeting moment in time. The others no doubt see it differently. Oh, and do pardon my ignorance, the name is Stanley Bruce-Patterson and this fine lady is Dolly, my dear wife."

With the level of intensity abating, I again took my seat and smiled.

"Of course," said Dolly, "life isn't always as it appears. Isn't that right, Stanley?"

"Oh indeed, dear Dolly, or one could go further and ponder, if it is as it appears, then is it appearing as perhaps it should appear?"

"Quite," replied Dolly, as she tilted her head downwards slightly, in recognition of such a profound response to an equally profound statement.

Events were now becoming slightly surreal.

Stanley continued, "you see, sometimes we seem to drift in and out, around and high, out and about. Why, sometimes, we aren't entirely sure, if we are meant to be here or indeed anywhere."

There was a flowing, almost musical rhythm, to the way he sounded. I was mesmerised. I could feel myself being drawn closer to this effortless, free-flowing assonance.

"Ah yes, dear Stanley," chimed Dolly. "Out, around, high, and about."

Stanley smiled, gently tapping his hands on the table. "Indeed, my dear, sweet, Queen Dorothy," as he joined her.

"Out, around, high, and about! Out, around, high, and about! Out, around, high, and about! Out, around, high, and about. Out, around, high, and about. Look out on Mother Thames. Look out and drift out far. Look out and drift out wide. Look out and drift out wide."

I was in a trance-like state, unable to avert both my mind and presence away from their rhythm, which had become quite intense. Suddenly they stopped. Stanley looked over at me smiling. "Did you know young Alastair, that rivers have such ethereally enhancing, enriching qualities? And none more so, than the most majestic of all rivers - Mother Thames. She has a voice. If only one would listen. If only one would listen."

"Ah yes," continued Dolly, "one must listen to Mother Thames. She does have a voice. Sadly, too few have neither the spirit, nor the resolve to hear it. But I would imagine, you Sir, are of the spirit." She then leant forward, and resting her hand gently on mine, continued, "do this, Pudkin. Shut your eyes briefly, open them, then look out upon her, and listen for her voice. You must do this now." She seemed quite insistent.

This was all getting a bit weird now, but in the interests of diplomacy, I did as instructed. I closed my eyes briefly – not more than five seconds, opened them again, and then looked out onto the Thames. As expected, I didn't hear a voice, but to my total astonishment, when I turned back, they were gone. I couldn't explain this. I hadn't heard any noise to suggest chairs being pulled out, or glasses being lifted. The table, apart from my half-finished glass of wine, was now entirely empty.

Hastily, I fixed my coat back in place, picked up my satchel, and moved rather speedily towards the exit. On the way out, I asked the passing waitress who had served me earlier, if she had seen them leave. With a confused expression, she replied that she hadn't seen anyone else at the table all day.

I wasn't sure if I had imagined the whole thing, or, well the other possible scenario really was too implausible to contemplate.

The experience that day had left an indelible mark. I would never view the Thames in quite the same way again. It still had a strong power, which could draw me in. Just simply looking out onto it sometimes is such a calming, enriching experience. So it was decided. I would see out my last day by it. I would do this tomorrow. Not a single more day was to be wasted.

As my GP had ceased issuing me with prescription sleeping pills, I would do it on "Nytol". I reckoned two packets should do the job. I would crush them into powder form, and over the course of the night ingest it, all washed down with silly amounts of Bin. The plan was I'd call in sick tomorrow morning, buy a tent from Millets, pick up two boxes of Bin, and head to Caversham. At some point during the evening, I would warmly drift off, and by the morning I'd be dead. As the tent would shield me from any ravenous rats and waterfowl, my body at least on the periphery would remain largely intact. So, when some poor unfortunate did discover me, my otherwise intact body would lessen the impact. Well, that was the hope anyway. I didn't fear death. I now embraced it, but I did feel a strong sense of guilt when faced with the prospect of a poor innocent coming across my corpse. Whatever way I looked at it, and however I attempted to rationalise it, the fact remained that I was going to do it, and whatever form that took, someone, some innocent person who had caused me no harm whatsoever, would have to deal with the impact. Honestly, if there was a different way – simply disappear into thin air, or even spontaneously combust – that would have been my preference.

I folded the now full A4 sheet of detailed plans and slid it into my inside pocket. Mentally, I was now fully ready. As I now had firm plans, all traces of fear and anxiety evaporated. The only negative feeling that remained now was impatience. As this evaluation would be taking on no significance whatsoever, my impatience at this whole pending process was building.

I was in two minds whether to stay and grind it out, or simply get up and leave. After all, what was the worst that could happen? They'd sack me?! But something was urging me on to stay, for the time being at least. If I left now, then I would be drawing attention to myself. This would raise questions – many questions. It was best to start the day off as normally as possible. No one would question me ringing in sick, given my current situation. In fairness to management, they had shown a surprising compassion, and had said that I could take as much time off as I needed.

Just as I was beginning to relax again, the door went, and in walked Daniel. What was he wearing this time!? Apart from his usual smug grin, he was dressed head to foot in what can only be described as princely attire. This was all complemented with a highly stylish light-brown mohair overcoat. It seemed that every time we met he was wearing something new. I wish I could say that he smacked of the nouveau riche, who in an attempt to impress "their friends", throw money at impulse purchases, without due consideration for taste, but this wasn't the case. He was a man of impeccable taste, at least when it came to dress sense, but this was where any semblance of finesse ended. I wondered how long it would be before he filled me in with all the details of his latest conquest.

"El-Puderino Sir! How's it hangin' my friend?"

I hated being called that, and I wasn't his friend.

"Mucho apologies for the lateness fella. I got accosted by yours and my favourite nutter, Pissycombe! What is that bloke on?!"

Daniel was referring to Gerald Piscombe. Gerald wasn't in any way mad. In fact, he was the ultimate conformist. All his "mad" actions were nothing of the sort. These were actions sanctioned by people like Daniel, and the rest of middle management – in-jokes. He didn't dare to come up with his own ideas of madness. He was far too mindful of eventually one day reaching the zenith of that greasy corporate pole.

He removed his overcoat, and on a table of 10 seats, placed it over the one next to mine.

Great, I thought.

He then, as if making some sort of statement, slammed his briefcase down hard on the table, unclipped the clasps, waited for it to spring open, then removed a bundle of stapled A4 sheets.

"Anyways, Mr El-Puderino. How ya diddling? All good, fella?"

I forced what I thought was at least the semblance of a genuine smile.

"Yes. All is good chap. All good."

He smiled in response. "Cracking! Anyway, as I is running well late, I'm going to keep this as brief as possible. That Pissycombe has a lot to answer for. I tell ya."

I really was in no mood to engage with someone I didn't have a lot a time for, and about someone whom I had absolutely no respect for, in this faux banter.

"Yes, he really does have a lot to answer for. What a nutter indeed," I responded with a smug indifference.

"Ha, ha Pudds. You do crack me up, man!"

Pudds, this time?!?

"Basically, we have a file on you, and we need to address a few points – a few areas we have identified that need improving. Only joking! Your face, mate! Priceless! No seriously, I don't think you need me to tell you this, but you are the best of all repeat sales. Your stats are off the scale fella!"

This time, I was genuinely surprised. Strangely also, it felt quite heartening to be hearing this, even though I hated my job. I had been doing this now for three years, although it felt a lot longer. Yes, I was good at what I did, but I wasn't the best – far from it. He was being nice. There was a good chance that he was right though. I had hit the highest figures in this period. Considering that Dim Dave was off on his honeymoon, Pookesh and Steve were off "bashing it" over in Ibiza, this just left old Mike Tyler, and he was a trainee. So, all things considered, it wasn't that much of an achievement. Still, I'd take it, all the same.

It's quite funny how things can go full circle. It was twenty years since my school days ended, yet here I was in a job in which I was required to wear a uniform of sorts. It was compulsory to attend classes. We were constantly berated by management for not keeping our areas tidy, and when the big bosses were on conference calls, we were berated for not being quiet enough!

"The only thing I will say what might sound negative, and I don't want to say it, trust me, but them upstairs…"

He loved saying "them upstairs". Oh, he must have felt so empowered, when an opportunity arose to use that term.

"Upstairs have told me, that you need to start using the script mate. You use it sometimes, but you need to use it all the time. It don't really present the type of image that we like to project here at "Fastend Telefonic". That's all. Apart from that mate, you are smashing it. It just remains for me to get you to sign what we've discussed."

What WE'VE discussed?! I thought. Aren't discussions meant to include more than one person?

I leant forward and signed, Daniel countersigned, and that was it. With a decided lack of nonsense, my quarterly evaluation at "Fastend Telefonic" was concluded, for the final time.

"Laters Pudders," said Daniel, as he pulled the door handle. "Oh, yeah! I forgot to tell you. You know that bird I was telling you about? The one down "The Grapes"?"

Oh here we go! I thought. "What? The one with the big tits, and that dirty smile? Misty, isn't it?"

"Yeah, that's the one."

"You may have mentioned her once or twice."

"Well, she came back to mine after kicking-out time, and I smashed it – all night mate! Every angle played, both holes filled! She couldn't get enough of the Witters-man!"

"So, will you be seeing her again?"

"Will I fuck mate! I need to share the love! Laters fella. Must pop!" He then left.

I drained the last of my coffee and placed the cup back on the table. Relaxed and confident in my plans, and with my last ever evaluation at this place now behind me, I left Kennet side meeting room. Recently, "them upstairs" had decided that in the interests of "transparency" and "going forward", it would be a nice idea to re-arrange the whole office into an open-plan model. I really fucking hated it. Accounts were now staring at Procurement. HR were now staring at PR. And we in Sales were now being stared at by Strategy and Planning.

As I approached my desk, it suddenly struck me that today would be the last time that I would ever have to face such a sorry sight of losers ever again. More importantly though, I really had no idea where Millets was.

Chapter 3

Fortunately, Millets was easy enough to find. Phoning in sick had gone as I expected it would. No awkward questions had been raised, when I told them that I'd had a relapse, and that I needed more time. Ben – my new line manager – had simply told me, "don't worry about this place. You need to concentrate on getting yourself right." This kind response had almost moved me to tears. It had also made me feel guilty, especially in light of what I planned to do today. Still, I knew that if I was going to go ahead with it, I'd have to block any feelings of sentiment.

I didn't realise how close Caversham was to Reading. The taxi driver, when hearing where I wanted to go, had refused to take me. This was a first for me, but when he told me how close the place actually was, I understood why. It wouldn't have been worth his while. He finished it all off, by lecturing me on the subject of laziness. I didn't have to listen to him. I could have just walked away, but his indignation had compelled me to stay put.

The distance between Millets at Reading Retail Park to the Caversham side of Reading Bridge may well indeed have felt short, if not weighted down with a tent, a sleeping bag, a rucksack, and two boxes of wine. On foot, it should only have taken five minutes tops. But as I had to stop every few steps, it felt more like twenty.

Wearily, I made my way slowly and awkwardly down the granite steps of Reading Bridge. It was a slightly overcast morning, and it looked as if the heavens could open up at any time. I had hoped to go out in effervescent blazing sunshine, but right now, my main concern was where to pitch the tent, and to do so before the angry sky vented. I wasn't the best at putting up tents. On a good day, it was an exercise in extreme boredom, but this time, unlike Glastonbury, there would be no friends to erect it for me.

I noticed an upturned tree. Erosion had, over time, fashioned its trunk into a perfect seat. The flailed outstretched branches formed a natural boundary. It was perfect. I had found my final resting place.

I placed all the kit down neatly in a pile and looked down along the river. In the distance I could see an identical bridge to Reading Bridge. Both created the perfect vista. The nearby tennis courts, due to the early hour and the inclement weather conditions, stood empty. Across the river, the lights were being called into play, as the nearby offices of Thames Water and Reading Mutual slowly began to come alive.

In the near distance, the straight continuous line of river was interrupted slightly, by what appeared to be a small island, covered in dense thicket.

It was too early to pitch up now and just sit around. I didn't feel right starting on the wine at such an early hour. Besides, if I started now, then it would be gone by eight! I was determined to get as many hours in as I could, before drifting off for the final time.

I wanted to venture upstream along the towpath and explore. My mindset certainly didn't feel like that of one about to kill himself. I was very excited.

I moved my pile of kit off to the back of the trunk and covered it up with some branches. I felt that it was in a safe place and would remain undetected, whilst I ventured upstream. It didn't matter if it rained now; everything was protected, and I didn't mind getting wet or even drenched.

The lure of Mother Thames really was quite strong now. I felt very much at home here, and ironically now, very much at peace. I couldn't have chosen a better and more appropriate place for my final day. It was less built up then the Kingston part of it that I had visited many times. One side was populated with a small cluster of low-to mid-rise offices and some rows of townhouses.

Pockets of moored vessels bobbed and swayed, fuelled by a determined breeze. The side that I was on, apart from a group of four tennis courts, seemed mainly populated with willow trees, their outstretched limp branches sweeping gently in from the river's edge.

I went back to the pile, and covered it with yet more branches, just to be on the safe side. Although it felt as if I had all the time in the world, I didn't. Before long, this day would pass and that would be it. I would fill my last day with wine, tobacco, and nature. *Fuck it*, I thought. I can always get another one, as I pulled one of the boxes of Bin from my rucksack.

I hastily punctured the seal, pulled the plastic nozzle out, and brought it to my lips. I pressed the nozzle and let the nectar flow down. If I wasn't about to kill myself, the ease at which the wine flowed, would have given me great cause for concern. I must have drunk the equivalent of nearly two large glasses in one go. It was a good rush! I was now ready to start traipsing.

I wondered how it had all come to this. It seemed rather poignant that only four years ago, almost to the day, I was standing in front of the registrar, alongside my beautiful bride-to-be, Tanya Matterelli. My mind was infused with all manner of chemicals rushing through my bloodstream at that moment. I had never felt so enlivened in all my thirty-two years on this planet. Such was the extent of my emotions that day, I had struggled to prevent a deluge of joy from breaching my walls of pride. The love that I felt had been beautifully intoxicating. I had wondered if she too, had been experiencing the same, or even similar levels of ecstasy.

I have never been a believer in the concept of fate. At best, I've been a sceptic and at worst, I've dismissed it entirely out of hand. However though, the fact that we even met, contained far too many variables for me not to at least consider it.

We met at the University of Hertfordshire. Now that in itself doesn't sound like the workings of fate until you consider that unlike the vast majority of students who ended up there through the clearing process, we had chosen to study there, or in my case, I had chosen to stay there for four years. Then, there was the small matter of Tanya's engagement breakup. Had that not happened, she would have followed her husband all the way over to the Gibraltar naval base. Instead, she chose to temporarily break her own heart, in the interest of personal development. Besides, twenty was far too young to be throwing one's life away on marriage. At that age, there are still a great many more mistakes that need to be made.

She was the perfect embodiment of a union between an Indian mother and an Italian father. She had taken great delight in showing everyone family photos – in particular ones of her parents when they were "our age". It wasn't difficult to see how she had turned out the way she had. She was tall and elfin-like, with blemish-free light-brown skin, topped off with a mane of silky, straight black hair and punctuated with deep almond-shaped, brown eyes.

Although my behaviour hadn't exactly lent itself well to the continuation of my marriage, I felt that she had just given up too easily. I'd agree, I wasn't the easiest person to live with. I was moody. I could switch at just the slightest provocation. I was prone to bouts of depression. I smoked. I drank too much, and on a couple of occasions, I had even gone off the radar for days on end. All this in her mind were the actions of a very selfish man, who was never prepared to put her first. I could see how taking all these into account, she had arrived at that conclusion. I even put myself in her position, to imagine what it would be like to be on the receiving end of this. I had concluded that I too, couldn't live with "me!". Still, she could have tried harder. Who was I kidding? *She really couldn't have tried any harder than she did!*

I passed on down by the side of the tea hut, and under the giant canopy created by the branches of the nearby willow tree. Yellow spears of sunlight were beginning to pierce the clouds, so perhaps I would get to depart in glorious sunshine after all. As I followed the meandering pathway, the willow trees were joined by a mixture of evergreens and deciduous, in various colours, defining and enhancing the manicured landscape of the nearby park.

Before long, I had arrived at the beginning of Caversham Bridge. To the right of me stood a War Memorial, with rows of poppy wreaths laid neatly at its base, and to the left of that was an interesting waterside pub and restaurant. I could almost picture the crowds of young men and women, high on the excesses of a typical weekend, give each other the "glad eye" across the room. I wondered, statistically, how many of these encounters had led to marriage, and of these marriages, how many had ended in divorce? And out of these divorces, how many sad, lonely losers had taken that ultimate leap of doom?

I stepped onto the bridge and waited until a gap in the traffic presented itself, allowing me to cross the busy road. I looked down towards the continuous expanse of the river. It really was quite sublime. The sun had now fully broken through, and the bright blue sky framed all in view, perfectly. I carried on down the side of the Crowne Plaza hotel. It was now close to ten, and the aromatic smell of freshly ground coffee beans hung tantalisingly in the air, near a café ship. As I passed by it, a friendly couple in their mid-twenties smiled and nodded at me. I returned the gesture. I suddenly felt a lump in my throat. This seemingly simple gesture from people who didn't know me had moved me greatly.

The benefits of being dead soon far outweighed those of deciding to battle on through my depression. It wasn't a decision that I had taken lightly either. I honestly couldn't see a way out of this dark cloud popping up whenever it felt like it, making my life hell. With the occasional welcome respite, this cloud was a constant in my life. I was of no use to anyone in such a state. What would be the point in continuing, just so I could exist for the sake of others? I wouldn't expect anyone to live simply because it was what I wanted, if they felt that they couldn't. I had tried. I had been staring into the abyss now for far too long and I'd had enough.

I didn't fear death at all. I used to when I was younger. Growing up Methodist, like all in my flock, the virtues of restraint, devotion, prayer, guilt, and the controlling of one's desires, were constant themes in my life. To attain salvation seemed an unrealistic goal. So, one day, I simply stopped believing or at least started expressing doubts. I couldn't go fully into the atheist camp though. That seemed a little too final. I was quite happy staying agnostic, but now I was having doubts about that stance too.

All animals, including humans, are a series of sinew, muscles, bones, and organs, all connected with a network of interwoven tendons and arteries. How arrogant to think that only we can have a higher force called God, and the rest of animal kind don't! What makes us so special? What makes us so important? Is it because we can walk upright and design guns? No, none of this makes any sense. No, tomorrow, there will be no man with a long beard, wearing robes, framed in radiant, effervescent light, sitting on a throne, waiting there to judge me.

I had planned this well. When I got home last night, I had crushed up my Nytol, and divided it into five bags. When I got back to base, I would set up my tent and hit the wine – hard at first – and then sip slowly over the course of the night. At around 6 PM, I would start introducing the powder, one bag at a time, on the hour.

This place really enlivened me. I felt far more alive right now than I had done in years! If such a place did exist, then this would be the Garden of Eden. Most people who top themselves, do so in dingy rooms or in litter-strewn, piss-drenched alleyways. I really did feel privileged to be going out in such lush surroundings.

Across the river, the bells of an old stone-clad Norman church sounded its celestial greeting, far and wide.

Along the way, I found another fallen tree with an even better-crafted natural seat. I was tired, so I went over and sat. The Thames was now beginning to fill up. Boats of many different sizes, functions, and colours joined the collective of waterfowl, on this glorious day. I honestly could not remember feeling this happy before. The fact that on this day, a day of such heightened joy, I would choose to end my life, would to most rational people, sound like a waste – ironic perhaps, but not to me. It all made perfect sense. I can't imagine that there is a single person alive who would wish to leave in any other state of mind. The only difference with me was that I was bringing this process forward. *If there is a God, then perhaps this is his way of telling me that he absolutely understands why I am doing this. Perhaps today is a glimpse into what I can come to expect when I do pass. If there is such a place as paradise, then I can't imagine that it's any more splendid and sublime than here.*

A bright garland-adorned paddle steamer sounded its horn as it passed by me. It was full of people all holding glasses, in celebration of a glorious and perfect day. I felt a strong sense of fellowship with them.

OK. This was it. I was ready. I had satisfied my curiosity. I hoped that I would be seeing this place again after tonight. If I wouldn't be, then that would be OK too, as I'd be dead and it wouldn't matter.

I had now lost all concept of time. I must have been sitting on this tree for about two hours, and I had no idea of where the time had gone.

All had now become still. I was excited. It was a great source of relief, that the black cloud would and could no longer stalk me.

I passed by the café ship. There were now a lot more people on board, no doubt enjoying their cream teas in the sun. That nice friendly couple from earlier though had left. I said a silent prayer in tribute, wishing them well for the journey ahead. I wished them fine children. I wished them understanding, and I wished them longevity.

I passed under the tunnel of Caversham Bridge and back along the towpath. Across the way, groups of kids were playing football. Jumpers and coats provided the goal posts. Their sound of laughter, shouts of enthusiasm, and sheer enjoyment, seemed to bounce off all sides of the bridge and then back again.

My mind was cast back to the days of playing football in my local park in Edinburgh. As was commonplace in that part of the world, it often rained. It seldom bothered me though. It was never anything more than a slight inconvenience. I could almost hear the frustrated calls of my father, resonate loudly as he told me "get back in the box son." "Use your instep!" "Ah for fuck sake SON! Use that instep! Christ!"

I passed by the offices of Thames Water. It was lunch time and crowds of office workers were out, enjoying the sunshine and making the most of their single hour of freedom.

As I stepped out onto Reading Bridge, I was met with a soft soothing breeze. The tall, symmetrical line of pine trees at the back of the tennis courts rustled, as their tips swayed gently in unison, like a conductors' baton.

I arrived at my base, calm, focussed, and ready. I brushed aside the branches and leaves and picked up my tent. Usually, this would be a real pain, but now it wasn't. With ease, I slid off the sleeve containing it, and threw its contents to the ground. Assembling this would be much easier than I thought.

As I pushed the poles through the sleeves, I wondered what the problem had been. It was easy. Before long, my tent was up, and with the guy lines secure and taught, the process could now begin.

I lifted up my box of Bin and poured a large glass.

With the tent entrance facing the river, I sat on my trunk seat and looked out. With their liberty from servitude concluded, the office workers had gone back to continue dispensing their various duties.

I suddenly felt lonely. *Ah well. This is it now*. Bin was gradually taking effect and I began to relax happy into my self-induced destiny.

The hours had just seemed to fly by seamlessly, and before I knew it, it was nearly 10 PM. The line of art deco lights of Reading Bridge and the dimmed office lights nearby, combined to cast a colourful, flickering image of tranquillity upon the river. I felt at peace. Ready now to depart.

I pulled out my phone to check the time. There were a few texts, but I didn't bother reading them. There was no point. It was 10.05, time now to take my final bag. I shook the remaining of the boxes to see what was left. Judging by the sound of it, I reckoned there was the equivalent of a large glass in there. Silly amounts of Bin and what I had ingested of the powder, had combined perfectly to sufficiently numb my senses. *All the same though, I may as well take it, just to be on the unsafe side.*

I removed the remaining small translucent bag from my jeans, pulled the strips apart, and brought it to my mouth. This was it. *Goodnight. Goodbye.*

Chapter 4

~

A sunny Broad Street was humming to the sound of the weekend. The various street-vendors heralded their own "absolutely unbeatable bargains". The laid-back Saturday strollers sauntered nonchalantly along their way. An eclectic band of buskers, from pan pipe players rasping their haunting Andean melodies, to a rather nervy elderly magician, and an "Axe God", metal guitarist, were performing to impress, and in the rock-seated mini-auditorium outside M&S, the stage, or rather the altar, was set. Mayfly was up next.

You always knew where you were with Mayfly. He had a great ability to delve deep down into the very soul of people, and extract honesty as skilfully as a miner brings precious minerals to the surface. He had all the attributes necessary and associated with being a very effective street preacher. He was blessed with a combination of boundless energetic charisma. He was fearless. He was empathetic, and to top it all off, he was a thing of incredible natural beauty. With a dark blonde flowing mane of shoulder-length curls, chiselled features, and deep hypnotic brown eyes, he had the air of a Jim Morrison about him. To the outside observer, he had it all, but to those who knew him, who really knew him, he had very nearly lost it all.

It happened roughly two years ago. High on the excesses of a great night out, he and his flatmate Ben Jerem were making their way down Zinzan Street, when calamity struck. A BMW suddenly mounted the pavement at speed, hitting Ben head-on. He had just bounced off the bonnet and down into a nearby basement, his flesh being ripped apart by the rusty gables, down along the way. The outcome was never really in doubt. Death was instantaneous.

Giles Kingston, as he was then known, was never the same after this. He availed himself of every free counselling session on offer. All had proved fruitless. Before long, he found himself sectioned – an unwilling resident of Prospect Park Hospital.

Then, one day in May, his salvation finally arrived in the most unexpected of guises – a mayfly. Lately, he had been showing steady and gradual signs of improvement. The most recent cognitive analysis had indicated that he was making steady progress, and it was agreed that they would build him up towards release. What this meant was that they would gradually re-acclimatise him to aspects of the "Non-Prospect Park World". On one such day, supervised of course, he was walking by the River Kennet, along the "Oscar Wilde Walk". This was one of his favourite places. When he was a teenager and ultimately too young to get served alcohol in pubs, he'd come down here with Ben and a few others, and indulge in what they called, "a bit of naughty drinking". As he got older, he began to appreciate it in other more ethereal ways. He liked the serenity if offered.

So, many years later and with many sessions of naughty drinking behind him, he was back for a different type of therapy.

The fact that they felt he had to be chaperoned really irritated him. Although in the interest of simply getting out of Prospect, he was prepared to play the game, so he kept his annoyance well hidden. Besides, it wasn't Marta's fault. She was quite sweet really. She also loved to talk a lot. He didn't really mind having to listen to her endless stories of her "bastard fiancé", who had jilted her – and at the altar, the reason she had left Poland vowing never to return again. She didn't seem to have any other stories, such as why she had chosen to move to England and whether she even liked it here. No, there were only two stories. She did modify them, and sometimes small details of the stories may have appeared different, but slight deviations aside, they always came back to the same two. He sensed that perhaps she may be harbouring a sense of bitterness.

Once again, she was in full flow, raging at the injustice of being left at the altar that day. Giles, being the considerate polite person he was, feigned interest. Usually it wouldn't be much of an issue, and he could almost watch in silence, filtering out most of the minutiae. This time it was different. He felt drained and fatigued. He suggested that they sit for a short while to refuel. He wasn't very hungry, but he thought that if he did something different, even simply opening his lunch box, the sound it might make might interrupt her train of thought, and she'd stop talking. Just as he was reaching into his satchel, something small landed on the back of his hand. He didn't recognise it at first. Just as he was about to flick it away, he paused to take a closer look. It was a mayfly.

He, like most people, knows the story of the mayfly. How, after much time growing as larvae, they emerge colourful and full of life. They gather first in groups, in communal celebration of the gift of life. They inject everything that they possibly have in their being, into this single day, making the most of their brief time here. Then, as the day progresses and their strength begins to wane, the group slowly fragments, and off they go alone, to see out their final hours, while desperately trying to hold on. The intensity of their wings flapping, and their bodies writhing, shows how much value they place on life, and how desperate they are to cling on to it.

Giles sat there mesmerised, with his gaze fixed upon this little creature, as his movement began to cease.

Given that he was literally watching the struggle of life and death being played out on the back of his hand, Marta's outpouring of seamless self-pity was beginning to grate. He didn't want to engage her. This would only encourage her. Instead, he continued to watch helplessly as his little friend fought with all the energy that it could possibly muster, desperately trying to hang on – each second as precious as the last. He remained mesmerised and helpless all throughout, until finally, all movement ceased.

This was a defining moment for him. It was his epiphany. Watching a scenario of life and death play out had a profound effect on him. From now on his belief was, we only get one chance at it. Life is brief. Life must be lived to its fullest extent possible, and in the short time we have, we must do the best by others that we can possibly do. There is no second chance. There is no afterlife. No one will judge us but ourselves. Live up to our own expectations, and set these expectations high.

That day he decided that he would from now on convey this message as strongly as possible, and with the same unrelenting vigour he had witnessed so many times, from the street-preachers of Broad Street. Someday soon, he would take his place alongside them, as a preacher – as an atheist street preacher.

That day witnessed the death of Giles Kingston, and the birth of "Mayfly".

A week after this profound encounter, he was out of the Park, and a most willing guest of the Salvation Army.

He approached the stand with his usual confident swagger. A slight breeze lifted the trailing mane of curls off his shoulders, revealing the long contours of his bronzed slim neck.

His was the last pitch. (Self-proclaimed Rev) Viglind Hythe had just finished. Her delivery had been rather pedestrian and lacking in any real zeal. Few in the crowd had appeared inspired. Others had simply walked away in disappointment. She wasn't her usual buoyant, "happy-clappy", hippy Christian self that most had come to know and love. At one point, she had even dropped her tambourine. No, she wasn't having a great day. Mayfly felt for her. For what it was worth, he would minister to her later…

"People" (he paused) **"I have something to tell you!"** (this time, another, slightly longer pause). **Live life! Celebrate live. Engage! Help! Love! There is no second chance. There is no afterlife. No one will judge us but ourselves. Live up to our own expectations, and set these expectations high! People, rejoice! Rejoice, people. Rejoice in people. Rejoice in the great gift of humanity. Brothers! Sisters! Rejoice in this belief! People! Rejoice in disbelief!"**

A few early gigs aside, when finding his voice in what can be a very tough, sometimes unforgiving arena, he was seldom heckled. He had honed his skills well. All who heard him seemed mesmerised. It wasn't just atheists or doubters who turned up to listen. His congregation was very much a broad church. It helped that he was a master in self-promotion. From the local vendors, he would buy a copy of "The Big Issue", but not take it. In return, they would slip his fliers into their copies. Before long, he had become second only, in local folklore, to the much loved "Reading Elvis".

His evangelical zeal was building. He continued… He lifted his book of Dawkins high for all to see.

"You see this book? Yeah? Do you see this book? I could quote from this. I could quote from it chapter and verse. I could tell you for example, that we all come from the sea. I could tell you that there is empirical evidence to prove, that this world is much older, FAR MUCH OLDER than what is contained in the books of Abraham. BUT I WON'T! There is no need. READ ALL THREE. THEN DRAW YOUR OWN CONCLUSION! Or read none of them. It doesn't actually matter. Do you know my mantra? Would you like to know what I feel is the most important tenet of humanity? WOULD YOU?!?"

"YEAH," came a strong collective response.

"DO WHAT IS RIGHT! HELP PEOPLE WHEN YOU CAN! LISTEN CAREFULLY TO THAT DEEPEST PART OF YOUR HEART! DO WHAT IS RIGHT BY YOUR CONSCIENCE! THERE IS NO DEEPER STUDY REQUIRED. BE DECENT!"

He paused briefly, sighed, and then brought his book down, clasping it gently. His voice was tired and his output changed to reflect it. He continued.

"People. No book, not the one that I hold right now, nor the ones that my friends who preceded me, held today, can teach you humility. Recently, I saved a man."

"YEAH!"

"We can all save people. Yes it is true. Two weeks ago, I saved someone. Not his soul. Not his salvation. BUT HIS LIFE! He was drifting off slowly. I went over to him. He was sitting by a tent by the river. I talked to him. I listened to him. He told me that he had decided to give himself up to the river. I asked him why. He told me that he couldn't see any other way. I told him that he was wrong. And do you know what? DO YOU KNOW WHAT? THE RIVER IS GONNA HAVE TO WAIT A BIT LONGER FOR THIS MAN! YOU ALSO CAN SAVE PEOPLE! IT IS TRUE. All you have to do is reach out. It doesn't matter if you know a person or not. IF YOU CAN HELP, THEN YOU ALL CAN SAVE. MY MESSAGE TODAY IS SIMPLE. DO THE

RIGHT THING. DO IT WELL, AND DO IT WITH LOVE. THANKYOU!"

He then bowed. A great applause ensued. His sermons weren't particularly long, but they didn't need to be. What he had to say was basic and simple. Yet it was powerful. He knew this. He could never really understand why people preached book in hand, referring to it, in order to emphasise a particular point that they had just made. Surely, if they were secure in their beliefs, then they wouldn't need backup. Yes, he too would preach book in hand, but that was only for show. Just like his weathered suede jacket and Alice-band, it was another prop.

As he made his way through what was left of his congregation, mainly women, and with his sermon on the celebration of life concluded, he felt privileged to be alive, on this, such great day to be alive.

Chapter 5

~

After taking the final bag, the rest of the night was a dream-like blur. What I do remember though, is being slapped across my face repeatedly, by a considerate stranger. I hadn't made it into the tent. He had found me, passed out by the tree. He wouldn't stop talking. That bit I do remember. I can't recall what we discussed, but he must have asked what I had taken and why, because I have no idea how I could have made it home, given the state I must have been in.

I had slept for three days solid. I was actually relieved that my attempt had been so lame. I should have known really. There's a reason why over-the-counter stuff is as the name suggests, readily available, and why other stuff requires a doctor's note. It turns out that if I had taken five, even ten boxes, it still wouldn't have worked.

Once I had fully awoken, and having processed what I had attempted, I decided that I would never again attempt to take my own life. I also decided that no one could ever know of this. If they did, then they would never view me in the same light again. They would be constantly looking over their shoulders, wondering when the call might come, or when a message would appear on Facebook.

I made a promise to myself that day, and to a God whom I barely believed existed, that I would never try this again. That said, I had to be realistic. I owed it to myself to be entirely honest. I was still in a bad and dark place, and one way or another, I would have to navigate my way out. The fact still remained, that the only reason I had for not killing myself, was to spare the grief of others. That one reason, the only reason for remaining alive, couldn't sustain me indefinitely.

With a further suicide attempt ruled out for now, a few options remained. I could admit that I had a problem, and then seek all the help available to me. One option would be to seek independent counselling sessions, but I had tried this a few months back, and had found the experience to be a complete waste of time. I don't know what I expected to gain, by telling some stranger what had happened in my life to get me to this point. Another option would be to declare myself already dead on the inside. The more I thought about it though, the more ridiculous it sounded. A declaration like that would change nothing. I always viewed the stance of "I think therefore I am" to be simplistic nonsense. This left me with just one option, and it seemed the only viable one.

I would indulge any form of sensory pleasure that came to mind, to the fullest extent possible. If I filled my life with whatever form of pleasure I could, there would be little room left for sadness. I would in effect go into a kind of self-induced state of hibernation from Monday straight through to Friday evening. Then for the entire weekend, I would hit the wine and drugs recklessly.

Although on the whole, I disliked my job, I found it easy. There weren't many variables in what I did on a daily basis. Therefore, there was very little concentration required. This meant that I could merely exist in a void of sorts. I had been back in work a week now, and that week had seemed to pass by seamlessly, and without incident. Somehow, I had managed to push this cloud to the back of my mind.

As soon as I got in from work, I would grill some fish fingers, collect one, sometimes two, bottles of Bin, head straight to my room, and put on my music. Eventually, with the properties of wine and sounds in great fellowship, I would pop a couple of Nytol, and then await peaceful oblivion.

Jacques and Adri had really looked out for me over the past few weeks. Adri knew that at the best of times, I had the appetite of a sparrow, but that didn't stop her from calling me when they were sitting down to eat the evening meal. Sometimes just sitting with them, having to drag myself away from my thoughts, helped stem these feelings of despair.

Sitting with them and listening, as they discussed the trivia of household chores, and upcoming holidays, I would feel elevated to the position of a family member. The more I dwelt on this, the more I realised that we were a family of sorts. Although younger than me by two and three years respectively, they were by virtue of a greater maturity, my elders.

With these two dear people in my life, I knew that I at least had a chance.

Chapter 6

~

Friday evening had finally arrived and I was on it! I was with Pookesh and Steve, and I had taken roughly half my bag of MDMA. We were in this rather edgy, Bohemian-type club, dancing like lunatics to house music. The place smelt of stale beer, body odour, and a cocktail of cheap perfume, and patchouli oil.

It was the kind of venue some would refer to as alternative. It was quite the mix. There were hippies, trendies, goths, a couple of very unconvincing trannies, some designer-punks, and a group of denim and leather-clad rockers, all mixed in with the usual non-descript generic clubbers. In all my thirty-six years on this planet, I had never experienced such a hive of raw anarchy! I had to say that this place was just a bit superb!

On weekends, my alcohol consumption had shot right up. At a guess, I was doing roughly two boxes of wine, eight–ten pints of beer, a small bottle of vodka, shots of some disgusting green liquid, and generally whatever was close to hand. As planned, illegal substances now formed a staple part of my weekend diet. MDMA was an occasional treat. At £60 a bag, it wasn't a luxury that I could afford to indulge in on a regular basis. Speed in comparison was by far the poorer relation, but at 10 quid a bag, it was at least financially sustainable. This was the perfect therapy. If I didn't need to work, then I could quite happily stay permanently in this state of euphoria. Nothing could touch me here – not sadness, not anxiety, and not panic. It was only when Monday came around, that the reality of my situation would hit home, reminding me yet again, that nothing had changed. But that was fine. I knew Friday would always come back around, and with that, a complete change of spirit and mood. The weekend provided the perfect foil and reward for the sadness, fear, and despair of the preceding four days. It was the perfect balance, and one that I fully deserved. I knew the likelihood was that this was a cycle that would most likely continue indefinitely. I took solace in the knowledge that this was the same for everyone. Life is by its very definition a cycle. We all have duties to fulfil, and some of us are fortunate enough to have rewards awaiting us, at the end of it all.

I surrounded myself with likeminded hedonistic people – those whose only concern was embracing pleasure and getting twisted in the process. If I could have scripted how my weekend usually played out, then it would be exactly like this. My circle of party people had grown significantly over the past few months, and I owed this all to Pookesh and Steve. We all had the same agenda. Also, they had the ability to play dual roles of counsellor, and prescriber of mood-enhancing chemicals. My GP had failed to play the latter role, refusing to prescribe me Valium.

I had now reached the point at which I was fully dependent on artificial highs – legal and otherwise, in order to secure my happiness. Choosing to sit back and do nothing wasn't an option, as it would leave me exposed to the dark elements.

The MD had now fully kicked in. The music seemed so sweet, as if being performed by angels on the most radiant of clouds. Everyone around looked so happy, so beautiful, and totally alive. As the light danced across Steve, and I caught a glance at his saucer-sized pupils, I felt a strong all-encompassing feeling of love and affection for him. Right now, I was overcome with absolute love for everyone, in what I truly believed was a venue of Gods! I loved this place! I wondered why they hadn't brought me here sooner. Perhaps they were building me up for it, and the previous months had been a training of sorts, preparing me, priming me for this night. I couldn't stop smiling. My jaw was beginning to ache somewhat, and although I wasn't particularly hungry, I couldn't stop chewing the inside of my mouth. But it wasn't causing me discomfort. *This stuff is fucking excellent!* I thought.

My pledge to Mistress Hedonism had been duly honoured, and with great enthusiasm. As I cried out in hopeless despair that dark night, a few weeks before tonight, I vowed that I would fully embrace any form of sensory delight available to me. There was one though that I hadn't factored in at the time, as it hadn't been a consideration. It was now. Sex. Since embarking upon my weekend activities, I had rediscovered my long-lost libido. This was in no small measure down to the consumption of MDMA, and to a lesser but not insignificant extent, speed.

I looked around, scanning all in sight. Nothing. Everyone seemed coupled up. What could I do? I had to get something. I knew it was wrong, but I was now considering even going down Oxford Road, to satisfy this sudden lustful craving. There was always an option there, if all else failed. It was something that I had never given serious consideration to before now. The more I thought about it, the more sense it seemed to make. Even still, it went against everything I believed in. Most prostitutes are junkies, chasing their next fix. They are trapped in a spiral of decay, squalor and low self-esteem. They run the risk of being attacked, every time, they step out of the shadows to ask, "are you looking for business, love?" I had lost count of the number of times I had been asked this lately. It was almost a daily occurrence. But perhaps, it wasn't all sad and depressing. Maybe some of them do actually do it through choice. Yeah of course, Alastair! Isn't it just a lifestyle choice? I knew I was deluding myself though, trying desperately to keep hold of even a small scrap of morality. However I tried to dress it up, what I was considering was wrong, very wrong, and couldn't be justified. Still, I needed a jump.

I gently and with due consideration, nudged my way through groups of sweaty bodies, in search of Pookesh and Steve. They had gone to the front to try and get served at the bar. It was nearly 3 AM, so the place would be closing soon. If I was going to do this, then I'd have to leave now. Pookesh and Steve lived on the Tilehurst Road, which meant that if we left together, we'd be walking home together. If this was to happen, then I'd have to reconsider my plans. I couldn't risk dear friends being privy to such murky intent.

I reached the exit and looked around. I couldn't see them anywhere. The place was slowly beginning to empty. Perhaps they had already left, and, in their heightened state of euphoria, simply drifted off back along their way. This suited me perfectly. I could now seek out my fix.

Gun Street was jammed with crowds of revellers filing out of the nearby clubs. Groups of impatient clubbers jostled for position at the taxi rank. Others, high on excess, nestled their weary heads into friends' shoulders for support. I must have drunk the equivalent of three bottles of wine and had numerous shots of some disgusting pink liquid, but I didn't feel even slightly drunk. I did feel high though. I felt absolutely connected with all around me. The various colours of the street seemed to combine perfectly, illuminating slightly, all in view. Right now, the sadness, panic, fear, and any feelings of dislocation which were usually a constant in my life, seemed a distant memory. I had indeed chosen the perfect course of therapy. I had no idea what damage my body would sustain if I continued along this path, but I couldn't risk the damage to my mind, if I didn't.

I crossed over by the church. With the flood lights and the various colours from the nearby clubs bouncing off its walls, it seemed like a celebrated, distinct entity. Considering what I was about to do, it felt wrong to be walking through its grounds. But I had to; its lure was too great. As I continued along with lustful purpose, I wondered if absolution really could be administered retrospectively. I continued down along the side of the church, on past the giant oak tree and through the graveyard. The tree, with its bulky presence and outsized branches, seemed animated. I looked up and along the church's gothic, rather eerie, splendour. There was light within its dark façade. Guided along by the gleaming lights and nocturnal activity of the surrounding streets, I reached the end of the pathway. Oxford Road was now within sight.

Chapter 7

~

Monday had once again arrived, and with that, the usual gloom. If this wasn't bad enough, we were sitting in a minibus on our way to the annual exercise in pointlessness – "team building day". I hated such days. I really resented being forced to listen to some corporate slave spout nonsense about "our collective value", "the sum of our parts", "valuing the team", "synergy", "out of the loop", "gap analysis" and "value added". Did anyone actually take this nonsense seriously? I was sure it was just some game.

I had my own theory – one day, some canny opportunist, bored and with thoughts wandering, came up with a simple, effective, and cast-iron way of amassing a great wealth. Of course for this to work, he or she would need to have a large pool of easily impressed, gullible fools, from which to draw. The plan was he/she would package everyday phrases, words, and sound bites, put them in a book, and then sell this book on to companies, emphasising how attending such courses was imperative to commercial success. He/she, whoever he/she was, had done incredibly well. The captains of industry had been skilfully duped.

However, my troubles didn't end there. I had, for some reason, felt it necessary to furnish Pookesh with the details of my Oxford Road early morning lust-fuelled escapade. He wasn't impressed.

"Mate, do you know what these birds are about?" he said. "As well as what you might catch, it's actually very bang out. These people are damaged mate, and you're just adding to it."

"It wasn't like that though," I replied sternly.

"Oh, get you! All defensive! Oh, how was it then? Oh, so you took her out to dinner? Or do you plan on taking her to the Hexagon? I hear Dream Boys are back in town. We all know walkers love a bit of Dream Boys."

"I actually liked her, in that I thought she was nice. I didn't expect that would happen. I just thought I'd have a quick in and out, squirt, and then go."

"Mate that really is too much information! Actually, forget that. I'm curious. Where did you do the deed? What was she like?"

"She has this little bedsit on Russell Street. We went there. Her name's Lynn. She's lovely. She's really quite sweet."

"Lovely? Sweet? Are you sure?"

"Seriously. She is. After the deed, she asked if I would like to stay on for a bit, so I did. She said that I was her last job of the night."

"That was really nice of her!"

"Yeah, I thought so too. It wasn't even about the sex after a while. We talked for a bit, and then fell asleep. She shares the room with her friend who was out for the night, so I left at around 6. I can't wait to see her again. I think I've got it bad."

"Well, it's probably not as bad as you think. Go and see your GP. He'll sort you out with some cream. Is it itchy and a bit red?"

"No! I don't mean bad in that way. I mean that I've totally fallen for her. She's also rather attractive – long legs, tanned, brown wavy hair. She's definitely not your usual, as you so eloquently put it, walker. In fact, I'm taking her out on Wednesday!"

"Mate!" replied an aghast Pookesh. "Are you fucking with me or what? She's a walker, bruv."

"I know, and I have seriously fallen for her. Work is work. We all have to earn a living. Actually, we had a chat on that very subject. We exchanged views. I didn't hold back either. Not in a rude way, but I just let it be known that despite what had just happened between us, and we had shared a rather touching, beautiful moment, that perhaps it may be wise for her to consider perusing other less problematic areas of employment.

"How very public spirited of you, Mr McLeish-Pidkin," replied Pookesh. "If only others took such a caring stance, the world would be in a lot better shape. That's for sure."

This made me smile. What he said was absolutely correct; he didn't have to say it though.

I looked around. More and more people were stepping on board. "We'll pick this up later," I whispered. "More ears are about now. Thanks for the chat and the kind words fella. Cheers."

"Yeah, no problem mate," he replied. "Anytime!"

I recognised most, but not all. Alesandra, the stunningly beautiful, Italian PA to Boz Neilson, was sat opposite me. She was flicking her light-brown corkscrew hair and applying her lipstick. Even the most basic actions such as these had an eroticism when she performed them.

Gerald Piscombe had just stepped on. *Shit!* I thought. *Stay up the front. Please stay up the front. None of us think you're funny.* My energy levels were too low to be able to absorb his corporate-inspired buffoonery. In a vehicle of 15, he was probably the only one actually looking forward to this. He was made for such days. Luckily, as if somehow picking up on my subliminal vibes, he took his seat just behind the driver's seat. *Phew! Lucky escape!*

Steve was the last one on. He made his way down towards us. As he passed by Alesandra, she flashed him one of her smiles. It wasn't just the normal smile either. It was her, "take me to bed and rip off my clothes" smile. I can't put into words how jealous I was right now. The thing is, she had flashed me that exact smile only last week. It never meant anything though. It was just a game to her. Perhaps the attention empowered her. And why not?

Steve took the window seat behind me. There was plenty of room down this end, so I stretched out over the two seats. Almost immediately, Jacques jumped in the driver's seat, and we were off – the beginning of our journey into nonsense. *At least the half hour or so it takes to get to Newbury will allow me to drift off*, I thought – with the weekend excesses stubbornly lingering.

Before I knew it, we had arrived at the entrance to "Great Providence Togetherness Solutions". As this was an annual event, I recognised the place straight away. The main building, side buildings, and overly landscaped gardens, had a veneer of blandness about them, which to my recollection mirrored that of its staff. This was going to be one long day indeed.

Jacques presented the security guard with the token, the barrier went up, and in he drove. He was lucky. He didn't have to attend this. His job for the whole day, was to deliver us here, then seven hours later, return, and take us away from our torment. He really had avoided the short straw. *Lucky Bastard!* I thought.

He turned to face us. "Well team, what can I say? I'm gutted that I won't be able to join you, in what I'm sure will be a life-enriching experience. Do listen very carefully to what the trainers, coaches, or whatever the fuck they call themselves, tell you. Observe them well, and take this knowledge away with you, to help make Fastend Telefonic the great company that it truly deserves to be... now get out of my van."

One by one, we did as instructed and vacated "his" van. The entrance was in view, and standing just inside it, was the silhouette of a large man, dressed in what appeared to be a purple and grey tracksuit. We made our way over, and carefully in through the revolving doors.

And there he stood, armed with a clipboard, and bearing the name badge, "Coach Richard Stanner".

"Stunner more like!" whispered Alesandra. I grudgingly accepted that she may be right. *Has she got it in for me!* To women of a certain age, I admit that he would appear somewhat attractive. With a 1980s-type brush tach, and a stance which shouted, "look at me! I am strong! I have an abundance of self-confidence. I am THE Alpha Male!" How could any woman of that certain age not swoon? Here before us stood Magnum, for the new millennium.

"Hello there, guys," he began, "welcome to the European headquarters, of 'Great Providence Togetherness Solutions'. It's really great to have you here. God, I feel excited about today. Yeah. There's some really good energy coming from you. I can feel it. I am your coach, and my name is Richard Stanner, but you can call me…"

It struck me that perhaps Rick, preceded with a slightly clipped P, would be far more fitting. It was obvious at least to me anyway, that here was a man constructed almost entirely of plastic. Nothing seemed genuine about him. Everything about the man seemed fake and affected, especially his poor attempt at a generically average American accent. Perhaps it was my new town Edinburgian snobbishness, but his vowel sounds seemed far too rounded. He couldn't possibly be American. He was nothing more than a "wannabee".

He continued, "But you can call me Richard. Let's do this yeah?! A-GAME! A-GAME!"

Once in, we were issued with the obligatory, plastic clip-on visitor badges. We followed (P)rick over towards the entrance to the main open-plan office. It was vast. Signs stating, "Together we can reach our targets!" "Be your goal!" "Quitting is the highest form of failure!" and of course, no temple of corporate evangelism would be complete without the obligatory, "There's no *I* in team!" hung throughout. There was a bland uniformity about the place. Numerous potted plants, some of which may have been real, provided the bulk of the décor.

We made our way over towards what was known as the "chill out zone". This "zone" comprised two large beanbags, a coffee-making machine, a plasma television devoid of sound and a counter, upon which sat four glass jars, filled to the brim, each containing various delights, such as jelly beans, chocolate chip cookies, jelly snakes and pistachio nuts. On one of the beanbags sat a woman in her mid-to-late twenties. She was slim, pretty, and wore purple-rimmed designer glasses. Her long brown hair was tied in "bunches", which hung to meet the straps of her yellow dungarees. On the other sat an overweight, bald man in his fifties. He was wearing a t-shirt stating, "AVOID HANGOVERS! JUST KEEP DRINKING!" Both appeared engrossed in their tablets. I recognised them. "Team," said (P)rick, "I'd like to introduce you to Gina and Brett. I must warn you, they are a bit mad. There, you've been warned." Gina and Brett stood. "Don't listen to him," said Brett. "We're not really that mad, are we Gina?" "Err, no," said Gina, "I mean it's perfectly normal to go around in one of, if not THE, biggest motivational training companies in the world, wearing a t-shirt like that...NOT!"

"OK Gina. Fair cop," said Brett. "Well you're not exactly the sanest person yourself." They then faced each other, paused briefly, and laughed in a way which suggested that it may have been rehearsed. I wasn't convinced that in fact the whole thing hadn't been contrived. It had all been unbelievably spontaneous. *Only professional comedians have that type of timing*, I thought. The likelihood was that this whole thing had been planned – right from the choice of that "wacky" t-shirt up to the delivery of their respective lines. *Corporate-sponsored wackiness at its finest,* I observed, rather smugly. They reminded me, in some way, of those other "wacky" and highly irritating "118118 boys", who invade our TV screens, breaking the continuity of a great film, with their "out there" antics. "OK gang," said (P)rick, "help yourselves to coffee, tea, OJ, Vodka, err sorry not Vodka, it's only ten! I'm so out of control sometimes! Cookies, jelly snakes, and nuts." He turned to us and placed his hand over his mouth, as if trying to prevent a deluge of laughter escaping, at his having said "nuts". Fortified with ample amounts of various goodies, and clasping our beverages, we followed Mr Moustachioed Tracksuit trainer and the "mad" Brett and Gina, over towards "The Motivation Chamber".

My stress levels were now rising by the second. Usually, I could bury my darkness under a series of repetitive tasks which didn't require any interaction and concentration. This, however, was a very different proposition. Where we were going now, and the tasks we would be expected to engage in, required absolute concentration, and interaction was central to the perceived success of it all. *Anyway, who is this track-suited charlatan? I can't stand his type. Pretentious fools – actually not a fool. I wish that was the case. The real fools are those who place importance on such people and on such days. Oh why do they have to put us through this? Have they honestly no idea how pointless this whole thing is?*

Accepting that there was no point in fighting the inevitable, I took my seat, and awaited my fate.

Chapter 8

It was Wednesday evening. Adrenaline was shooting through my bloodstream at a furiously quick speed, causing my heart to beat arrhythmically. Both my palms felt furry and damp, and that small crevice at the top of the buttocks, and just below the spine, seemed moister than usual. Tonight I was meeting Lynn – my prostitute. Given her line of work, I wasn't sure if this was going to be a date or a transaction. As we were going out to dinner and I was paying, it definitely had the feel of a date. I suppose the real test would be if after the pub the mood took us, we went back to hers for afters, and she charged me for the afters. Then that would make it part date, part transaction. In which case, the money and time spent on the date would have counted for nothing, and I would be out of pocket. If I factored in say 40 quid, 15 on food, the rest on libations, and then her standard rate of 15 for a jump, I'd be out of pocket by 55, or I could just proceed straight to the afters, and save myself that cash, or perhaps better still, I could tell that annoying, over-analytical voice in my head to shut it! So that's what I did!

Unsurprisingly, given my rather sheltered, socially privileged upbringing in Edinburgh's new town, romancing, or even engaging in a transaction with a lady such as Lynn, was a departure for me. Prostitution certainly wouldn't have been among my parents' favoured choices of occupation, for their eldest son's love interest.

Pookesh's pronouncement of prostitutes as damaged and vulnerable victims was pressing down hard on my conscience. He was of course right. They usually are, but I knew all this anyway. I certainly knew this as I marched with lust-filled purpose, along the Oxford Road that night. Tonight's date though, or at least my desire to see it as such, would surely demonstrate to him, and to anyone who was interested, that I wasn't one of those amoral opportunists who prey on such victims. I had depth enough to want to know the person, and not just see her occupation.

So now here I was, tapping my face with drops of pound shop Adidas aftershave, on my way to a Wetherspoons pub, to meet my date, or engage in a transaction. *My parents would be so proud!* If my intention was to somehow create conditions necessary for a date, then it turns out that I was off to a good start. My suggestion of taking her for a meal in 'The Back of Beyond' was met with the response of, "wow! You really know how to treat a girl." So there it was, the perfect conditions for a hot date, in place.

I shut the front door gently behind me. Jacques and Adri were having their own romantic stay-at-home date night, complete with candles, symmetrically placed red tablecloth, and accompanying atmospheric music. *Best not break the moment*, I thought.

I turned out on to the Oxford Road, and started the journey towards town. It was just after 7, and there was a crisp, fresh bite of energy in the fading, evening sky. The mood of the road seemed relaxed, tranquil even, which appeared out of step with its usual sense of pace. Directly in front of me was a red kite, impatiently pulling apart a chuck of bread. Immediately, this struck me as strange. Pigeons aside, birds are timid and unless trained, usually keep a very safe distance from people. It is no accident of nature, that when needed to do so, they can take flight into a safe space, high above us – except of course, chickens, who really are firmly down, perching awkwardly on the foot of this particular pecking order. Birds in general are usually so far away that you can barely recognise their species, never mind their markings. But this kite was so close to me, that not only could I recognise it as such, but I could also make out what appeared to be distinctive markings. I say distinctive markings, although prior to this, I had only ever seen kites soar and glide gracefully high above me, or in the near distance. But it struck me as unique that this particular one appeared to have a purple trim around the base of its neck. I knew that red kites weren't entirely red, but it did seem odd that purple would be among the collective of different hues. I was struck with the sheer majesty of this beautiful little creature. I felt privileged, that among the varied souls of Oxford Road, it would wish to single me out with its presence.

Suddenly, everything seemed frozen in time, framed and captured, as if saved in a sort of snapshot. It felt weird, but not eerily so. I was quite simply mesmerised. Mr. Kite couldn't have been standing more than three or four feet away from me. He seemed to be the only thing moving. I was fixated, glued to the spot, as he dragged this mouldy chunk of bread, bouncing it against the concrete, dragging it furiously from side to side, in a bid to break it up into manageable bite-sized pieces. Then suddenly he stopped, dropped the bread, and began to move slowly in my direction. I literally couldn't move. Then as sudden as the time had frozen, and the traffic had halted, and grown silent, and a sense of stillness had fallen upon this street-road, all life resumed. Once again, the traffic was moving, the strollers strolled, and the pigeons went about their business. Above me, I heard a sharp squawk; I looked up and he was gone. I knew it was him though. I was sure of it. Wasn't I?

I reached Broad Street. Outside the coffee shop on the corner a group of teenagers with devices held high, jousted with mobile phone egos, boasting of their latest "well cool" apps. "Mate, this app is sick fam. It is totally well sick," one of them proclaimed. If this was a battle of egos, I felt that this particular lad had got off to a very bad start. Never reveal your weakness. That's hindsight for you, I guess. You don't always know if something is going to live up to its billing. Still, personally, I'd have waited to use this one or, better still, kept this particular poor choice in app to myself.

As I passed by the library, I was approached by a 60-pence-boy. This was an interesting collective, who lived off their wits, harvesting the decent, the gullible, and the weary, from Reading's streets. They were harmless really. I couldn't help but admire their resolve. It takes real balls to approach the same people, sometimes twice in a day, telling them of being stranded in town and requiring just 60 pence to get back to Wokingham, Bracknell, or wherever it was they needed to get back to. Before moving here, I had of course been approached by beggars, but those ones generally didn't provide reasons for asking for money; they simply asked. Of course, Reading too has its fair share of generic beggars just like any other place, but no other place I had ever encountered had 60-pence-boys, or even a similar monetary equivalent. You certainly get a more resourceful form of beggar here, I mused. This particular 60-pence-boy probably lived in a shared flat, somewhere off Southampton Street, with presumably other 60-pence-boys. So unless he had holiday homes in Bracknell, Wokingham, or Henley, he was lying. I didn't care though. He seemed a decent sort.

"Hey bruv. Listen. Sorry to bother you mate, but you wouldn't have 60p? Would you? It's just that I had to lend my girlfriend a bit of money and forgot that I need to buy a ticket to get back to Oxford. It turns out, I'm short by 60p."

Oxford now! I thought "Goodness. That really is unfortunate," I replied. "I suppose the good thing to come out of this, is that you did it helping someone. You can be rightly proud of yourself, that's for sure. Of course, I'll help you get back to Oxford." I put my hand in my pocket, pulled out two pound coins, and placed them gently in the palm of his outstretched hand. "Here you go, get yourself something for the train too fella."

"Ah, nice one bruv! Cheers!" replied Kyle.

I continued on. In roughly five minutes time, I'd be sitting, drink in hand, facing my prostitute. The whole thing felt paradoxical. On one hand, I was excited – really excited! I was meeting a very attractive lady, who was also a prostitute! *If this isn't rock and roll, then I don't know what is!* On the other hand, I hadn't been with anyone since Tanya. Well at least, not in "that" way. Last Saturday didn't count, because it had been a transaction. At least that's how it had started out. But this was different. I had formally asked her out on a date. Although the sense of loss which had been suffocating and overwhelming at first, was now far less acute, Tan's memory still lingered. I could still picture her as if she was here, standing right in front of me, her almond-shaped hazel eyes feeding my soul. I could still smell her sickly oil-based musky perfume, and I could still hear her say, "you know what, you silly precious acting Scotsman – my, silly precious acting Scotsman, I bloody love you." Here I was doing it again – overthinking. *Stop this now! Back to now.* How should I play this? Should I hold back? Should I choose transparency? And if I found that I was falling deeper and deeper as the night went on, should I choose pride over emotion? It was no contest really; of course I'd choose pride!

I entered BOBS - the drinking emporium. As Wetherspoons pubs go, this place was a very fine den of inequity indeed. I was surprisingly impressed with the scale of it. With a high ceiling, and wide expanse, it seemed vast. This combined with the neutral colour scheme, gave it a nice sense of airiness. The oak finished furnishings kept it grounded in a traditional context. I liked the contrast.

I looked around but couldn't see her. *Where is she?* I wondered. *Where is Lynn, my prostitute? Actually, probably not a bad thing if she's a bit late. It'll give me time to top up.*

A hipster dude, with woodcutter beard and 1950s imitation NHS black-rimmed glasses approached me on the other side of the bar. His demeanour seemed welcoming and relaxed.

"Well, what's you poison young man?" he enquired with a warm beam.

"Oh," I replied. "Do you have any Bin at all?"

"Ah yes. But of course we have Bin."

"Do you have Chardonnay Bin," I replied.

"But of course. How many glasses would you like?"

"Oh, just the one please. I'd like one large glass of Bin Chardonnay please."

"Ah, but we only do Bin by the bottle. We do have one that we do on tap though."

"Tap wine," I shrieked. "I don't think so!"

"I don't blame you," he replied. "Tap wine is rank. This stuff is particularly rank if I'm honest. So how many glasses would you like for now with your bottle of Bin Chardonnay?"

"Oh, just the one for now please. I'm not entirely sure what my pros… I mean friend, is drinking."

He smiled and went to the cooler to collect my libation…

I hadn't settled in long when I felt a tap on my shoulder. And there she stood – she struck the perfect balance between classy and sultry. Looking at her right now, I felt a strong desire to proceed straight to the afters. Indulging in the obligatory small talk suddenly felt like a very tedious proposition. It was all about the main event. I knew

I was staring, but I didn't care. Who was I to challenge nature? Her eyes were adorned with smoky mascara and brown eyeliner. Her lips were a bright pink, and she wore a long black skirt which hugged a little too tightly, even for her slight frame. I wasn't sure if I was in love or in lust, and then she spoke, and then I knew that it was most definitively, just lust.

"Where was you? I should have known you was the show up late, kind of bloke."

Where WAS you? I thought - *mustn't correct her. Don't correct her. You'll come across as strange.* Sex. Think of the sex.

"Anyways," she continued. "Minds if I sits down?" she asked jokingly.

"Of course," I replied. "Please. I don't minds at all." So she sat, and we talked, and we laughed, and we joked. A few hours later, we were staggering down the Oxford Road heading to her place, for afters. "Listen," she said, "Ali. And please don't take this the wrong way, but you ain't my usual type."

"None taken," I replied.

"It's just that I don't usually go for posh boys, and I know that if I ever takes you home, my old Dad won't like it. He won't be happy. But it feels different wiv you. You ain't the usual posh boy type. I doubt if he'll see it like that though. He's a bit stubborn. Set in his ways like."

"Ah well, not to worry," I replied. We then stopped, smiled briefly, and embraced. It was a slow and gentle embrace. Afters were indeed forthcoming, and there was no charge incurred. So this made it a date and most definitely NOT a transaction. All she asked was that I compensated her for lost earnings, while we engaged in afters. So, the standard sum of £15 for a jump was agreed, plus a four-pack of Redbull. She still had a few clients to see, so it was important that she kept those energy levels up. Ah, my Lynn – my prostitute!

Chapter 9

It was just after 8 PM, and "Friday Kitchen" was in full session. We were all in. Our bright narrow kitchen usually provided the focal point from where our weekend activities would begin. I would join my family in music, alcohol consumption, and a general catch up of the past week, before heading out. It was never planned. That was the beauty of it. It was entirely organic. One by one, we would arrive and prepare our Friday meal. Adri always made Hoender (angry chicken) as a Friday treat for her and Jacques. Once she had finished, I would carefully remove two, sometimes three, fish fingers and, with great precision, place them under the grill. Food still didn't play a significant role in my life, so the key here was simplicity.

My Reading odyssey was now roughly six months in, and our family had grown by two. The double room which once held in it the entire contents of my life, was now inhabited by Karl and Abbi. They were a pleasant couple in their late twenties. Abbi wore long flowery hippy-style skirts, and smoked roll ups in liquorish Rizlas. Karl had a sinewy well-toned physique, which legitimised his wandering around open shirted. Seventies retro mutton chops adorned his sides, and he wore yellow-shaded John Lennon-style glasses. He was a bit cool – they both were. With Jacques and Adri in their early thirties, this made me the elder statesman. I didn't mind though. A lack of personal maturity, and an ignorance of the concept of responsibility, more than compensated. We were a strong collective, bound together by common interests, such as music, going to the pub, curry nights, watching "Desperate Housewives", comedy nights in, and indulging in far too many units of alcohol as deemed officially safe.

Monday had been horrendous. In the weariness stakes, it had surpassed last year's. Considering how horrendously draining last year's one had been, that certainly took some doing, but last year's group didn't have (P)rick at the helm. Our group had been force-fed irresponsible and dangerous levels of corporate cheese. Fortunately, I seemed to be over the worst of it, with the last remnants still lingering. I don't think that I had ever met anyone quite like (P)rick, before. Of course, I had met his type, but he was an exaggerated caricature of this type. He really was quite an elevated form of wanker. To defend ourselves, well as much as we could under this avalanche of cheese, most of us played "bullshit bingo". It works like this – to participate, two things are required, a sheet containing a list of corporate buzzwords and/or a pen/pencil. In the interests of authenticity, I generally favour the pencil. It is similar to conventional bingo, but instead of numbers being called out, it's buzzwords and platitudes. Blinded, or perhaps shielded by his own misguided arrogance, (P)rick glided along, oblivious to our little game, spouting platitude upon platitude, buzzword upon buzzword. We all need to be more, PROACTIVE – Tick. Let's help each other break through this "GLASS CEILING" – Tick. Don't let some "GRANULAR" – Tick – "GOOGLE JUICE" – Tick – "RESULT-DRIVEN" – Tick, "CAN DO MAN" – Tick, tell you that you can't achieve "OPTIMUM" – Tick "SYNERGY" – Tick. Instead focus on "THE BIGGER PICTURE" – Tick, to produce a "ROBUST" – Tick, "FRONT LINES" – Tick, "BUSINESS PLAN" – Tick; otherwise we'll find ourselves "HERDING CATS" – Tick. BULLSHIT! Well, at least I think that's how it played out.

"So anyway," asked Jacques, "what is this big turn up you've been dying to tell us about? The one with Gerald?"

"Oh yeah, that," I replied.

I squeezed my roll-up tightly, allowing for maximum inhalation, and then pulled hard, filling my lungs to capacity. I coughed, almost shooting out deposits of lung-butter, over towards Abi.

"Well," I said, after I had regained my breath, "he dropped me."

"Gerald dropped you," replied Jacques.

"Yeah, he dropped me."

"Dropped you from what?" asked Adri. "From a great height? From a table?"

"Well," I continued, "we had reached the final stage of the bullshit. I checked my phone and saw that it was ten to five, which meant that if we finished on time, then we only had ten minutes to go. I say only, but ten minutes in that place would seem like an hour anywhere else…"

"Yeah yeah Alastair," replied Jacques, rather abruptly. "We get the picture. So C'mon! What happened?"

"Well, the last game of the day was entitled, "A demonstration of trust".

"Wow dude," said Abi. "That sounds cool."

"Maybe," I replied. "It certainly wasn't cool for me though. Well, (P)rick…"

"Prick?!" replied Adri.

"Well, Richard is his real name, but I call him Prick. Rick short for Richard, yeah? Then Rick, preceded with a slightly clipped P. Anyway, he paired us off and linked me up with Gerald. The object of this pointless exercise was to demonstrate trust in the team."

"Cool!" cried Abi enthusiastically.

"No Abi. Not cool," I replied. "It's cheesy and pointless. Anyway, we left the motivation chamber and followed (P)rick over towards the chill-out zone."

"The motivation chamber?! The chill-out zone?! What the fuck…?!" exclaimed Karl.

"Yeah, I know!" I replied. "Anyway, the motivation chamber, ironically named, as it didn't motivate me one bit, is where most of the sessions took place, and the chill-out zone is as the name suggests, where folk go to chill out. It's a typical example of corporate bullshit, trying to be cool. When we arrived at the chill-out zone, that was when (P)rick paired us off. I couldn't believe it. Of all the people he could have chosen to pair me off with, he chose Piscombe. I mean Gerald. Sorry."

"So you go into this motivation chamber, link up with Gerald. Then what?" said Jacques, whose impatience at this whole exchange seemed to be building.

"The object of it all," I continued "is that one person falls back, and the partner standing behind him catches him, thereby demonstrating in a most obvious puke-inducing way, that you can trust this guy, that he literally "has your back". Anyway, I fell back, Gerald caught me, briefly held me, then let me go. And then I fell."

"But why do such a thing?" replied Adri, sounding concerned. "Were you alright? Did you hurt yourself?"

"Thanks for the concern sister. Well, (P)rick asked him why he did it, and what exactly was he trying to demonstrate, by initially catching me and then letting me go. His reply, I have to admit, was brilliant, and considering that he had just humiliated me in front of not just my colleagues, but passers-by too, this was some achievement. Simply put, he said that he agreed fully, that we should have trust between colleagues. But sometimes there will be times when you can't trust anyone, and you must be prepared for that. And no, I didn't hurt myself. Well at least not in the physical sense anyway!"

"That's a relief broer," replied Adri. "How come? How come there was no pain?"

"Well," I replied. "I landed on a beanbag – a bloody beanbag!"

"Sorry mate!" replied Jacques, with great enthusiasm. "That is fucking excellent! Haha! Who'd have thought it eh? I didn't think old Gerald had it in him! I see him in a whole new light now bra! Or should I call you, beanbag man! You've got to hand it to him man."

"No," I replied laughing. "I don't!"

Actually, I probably did. Perhaps, just perhaps, I had got him wrong all along, and there was a great deal more to him than I thought. I certainly wouldn't have had the balls to do what he did. However much I'd want to. My defiance was out of sight and underhand. His was unashamed and transparent. I turned to Jacques and smiled, grudgingly accepting that he was right. I really did have to hand it to him… perhaps!

Chapter 10

~

It was midday – the afternoon after the night before. And what a night it had been! Somewhere in between though, there had been a memory lapse. This wasn't the first time that it had happened. It was beginning to give me a slight, but not major cause for concern.

We had left the "After Dark" around 3, gone back to Wonderwoman's place, and stayed up doing coke for a bit. At around 7, I'd left them to it and set off for home. I don't remember the journey at all. The next thing I remember was waking up fully clothed in my bed at 11. I had a strong feeling that I had gone off somewhere beforehand, but couldn't be certain.

To my surprise, Lynn was beginning to make good on her pledge to give up the game. She wasn't quite there yet, but she had cut back. She now only entertained established clients, and had given up walking completely. The income from her clients was bolstered by some shifts in Tesco. Her eventual aim was to go full-time there, allowing her to quit the street completely. Still, despite all this, I couldn't take our relationship seriously while she was still entertaining.

I was meeting her today. We had no firm plans. But it was during the day rather than the evening, and it would involve shops and not clubs. It was her mother's birthday soon, and as she wasn't the most decisive person, it was likely to involve quite a few shops until she finally decided on something. This to me was a nightmare scenario. Usually by now, I would have been a few cans to the good, with a good session of wine consumption and drug taking close on the horizon. On a positive note however, she had a client coming at 5, so she'd have to be back at 4, to make herself even more attractive than she already was. I reckoned I could just about make it to 4, but not far beyond.

My reason for taking such a casual approach to the whole association wasn't just about the relentless pursuit of hedonism. This was the main reason of course. Hedonism was my number one priority, and my number one love. I had yet to encounter anyone who could come even remotely close to challenging such weekend staples. The other reason was of a more cautionary nature. I couldn't, and wouldn't allow myself to fall too deeply for her. If I didn't remain vigilant, I could quite easily find myself back where I was nearly a year ago. Given that the dog was never far away, it wasn't a risk that I could afford to take. I tried to frame this dog of mine in some sort of image. I imagined it to be to one of those annoying little fox terriers, irritatingly snapping at my heals. The likelihood though was that he was some towering wolf-hound, saliva drooling, threatening to pounce at any given time. Or maybe it wasn't a dog at all. Perhaps it was a person who masqueraded as a cloud and could suddenly take human form. I imagined this person to be either unassuming, with hidden depths of terror, with perhaps an equally unassuming name, like Nigel or Colin. Or perhaps he was some fearsome demon. My parents always warned me to be on my guard around the quiet ones, remarking that you never knew what level of terror lay beneath such a clam exterior. At least with the physically imposing ones, or those with a crazed expression, you knew what to expect, so you could plan accordingly. You couldn't really do that with the Colins and Nigels of this world.

It was getting cold now, and the dark overcast sky looked as if it could vent at any moment. Despite these conditions, it hadn't kept the usual mix of humanity away from all that a Saturday afternoon along Broad Street has to offer. As I approached the top of the street, I was met with the usual fear-mongering output of that uber-animated, physically imposing, street preacher. He and those of his ilk confused and unnerved me. To me his methodology was a wasted opportunity. It's a shame really, because the core message is warm – Jesus loves you. God is love. Everyone should have the right to free speech, up to a point, but I had a real problem with people shouting out angrily, about how much God loves us, yet telling us of the ghastly fate that awaits us if we don't believe this. My mind was a long way off from being right, and although logic dictated that he may be wrong, I was best served in moving on.

I carried on past him, and over towards a far saintlier sound. Enthusiastically and with great panache, was this really cool and stylish guitar wizard knocking out sublime riffs. He was playing an all-time favourite of mine – "Don't fear the reaper". I took my place among the small assembled crowd and just stood there mesmerised. For a brief moment, I felt pangs of jealously. Here was someone who not only had real talent, but appeared to be lost in his brilliance. I tried to think of any hidden talents that I may possess. They were either non-existent or, else, too well hidden.

This guy was amazing! And to top it all off, he had an incredible voice! I tried to look for imperfections in him, but I couldn't find any. He didn't say much. He didn't need to. It was the subtleties that defined him – his smile, the slick way he moved his head from side to side, resulting in a slight movement of his bleached straw-like mane. I hated him. I loved him. I loved him more than I hated him. I wanted to be him. I wanted to be with him, and so on, he continued.

> "Come on baby, don't fear the reaper
> Baby take my hand, don't fear the reaper
> We'll be able to fly, don't fear the reaper
> Baby I'm your man"

I was now in a state bordering deep hypnosis. Right now, the last thing I wanted to do after this, would be to wander aimlessly and without any real purpose, from shop to shop, having cheesy, mass-produced crap played at me through cheap stereos. I couldn't do it. I was meeting Lynn in an hour. This would give me plenty of time to construct yet another spurious reason, for not being able to meet her again. The last one was a classic! I didn't even call her. I just texted…

"Hey babe. Not great. It appears that I have picked up that ghastly bug that's doing the rounds. So, regretfully, I won't be able to make it out tonight. Catch up soon. Alastair X."

I best do it now, I thought. I reached into my pocket for my phone. There were a few messages. *Ah, Who is it now?*

Jacques, Abi, and Karl had all texted me last night, wondering where I was. I was hoping that it may be Pook or Steve, planning yet another cracking night out! It wasn't. To my surprise, it was Lynn. *Strange*, I thought, *she hardly ever texts. Anyway, we're meeting later.*

It turns out we wouldn't be meeting later, any time soon or, perhaps, ever again. She wasn't happy. I was also now able to account for those lost hours, and it made for very uncomfortable reading.

Text 1
"Dear Alastair. I use the term 'dear' loosely. Who the fuk do you think you are? I'm getting really fukd off being treated with no respect. My clients treat me with more respect that what you do. When we met, I thought you was nice. You seemed different from the kind of men I usually meet. But it turns out, you ain't. You's just the same as them. Actually your worse. For a start, they don't come round my place at stoopid o clock in the morning, banging on my door and shouting. Like a fool, I let you in. Listen, I may be a 'fucking hore' as you said, but at least I don't go round out of control being nasty to someone I'm suppozzed to care about. It ain't just last night either."

Text 2
"You probly wont care anyways. Your always finding ways not to see me. Alls you care about is getting shit faced with your mates. You don't give a fuK about me. If you did, you wouldn't treat me like this. I really think you need to get help and get your life sorted. The sad thing is when your not on that shit, whatever it is you take, you ARE really nice. But I never see you when your ain't, no more".

Text 3
"I'm sorry Ali, but I can't take this no more. And I wont. I hope you'll be ok. But please, just stay away. Don't even text me and definataly don't call me. I do hope you don't pick up any ghastly bugs anytime soon! Good by. PS, FUK U!"

I was in shock. I hated myself now, more than ever. I may well have many flaws, but I didn't think being aggressive was among them. I felt sick. *How could I treat someone like this? Calling her a fucking whore? Shouting at her? I didn't give a shit about what she did for a living. Actually, I did a bit, but only because it's a dangerous line of work to be in. If I didn't care, then why would I have advised that she gave it all up? If she was a junkie, I would have certainly judged her on that, and not gone anywhere near her. She could never be my intellectual equal, but that didn't stop me either.*

Whatever way I tried to rationalise it, and attach some semblance of justification to this whole affair, I couldn't. I was wrong to even try. There was a demon in me. I knew all this anyway. I was playing the only option available to me – containment. All I needed was a bit of tweaking – a bit of fine-tuning. I couldn't continue with these blackouts though. *God only knows what I might do next time I black out.*

If I was serious about tackling this, then I would have to visit my GP. Not only that, but I'd have to be entirely honest about what I was taking. I wasn't worried about them going to the police – they wouldn't have any proof. But I was seriously worried if they told me that what I was taking was causing these blackouts. Because then, I'd have to stop, and if I stopped, then almost certainly the suicide option would resurface. I really had a lot of thinking to do.

Strangely enough, I was beginning to feel less guilty. *Of course, I should never have gone around to her in that state and abused her like that, but in reality, I wasn't in control. I wasn't aware of what I was doing.*

The realisation that I wasn't in control, or indeed aware of my actions, had suddenly seemed to alleviate most of the guilt. Now, I didn't seem to mind not seeing her today. After all, I had been dreading doing what we, or rather what she, had planned. The fact that whatever it was we had, had come to an end, now didn't seem to bother me. On the contrary, I once again felt free. Although I had many complexities, I realised that a part of me had now become incredibly shallow.

Right now, I needed to direct my thinking away from all this. Whatever happened, whatever I did, it was still the weekend. Before long, Monday would be back, proclaiming loudly that once again nothing had changed, and that my situation was as dire this week as it had been the previous week and so on.

The plan was, I would continue walking, find a decent pub, and get on it, hard. I walked over to the music man and dropped a fiver into his guitar case.

"Well done chap! Pleasure watching you work!"

He smiled and nodded in response. *No one has the right to be that cool!* I thought. The healing properties of great music can never be exaggerated. Once again, my euphoria was back to the usual weekend levels.

Just like my mood, the sky had brightened up considerably. I felt a renewed vibrancy. I continued on down towards M&S, on my way to The Coopers Arms. From there, I would phone Pook and Steve and try to get them down here, much earlier than usual on a Saturday. When I left, yesterday, they were enthusiastically on it, so goodness knows what time they got back in, or if they had even left Wonderwoman's.

Directly ahead of me, was a fairly sizable crowd in the mini-auditorium. They seemed buoyant. I was intrigued to know why and how. Who was doing this to them? Who was drawing them all in? As I got closer, I noticed that most of them were women, and rather attractive ones at that. I carefully nudged my way in, closer to the front.

Oh no! I thought. *Not another Bible basher! And this one's standing on a stage!* I felt compelled to watch for a bit. This guy didn't seem like your usual street preacher though. For a start, he appeared younger than the average. At a guess, I would say that he was early-to-mid thirties. Also, he was smiling, and seemed to have a great warmth about him. He was indeed preaching, but not in the usual way, and it wasn't the material usually associated with street preaching. I now knew the source of this great energy. He began to speak, and then something really quite profound happened.

"People"! Be lovely! Be good! Be decent! Be blessed!"

Enthusiastic applause from the crowd ensued.

"We can all do it. We can all feel it! Each and every one of us has it in us, to be nice. Don't be fooled into thinking that you need to believe in any book to know this, and I mean no offence to my good friends, Rev Vigland or Hassim Abdul, but goodness is found in the heart, and words are found in books.

Look around you. Look around you today. Simply open your eyes, and you will see broken people. You will see people who have been pushed to the margins of society. Don't judge someone who begs, even if it is to buy that can of brew. That one can of brew that for even one hour, will take him or her out of the misery that they are in. Who are we to judge, as we walk past these ghosts and back to the comfort of our nice warm homes, and our nice warm families? Be blessed for what we have. Don't judge."

Now, society would generally view such people as mad, and therefore socially disconnected. I took a different view. I loved what I was hearing, and he was absolutely connected! It was having a very positive effect on my mood. Yes, he was stating the obvious, but it was how he was stating it – the tone, the passion, and the warmth. The main point was that he was standing there like a preacher, sharing his views on society. Every utterance was warm and positive. This was at sharp contrast to my earlier encounter. For me, right now, it seemed far more believable and logical to hear someone express kindness, rather than listen to some deranged maniac tell me that some invisible man in the sky loves me so much, that he will punish me if I don't accept this fact. I needed to absorb positivity, rather than stand there, listening to kindness being expressed aggressively.

My earlier uncertainty which had led to sadness, guilt, and panic, had now completely evaporated. I couldn't deny that something in me was fundamentally flawed and needed addressing. I would tackle this – one day, but for now, I would keep the dog at bay by applying positivity to my wound, whenever the chance presented itself.

I had no choice. I couldn't wing happiness. I had tried that. I had to work at it. Right now, I had my weekends – wine world, music world, and illegal drug world – but sadly for now, no sex world. The latter was really the least of my concerns. This would be remedied in due course. No need to panic on that front. And now I had this man. There was a strong familiarity about him. I felt as if I had met him before, but I couldn't quite place him, and then it happened…my epiphany!

I suddenly felt as if not just for now, but forever – for the rest of my life, and, quite possibly, for a life beyond that, everything would finally be still. Something or someone had transported me off to a place where the black dog could no longer gnaw away at me. I could offer no explanation as to why this had happened, or indeed how, but I had a strong feeling that this ridiculously handsome and kind-spirited man that I was looking at right now, had played a part. I felt a high, far better, far stronger, and far purer than the effects of the best MDMA or coke. It felt ethereal. It felt warm, and it felt honest. Blood was coursing through me at a furiously quick speed, administering close to dangerous levels of dopamine and serotonin. I was high on joy, almost to the point of collapse.

As I attempted to compose myself, I wondered who this man was. I wondered why now at this moment, he had been sent to me.

Chapter 11

~

Despite living just off the Oxford Road for close on 8 months now, I hadn't really experienced much of it. It was a daily event in my life, but only in a peripheral sense. I only really ventured out onto it on my way to work, on my way back from work, and on my way to and from town on the weekends. Of course, I had sampled the delights of the famous "Star" kebab on a few occasions. I had nodded my greeting to familiar faces. I had witnessed trains at speed, rattling the cast-iron structure of West Reading Bridge. But beyond all that, I had yet to delve deeper into its fabric, and find out for myself, the reason behind its legendary status among my Readingites.

I hadn't stopped ingesting potentially life-threatening powders completely, but since my epiphany, it was now an occasional treat, rather than a necessity. Curiously enough, the dog hadn't visited once. Stripped of all forms of irrational fear, I was now able to enjoy pain, disappointment, and despair, on the same footing as everyone else. As with my drug taking, I now only drank for pleasure and not to deflect non-existent attacks. Even still, I really couldn't have expected to indulge to the extent that I had, and not expect some form of recompense. I had been left with the legacy of addiction. Luckily, it was just to alcohol. I was fortunate in that it was manageable and not all-consuming. It didn't affect my job and my relationships, and it hadn't affected my health. I was particularly relieved about the latter. I had indeed taken well to my role of functioning alcoholic.

For weeks, I had been putting off going to the doctors to ask for that dreaded blood test. Then for the following week, I had been anxiously text-watching, for the news confirming my worst possible fears of liver damage.

I had texted Lynn, expressing sorrow and regret, thereby completely ignoring her wishes. In credit to her, and far more than I deserved, she had accepted my apologies and agreed to meet me today. After telling her what my plan was, she had with great enthusiasm suggested that as she is the "true local", she would give me the grand tour of the "Okki Road". I didn't have the heart to tell her that another true local had given me quite an interesting, albeit brief, insight already.

Derrick told me that as a boy during the war, the trains en route to Reading Central would often pull up opposite the side of his house, which was beside West

Reading Bridge. Excitedly, he would scramble up the garden hill, and on to the track, furnished with the latest batch of his mother's home-made lemonade and accompanying cheese and pickle sandwiches. In return, they would let him travel up front with them, the short distance to Reading, then drop him off on their way back to Newbury. In the midst of such violence and uncertainty, this story of innocence and decency resonated strongly.

Looking now at that very same bridge and at that very same house, I could almost picture this excited young boy scramble up this hill and on to the tracks. I wondered what that same boy and not the man as he is today, would make of the place now. I passed under the bridge, as a speeding train screeched along the rafters above me. I couldn't imagine train drivers these days stopping off for lemonade, no matter how celebrated.

I carried on past the bus stop alongside Lidl, remembering my first morning, as I watched those waiting there in the rain. In my now more relaxed and still state of being, I wondered why it had taken me this long to revisit it. I guess I didn't see the need. I had moved on. I mean, why would I walk down a road, just like any other road, the length and breadth of the country, just for an experience? But standing here now, breathing in all around me, I was struck by a strong realisation that it may well indeed resemble similarly sized urban thoroughfares, but that is where any similarity ended. It felt soulful, an entity all of its own - as real as those who trekked along its path.

As I continued along, a sharp wind stung my cheeks. It felt prophetic - as if warning me, preparing me for the uncertainty that lay ahead.

Although the text from Lynn was polite and seemed cordial enough, I still wasn't entirely sure what reception awaited me in the pub. I had behaved like a boorish, arrogant shit – the type of person that I usually despise. There could never be a repeat of this.

I continued on down, surveying all around me. With a turbulent mind as it was back then, I had seen, but never really looked, and never really felt. The petrol fumes, the vibrancy, the mix of personalities and cultures. It seemed as if the whole world had descended upon this part of Reading today.

I stopped briefly and decided to look, rather than just see.

Exotic mini-marts were, by their very presence, enticing people in to sample other worlds. As I looked closer at the buildings, it was apparent that the façade of modernity partially concealed striking solid structures from a proud architectural past. The rows of once purely residential Victorian red-bricks, somehow seemed to have married well with the neon shop-signs. Restaurants of varied cuisines, blending in nicely, were furnishing those present with a tantalising aromatic treat.

If an actual place could be described as having a rhythm, then this place would be it. I've long believed that Reading as a whole has this. I believed it almost since the time that I arrived here. All that needed to happen, was for some of the mist to lift, even if only slightly, allowing me the clarity needed to see this. I never believed that a town could have a voice and a unique feel. It's an absurd theory really, but Reading has. And this part of Reading appears to have its own voice within Reading! Amazing!

'Franco's Italian Trattoria' – 'Mo's Burrito Delight' – 'Happy Mimi's Jerk Delight' – cheeky! 'Blue Jade Chinese and Malaysian Take Out' – 'Perfect Fried Chicken' – Is there any other kind? 'Sea-spray – Fish 'n' Chips'. Reading certainly won't be going hungry any time soon. That's for sure!

Groups of people were gathered outside shops, chatting away in various lingos. I wondered what they were all saying or planning.

If only Babel hadn't decided to build that bloody tower! What was he thinking? Who was he to challenge God? If it wasn't for him and his arrogance, then I'd be able to understand what they're all saying!

I was meeting Lynn in a pub she had suggested, towards the top of the road.

She said that back in the day, it had been an old coaching inn. Her interest in history had surprised me. That was me all-over though, pre-judging others based on my warped sense of criteria. I mean, what would a walker be doing, knowing of such things?

Ten minutes later, I had arrived. With an extensive backyard, and a wrought-iron two-storied frontage, it did indeed have the feel of a former coaching inn. Slowly, I slumped in, with a certain degree of dread. With carpet-textured walls and loud colours, it was like stepping on to the set of a 1970s sitcom. The only thing missing was a slightly overweight barman, sporting a brush moustache.

Over towards the end of the room sat Lynn. She looked deep in thought. Suddenly a rush of energy jolted through me, almost knocking me over.

Attempting to at least project a confident façade, I made my way over towards her. She looked absolutely gorgeous, but not in the usual sultry way that I had grown to know, love, and fantasise about. It was as if someone had taken her off to one of those makeover farms and knocked all the rough edges off her. Here now sat a woman transformed, and now slightly out of my league.

She stood and approached me, offering a single cheek for me to kiss. I was intrigued to know what had brought about such a metamorphosis. Her make-up seemed more subtly applied than usual, and with a purple chiffon scarf resting on the exposed neckline of her long, slim-fitting cream dress, the picture was complete. I felt numb. I could barely speak.

"Ello darlin'," she said. "Nice to see ya."

At least she still SOUNDS the same!

"Really great to see you too loveliness," I replied, rather earnestly, "especially given my shitty behaviour. I really am so very sorry."

My remorse now was very raw and exposed. I was carrying a heavy burden. I felt so ashamed. *Why is she even giving me a second chance?* I thought. *I certainly don't deserve one.*

"Oh, Ali. Please love. Listen, there's no need. Shush. Your face tells me alls I needs to know. That was the test for me. I told myself that as soon as I saw it, I'd know for sure, whatever IT was, I wasn't quite sure. But now I see it."

"I'm so sorry babe," I replied through blurred tear-stung eyes. "I can't believe that was me back then."

She leant forward, gently cupping my hands in hers.

"It's OK Ali, please love. I know that weren't you back then. That's why I'm here."

She removed a tissue from her tasselled tan leather bag, and gently dabbed the corner of my eyes.

"We'll be fine babe." Her voice resonated with such rich warmth with a kindness that I didn't deserve. "Now get yourself up to the bar. Have you never been told that it's rude to keep a lady waiting? Go on. I'll still be here when you get back."

I really hope that you will. I couldn't really be sure of anything right now

You better not mess this up again laddie. Seriously man, I thought, as I hastily made my way towards the bar.

Time had seemed to pass by all too quickly. The yellow streetlights by the lane outside danced on the puddles made by the earlier fall of rain. Acknowledging that we could only fully appreciate the various attractions and landmarks that Oxford Road had to offer during daylight hours, we bilaterally agreed to continue our discussion back at mine. Yes, we were comfortable here, enjoying generous amounts of Bin. Still, we needed a jump!

Chapter 12

It felt somewhat surreal that my girlfriend, my soulmate, and the love of my life was now in large part at least, a former prostitute. We had gone back to mine that night and stayed in bed for two days, getting up only to eat or to use the bathroom. That was four months ago. I had never known love like it.

She promised that her plan to eventually give up the game would continue apace. She was now largely client-free and had made assistant manager at Tesco in Kings Meadow. They even had her enrolled at Reading College on day release, studying for her manager's qualification. From the outset, she had been transparent about all aspects of her life. Rather than this prove to be a barrier to success, her honesty and her desire to turn her life around, had earned her great respect. The fact that she used to toss clients off at the back of Reilly's for a tenner, had actually worked in her favour. This spoke volumes of HR.

For my part, although I didn't feel I needed them, I had agreed to attend anger management sessions. In fact, I knew I didn't need them. I went anyway, just to keep the peace and to ensure she stuck around. My fellow attendees, to say the least, were an interesting lot. There was one in particular who stood out from the rest. His name was Andy. He was ex-Special Forces. He'd been through a lot and didn't mind sharing this with us. His harrowing tales of what happened to him, at the hands of his Serb captors, were both moving and very disturbing. All throughout though, I never once sensed any anger or aggression coming from him. There was only sadness. Like me, he too seemed out of touch with the general mood of the group. There were some unsavoury and downright nasty types here, who absolutely fitted in. I told Andy that I couldn't understand why he was here and suggested that he had perhaps filled in the wrong form, and that cognitive behavioural therapy might serve him best. He agreed, but like me, it was his girlfriend who had driven the decision. From what he said, he had never shown her any aggression and most likely never would. It was just that knowing his story, she thought it may be a good idea to learn coping techniques, should that situation ever arise. The selfish part of me liked having him around, as his presence in an otherwise thugs' cauldron, put me somewhat at ease.

My depression now seemed firmly rooted in the past. I think it was down to a combination of things. The fact that I would without warning and reason suddenly come under attack, suggested that it was a chemical condition, rather than a situational one, but I wondered what had happened to fix this imbalance. What had been the trigger? Without a doubt, hearing that kind-hearted street preacher had played its part, but was it just that? I couldn't be sure. What I did know was that whether it was his words, the way he conveyed his message, or quite simply the man himself, the foundation had been laid that day. From there, this allowed me to gradually claw back what I had either lost or thrown away.

We had both agreed that in order to give our relationship the best possible chance, we would have to be completely honest with each other. There was no way I was going to burden myself with impossible and unrealistic promises to her. I had been upfront from the beginning. I had told her that I would find it very difficult to give up my hedonistic sessions completely, but if it was a deal-breaker in her eyes, then I would try. The fact that I was willing to do this just for her, was all she needed to hear, and so a compromise was reached. She didn't want me to change completely, as then "you wouldn't be the one what I fell in love with." All that was required was some form of tweaking.

Most people by now would be planning to move in together or at least, would be having the conversation. With us it was unwritten. We had each become used to living by ourselves. Apart from a brief period of a month, when putting her friend up on her sofa, Lynn had lived by herself in the same ground floor flat on Russell Street, for nearly five years. It was hard to see her ever moving out. Why should she if she was happy? All of this raised the question about our future together and our subsequent living arrangements. I had read recently about a married couple who although very much in love, still retained their singular living arrangements. Perhaps this was the secret to a successful marriage.

I was in my fourth anger management session. It was the same format each time. It was predictable, pointless, and boring. I was getting nothing out of it. I couldn't see this ever changing. Mike, the person chairing the session, would once again introduce himself to us, and then give us the same brief overview of anger and its many pitfalls. He would then invite some meat-head to stand up and give us his sob story as to how his upbringing had compelled him to kick the shit out of his "domineering" girlfriend. It was as grating as it was tedious. Apart from Andy, whom I liked and admired, I felt absolutely no empathy with any of them. Mike seemed nice enough, but he was probably a reformed beater himself. That's generally how these things follow – a former alcoholic chairs

AA meetings, a junkie, NA meetings, and a thug, anger management ones. It was safe to say that I had no respect for this man.

It was Andy's turn to speak. He was a glaringly obvious exception to these wankers. It was the one time I would sit up and take notice of anything. He was every bit the warrior. His broad 6'7" frame was lean and his expression sullen. The more he spoke though, the more it enhanced my view that he, along with me, was in the wrong support group.

"You see," he continued, "once you're out, you are out. That's all there is. It doesn't matter that you fought for your country. That you were willing to die for your country, or even that you killed for your country. One minute, you're behind enemy lines, shivering with fear and sometimes even shitting yourself – literally. The next, you're tied to a chair being beaten with a rope. Then one day, you're discharged under grounds of stress or fatigue. After arriving back in my hometown here in Reading, do you know where I ended up sleeping? YEAH? In a car park. In a fucking car park! I've got a place now and the love of a dear woman, so I'm doing OK. Well, as OK as I can be anyway. It's no thanks to anyone though, especially not the politicians that send us out there to fight their poxy wars – their man-made, all-for-money, pointless wars. I fought for this country and was willing to die for it. Can any of you say the same?"

Of course we couldn't.

As much as someone who hasn't experienced anything like the horrors he had could, I really did feel for him. The same couldn't be said of the others. They were just sitting there - fidgeting, staring aimlessly into what little space occupied their minds, totally disinterested in what they had just heard. Were they really that shallow? There didn't appear to be even a shred of decency among them. What he said may have been harrowing and difficult to hear. But at least it was real and not some banal "poor me" attention-seeking bullshit. Their ability to deflect any wrongdoing and accountability away from themselves, was matched only by their ability in painting themselves as the victims. They were pathetic.

I gestured over to Andy, nodding gently. These pointless sessions were doing neither of us any good. We were clearly in the wrong group. Listening to the relentless procession of self-righteous, self-important twits, expressing remorse with such insincerity, really was grating. I decided that day that I had had enough. I was sure that if I explained the whole set-up to Lynn, thereby illustrating exactly why it wasn't working, and that it never will, she would understand. Besides, I had enjoyed two absolutely full on sessions of hedonism, and not once had I felt compelled to either text or call her. It was clear that I was making progress.

"Thank you, Andy," said Mike, "for this, such a riveting insight into life in HM forces. You really have been through the mill. So, that's what happens then, when you put your life on the line for your country – thrown on the scrap heap. It just isn't right. In fact, it's all really, very wrong."

It was clear, at least to me anyway, but hopefully not to Andy, that Mike hadn't meant any of this. He was just going through the motions in delivering what he felt Andy wanted to hear. It felt false. I hadn't fully made my mind up about Mike, but my instinct was not to trust him. I'm sure he appeared charming to those with less of an ability to see beneath the surface. His voice was too calm and measured for my liking. It seemed devoid of emotion and expression – the classic signs of a sociopath.

I looked across at Andy. He seemed worlds away. I suddenly felt helpless and totally useless. Being surrounded by psychotic narcissists clearly wasn't working. These people really didn't deserve to be even in the same room as him. And I certainly didn't deserve to be in the same room as them.

I had decided that under no circumstances was I ever returning to such a toxic environment. Lynn would surely understand. Wouldn't she?

Chapter 13

~

Friday evening had once again arrived. I had decided to give Friday kitchen a miss tonight. There was a good reason for this – Dream Boys were back in town. Tonight they were playing the Hexagon and I was taking Lynn to see them. I can't believe that a rather lame attempt at humour had backfired on me so spectacularly. Remembering Pookesh remarking that "walkers" love a bit of Dream Boys, I asked her if this was true. I don't know what I expected her response would be, but I certainly didn't expect her to say, "yeah it is true. Your mate's spot on. Us walkers and even former walkers, certainly do love a bit of Dream Boys. Actually, they're coming to town soon. Fancy taking me?"

I couldn't really say no after that. So now here I was, splashing my face with drops of Paco Rabanne, getting ready to take my assistant manager girlfriend off to see Dream Boys. There was absolutely no way I was going in dry though. I'd need something naughty and illegal beforehand. A very challenging night lay ahead of me, and if I was going to come through this, then I'd need the correct minerals. My illegal drug of choice tonight was cocaine. I hadn't seen Charlie for quite some time – I'd missed him. In doing drugs tonight though, I had broken a promise that I had made to Lynn, shortly after our reunion. She had taken a very pragmatic approach to the whole area of my drug taking. She was pleased that I was no longer dependant to the extent that I had been, but she was also realistic. She knew all too well that such behavioural traits can't be erased overnight, so she put a proposal to me. This proposal was - I could have one weekend a month in which I could do exactly as I pleased. If this involved taking drugs and drinking all night, then so be it. But at no time during this weekend was I to even think of contacting her. For the weekends we were together, I wasn't to touch illegal drugs, and if I must get wasted on alcohol, then I was to do it with her. I didn't hesitate in whole-heartedly agreeing to her terms and, up until now, had honoured them. But tonight was different. Well, at least that's how I tried to justify it to myself.

It was twenty to nine. I was meeting her in the bar of the Hex soon. I had hoovered up half my bag of coke, drunk two cans of Amstel and the dregs of a bottle of Bin. I felt great, but not wasted. If I refrained from random outbursts of elation, then she wouldn't know that I had taken any naughty stuff. As for the alcohol intake, I was seasoned, so my capacity was rather impressive.

It now seemed that all aspects of my life appeared to be falling nicely into place. I couldn't believe the change in me. The cloud's visits were becoming a lot less frequent, but when it did show up, it still brought great sorrow and distress. I had given this cloud of mine a name – Jeremy. I have no idea why I chose that name. I didn't even know any Jeremy's personally, but there were of course the famous ones. There was Jeremy Paxman, the stalker of and feared grand inquisitor of politicians. I found his direct style to be unnerving, yet beguiling. There was Jeremy Clarkson and his thuggish buffoonery, masquerading as a worthy foil to the excesses of political correctness. The latter I loathed, and the former I feared. I had read somewhere on one of these self-help forums that naming one's darkness or fear helped focus the resolve to overcome that fear. Perhaps this was partly to explain why "Jeremy" now seldom showed up. I had a feeling that he knew I was onto him, and that one day, he'd just decide that there was no point in pursuing me any longer.

The connection with my Reading family, which was strong and seamless to begin with, was growing by the day, as was my love for Lynn. I had now fallen so deeply for this lady; I struggled to imagine my life without her. This in itself presented a huge dilemma. I'd been here before with Tanya, and the breakup with her had literally nearly killed me. I had tried to pull back from Lynn emotionally, but it hadn't worked. I had regained her trust in me and really shouldn't do anything to compromise this. All I could do would be to continue to treat her with the respect she deserved, and to do all those little things which really end up being big things. Things like texting fairly regularly and remembering to finish these texts off with a X or two but never more than two. It was important to show that I cared, but not too much. Although I didn't believe in the predications of astrological charting, she did, so it was important from time to time that I enquired as to what the stars held for her. These things showed that I cared, and although she didn't divulge it in precise details, she sometimes alluded to a not particularly caring upbringing. I never pressed the issue. So apart from Jeremy's spasmodic incursions into my life, everything seemed solid and in order. Everything except one important aspect – the blackouts had returned. Once again, I was waking up unable to account for a whole section of the previous day. On one such occasion, I had woken up clutching a golf club. I don't even like golf and haven't a clue how to play it well.

I turned out on the Oxford Road. The sky was overcast, with a soft pink glow just about visible on the horizon. The road appeared calm and relaxed, as a gentle murmur of engines rose up into the night's sky. In a strange way, I was looking forward to this. When I told Pookesh of my plans, his kind response was that he always had his doubts about me, but that it was OK to admit that I was gay. He said that it wouldn't change anything between us, but he always knew. I wasn't sure if he was joking – I think he was – but you could never really be sure with Pookesh. His sense of humour was so dry and irreverent, that he could sometimes make Frankie Boyle come across as caring and sensitive.

I approached the Hexagon. It was beautifully lit up in blue, interspersed with clean lines of purple around the edges. It seemed framed, for a perfect night of man-worship.

I approached the ticket office. I was greeted with a smile by a pretty twenty-something woman of a sallow complexion.

"Name please," she asked.

"McLeish-Pidkin," I replied.

She tapped away on her keyboard for a few minutes until…

"Ah yes, Mr Alastair McLeish-Pidkin. Two tickets. Fully paid."

She handed me the tickets. Feeling somewhat self-conscious, I placed them awkwardly in my inside pocket.

"Enjoy the show Alastair. Nice mans. Lots of nice handsome mans. Enjoy. Next please."

Alastair? I thought. That's just a tad overly familiar.

I entered the spacious bar area. It was just like any other theatre bar that I had been in before, only bigger. The carpet was a lively crimson, the walls black, and this rather kitsch ambiance was punctured slightly, with wall-height mirrors behind a well-stocked bar.

Surprisingly, given that I was ten minutes early, and she tended to favour a fashionably late arrival, Lynn was in. She was sitting over by the jukebox. I went over and sat opposite her. She appeared to be holding a programme of tonight's event.

"Oh, hey Ali," she said. "Soz, I'm a bit early. C'mere you."

She leant forward, grabbed me by the collar, and pursed my lips with hers. It was like those exaggerated cartoon kisses that end in a loud squeak. I didn't want it to stop. Arousal was instantaneous.

"So," she said. "Looking forward to it? 'Ere, 'ave a look at what's in store for us tonight."

She handed me the glossy official programme. The page was opened on a spread of the entire cast. I was particularly taken with the image of "Jason – the man who gets things done!" as the caption read. "Wow!" I exclaimed. "What an absolutely powerful accolade," Jason, sporting a naval officer's cap, jacket open to reveal, not a six pack, but an eight pack, seemed almost as wide as he was tall. He wasn't that tall actually, so I could see how this was possible. He certainly didn't look like someone to trifle with; and only a fool would attempt to hinder him, as he went about the business of "getting things done".

Curiously enough, I was looking forward to this now. Granted, not in the same way that Lynn was. Before we could finish our bottle of Chardonnay, an announcement came over the tannoy, informing us that we had five minutes to performance, and to make our way promptly to our seats. I had left the seating arrangements up to Lynn. She had done well! We were two rows in from the front and practically central – right in the line of fire. *Brilliant! Not really!* I looked all around. I couldn't see a single empty seat. This bubbling cauldron of oestrogen was spilling over! The excitement was palpable and building by the second. Then the screams…Dream Boys were on!

Although my reasons for being here seemed to differ from those of the majority, I couldn't help but get caught up in this electric atmosphere. Its energy was infectious. I almost felt like screaming too. I very nearly did, but stopped short just in time. I was glad. I think it would have confused Lynn.

The show seemed to follow a generic format. I knew this, not because I had been to see male strippers before, but I had seen the female equivalent once, on a friend's stag do. Marshalled into position by Jason, the lads would come bounding around the stage, in various different costumes. Judging by the level of screams emanating around this cauldron, the naval uniform seemed the clear favourite. This was followed closely by seven oiled up Poldarks, two Terminators with jackets unzipped, revealing yet more perfectly oiled torsos, and for the finale, ten overly enthusiastic New York PD officers, moving gracefully up to the bumper, at the behest of Grace Jones, and ushered in to position by Jason.

This was just a bit superb! I'm not sure if it was down solely to the minerals, but my enjoyment levels were such that I was struggling to keep the laughter in. This was absolutely hilarious.

Smiling broadly, I peered over at Lynn. She seemed so content, so happy, and I hoped now, totally valued. I was absolutely high – not just on minerals, but on a love the power of which I had never before experienced, nor thought possible. Looking at her right now, I couldn't believe my luck, that this kind-hearted, beautiful, stylish, and highly resourceful human being, had agreed to let such a boorish arrogant shit back into her life.

I was glad she was enjoying tonight's surreal display. At least to me it was surreal. I hoped she was enjoying this fine exhibition of manhood being played out before her beautiful leering eyes. I hoped that every single sinew in her being, and every single receptor, was receiving the highest possible amount of stimulation. She was worth this, and so much more. Ah my Lynn, my assistant manager, at Tesco Kings Meadow, Reading!

Chapter 14

It was Monday morning. Jeremy, after a decent lapse in time, had decided once again to pay me a visit. I wasn't impressed. His timing couldn't have been worse. Mondays were tricky enough for me at the best of times. It wasn't as if he didn't know this. *How inconsiderate of him,* I thought. *Woe is me right now.* Anyway, he wouldn't be staying for long – he seldom did. Still, with him around hovering over me with menace, I wouldn't be of much use to anyone today, so I had called in sick.

I had laid the blame firmly at the steps of "Flavour of India" – again. I forgot that I had blamed them the last time too. I wasn't known as someone who regularly threw "sickies". Therefore, I was fairly green when it came to spurious reasons for my lack of attendance. Others though were well primed in this area – none more so than Todd Bicknell in Finance. June from HR told me that poor old Todd, in this year alone, had witnessed his dog being hit by a car and killed. He had been dumped by his fiancé, and worse still, had witnessed the mugging of an old man. To his shame, he had stood by frozen to the spot, unable to intervene. There were reasons for his other twelve Mondays, but these three had seemed to stand out in terms of severity. All these events understandably had traumatised him. In fairness to HR, they had demonstrated great compassion. Each time they had given him as much time off as he needed in order to process these traumatic events. His powers of recovery though, seemed incredible. He usually didn't need more than a day to bounce back. It did seem odd that these harrowing events had all taken place late on a Sunday evening. Thankfully, he had never experienced food poisoning at "Flavour of India", this despite him being a regular patron there.

I had decided to get out of the house. It wasn't often that I had the whole place to myself. This meant temporary ownership of the remote. Not that it counted for much though. Yes, we were hooked up to a magic box, which gave us access to countless channels, but no amount of channels could blunt the pain of daytime TV. My choices today were property programmes, talk shows, documentaries, and reruns of "Blue Peter". None of which were doing much to lift my spirits.

I had decided, rather than just meander around the streets aimlessly, casually window shopping for items I had no intention of purchasing, or getting wasted in some town centre pub, that I would go on a bit of a trek. I was going to walk along the Thames to Pangbourne. Another reason for going by the Thames was that Jeremy didn't seem to like it there. I knew this because whenever he visited, I would feel a strong pull towards areas of water. Last time he visited, I went for a stroll along the canal, and by the time I had reached the confluence of the Kennet and Thames, he was gone. Actually, the more I think about it, he probably didn't care much for the Kennet either. His presence seemed to diminish as soon as I stepped out on to the Oracle riverside.

As I crossed over by the Crowne Plaza, and the majesty of the Thames came into view, Jeremy departed. Drops of light rain, falling from this slightly pale soft sky, ensured that he wouldn't be returning, at least anytime soon. The feeling of relief, and a sense of liberation I felt each time he left, was a perfectly formed paradox. The initial few hours post-Jeremy seemed to allow me a connection, a heightened sense of awareness that others who didn't have a Jeremy in their lives could never fully comprehend. It was an ethereal gift, born out by an acute sense of relief.

I passed by the tea boat. I smiled when I remembered that kind young couple and their warm beam that they gave me that lonely day all those months ago. I wondered how they were doing. Were they still together? Were they still absolutely precious to each other – more so than anyone else? I hoped so. Were they still enriching the lives of casual strollers, with that nice rich warm beam?

I passed by the boathouse, as a couple of enthusiastic lycra-clad boaters, slowly lowered their double-cox into the slightly choppy Thames. The air felt crisp and fresh, as the soft delicate sheets of rain swept gently along the river's edge, brushing the overhanging clumps of grass. There was magic in the air – I could feel it.

I continued on past the perfectly formed "tree seat" that I had sat on all those months ago, whilst pondering life, death, and that uncertain grey area either side. *You silly boy! And for what? This wasn't you back then. It wasn't a life that you were cut out for at all. Sadly, sometimes we need to go through some pain to get to where we need to be. Ah well.*

Experience had shown me, once Jeremy had left, that would be it for the day. I sat on my tree seat, happy in this knowledge. I unzipped my holdall and removed my flask containing fortified coffee that I had prepared earlier, whilst watching reruns of "Blue Peter". I had it on good authority that no one in West Reading could mix brandy with coffee quite like I could. There were an additional two key ingredients – Demerara sugar and Haribo Tangfastics. They had to be Tangs. Otherwise it wouldn't work so well. The beauty of it all was largely in the contrast of sharp with sweet. This was why Starmix, although pleasant enough, wasn't quite up to the job.

I poured myself a generous serving of the burnt bitter-sweet dynamic nectar. I closed my eyes, and then poured slowly and with precision down my expectant tube. *Ah bliss*, I thought. *This is perfect.*

"It definitely smells nice," came an unfamiliar voice from above. "Although I'm not much of a brandy-man myself. It makes me gag. Actually, that's the same with all spirits if I tell the truth, 'cept Vodka. That just slips down nicely, that does."

Quickly I opened my eyes. Standing about two feet away from me was a man with shoulder-length shaggy raven hair, wearing what appeared to be a 1970s Reading FC top. He looked early-thirties, and his causal relaxed demeanour, suggested a strong inner confidence. He had the air of a George Best about him. He looked familiar. I'm sure I had seen him before. I was struggling to recall where that was.

"Sorry, but do I know you?" I replied, rather abruptly, clearly irritated by this sudden invasion of personal space. Few things vexed me more.

The man gave a mischievous smile. "Yeah, you could say that, as it goes. I certainly knows you. That's for sure. Listen, I'll tell you all. But you must promise me that you won't lose it, yeah? 'Cos this is going to sound well weird."

"Sure," I replied.

"Right, me name's Dave. And please NEVER call me David. I don't like it. We'll fall out. Comprendez vous?"

"Sure Dave. Comprendez vous. Please carry on. I'm intrigued."

Dave smiled. "Now remember what I said, yeah? Keep calm. You must keep calm. I've watched your struggles with Jeremy. What is that pilchard about eh? Just showing up whenever he likes, making your life hell?"

Dave was right. This was indeed getting well weird.

"I know about the blackouts too; well at least some of 'em. Guess who's behind these blackouts. Yeah?"

"Errm, it wouldn't be Jeremy by any chance? Would it?"

"Spot on!" he replied, sounding rather smug. "You see, stop Jeremy, and you stop the blackouts. Stop Jeremy, and you stop the fear. Stop Jeremy, and you stop the sadness. Well, I'm here to stop Jeremy."

"But I'm really confused," I replied. "I haven't told anyone about him, so how could you possibly know all this?"

"Right," he replied. "This is where it gets well weird."

"What!?" I exclaimed "Of course none of this is weird at all."

"OK, fella, now remember what you promised. Don't lose it now. Yeah? But I know all this, because well… I'm a part of you. Put it this way, I know you better than anyone. I even know you better than your mum and dad. We are the same, yet very different."

"But," I replied, desperately trying to make some sense of this madness.

"It was the golf club episode. I thought the other stuff was bad."

"What other stuff?"

"Well, dancing with your top off, at two in the morning in the Abbey ruins. That place is sacred man. Then there was the time you took the late train to Bristol, dressed up as a sailor. You were dancing then too. Actually, you seem to enjoy dancing quite a bit. Haha."

"I'm glad you're finding all this funny Dave, because I'm certainly not."

"Ah lighten up mate. It's all good. It's just a bit of fun. Anyways, on the way home at two o'clock in the morning, walking down the Ocki road holding the golf club high for all to see, that's when you cried out, and that's when I listened. "Die Jeremy, die. Please die," you said. "Please help me to kill Jeremy. So here I am, here to kill Jeremy, and I will."

Being fully aware now of my less than robust sanity, I knew that this person standing in front of me, Dave, was my creation. Strangely enough, I wasn't in the slightest bit nervous. This was Dolly and Stan all over again, albeit a decidedly cooler version. Luckily, there was no one around to witness a stranger swigging something out of a flask, talking to himself. *Thank God for rain*, I thought. Not exactly to everyone's taste, but it does have its uses.

Dave continued, "look, I won't always be here. The deal we made is that I kill Jeremy and then go. How I do this is down to me. You said that you didn't care how I did it, just that I did it. Listen mate, I have a good feeling about this. I think we're going to get on fine. Listen, I've got somewhere I need to be, so I'll love you and leave you. Enjoy Pangbourne. Please close your eyes, count down from 10, and then open them again. The deal is you don't see me arrive, and you don't see me leave. Agreed?"

"Agreed," I replied. I closed my eyes, counted down from 10, and opened them. True to his word, Dave was gone.

There was a striking irony here. On one hand, what I had just experienced was an episode of acute psychosis. There was no question of it. But it seemed benign. What happened really should have traumatised me, but it hadn't. In fact, I'd enjoyed our little chat. Dave seemed nice enough. As we had just met, I thought the best course of action would be to take him at face value. I had yet to meet a Dave I didn't like, and this Dave seemed no different. After all, everyone needs a Dave.

Chapter 15
~

Roughly eight months after my one-to-one with Daniel Witterington, I was back here in Kennet meeting room for another meeting in pointlessness. Fortunately, this time around, it was a team meeting. This meant that the painful burden of having to be in the same room as him could be distributed equally among us. Witters was sat at the top of the table. Facing him down at the other end was Jacques. Jacques's polar positioning to Witters wasn't due to ranking, but was down to his unofficial status of alpha-male among us in the group. Alesandra was sat opposite me, gently twirling the ends of her corkscrew hair. This time it was me she was flashing that smile at. I can't put into words how absolutely turned on I was right now. It's a good thing I was seated. Sat next to me was Gerald Piscombe. Since that other day of pointlessness, I had developed a grudging respect for this man. To say that we had become the best of friends all of a sudden would be an exaggeration, but we had grown close. I'd even been around to his rather plush dwellings in Eldon Square for dinner with Lynn and Pandora – his fiancée. In the interests of continuing reconciliation, I had gone against my dislike of all things formal – I hated couples-only evenings. Gerald was quite the host though, especially after one too many of his fine collection of single malts.

There had been a trade-off of sorts between Gerald and me. Life isn't always as it appears to be. That includes people. Gerald, it turns out, was a chameleon – a game player of the highest calibre. His perceived beguilement of all things corporate and all things management, was precisely that – a perception. It was a perception that not only myself, but my colleagues who had baited and goaded him on an almost daily basis, had failed spectacularly to spot. And like all players, Gerald had a back story.

His humble upbringing in the Tigers Bay area of Cardiff's docklands, contrasted sharply with Pandora's socially privileged one in Henley. In her parents' eyes, especially in those of her father, this particular Welshman was not even close to being good enough for their classically trained princess. It was inconceivable that she could even fall for this man, never mind agree to become his wife. She was their only offspring, and the thought of their well-cultivated gene pool converging with his murky one, horrified them. They had tried everything that they could think of to put a stop to it. They had tried to set her up with a highly successful securities dealer, who owned a fifteenth-floor penthouse and drove a McLaren sports. When this failed, they had tried the dramatic approach, with an emotionally charged phone call from her mother. As a last resort, they had threatened to disinherit her. Judging by what Gerald told me, she stood to lose a few million. The fact that they didn't follow through with this threat really was irrelevant. She was prepared to bare those losses. This underpinned the extent of her feelings for him. Faced with such a loving resolve, her parents' pressure gradually subsided. I hadn't met her parents, and for Gerald's sake, it was probably best that I never did, but I knew their type. They were nothing short of aggressive thugs, masquerading as respectable pillars of society. I felt both saddened and ashamed; that not only had he to content with their nastiness, but he then had to field the snide pathetic sideswipes from us too. He told me that despite how it all looked, and he did admit that he must have come across as a spineless sycophant; he was doing all this motivated largely by pride. One day he said he would show this spiteful couple of worms that he could become at least as successful as them. If this meant that he had to come across unfavourably in the eyes of his peers, then so be it. He was playing management manipulation to get where he needed to be. Management probably knew this. If they did, they probably didn't care. This all played to their incredibly unpredictable egos. This was his plan. It was a plan fully endorsed by his beloved Pandora and unknown to his spiteful, future in-laws.

"Right then team," said Daniel. "I'm running late and have another team meeting in Newbury. If I'm honest, this is one of the last places I want to be today– with you lot. And you think I'm joking."

Wow! What an opening! I thought. *Nice and powerful. It's definitely got me engaged!*

"Anyway, let's crack on, and let's keep this brief. Look, what I am about to say may come as a shock to some of you, but please bear me. There's no easy way to say this. There's going to have to be some redundancies."

"Fuck! No! Really?!" exclaimed Tommy from sales. "Apologies, people. Sorry. I didn't mean it to come out quite like that!"

"No Tommy. Don't apologise. You've got every right to voice concerns. This is big man. Really bloody big," interjected Jacques. "So, Daniel," he continued, "c'mon then. Who's for the chop?"

"You know I can't say. It's unprofessional. Even if I knew who it was, I wouldn't be allowed to say. Them upstairs have told me to give you the heads-up, so you don't panic when a certain letter drops on your mat. I'm really sorry. For what it's worth, I think it's pretty shitty that you have to hear it this way. I'm sorry that I have to be the one to deliver this shitty news. Oh seriously guys, fuck this. I know I'm not meant to swear or slag them off, but

I'm past caring now. I've been looking elsewhere if truth be told. Not that I had prior knowledge. I could just sense that this was going tits up. This company has got great potential, or rather had great potential. But do you see those dicks upstairs giving two shits about you lot? No you don't. And that's cos they don't. They pretend to. But the truth is, they would sell you down the river first sign of problems. I've had enough. For what it's worth, I wish it was different. I'm sick of playing their stupid games."

"What sort of games would these be then?" asked Alesandra.

"Oh you know, that whole cool image thing. They think that I'm a bit of geezer. I like to enjoy myself. I like the finer things in life. Things like nice hotel stays, nice clothes, the occasional bottle of bubbly, weekends away. I think perhaps they look up to me in some strange way. They're always inviting me around to theirs when they're having big get-togethers. They parade me around to all their friends, as if I'm some sort of rare pedigree dog. It's embarrassing. I really can't stand that lot, despite all I've said.

"Seriously?!" I gasped, with perhaps too much excitement. "Why? I don't understand."

"I'm not sure I really do. Perhaps I have something about me – a swagger, a sense of style, a spark. They assumed I was a player, so I played them. I played along. Maybe being married boring and dull, they needed someone to play out their fantasies, so I obliged. The truth is, women, bints, birds, whatever you want to call yourselves, have never really appealed to me; well at least not in THAT way. Men on the other hand do – big time! I was living a lie. And for what? For them?"

And that was it. Shortly after Daniel's fine monologue, this perhaps not-so-pointless meeting of pointlessness was concluded. Looking around at the collective look of disbelief, as we all filed out of the room, it was collectively agreed that what we had witnessed today was a bit unexpected and somewhat strange – very strange in fact.

Chapter 16

~

It was Tuesday morning. There was a hum of anticipation around the office. Some of us had received letters. Others remained in limbo awaiting their fate. This struck me as just a bit unprofessional. Witter's analysis of them upstairs was painfully accurate. Surely given the collective uncertainty that stalked us, the decent thing would be to bring us all crashing down in unison. But that was it; they had no understanding of such a basic concept as decency.

To my surprise, I was one of the anointed. More surprisingly, Gerald was one of those in limbo. This was the ultimate irony. I made no secret of the fact that although grateful to have a job, it was a job that didn't really inspire me a great deal. I did the bare minimum, delicately straddling the worlds of compliance and accountability. I did just about enough to keep my job but not too much to push for promotion. I seldom joined management for Friday drinks and only attended company socials, if absolutely necessary. Even the promise of a free bar all night didn't seem a price worth paying, if it meant having to listen to a collective of self-interested, self-serving pricks, displaying their misguided sense of superiority. I didn't laugh at their jokes, but I did laugh at their starched pressed shirts and their boasts of golf handicaps and trophy wives.

Gerald by contrast, not only joined them for Friday drinks, but sometimes even organised Friday drinks. His enthusiasm or rather what people perceived as enthusiasm for company socials was amplified to the extent that stores could pick up on it. Sales, at least this area of Sales, seemed to come easy to me, but he had to work for everything he got, and it paid off. The end of month sales figures were a testament to this. He straddled the worlds of enthusiasm and diligence perfectly, and of course, he laughed along with "them upstairs", as they entertained their subordinates, with tales of excess and the trappings of success that seemed out of reach to most of us. But I knew better. He was laughing at them. They didn't know this though, so what was their excuse? What was their justification in keeping such a loyal servant in a limbo he didn't deserve to be in?

The biggest subject of conversation and considering the general mood of uncertainty here, was the revelation of a certain Daniel Witterington. If any man couldn't possibly be gay, it had to be him. He was the best-dressed man in Reading. His grooming was impeccable. He drove a Porsche Boxster. He was the epitome of subtle understated coolness. There wasn't a single person among us that day that had a problem with his sexuality, but there wasn't a single person among us who wasn't surprised. This man could with the exception of perhaps Jade in Accounts, have his pick of any woman, yet it wasn't his thing.

I was meeting him later. He said that although he was accepting of his newly voiced preferences, he did need a friendly receptive ear. He also said that he always had a bit of a thing for me. I wasn't entirely sure what he meant. He said that he had never really connected with the others here quite in the same way that he had connected with me. I was flattered, if just a tad apprehensive.

I had told Dave of my plans for tonight. He told me that it was good of me to take the time out for a mate. I told him that he wasn't a real mate, at least not in the sense that Dave was. Dave had told me that none of this mattered, as it's always nice to be nice. He did advise caution though, warning me that perhaps things could get well weird.

I checked my watch – *shit!* I thought. *It's half four, and he's picking me up from mine in an hour! Better get a move on, if I'm to jump in the shower beforehand.*

Chapter 17

~

It was just after 6 AM. Dave had decided once again to pay me an early morning visit, and engage me in a most bizarre Q&A session.

"Oh, I don't know Dave," I replied abruptly. "What kind of question is that? What would you do?"

"Yeah but it ain't about me. I'm fine. I'm not the one with issues!"

"Fair enough. But what would anyone do, if they were locked in a room, and the key to this room was in a bowl of slime, and they had to eat the key out?"

"Of course, I'd eat the key out. Happy? You need to stop watching 'SAW'. It's mental!"

"Yeah, but what if after eating through all that rancid slime, you puke your guts up, you put the key in the lock, only to find that it don't fit? All that puking, and for what? The wrong key?"

"OK Dave. Cheers. But what is the point to all this?"

"The point is, my posh Jock friend, that it's all about problem-solving. Look at it like a workout. Yeah? The harder you work out, the more impressive the results will be. A lot of people just go through the motions. They hit the gym and dick about on the treadmill for a bit. They've got the headphones in listening to tunes, just waiting for time to go by, so they can head to the pub and tell everyone that they've been to the gym. Then they wonder why they don't see any results. Then there's the guys doing free-weights. These peeps know how to work out! You see them strutting around, bigging up their chests and flexing them guns. What I'm saying here is, I'm your personal trainer, and I'm gonna get you some guns."

"What?"

"Guns mate. You'll get guns. You'll get strong. That's the same for your mind. That's the whole point of these early morning questions – to strengthen your mind. Trust me. You'll thank me for this."

Perhaps I would thank him, but not right now. This was the third time in a week that he had woken me up earlier than I had to be up – two hours earlier, just to ask me stupid questions. I knew he meant well, but it wasn't helping. I was now finding it difficult to concentrate at work. The one good thing about my job was the fact that I could perform basic duties without ever really needing to concentrate. He told me that this wasn't necessarily a good thing, as it made me complacent, and that waking me up with such cryptic questions early each morning was sadly necessary.

What kind of monster have I created?

"No offence Dave, and I know we're mates, but can you piss off now and let me try and get some sleep? I've got a while yet before I have to be up."

"OK! OK!" he laughed. "Fair enough. I think we'll wrap up today's session. By the way, you're doing well. I'm proud of you mate. I need to be heading off now as it goes. Right, you know the drill. Please to be faces to see. Catch up later yeah?"

"Sure Dave. Yeah. Catch up later."

I shut my eyes and began counting down from 10, 10… 9…8…7… I was out.

Very little time seemed to have elapsed before I found myself sat behind my desk, totally hanging from the night before. I shouldn't have been surprised really. Witters may indeed have lied about his sexual orientation, but he certainly hadn't lied about his ability to smash off! That man had a freakish capacity for alcohol consumption.

As school nights go, I had been somewhat irresponsible. In fact, I had been very irresponsible. Over the course of the night, I had drunk a box of dry white, or a gay drink, as Witters liked to call it. I had also faced him square on and accepted his spirits-challenge. Bad move. One look at the contents of his drinks cabinet should have told me all I needed to know. The fact that he even had a drinks cabinet at all should have told me all I needed to know. I needed to see for myself if there was any truth in these boasts of extreme capacity. I mean, if he could lie about something as big as his sexuality, then potentially he could lie about anything. He hadn't lied about this, sadly.

He was the consummate host, and I had enjoyed chatting with him. Well, it was mainly him doing the chatting, with me on hand, as a sympathetic non-judgemental ear. There was nothing to be judgemental about anyway. He had concealed his sexuality – hardly a serious crime. He wouldn't be the last. He couldn't stop thanking me for spending time with him, and just as in Gerald's case, he had revealed himself to be a decent, yet troubled individual. I wished that wasn't the case. Sometimes otherwise decent people are forced into evasive action, in the interest of self-preservation.

I was now on my second coffee – espresso of course. I had swallowed nearly a half box of paracetamol, drank roughly two litres of water, and I still wasn't right.

There was something else troubling me. Why hadn't he tried it on with me? *OK, I'm not exactly James Bond, but some have commented that I bear a bit more than a striking resemblance to Kevin Keegan. Why didn't he try it on? What's so wrong with me? Not having had time for a shower won't have helped, I guess. He on the other hand smelt fresh. Then again, he wasn't working yesterday, so he had all day to prepare. I didn't even slap any aftershave on. He was wearing that same scent that he wore when we had our one-to-one. It was a fresh aquatic type of scent. I liked it. If he hadn't had a decent shag for months, like he said last night, then why didn't he at least try it on? I don't understand. It's not as if I would have taken him up on it – definitely not. Still though, it would have been nice to at least have been propositioned.*

Gerald was in good form today. It turns out that there was more than a legitimate and justifiable reason for the delayed letter – he had been offered a new and improved contract. It takes time to iron out the small print, the finer points, and the points that no one really cares about. Such was their faith in him, rather than just kill off his current position; they had created a whole new level of bureaucracy – just for him. His new role was to act as a bridge between Sales and Strategy and Planning. As this was an open-plan office, he didn't have his own office, but he did have a desk all to himself and dividers on three sides. This at least gave him the feel of his own office. He was now "Branch Liaison Sales and Strategy Officer". He had played "them upstairs" with a deft touch and skill. I was proud of him. If I had even just a modicum of his resolve, then I too would be busy crafting my own escape tunnel. Even if I did, I wouldn't know in which direction to dig. This was why I was sat here calling people I didn't want to have a conversation with, trying to drum up business for a product I didn't fully believe in. There were far better products out there than the one that I was trying to flog. Still, they kept buying it. Repeat business suited my indifferent character.

Gerald looked over at me and smiled. It was a smile of confidence. It was a smile of contentment. It was a smile that said, "it really was a struggle at times, but I got there. I've made it. All this game playing really has paid off."

I returned the smile. I was pleased for him. He'd actually done it. This man had revealed himself to be highly resourceful, with a great depth of character. As he went about the business of attempting with Alesandra, to prize a sheet of trapped A4 from the photocopier, I seriously wondered what game I needed to play in order to reach somewhere even close to his level of contentment and peace.

Chapter 18

~

"Wakey, wakey! Rise and shine matey!"

It was Saturday 1 PM. I had seriously overslept. Fortunately, Dave had decided to act as my alarm call.

"Mate, are you sure this is a good idea? Guildford? Really? Are you sure mate? Yeah? 'Cos I don't think you're ready yet."

"Probably not Dave. But then again, when do I ever come up with good ideas?"

"This is true me ol' Jock mate. This is true. Just be careful, yeah? I worry about you sometimes. I really do. Right then, time for me to crack on – places to be, faces to see. You know the score."

"Fair enough Dave. Many thanks for the alarm call. Catch up later fella."

I shut my eyes and counted down from 10. 10… 9… 8… 7 … opened them, and he was gone. I was seeing a lot of Dave lately. His visits, even his random incursions into my sleep pattern, were generally welcomed now. His presence here seemed to have a calming effect on my otherwise turbulent mind.

A short while later, I was sat on board a Great Western bound for somewhere far away.

I hadn't seen most of the gang since moving away. A few had come up to visit, but I hadn't been back once.

I was disappointed that Lynn couldn't travel down with me. She was on 'til 6 tonight, but was planning on traveling down afterwards. I really hoped she'd make it. I was looking forward to showing her off.

This whole thing reminded me of "Born Free". Long after Elsa had left the compound, she just drops by one day to pay them a visit, with her cubs in tow and her regal suitor - his golden shaggy mane swaying gently as he watches proceedings from his rocky outcrop. The setting might be a lot different, but the sentiment was the same. Today after setting up in my new town, I was returning nearly a year after I fled the old one. I was returning to proclaim proudly that not only had I survived, but I had prevailed. The only thing missing from this picture was returning and walking into the pub, hand in hand with my beautiful girlfriend. They'd see her soon though. Then they'd know for sure.

Last night had been a late one – too late. I was paying for it now. I had realised some time ago that while it was still possible to party like someone in their early twenties, I certainly couldn't recover like one.

Although Lynn couldn't travel down with me, and Dave was elsewhere, I did have Mandy for company. This mistress never disappointed. She was always there for me whenever I needed her. I took a gentle pinch and swirled her brackish, crystalline charm around my mouth, numbing slightly my gums in the process. It wouldn't be long before her ethereal properties kicked in.

A short announcement from an incredibly muffled tannoy system went up, informing us that the train would now be leaving Reading, with Gatwick our final stop. She also mentioned engineering works, and having to go via Bracknell.

With great enthusiasm, I removed my plastic water bottle containing my travel wine, took a long deep squeeze, and then sat back. I enjoyed the gentle rumbling as the coach vibrated slightly, as it began to move slowly along the tracks, leaving the platform behind. My journey into uncertainty had now begun.

The 14.34 First Great Western to Gatwick airport was populated with the usual mix of holidaymakers, some with baggage lazily dumped in the aisles. Straight ahead towards the end of the carriage, rocking and swaying to the rhythm of the train, stood Posh Pikey. He was named as such because it was commonly believed that he was a gypsy. I wasn't convinced. He was probably homeless, or at least portrayed himself to be. To some though, I suppose, he could come across as posh. In fact, being punted to by him sometimes amounted to an audio treat. His pitch had it all – the cadence, the tone, the diction. I had lost count of the number of times he had pitched me. He seemed to favour the honest approach. Unlike the 60-pence-boys, there was no being unexpectedly stranded, and needing just a small sum to get back to Wokingham or Bracknell. It wasn't even about the need for sustenance, in the form of a kebab or a dirty burger. He was after sustenance alright, but it was of the alcoholic variety, and his delivery was charming. It went along the lines of … "Excuse me Sir, I'm terribly sorry, but I seem to have developed a rather acute addiction to alcohol, and I'm wondering if you would be so kind as to gift me a modest sum to procure a beverage, or preferably, bev-er-aaa-ges." I liked him and usually gave him the means to buy more than a single can of brew. For a member of Reading's homeless community, he was very well turned out in terms of attire, and this was complemented with a neatly trimmed grey Royal beard. This was all very well, but what on earth was Posh Pikey doing on a train?!

It turned out that he wouldn't be on the train for long, as he stepped out on the platform at Winnersh. I waved, as the train passed alongside him. He returned the wave, accompanied with a broad sunny beam. *Ah the little things and gestures, that can enhance life,* I thought, as I mirrored his beam, or at least tried to.

I peered out the window as we left Wokingham. To the right was a patchwork of allotments, backing on to horse paddocks. To the left was a neat bunch of "red-bricked starter homes". My mind was cast back to viewing one of these before moving to Reading. Back then, I was still at the point of commuting in. It was all too raw. I simply wasn't capable of concealing my emotions, and invariably, what little resolve I did possess, would give way to at first a trickle and then a deluge. I didn't care though. Back then I resented being alive, and right now, I was beginning to question the merits of making this journey. Dave was right. I wasn't ready.

And surely this was the whole point? For a variety of reasons, a big part of me really wanted to travel back and see everyone. It had been long – perhaps too long since I was there. Why hadn't I wanted to travel back before now? Maintaining the contact with my people there had been paramount – vital even. For weeks I had been looking forward to travelling back to see the old gang, and to find out what they had been up to. I had been looking forward to immersing myself in the "big news" events, right down to all the generic trivia of job promotions, house extensions, loft conversions, exotic holidays, and family additions – the lot. *How are they getting on these days? Has Seb been able to secure access to the balcony at Lords again? He seems to have an uncanny knack at charming his way on past the stewards. In fact, he could charm his way into pretty much any desired situation. Have Sally and Malcolm become pregnant yet?* I had maintained contact with both, but I hadn't seen any "big" announcements on Facebook lately, and I hadn't received a text from either confirming or otherwise. *Something this big though should never really be communicated via text. That's something that you can only really do face-to-face. There are so many questions I want to ask all of them, and so many conversations I want to have. Not now though. I miss you people, but I'm not really ready to travel back just yet. I will be for sure; only just not now. I've made good progress in my time here in Reading. You see, I'm worried that if I go back now, I'll be reminded of my past failings. I'm not ready to be reminded of my past failings yet. I will be though, at some point. Right now, I need to get back to Reading. I can hear Mandy and Wonderwoman calling, loudly – very loudly in fact! See you soon people – really soon – hopefully.*

A few minutes later, the cherry red signage of the Fujitsu tower came into the clear view. "Bracknell! Oh Bracknell! I love you!" I exclaimed loudly and without reservation. "I never thought I'd be so happy to see you! You crazy mixed-up erratically planned gem of a town! Oh Bracknell!"

Chapter 19

~

I rushed impatiently through the barriers at Reading Station, snagging the straps of my satchel. Something – a force, an instinct, a presence, was pulling me towards Broad Street. I felt that I could pass out at any time. But still, I continued. I crossed over to Malmaison, nearly tripping over the curb. I steadied myself against the wall. I was wheezing and struggling to catch my breath. *I have to get a grip – must get a grip. I need to compose myself. This is mental. What is happening?* I gazed around at the crowds of busy people, as they hurriedly darted from side to side. *I can't focus. Everything looks blurred. Think of good things. Remember what Warwick said. Remember he said that if you put good things into your mind, then your mind will produce good back. Remember? You must remember that. Surely? OK OK. Good things? Nice things. C'mon chap. Nice things. People in my life. Good people. Lynn, ah Lynn! My lady! Jacques and Adri, my housemates, my dear friends, my mentors! Freddy and*

Bernice, Kaz, Ros, Steve, Pookesh, Simon, Hippy Steve, great friends! Friends who have always been there. You see? You're not alone in this world. You're not alone. You are not alone. See? Yeah? But, but, it's not that. What is this? It can't be Mandy, as I've only taken a pinch. What is it? Eh eh, what is this? And suddenly, it struck me. I knew what this was, and it was actually a good thing, and now I was here. Suddenly, I was still. I had read somewhere that when the last remnants of poison leave the body, the residue that seeps out causes the body more discomfort than when the body was at its most poisonous. It's a bit like a parting shot to say, "OK, I'm leaving, but I don't want to, and I'm going to make you suffer just this one last time!" At Wokingham, I had decided that whatever was left of my past life in Guildford within me, finally had to leave. The poison escaping out of me was all the failure of a past life that I was expunging. This poison wasn't Guildford. Of course they were still my people, and of course I'd visit Guildford again, one day, but just not today. It wasn't Tanya. It was my past association with these aspects of my life. These aspects had held me in a bondage that I had never been fully able to escape from, until now. These factors were keeping me from moving on - from really moving on. What happened on the train had to happen, and if I was able one day to get beyond my agnosticism of such theories, was perhaps meant to. *Hey Tanya, I'm really sorry for messing you around and denying you the happiness that you truly deserved. I honestly didn't mean to. When I think about things, when I really think about things, not clouded by outbursts of emotionally charged expletives, I can actually understand why you did what you did. And you know what? I also know that you only did this 'cos you felt that you had exhausted every possible option of us remaining together. But you know something else? I'm over you. In fact, I have been over you for quite some time. Not only did you liberate yourself, you liberated me too. You liberated me from a life that I could never fully work out, and let's face it, trying to make someone else happy if you're not happy in yourself is virtually impossible. The truth is I had to fall very far down in order to rise. I had to experience severe dislocation in order to connect with who I really am, and I have connected. Now, possibly for the first time in all my adult life, I absolutely know who I am. I needed to come here to Reading for this to happen, and your brave actions that night all that time ago have helped get me here. Thank you! Bless you!*

I was now ready to embrace Reading and my Readingites in a way that up until now I hadn't been fully able to. I'd need a beverage or bev-er-aaa-ges first though. Things needed to be put into perspective, but not before some serious reflection. Reflection – it's important you see. Malmaison, what better place to start these reflections, and it's not too shabby either!

Two generous servings of Bin later, I was sufficiently, but not overly, fuelled. I picked up my pace and joined the fast pacers, the strollers, the loafers, and those aimlessly meandering along the flanks of Station Road. I was high, but in the way that I liked. It was an ethereal high, connecting me with all around me. It felt a privilege to be alive right here at this second, at this hour, on this day, in this great town.

I crossed up onto Queen Victoria Street and looked up. "Always look up when walking around this town," Gerald had told me. "That's the problem, see. People walk along, looking at the ground, at other people, or just straight ahead, but seldom do I see people look up. You must look up, see?"

And I could see, see? I was now controllably overwhelmed. Such ornate Vermilion carvings! For people of their day, the Victorians built high. Vermilion mixed in with yellow-bricked finish and then the zenith – small framed windows, high on their perch, looking out onto my town. *So, what happens now?* I wondered. *What should I do? Shut up, Pudkin! Shut up! Just continue on. This is your day. It is THE day.*

Energised, I made my way down towards Broad Street. The pull was now so strong. Straight ahead a crowd encompassing the mix of humanity that comprised this town stood in expectation. The colours were vibrant, and the people varied. Some were adorned in an interesting array of head gear – baseball caps, some worn at a jaunty angle, others back to front. There was a small group of

African ladies in traditional dress, with multi-coloured headdress. God, they looked stunning. There were Hippies, Goths, Trendies, and Hipsters with bushy beards, holding paper cups, most likely containing soya lattes or frappés. Women with prams moving gently, back and forth, were steadying their little ones. "Hush now hush, the man is about to speak." And there he stood, brooding and swaying slightly, building the moment. His presence crafted with great precision. And then he spoke…

"People! Friends! This world is infinitely precious. Each and every one of us standing here, is precious. Life is precious. We won't be here forever or anywhere else for that matter. So now is all it is my friends. Smile to strangers. Offer solace to those in distress. Listen to the stories of others. You never know, they might tell of something, a little thing that may not be so little, once you get back home to the comfort of your castle. Value such strangers, because to them you are the stranger. We here, standing in this fine public space, in Broad Street, in this fine town of Reading, know the truth. This truth is nothing bad will happen to you if you don't believe what I say. This is now. Now is all there is my friends. Carpe diem! Seize the day!"

Again, just like the last time, I felt as if I knew him. This time the feeling was stronger – much stronger. *Think man, think. Where have you met him? And I don't mean standing here performing. You most definitely have met this man before – the voice. The voice! That kind voice! Yes, could he have helped me? Or have I imagined this too? I don't think I have. Think. I know it's strange to say you can tell someone's character by their voice, but you can in his case. Look at him standing there. He doesn't have to do it. He could be out having fun, just like most do on the weekend. So, what kind of person would stand in front of strangers and risk being ridiculed. I'm sure most see it as a form of entertainment, and it is, but it's genuine too, and if he can send one person to their bed tonight smiling, thinking that perhaps life isn't so bad after all, and to keep hold of hope, then this man is worth more than he will ever really know.*

The man continued…

"Isn't it the little things that make life great, people? We take so many things for granted, don't we? Most of us, and I speak from experience, as I'm prone to this too, simply meander through life. We don't really look. We don't really feel. We don't really listen. But it doesn't mean that it isn't here. Just because you can't hear something doesn't mean that it doesn't exist. Just because you can't see something doesn't mean that it doesn't exist. It does exist. It's in the wind. It is in the rain. It is a fresh crisp spray on a bright spring day. It is birdsong, and the haunting chirps of the moorhen, as she calls forlornly out for her mate. It is a gentle stroll by the riverside on a calm peaceful day…"

I suddenly felt a jolt shoot through me. It caused me to stumble. The collection of different colours seemed to fade into one. Time too seemed to speed up. The street fell silent. I had definitely met this man before, and now I knew where it was that I had met him. *It was the river. It was that night. It was that night when all had seemed lost. It was that night when I had decided that I had fought my final battle, and that it was time for me to leave. Then off I drifted into nothingness, happy to rid myself of this world. Then he came along. He had other plans. He didn't know me, yet he believed in me. He dragged me from this pit. He cradled me. God, I remember this now.*

I was looking at the man who had saved me. My eyes were stinging. Streams flowed down my cheeks, off my chin, and then on to my collar. I was weeping in clear sight. I didn't care. Something far more important and far more significant than my pride was at play here. This was a defining moment which needed to be respected with naked honesty. Slowly, I walked towards the man. He was in peaceful oratory. Up close, I could see a kindness of expression. I never really believed that a face could be described as kind, or indeed mean; but now I believed this. His had a kind face. It was a compassionate face. I had a strong feeling that something or someone far more intelligent than anyone past, present or future, had designed this moment long before I ever existed. This Supreme Being had deigned that this man found me that night by the river, and had drawn me here to him today. But why had HE drawn me to someone who didn't actually believe in HIM? I wasn't entirely sure in the existence of "HIM" myself generally, but unlike this rock star preacher, I hadn't ruled it out. What was important was that I was here now in his presence.

Suddenly he stopped mid-sentence. He appeared startled, as if he'd been ambushed. Then he smiled warmly… "Man of The River. We meet, once again."

Chapter 20

I was sat back on my recently made creaky bed, drifting off once again into my over-analytical mind. The golf club thing bothered me. How had I come by it? I didn't know anyone who played golf, apart from my dad, two of my uncles, and Knoxy who drank in the Rose. As I hadn't been back to Edinburgh in roughly a year, this ruled out my dad and my uncles. Knoxy had invited me out to join him on one occasion, but I had politely declined on the grounds of being rubbish. This was of course true. But what I hadn't told him was that I found the idea of hitting a tiny white ball hundreds of yards around fields, at best puzzling, and at worst, just daft.

Although I found him to be a very charming fellow indeed, I couldn't completely work Dave out. Certain things just didn't seem to add up. *How does he know of all my mad adventures? If he was a figment of my imagination, then that would make him my subconscious. But during those incidents, the person doing these things has to be my subconscious mind and not my conscious one. In which case Dave couldn't possibly be my subconscious. The only way he could, would be if I have more than a couple of personalities. No, that couldn't work. My understanding is that it isn't possible for different subconscious minds of the same person to converse, but it is perfectly normal for the conscious mind and the subconscious mind to. In which case, I, Alastair, and he, Dave, could quite plausibly have a chat. And why does he also always have to shoot off? Where does he go? And it's always he who instigates it. And when he does actually go off, where does he go off too? Is it into the back of my mind? It can't be anywhere else, 'cos if I have made him as Dave said I did, then I won't have him going off to chat to the conscious minds of others – he's my Dave; no one else's.*

I'd have to leave it here for now. All this overthinking wasn't doing me any good. It was only confusing matters. I had an imaginary friend who seemed very real to me, and I was fine with that. I knew that I really shouldn't be. Only children have imaginary friends, not childish grown-ups. I was using all possible resolve not to tell people. I was finding it increasingly difficult keeping this all to myself. I was considering telling Lynn. Surely, she would be fine with this. Besides, couples shouldn't really have secrets. I couldn't keep this to myself for much longer. The sheer pressure of keeping this in, was building by the day. Eventually, this pressure would force it out. If that happened, then the chances were it would be common knowledge before long. But if I told Lynn and just Lynn, then it would stay between us. That was it then. I would tell her. *Should I do this tonight? I mean, what could possibly go wrong? Perhaps I'll hold off for now. There's no point in burdening her with my madness, at least not yet!"*

Chapter 21

~

It was Saturday night. We were in Wonderwoman's place. I was next up.

"Whose line is it anyway?!" I screamed with great enthusiasm.

"Oh here we go!" laughed Wonderwoman. "Just do it, you daft Jock!" Neil D'mato was prolific when it came to encounters with the unfair sex. Such was his bountiful success, people **Wondered** which **Woman** he would wake up beside on a Saturday morning. A few others insisted on naming him "Need Tomatoes", but that was just lazy alliteration. Most agreed that Wonderwoman was far more appropriate -the perfect accolade for such deeds.

He handed me the straw. I smiled and took it from his outstretched hand.

I looked at this chunky line of snow on the mirror below me. To most, this would be the perfect line, but to me, it posed a challenge – it was too large. I favoured the thin, thread-like lines that most would dismiss as a light-hearted joke. I favoured the gradual assent, whilst most in my group wanted to reach the zenith with rocket speed.

Some joker had decided to stick "Dancing Queen" on. I think it was emotional John. He was new to this late-night after-hours club. He was stood facing the giant wall-mounted 70-inch screen, singing away, oblivious to the house etiquette.

I hadn't told anyone yet, but I had decided that tonight was to be my last after-hours club. I was coming off the gear for a couple of reasons. The truth was the comedowns I was experiencing after a good night on the snow were becoming more debilitating each time. Last month, I had to draw on whatever minuscule reserves of strength I had, just to drag myself out of bed. Also, although Jeremy could show up at any time unannounced, he was now guaranteed to show up after a session on the snow. A comedown plus Jeremy was proving to be a lethal force to have to contend with. Another reason was one of ethics. I had seen a documentary recently on YouTube, entitled "Sniff then Snuffed". This short film outlined how Charlie eventually finds his way to our tables. I knew about the cartels, and their contempt for all forms of decency, and a propensity for intense forms of violence. But nothing could have prepared me for what I saw that night. These reprehensible snakes were surely among the worst examples of humanity ever to draw breath. After that, I couldn't continue to be a cog, albeit a small one, in such a chain of misery and destruction. It did seem unfair though that someone could choose to drink themselves to death, but recreational illegal drug takers were subject to the supply and demand of narcissistic psychopaths. Anyway, here I was attempting to hoover up this fat juicy worm.

I was becoming increasingly anxious at the task that lay ahead of me. What should be an exercise in pleasure was now looking like a mission. *Should I break this up? If I do this, then it is breaking house etiquette. But if I don't, then it's going to hurt. Oh, just go for it.* I placed the straw at the base of the line and then paused. I was going to do this full-on. There was to be no separating it into bitesize. House etiquette could not and would not be compromised. I moved the straw quickly over the worm, drawing up this bleached powder, until I reached the end. There were no traces left – not a single grain. I felt great. "Dancing Queen" being inappropriately played, now didn't seem to bother me. In fact, I was beginning to enjoy it. This tune actually wasn't that bad. "Ooh see that girl, watch that scene, dig in the dancing queen". This really was even more than just a bit superb. I was seeing and hearing Abba in a whole new way now.

The video was circa 70s. Agnetha looked amazing, in those turquoise hot pants, as she swayed those hips from side to side. Muppet man – not the one with the beard – was in his element, twisting his Flying V up and down. And even the other lady, the one whose name few can remember, and the slightly less attractive one of the two, seemed radiant, as she beamed broadly and frowned provocatively.

"Superb choice, emotional John!" I shouted enthusiastically. There was no response. He was clearly beguiled by this superb choice of ditty and accompanying video.

I turned to Wonderwoman who was singing along rhapsodically to the chorus, "Dancing queen, young and free, only sev-en-teen, la la la la la la!"

He turned to me, "I wasn't sure at first," he said.

"Of what?" I replied.

"Of inviting the big man around."

"Here," I whispered, as I beckoned Wonderwoman towards the window.

"What was the reluctance about inviting him around? He seems decent enough".

"No, no, don't get me wrong mate, I like the emotional one, but he's only been in the area a short time."

"What's that got to do with anything?"

"A lot actually. He could be old bill."

"What?"

"I'm not saying he is or isn't, but we don't really know him. He's not been in the area more than, what is it? Six weeks? He seems to know everyone, and everyone seems to like him."

"That is exactly why he couldn't be old bill," I replied. "They have a certain manner about them."

"Exactly," replied Wonderwoman. "First they befriend you. They gain your trust. You let them in to your circle. They start to find out more about you – what you're into – where you like to go, and all the while they're making mental notes. The next thing you know they're showing up unannounced at your local and hanging out with you."

"That's called making friends. There's no mystery to it. Besides, look at him. Old Bill have to give chase when called upon to do so. Agreed?"

"Agreed."

"Well, he must be close on or even past twenty stone. Can you honestly see him in hot pursuit of a suspected felon, racing down Waylon Street?"

"Now that you put it like that, no."

"So, relax Wonderwoman. It's all good," I replied, as I placed a steadying hand on his shoulder.

But it wasn't all good. It was mostly good, but on the other hand it was really quite bad. I was going to miss this place. Of course I'd see Wonderwoman down the pub from time to time, but it wasn't the same. There was a bond between us. Being away from such an integral part of our dealings was surely going to have some impact. How could it not?

As I looked around at my merry group – Gillette, David, Wonderwoman, and emotional John, but especially Wonderwoman – I wondered if choosing morality over quality hedonistic time was indeed a wise move. One thing was certain though; this was all going to get very emotional.

Chapter 22

As far as I was aware, the only person to know of my golf club acquisition was Dave, and on that subject, he had some news that as he said, I was going to find "well interesting".

He had told me that, as he put it, "I have found the geezer whose club it is. You'll have to read about it." He said that it was on the Chronicle's website and well worth a read. He also said that it wasn't difficult from the description of the man, and that he was swinging a golf club, to see that this was the same golf club.

All day, I couldn't wait for work to finish. We were two down, so Gerald had taken me off repeat business and put me on new business. In effect, he had me continuously calling numbers in an effort to drum up new business. This really was the coalface of telesales, and I had hated every second of it. The fact that I didn't believe in the merits of the product I was trying to flog certainly didn't help. Because it was so relentless, I hadn't had time to check the article out. But I was home now. All Dave had said was to type into the Chronicle's search engine the words "Kevin Keegan" and "golf club". So I did exactly that, and here it was. I wasn't sure if I was happy to have had this particular mystery solved, or embarrassed to have found out how it had all happened.

The article

"An argument with her boyfriend and a legend with a golf club"

The Chronicle's Suzi Wickers recalls a night out in Reading, an argument with her boyfriend, and an extraordinary encounter involving a Kevin Keegan lookalike swinging a golf club.

"It was late, very late. It must have been after 2 AM. It was definitely After Dark! Sorry! A few of us had decided to revisit an old haunt of ours – the legendary "After Dark" club. I hadn't been there for years. So, I had called, texted, and emailed, suggesting that a visit was long overdue. The response was encouraging. Here we were, pretty much our group from back in the day, reassembled, solid as ever, and ready for a great night out.

As most Readingites will be aware, the "After Dark" isn't like other clubs. It has a uniqueness which sets it apart from your average nightclubs, pumping out the same generic soulless dirges. Its decor is modest, and its colour scheme subtle and atmospheric. It isn't trying to be bombastic like most clubs, and we like it that way. Anyway, enough of this trivia.

We had come from BOBS, where we'd been road testing the various G&Ts of the world. It is often remarked that travel broadens the mind. Well, this rather pleasant journey had certainly enlightened me! We staggered up the narrow lane way, which led to the familiar black-ink door of my early twenties. The centrally positioned stage was still there and, a good licking of paint and advertisement signs which revealed that we were in 2008 and not 1997 aside, little had changed. It was like going back to my childhood home in Whitely.

Shortly after though, this air of tranquillity was obliterated, when a band took to the stage. Now, those familiar with my work, will know that as part of my remit for being allowed to indulge my ramblings, I occasionally have to review bands. It isn't something that I particularly enjoy. The reason being that most bands I have to listen to are bland, unimaginative, soulless, and devoid of any real creativity. This band – Forbury – good name granted, sadly encompassed all these elements. With his lips brushing the microphone slowly from side to side, and his incoherent moody ramblings, the lead singer fulfilled the role of a substandard Jim Morrison with distinction. The drummer hardly kept in time. The bass player seemed disinterested, as did the guitarist, as he jingle-jangled his way through this laborious collection of "poor me" uninspiring dirges. What made this review unique, and even more difficult to sit through, was that this sad collective was managed by who was later to become my ex-boyfriend. He who shall remain nameless was less than pleased with my lack of enthusiasm shown towards his charges.

After the performance, we headed straight to the bar and stayed there doing Jager bombs and Tequila shots, until the curtain came down on what had been a great, yet troubling reunion. Sensing things weren't quite right between HWSRN and me, the others left, with promises to revisit this fine place again soon.

HWSRN and me left not quite hand in hand. It was more my hand on top of his hand, trying to hold his hand. Just as London Street came into view, he pushed me against the wall and began shouting obscenities at me. OK, I didn't like his band, big deal, but I don't think I deserved that. I was literally frozen with fear. Expletives kept raining down on me from his snarled-up distorted face. I had never seen him like this and was terrified at what he would do next. Then a most bizarre and surreal thing happened. Out of nowhere, a man who looked remarkably like Kevin Keegan emerged from the shadows swinging a golf club shouting, "unhand this fine lady! Unhand this fine lady or else!" This put me at ease straight away. I now knew that I'd be safe. My boyfriend though wasn't so sure and turned and ran, with my golf-club-wielding-hero in quick pursuit. Now I'm not sure if this young man would have used this club on my boyfriend, I'd say not, but the threat alone was enough to secure my safety. I will say this, Mr Kevin Keegan… I'd have loved it if you'd beaten him!

So, Kev, if you are reading this, sincerest thanks, I owe you one! Also, a certain Mr Timothy Phelan is missing a 7 iron. Kindly return it to him at the After Dark club any time after 6. There'll be a pint or two waiting for you, and perhaps a Jager bomb or three!"

Email – swickers74@readingchronicle.co.uk

And that was it, mystery solved. I had done many weird and wonderful things in my life, but this topped them all, even my dancing-sailor-train-antics. Of course, knowledge is power, but knowing that I now led a clandestine life as a clown didn't make me feel particularly empowered. But what was causing me concern other than my antics, was not remembering them, or what had caused me to behave in such bizarre ways. Even allowing for the lighter side of this story and any perceived heroics, it was now clear to me that my hopeful grip on reality was becoming more and more tenuous. This was now far from a joke – very far.

Chapter 23

The more I read this article the more I enjoyed it. It was a week since I had found it; or rather Dave had found it. I had read it obsessively most days. I was itching to tell people. As far as I was aware, no one, at least no one I knew, had seen it. The article was two months old, so I was puzzled to know how Dave had found it, especially given that he wasn't real. When I pressed him on this, he had seemed to get quite defensive saying, "oh I don't know; some bloke down the pub told me." Given that he was a figment of my imagination, that explanation didn't seem plausible.

So no one I know had seen it. This was all now about to change – "send". "Do you wish to send this email without a title?" asked Microsoft Outlook. Of course I bloody do! "Send", and that was it – link to article sent to ALL my work colleagues! This was going to give the gang a laugh or two. Friday drinks would definitely have an edge to them this Friday! And I was definitely going.

Right now, I was getting ready to visit the After Dark club to return Mr Phelan's golf club. I wasn't sure what reception awaited me. Judging by the casual nature of the article, I didn't feel that I had anything to worry about particularly. *Hopefully this Mr Phelan has a sense of humour.*

I turned out on the Oxford Road. There was a lively energy in the air, as petrol fumes mixed nicely in with the aroma coming from the nearby fried chicken shop, producing the perfect urban cocktail. The more I thought about it, the prouder I felt. I had after all, albeit in a most zany manner, played the role of hero, sparing a clearly talented journalist from a possible battering. In fact, this whole golf club element really added to the overall dynamic.

As I passed by Argos, I was greeted with a warm beam by Reading Elvis. It was impossible to live in or near Reading without encountering this legend. He was dressed in a turquoise tracksuit, holding aloft an album cover of the King, eulogising his greatness. *Reading certainly loves its characters and none more so than this man,* I thought, as I returned the smile.

Just as I turned down to the Butts, everything suddenly froze. I couldn't move. The streets fell mute. Shadows darted in quick-time all around me. They didn't seem to have human form, although I knew they were people – they had to be. The fact that I was still upright was a testament to resourcefulness I never knew I had. Then a familiar image landed close to my feet. This creature I could make out. It was a red kite and it was THAT red kite. It had that same purple stripe down the back of his neck. But why had he come to visit me again? There had to be some significance; but I couldn't work out what this was. What could it be? When he showed himself the last time, the world for me froze then too. I wasn't even sure if he was real. If I could conduct a robust friendship with someone whom I knew for a fact didn't even exist, then there was every possibility that I was imagining this whole thing too. Then as soon as he had appeared, he took flight and disappeared quickly up into the night's sky. And as soon as the Butts had fallen silent, the cacophony of sound returned, the strollers strolled, and the traffic hummed. *Best just continue on,* I thought, *I can analyse all this later.*

In what seemed like minutes, I was walking up London Street. I was slightly apprehensive now. I had spoken to Mr Phelan over the phone earlier, but it had been difficult to gauge his mood. Anyway, I was far better at reading people's faces, rather than their tone. I approached the top of the lane and looked down. It seemed an odd place to house a nightclub. *These places are usually street-facing and in-your-face*, I thought. With this dusky narrow laneway and small shadowy door, this had a certain "Potter-esque" enchantment about it. I reached the doorway and then pressed the bell. Tinkle, tinkle, *even the bell sounds quirky*, I thought.

A few seconds later the door opened, and standing there was a man dressed in a West Ham replica jersey, holding a baguette. "Ah, you must be Alastair, and that must be mine," he said, pointing at the club. "My treasured 7 iron! Come in. Come in."

I walked in. It was dimly lit or atmospheric as some may call it. Suzi Wickers had painted a most accurate picture indeed. *I'd love to do what she does for a living*, I thought, *rather than selling crappy, generic, telecoms solutions that don't really do much. If only I had even a modicum of her talent. Well even she had to start somewhere. It isn't like she became talented overnight, I guess.*

"Please, pull up a pew young Alastair, or should I say Kev?!" continued Tim, from behind the bar. "What's your poison? Heineken, London Pride, Chardonnay… ah, or how about a Jaeger bomb?"

"A bit early for that don't you think?"

"Nah mate. Never too early for a Jaeger bomb!

"Perhaps after a few wines or beers," I replied jokingly. "I'll start off with a Heineken then, if I may."

"Good stuff. Two of the finest Heinekens it is then."

He set the pints down beside me and then came from behind the bar.

"Well Kevin Keegan, let me fill in the blanks."

This was all bittersweet for me. Not knowing how I had come to be swinging a golf club chasing a man down the street was really bugging me. Well not just that, but I was also worried. On the other hand, did I really need to know the preliminaries? Surely it was all about the end result; and that had been a favourable one.

Sensing my unease, he straight away steadied my nerves as he placed his outstretched arm on my shoulder.

"Listen mate, it's fine. There really isn't anything that you need to be either ashamed of, or even worried about. You did a good thing here fella. Your actions came from a noble place."

"But how did I come by it? That's the bit that bugs me."

"Well it shouldn't. Honestly, it's all good. There's nothing to be embarrassed about at all.

"Well, that's a relief! So what happened then? Where did I get the club from? I obviously got it from here. But this isn't a place that you'd expect to find a golf club."

"This is true. Well, I had played a round earlier in the day up at Maple Durham. It was a shocking round. Apart from when I was learning how to play, I had never played as badly as that. Anyway, I was running a bit late. Knowing that I needed to set up this place, I thought it would be best to come straight here rather than go home. There's a flat upstairs which comes in handy sometimes. Anyway, I rushed through the door straight in here, dropped the golf bag down by the side of the bar here," he said, pointing to the side of the bar nearest the entrance. "I then rushed up to the flat, jumped in the shower, rushed back down, and prepped this place for the evening. Caught up in this whole rush, I completely forgot about the bag, and the rest as they say is history."

"The problem is," I replied, "not the end, but what actually happened in between."

"Oh yeah," he continued, "so, it's kicking-out time. Suzi's group starts filing out. Her boyfriend, who's name I won't mention, so as to protect his identity, is pissed off, really fucking pissed off that she hadn't liked his band – no one did."

"'Cos they were shit?"

"Absolutely! The lead singer was so full of himself, totally without justification, and the rest just couldn't play! Anyway, apart from you in your own little world, dancing on the stage all alone to WHAM, Suzi and that twat were the last to leave. She was trying to reason with him, but he wasn't having any of it. A few minutes later, the shouting started. It was deafening! Next thing, you're running over to the side of the bar, you pull a club out of the bag, and you run out the door, roaring."

"I guess that's not so embarrassing after all," I replied. "My reasons were honourable I suppose."

"Of course they were," replied Tim. "I also love that you continued giving chase down London Street. You'd never have caught him though. He's a keen athlete. I think he runs for Woodley Harriers. He's a good 200-metre man I hear."

"Thank goodness for that," I replied jokingly. "I dread to think what might have happened if I had done. I've tried lots of different kinds of shit in my life; but I'm not keen on trying murder."

"Well put it this way, Kevin Keegan; this article would have taken on a whole new angle. Can you imagine the headline?"

"'A night out in Reading, an argument with a boyfriend, and a killer with a golf club'."

"I think I prefer the original myself," I replied.

"Me too! I think it's got more of a ring to it! How about that Jaeger bomb now?!"

Chapter 24

~

It was Monday morning 10 AM. I was sitting with Gerald in the Avon meeting room.

I was intrigued to know why he had called me in for a meeting. I'd already had my evaluation.

In the eyes of management, upper, middle, and lower, I was now their golden boy – I literally could do no wrong. I wondered how it had all come to this. Actually, I knew how it had. "Them upstairs" worshipped at the golden altar of affluence. My perceived haggling skills were not only of benefit to me, but it helped solidify Fastend's position as the main player in local telecoms. Yet beneath this cloak of commercial success, lay the exposed skeleton of a man occupationally unfulfilled. Ironically, the better I seemed to perform, the bleaker my life at this place felt. I really had to get out - somehow.

Gerald sighed. "Listen fella, I hope you don't think I'm sticking my nose into your business, but I wanted to meet you face-to-face, rather than just send you an email; it lacks the personal touch."

This sounds ominous, I thought.

"You see, I don't know how to say this; so I'll just come out with it. I'm worried, man."

"About what?" I replied. "I've just had my quarterly evaluation. It went well. At least I thought it did."

"It did. It did, Pud. You're smashing it. Well done."

"So what is it then?"

"That link you sent. Yes mate, not good. I know we all had a laugh down the pub last Friday, but when I thought about it later, I realised that this is no laughing matter."

"So then, what's your problem? It's not as if you get a say in how I spend my weekend", I replied rather abruptly.

"Of course, I don't. There's no need to be so defensive chap."

"Sorry Gerald. I shouldn't have snapped."

"No that's fine. It's just that I've seen this before with my cousin. He was always getting himself into weird situations. Then not being able to remember how he got himself into them in the first place."

"What kind of situations?"

"Really weird ones."

"How weird?"

"Very. We were all worried. One weekend he woke up in a hotel room in Scarborough, lying between two beautiful naked women."

"Poor bloke!" I gasped. "That must have been a shock to the system! How did he cope?"

"He got through it. But the point I'm trying to make here is that he said that he left his flat to pop out for a pint of milk; the next minute, he's waking up in a strange town, with two strange beautiful naked women."

"Sorry again Gerald, but I'm seriously struggling to understand the problem here. He pops out for some milk and then wakes up in a nice hotel room between two naked ladies. In my book, and I would say in the books of men the world over, that's what you'd call a result. Can you let me know the next time he needs milk? Seriously, I don't mind travelling down to that magic shop in Cardiff – that magic shop that can transport men to hotel beds, populated with beautiful naked ladies!"

"It wasn't a nice hotel room at all. He said that the paper was peeling in places, and there wasn't enough shower gel for all three of them; but that's not the point. The point is he had no idea how he got there. Would that not cause you concern?"

"Listen, I woke up beside a golf club and I was confused. He woke up lying between two naked ladies. Granted, he may have been confused to begin with, but at least he had some consolation. So yes and no. In a general sense, yes; but if I was sufficiently compensated like your cousin was, then no, not really."

"You're not really taking this seriously my friend," he replied.

"I am. Hotel room, naked beautiful ladies, Scarborough. See, I have been paying attention."

"It doesn't end there though. That's just one example. There's plenty more, see."

"I'm all ears."

"Like the time he woke up, again, in a hotel room. But this time in Reykjavik."

"What? In Iceland?"

"Yes, Iceland."

"In a hotel room?"

"Yes. In a hotel room."

"A dingy hotel room, with ripped wallpaper, naked ladies, and not nearly enough shower gel?"

"Actually, the room was alright. He said it was clean and airy. There were no naked ladies this time though."

"Listen, I'm really struggling here," I replied. "You need to help me. I happen to like hotels, beautiful naked ladies, and I've always wanted to go to Iceland."

"It's not just hotels he found himself waking up in. One morning, he woke up in a park in Swansea, lying under a tree with his trousers down around his ankles. He said there was shit everywhere. Not so glamorous now, is it?"

"Was this his own shit?"

"He wasn't sure. Look, you're missing the point, Pud. It's not where he ended up, but how he got there. That's the common thread here."

"That's easy," I replied. "Well, for Reykjavik, I would imagine he took the plane. For Scarborough, I would imagine he took the train, or else was abducted by two scantily-clad lovely ladies and then driven up north."

"No, that's not what I meant. The point I am trying to make here is blackouts, memory loss – they're no laughing matter. The ones I mentioned to you are just some of the ones that Finlay told me of. He said there were tons more. The thing here, Pud, is if you are having blackouts and memory loss, then it shows that in those moments you aren't yourself and therefore not in control. Do you get it now?"

The laughter had to stop now. Gerald was clearly concerned. This was typical of me. I was using humour and evasion to mask my embarrassment and unease. I was running away from confronting this. It was difficult to argue against his stance. But what could I do right now?

"Look Ali, I know how this must look. I haul you into a meeting room on a Monday morning and put you in the spotlight. But you're a mate as well as a work colleague; well you're more of a mate really. Walking home on Friday, with a certain degree of clarity, it struck me that far from this being funny, it really was quite concerning. This was Finlay all over again. I know it all comes across as funny and exciting; but it really isn't. There wasn't a weekend that went by that we didn't worry about him, or where he'd end up. It was a constant strain. We spoke to him about this. He agreed that it wasn't right, and that he'd go and see his GP. That was two years ago. He hasn't had a blackout since; but sadly, he hasn't woken up between sexy naked ladies in hotel rooms. There's no way he could pull this off in his right mind – he lacks confidence."

This made me laugh. And smile. It also saddened me. I knew it was pointless harking back to past mistakes and unreliable behaviour, but right now, it was difficult not to. Here was someone whom I had goaded and tried to belittle with pathetic sideswipes on an almost daily basis; and here he now was, looking out for me, expressing concern for my well-being. I didn't deserve his friendship, never mind his kind consideration. I was finding this all very moving. I was close to emotional meltdown.

Best end this quickly, I thought.

I gave a respectful nod, in complete affirmation of my dear friend's sound advice. I couldn't speak. This seemed appropriate given the circumstances. It would have been rude. I now realised that I could no longer run from my demons. I couldn't go on hiding indefinitely. One day, they would be sure to find me; to really find me. Then what?

Chapter 25

~

"Ah, a very happy and joyous Saturday to you, my Assistant Manager at Tescos Kings Meadow! This has got to be the best day of the week. Of all the numerous days there are, this has to be the most amazing of them all."

"Actually," replied Lynn. "It's Tesco – not Tescos. I hate when folk get that wrong."

"True", I replied. "Sorry about that."

"Ah, that's fine luv. I'm only playing with you. Of all the numerous days? You mean all five of them?"

"Surely you mean seven?"

"Surely, I don't. There's five days in a week and two in the weekend; 'cos strictly speaking, Saturday and Sunday are weekend days, not weekdays."

This made me smile. "That's me told," I laughed.

It was Saturday 11 AM. I was lying in my creaky well-past-its-sell-by-date, single bed with Lynn. Her head was nestled nicely between my shoulder and arm – it was the perfect fit. This was bliss. I didn't get to do this with her often. She was on early shift most Saturdays. With this in mind, I had taken full advantage of her "stomach problems" last night, knowing that we had time to sleep things off.

"Ali, and please don't take this the wrong way, but do you not think it's time to leave your job? You ain't happy there."

"No shit, Sherlock," I replied jokingly. "But there's no point in leaving it. I don't have anything to put in its place. These palatial surroundings don't pay for themselves, you know. Even if I did leave, I wouldn't know what else to do. Nothing really inspires me, except of course you, my sweet."

"This ain't exactly true, is it?" she replied, sounding very sure of herself. "Those doodlings of yours; you know, I think you've got something here."

"Ah, you're just being nice now!"

"When have you never known me not to tell the truth, the whole truth, and nothing but the truth, darlin'?"

"I haven't, but then again, I've only got your word for that," I replied.

"Look," she said, with a mischievous grin forming, "I've seen it all, well not literally; but I have seen a lot. Remember when we met and you was leaving the next morning?"

"Yes, I was still buzzing from the night before. I looked into those deep killer eyes of yours, probably the happiest man alive, well at least on Russell Street. I was swept along for the whole day on the coattails of bliss."

"You see, that's what I'm talking about. Listen to you coming over all poetic! You asked me what kind of jobs I did in my job. You sounded so nervous and shy. It was sweet. So I gave you a breakdown. Hand jobs – blow jobs – sometimes back door."

"That was a bit naïve of me, when I really think about it, and very personal, actually," I replied.

"I didn't mind. But the point is I told you. I didn't hold back. If I can tell you that I gave hand jobs at the back of Reilly's for a tenner, then surely I can be honest when I tell you that these doodlings of yours are well good."

These doodlings to which she was referring, were a collection of songs and poems that I had written when bored at Uni. At the time of composition, I didn't think a great deal of them. I thought that they were reasonably well-constructed, but they certainly weren't going to set the world on fire. But I had kept them – all of them; and why would I have done that if I didn't rate them in some way? Perhaps she was right, after all. When I cast my mind back, when writing these little ditties, I was actually happy. I enjoyed the whole process from beginning to end.

"Lynn, my love, my former prostitute girlfriend, so you like my stuff; but how does that tie in with leaving my job?"

"A lot actually, as it goes. You asked me a few weeks after we met and I know you meant well, but you asked me if I was happy doing what I did. I said that I had never given it much thought. I went home that evening after work, poured myself a large Bacardi, sat down on my favourite seat, and thought about what you had asked. And I thought and I drank and I thought again. I realised that actually, I wasn't happy doing what I was doing. The next time we met, I told you. You know that day telling you that I weren't happy, helped get me to where I am today. Although you didn't say it in exact words, you asking me if I was happy doing what I did, was actually telling me that I can do other stuff; that I do have choices. Yeah, I worked hard to get where I am, but I don't think that I would've gone down this road if you hadn't asked me that question."

"That's really nice to say," I replied. I was quite moved by what she had just said. I had no idea that this one casual question could have played a part in the life she now found herself in.

"Thanks, that means a lot."

"You're welcome, lovely."

"And today, I won't ask you if you're happy, because I know you're not. So I say this to you. That article, you know the one in the Chronicle?"

"Oh, why do you have to remind me of that?! Not that I'll ever forget!"

"Well, you said when you went to visit the "After Dark" to drop the club back, you were impressed with how this bird, Suzi is it?"

"Yes, Suzi."

"You said that this Suzi had described the place in such great detail. You wished that you could write like that; or even be close to it. Well we've all got to start somewhere. Why don't you email her? See if she can advise you on how you get into that game. I'm sure she'll help. I'm sure she'll be more than willing to help her Kevin Keegan golf club man. After all, she owes you. You could say that you enjoyed her article, and fill it up with how good a writer she is. Then add other stuff. You've got a good imagination, you'll think of something. Then see what she comes back with. Once she does, then it opens the door for meeting up. Diya get me?"

If she was willing to consider other options, then why couldn't I? Only this time, she was going one step further in telling me that I wasn't happy, and that I should do something about it. Not only that, but she was advising me on what I should do. This made total sense. Here was someone who had gone from giving hand jobs, blow jobs, and other tricks, to organising strategy meetings in board rooms and overseas hotel conference suites. Now if someone as accomplished and as resourceful as this, could see that I had potential and pinpoint why, then really, who was I to argue against it? And the more I thought about it, the more I realised that she may be right. My technique though would need a lot of fine-tuning to be even close to entry-level. *Even the great Suzi had to start somewhere, I suppose.*

"Urm Lynn, well you know…"

Suddenly Lynn sprung up and straddled me. She slid her legs in behind my back, clamping me in a vice-like grip. I could barely move. I didn't want to move.

"You see babes. Always listen to Madame Lynn. She knows best. What am I to do with you? You've been a very naughty young man, questioning Madame Lynn like this. Haven't you?"

"But I haven't been questioning you at all, Madame Lynn. I think this is a great idea!"

"But you're questioning me now. Emmm, what am I to do with such an ungrateful little worm?"

"I don't think you have any choice, Madame Lynn. There's only one thing for it. You're going to have to punish me."

"Of course, you pathetic little worm. You know the payment for such behaviour. Now lie back, brace yourself, and take your punishment like a man; if that's possible for a worm."

So I laid back and accepted what punishment she deemed fitting for my dissent. After all, I did have it coming.

Chapter 26

Dear Suzi,

Kevin Keegan here! You know the one, the maniac with the golf club! How could you ever forget!? You'll be having nightmares for years to come I would imagine!

I just wanted to say that I read your article and thought it was brilliant! It also cleared up the mystery of how I came to have the golf club in the first place. I went back to the After Dark as instructed and reunited Tim with his 7 iron. He was most happy.

I recognised the place straight away from your description. Considering that I don't remember the event, the place had a strange familiarity to it. As that can't be down to having remembered being there, it has to be down to your superb and accurate description – the centrally-positioned stage to the up-to-date advertising, it was all there. I don't mind admitting to being just a tad jealous at your talent and having a job that clearly inspires you. My job just saps the spirit out of me – daily! I'd love to do what you do, but I'm no way near your standard. I used to write a bit at Uni – songs mainly and a bit of poetry. I didn't think much of it; but I still kept it in a folder all this time. My girlfriend Lynn, however, thinks it's good and that I should try and find a way to write for a living; or at least plan to. I'm not so sure, but you never know.

Anyway, Suzi, thanks once again for a really great article, and for solving the mystery of that golf club!

Cheers,

Alastair

I turned to Dave. "Well what do you think? Should I click send?"

"I don't know. I don't know. Can I read it again? You've got to get this right first time."

"Yeah, that makes sense. Yeah, if you wouldn't mind chap."

"Sure mate," he replied.

Dave looked at the screen, intently pouring over the content of my email. Each expression changing from smile to bemusement, from smile to bemusement, and back to smile, until...

"Overall mate, I like it. I think it says everything that you need it to say. You've come straight in sounding all friendly. You've added humour to it too; you've complimented her. That's a good move mate. I like the way you mentioned that you have written poetry AND songs. That shows that your writing is versatile. If I was her, I'd be interested in meeting you. So yeah, I like it. It works. There's just one bit that I aint so sure about."

"Which bit is that?"

"My girlfriend Lynn? Are you sure?"

"What do you mean?"

"Look, you've got to play the game."

"I don't follow, Dave."

"OK. Stay with me chap, yeah?"

"Sure."

"Right, Suzi reads this. It's all going well. You've got her attention. Then she comes to the bit about your writing."

"You need to help me here, Dave. Where's the problem? The main reason I'm sending

this is to draw her attention to my writing."

"No mate, that bit's good. It's very well done as I said. It's the *my girlfriend* bit. Not a good idea mate."

"But I love Lynn."

"That's all very honourable, chap. It's to be commended, but there's no need to mention you have a bird. It's creates a barrier straight away."

"But I don't have eyes for anyone but Lynn."

"I know this, but saying me bird thought this, me bird thought that, is basically saying, yeah, I'd like to meet you an' all, but don't get any ideas. Maybe you're not setting out to say this, but it can be taken that way. If you're trying to get her to help you, then if anything, you need to keep those compliments coming. Continue in that frame. Know what I mean?"

I paused briefly to take all this in. Once again, Dave was spot on. He had nailed it. I'm glad that I had got him to cast his ever so perceptive eyes over it before clinking "send".

"Dave, once again, you have been of a priceless help to me. I'll take that bit out.

The question is though, how do I tell her that someone thinks my work is worth looking at?"

"Tell her, my mate Dave who's quite well read thinks my work is good. Obviously, don't tell

her about me, you know that I'm a figment of your imagination. That'll sound well weird. Just

say Dave thinks it's good. She'll understand. But don't exaggerate. That smacks of desperation."

"Cheers Dave. I'll do just that"

"Nice one my son," he replied. "Right you know the drill. Places to be, faces to see."

"OK Dave. Thanks again. You've been a massive help, as always."

I shut my eyes, then counted down... 10, 9, 8,7... opened them and he was gone.

So, after a major, minor alteration, I was now ready to click "send".

Dear Suzi,

Kevin Keegan here! You know the one, the maniac with the golf club!

I just wanted to say that I read your article and thought it was brilliant! It also cleared up the mystery of how I came to have the golf club in the first place. I went back to the After Dark as you requested and reunited Tim with his 7 iron. He was most happy.

I recognised the place straight away from your description. Considering that I don't remember the event, the place had a strange familiarity about it. As that can't be down to having remembered being there, it has to be down to your superb and accurate description – the centrally positioned stage to the up-to-date advertising, it was all there. I don't mind admitting to being just a tad jealous at your talent and having a job that clearly inspires you. My job just crushes my spirit– daily! I'd love to do what you do, but I'm no way near your standard. I used to write a bit at Uni – songs mainly and a bit of poetry. I didn't think much of it; still, I kept it in a folder all the same. My mate Dave, however, thinks it's really good, and said that I should try and find some way to write for a living, or at least plan to. I'm not so sure, but you never know. Dave said he knows – he reads about two books a week, has read all of Shakespeare's sonnets, and has even written lyrics for Eric Clapton!

Anyway Suzi, thanks once again for a really great article and for solving the mystery of that golf club!
Kind regards,
Alastair
"SEND"

That's it! There's no going back now. I have nothing to lose but my pride. I guess. And that's pretty much shot anyway.

This was all very exciting the more I thought about it. *I'll check my Inbox later.*

As I lay back, content, happy and warm, into my creaky old bed, I felt a slight hum of contentment. I knew it wouldn't last long; it seldom did. I knew that I had to grasp such moments, recognise them for what they were, and then hang on to them as if my life depended on it.

I didn't really expect my email to lead to anything. If it did, then great; but it didn't, then that would be fine too. The simple act of composing and then sending this email had been very cathartic. In sending it, I had allowed myself to dream. A good dream can be very enriching indeed. It can be a source of great sustenance. A good dream can be remembered long after it has finished and the sustenance lingers for a little while after. I decided that I needed to have more dreams.

Chapter 27

~

I was meeting Mayfly shortly. Since the day, that day when it finally clicked where I had met him, and the circumstance under which we had met, I had seen him briefly. Given the sheer magnitude of "that day by the river", it was to watch him preach, but not much else. I was fearful of sitting down with him and the inevitable discussion of that dark episode, which was sure to ensue. But today for some reason, I felt at ease about the whole thing. He had asked that we meet by the river, at the Oscar Wilde walk by the Abbey Ruins. I liked it there.

I had discussed this meet up with Dave. He wasn't convinced that it was a good idea as "that conversation" was sure to happen. He didn't think I was ready. He said that I would be at some point, but not yet. I politely suggested that we agree to differ on this one. This was a first for me. I had never disagreed with Dave before. Perhaps this showed that I was making at least some form of progress.

Dave told me that if I must go, then he would be on hand to jump in, if he could see that things got a bit weird and tricky. I couldn't see how this was possible given that the deal we had was that he wouldn't appear to me in front of others. Not that they could see him, but because of the way that I had been brought up, I would feel compelled to respond to anything he said. To not do so would be rude. He agreed. He could see where this could be problematic, but said to trust him. What else could I do? He had yet to let me down.

I arrived at the side of the fenced off Abbey Ruins. The wind was gentle and pleasant, as it slowly moved a small bunch of moss and twigs along, as I walked alongside the perimeter of the prison walls. I walked slowly, savouring each step, down along the Oscar Wilde walk or Chestnut walk – to give it its original name. Both names to me had merit and legitimacy. The latter framed perfectly the essence of this small stretch of riverside, with symmetrical horse chestnut trees, right down to the gates bearing the image of a harshly judged genius. Looking up at the high perimeters of this stark dungeon, it seemed eerie to think of a broken, despondent Mr. Wilde looking out on to the same stretch of pathway that I now was standing on. Oh, how he must have envied the gift of flight of the geese, the ducks, the swans, the moorhens, and how he must have cursed his own miscalculated risk, sealed by his own profound arrogance. Still, little could right the wrongs of such a cruel fate. Binding his title to his familiar picture of freedom seemed both the ultimate irony and the ultimate accolade; as the lime-green painted gables proclaimed: "Oh beautiful world". How right they were.

Mayfly had said to get here ten minutes early, take a leisurely stroll by the side of the ruins, and on alongside the prison walls. He had expressly asked that I don't just sit on any bench, as he had a specific one in mind. He said that its quirky design would easily mark it out from the others. I had duly obliged and was now sat gazing out onto the river. This seat was unique. This wrought iron olive-coloured seat was by its very shape unfriendly. It was possible to seat two, but its zigzag shape precluded being able to sit side by side. It stood out defiantly, from the oft marble, low-set symmetrical others. I took my seat and peered out onto the river. My otherwise unbroken vista was blurred slightly by a small cloud of winged insects. Together they formed the perfect kaleidoscope, blue moving into green, green into red, and then back to blue. I was mesmerised by such a fine exhibition of nature's bounty.

"They're called Mayflies," came a voice from above. I looked up. Standing there with a flowing hazel mane which glistened in the sun, and that familiar kind beaming smile, was Mayfly. He looked criminally resplendent. He continued, "these charming little fellows don't start out as such, my friend. They live in mud banks as little grubs, for months, waiting, longing for the real journey to begin. Then one day, that day comes and off they go. Mind if sit down?"

"Not at all, please."

"Thanks, brother. You see what you are seeing here? It's a party. It is a celebration of life like no other. But this supreme celebration is tinged with a great sadness. After all this time stuck in the mud, yearning to break free from their own slime, they get one day! One day! Hardly seems fair, does it?"

"It's not fair at all," I replied earnestly. "It's very unfair actually."

"These little fellas don't want to leave. Look at that energy! Feel their life force! They don't wanna go. But they know that they have no choice. They can sense that their time is up. So they just go for it. Then when the time comes to go, off they go alone to die. I'm sure if we were privy to their methods of communication, we would no doubt hear them shout, "carpe diem friends, seize the day!" Why wait to celebrate life to the full when we are no longer able? Two years ago to the day, and sitting exactly where you're sitting now, I became Mayfly. I haven't looked back since. So how are you these days, man?"

"Things are good these days," I replied. "Recently, I made a new friend."

"Ah cool. Now you've made another one."

This man of such a kind gentle spirit that I had finally got to sit down and connect with once again, really had no idea how much I felt indebted to him right now. It was all coming back to me – that day, that night being played out, again with a stinging, haunting clarity. I knew this would happen. Dave knew it would happen, but I now realised that it needed to happen. For months, I had been delaying the inevitable, afraid of bringing to the surface the emotions that I had kept buried for the past eight months. Once again, I was feeling exposed and vulnerable.

I turned and looked at my benefactor squarely and with purpose. He smiled back.

"Come on," he said. "Let's have it. I know it's in there bursting to get out. Don't worry, we'll have "the conversation" and that'll be it. OK? I'll start off. Yeah?"

"Sure." I replied. "Yeah."

This man was a legend. Hundreds of people each week turned up to watch him preach, to catch a glimpse of him, and now I was sat, albeit with my back to him, inches away from having an audience with this legend. I felt privileged. "How are you keeping these days? C'mon, honestly."

"Much better than when our paths first crossed," I replied.

"That's good to hear. Really good."

"I just want to say thank you so much for what you did that night. It ended up being such a massive wake-up call."

"You are most welcome, brother. I just found you. You did the rest. For months, I wondered how you were getting on; if you were in a better, happier place. Reading's not exactly London, so I was surprised that we hadn't met again before last month."

"Well, actually we had. Yet we hadn't if that makes any sense."

"No sense at all. But go on," he replied jokingly.

"OK," I laughed. "Well, I had seen you preach a few times, but I hadn't been able to make the connection until last month. The first time I saw you preach was about four months ago, and although I didn't make the connection then, I made a different sort of connection. Hearing you, listening to you, watching you, strong almost overpowering waves of energy were rushing through me. But there was something else. I suddenly felt incredibly at peace. You really have such a powerful, priceless gift."

"Ah, that is such a nice thing to hear my friend," he replied. "It's both humbling and heart-warming. You see, it's all about positivity. A while back, I read a book on the power of positive thinking. I can't remember who the author is. It's not important. What is important though is the message it conveys."

"Oh, and what message would that be?" I replied mischievously.

"It conveys a strong message of positivity. It says that your mind is similar to the body. What you get out is the result of what you put in. If you eat lots of fatty foods for example, it shows on the body eventually."

"This makes perfect sense," I replied. I wasn't entirely sure where he was going with this.

"You're probably wondering why I'm telling you all this. You're wondering what relevance it has. But it does have relevance. It has great relevance. We don't always know that we're putting positivity out there, but we do it nearly every day. Positivity doesn't discriminate. It doesn't care if you're suffering depression; it still sends signals. Do you remember the tent you left?"

"I try not to," I replied, in a weak attempt at deflection. I really wasn't comfortable with this question.

"Well, I think you should think of it more."

"Why though? What good is it going to do? How can revisiting a past shame be of any benefit?"

"Because it shows people how far they have come. It teaches them not to repeat the same mistakes. Positivity can happen even when you're not aware of it. Most people would have gone back probably the next day, but definitely within a few days and taken that tent down. You didn't though. Why?"

"As I said, I didn't see the point. It's not as though it cost me a lot anyway. It was a cheap piece of canvas from Millets. Why traumatise myself over that?"

"And if I'm correct, I bet you haven't even been near Reading Bridge since then. Am I right?"

"Too right! What? And revisit the scene of the crime?"

"Well, I think you'll be pleasantly surprised if you did."

"Pleasantly surprised? Really? But how?"

"Because if you go, you will see a great example of your positivity."

"I don't understand this at all."

"Well, let me help you understand then. Because if you go down to Reading Bridge, you will see that your tent still stands. And that in your tent live a couple of decent folk that were once homeless, and thanks to your positivity, no longer are."

"What? They moved into the tent?"

"That's exactly what happened."

"And they've been left alone? In that no one has moved them on?"

"Yeah, they aren't harming anyone. They could be under John Lewis trying to keep warm on a piece of cardboard, on a cold concrete street. Instead, thanks to you, they're living in a comfy tent, waking up to the sound of waterfowl and looking out on to Mother Thames. People pay good money for riverside views, and you have handed all this to them for free."

"So how are they getting on?"

"They have flourished actually. You see, because of your positivity, they now have somewhere not so cold to live. Because they have somewhere to live, they have somewhere to love and because they have somewhere to love, they can now make plans."

"What kind of plans?"

"The kind of plans we all have. Because they now have an address, Kim the man was able to get sufficient sleep needed in order to be able to get back into working as a plasterer. Plastering is hard graft you know."

"I'm sure it is. But, err, why is HE called Kim?"

"Well, 'cos he's kinda in transition. Yeah, he's not altogether happy being male. He tells me that he hasn't been for years."

"And his partner?"

"Oh, she's really lovely."

"So, what's HER name?"

"Oh, she's called Fran."

"And what does Fran do?"

"She plays the guitar, mainly sitting around by the side of the tent; although I have seen her in Broad Street busking on a few occasions."

"Oh wow. Is she any good?"

Mayfly paused briefly. I could see that he was trying to choose his words carefully.

"Errm, I would say she puts a lot of passion into what she does. She has it in spades. I've seen far more technically accomplished musicians on Broad Street, and I've been bored to pieces."

"Well, you've got to love a trier," I replied. I had no idea why I had said this, other than feeling profoundly awkward when hearing such a subtly damning verdict delivered by one so kind.

"Oh, I'm not so sure in her case. I've been in a few bands over the years. Don't get me wrong – I'm no Hendrix. I know my limits. But she really does take the piss."

"Well, what can you do?" I replied.

"Nothing really, I suppose." The important thing here is that she now has a platform upon which to murder great songs, and this platform is down to you. So, you can be proud of yourself fella."

I smiled. In one sense he was right. Surely I could allow myself to feel a certain sense of pride. The fact that cross-dressing plasterer Kim, and Fran, the murderess of fine classic songs, now had a place to call home, was more to do with circumstance, rather than an altruistic gesture on my part. Still, I was in no great hurry to challenge Mayfly's kind accolade. It seemed a great paradox that the very place in which I intended to leave this world, now formed the focus of stability for others.

I turned to face Mayfly. "You know chap, it's brilliant finally getting to actually sit down with you. The next time though, do you mind if I choose the seating arrangements?"

"Sure," he replied. "Why so?"

"Well, as much as I recognise the aesthetic merits of this quirkily designed seat, I would be inclined to suggest one which is entirely and not partially, river-facing. I certainly don't intend changing views, should we decide to meet here again, and I wouldn't be happy to see you missing out. Nice place though, chap."

"Of course," he replied. "I know of a lovely marble one further downstream. Does that sound more to your liking?"

"It certainly does Sir! Marble one it is then!"

Chapter 28

It was 7 AM as I wiped crust from my eyes. Once again Dave in his infinite wisdom had deemed it necessary to pay me a visit two hours before I had to be up.

"So how did it go then? I wish I'd been around."

"It went well, Dave. It went really well in fact."

"What was it like meeting him? The bloke's a legend. Apart from Elvis and maybe Madejski, he must be the most famous person in Reading."

"He's definitely up there," I replied. "That's for sure. I enjoyed the whole day. I was excited and perhaps just a tad apprehensive to begin with, but once we got talking, I started to feel a lot more relaxed. He has such a calming manner about him."

"He certainly does. I've met him a few times. He's a good bloke."

"But how could you have met him? I created you. How could he possibly see you?"

Dave looked puzzled as if caught off guard. Then he smiled. "Your face! I had you there," he replied. "Don't pretend I didn't."

"Dave," I replied rather sharply. "Don't do that. You're here to help me, not mess with my head."

"Sorry mate. It was in poor taste. Won't happen again. Promise."

"That's fine, Dave. Look, perhaps I overreacted. It's just that, well you know, my mind isn't the most robust these days."

"The most what?"

"The most robust. As in the strongest. As in my mental health isn't exactly in great shape."

"OK. Fair enough. Look, I can see that you're fading. You need to get your head down for a bit, yeah? So, I'll leave it here for now."

"Are you sure? You really don't mind?"

"I don't mind at all. You've got a long day ahead of you. Oh, and check your emails when you get back from work. I think you'll get a nice surprise!"

"Really? Why? From whom?"

"Get you! From whom! Don't be a tart. Just trust me yeah?"

"Sure Dave."

"Good stuff mate. You know the drill. Places, faces, innit. Catch up later yeah?"

"Sure Dave." I shut my eyes and counted down … 10, 9, 8, 7… I was out.

A few hours later, I was sat at my desk phoning clients in order to secure ongoing accounts. Although on the whole I found it mind-numbing, there were some clients I enjoyed tapping up, especially Jesper Hampter. Jesper was a self-made man, who with a modest loan from his parents had set up a small, yet successful dating agency. His clientele was varied and far-reaching. I enjoyed our little chats, during which he contravened both data protection and overall general decency. I liked him.

"So, Ali darling, he's 56, yeah? He's obese. He's divorced. He has OCD. He's been inside twice for aggravated assault. I mean what other kind is there? Oh, and he lives at home."

"He sounds quite a catch," I replied.

"I mean how am I meant to sell THAT, to anyone?"

"There must be some desperate ladies on your books. Surely?"

"Well, I do have a few in mind. But it won't be easy. He is rich though, which is a selling point, I guess."

"Indeed, a rich mummy's boy. I'm sure you've got more than enough desperate shallow ladies on your books that would jump at the chance of meeting?"

"James. His name's James Tillman. He lives somewhere in Winnersh Triangle. I think it's near Showcase Cinema."

"Oh, I see," I replied. "Thanks for that."

"Pleasure. Anyway Scotty, yeah of course you can rely on my continued support of "Fastend Telefonic". I'll get that signed off today and then email you confirmation."

"Cheers Jess," I replied. "That should set me up for a few months."

"Oh, anything for you, Scotty. What about your own love life? Are you still with that tart?"

"Erm yeah, although, she's no longer in that line of business."

"Oh, that's right. She's working for Tesco now. Sorry, I forgot. Well, every little helps, I suppose. Toodles pet."

"Erm, yes, toodles, Jes."

And that was it. Although a relatively small company, this was a big contract. Landing this each quarter was worth four thousand to the company and based on my commission of ten per cent, four hundred to me. I was flying this month. The fact that I was still on repeat business was largely down to Gerald's canny intervention. I had almost become a victim of my own success. "Them upstairs" had suddenly taken a keen interest in my sales figures. They were seriously considering moving me on to new business. Gerald had put forward the counterargument that my ongoing success was down largely to my ability at nurturing strong client bonds. And that due to the attention and care given at solidifying these relationships, ongoing business now accounted for over 60% of all monthly sales. He had then posed the conundrum that if they did move me away from these clients, there was every possibility that they would take their business elsewhere.

I looked over towards Gerald's makeshift, slightly open-plan office. The combined journey that the two of us had been on really was quite immense. No one could have possibly predicted such a change; least of all me. Alesandra was stood over by the photocopier. She seemed in deep conversation with Pookesh. Rumour had it, that the two were now in the deep throws of a steamy affair. It was unlikely that it was anything official – Alesandra didn't do relationships. She just had fun. At least that's what she had told me a while ago. Part of me of course was happy for them, but the other part was slightly jealous. I was happy because Pookesh was a mate, yet jealous because Alesandra was the embodiment of my fantasy woman. With her long corkscrew hair, her fresh olive complexion and round hazel eyes, this made her my imaginary plaything. She also had an understated classy elegance about her. She moved with such grace, poise and confidence, as if the whole of Reading was a catwalk crafted just for her. Morally I had no justifiable cause to be jealous. My heart was bound hopelessly in loving servitude to Lynn, and that was as it should be. Fantasies though are an entirely different affair.

The buzz of having secured the sale with Jes still lingered. As far as I was concerned, I had done more than enough to justify my calling it a day. In the course of a single phone call, I had made more in a day than most do in a week. It wasn't far off clocking off time anyway. Surely Gerald would let me go early? *After all, we're mates now*, I thought.

"Hey Pud," said Gerald. "I really want to help you, but you're going to have to ask me in a different way."

"How do you mean?" I replied.

"Well, you need to help me help you. If the upstairs dragons ask why you have left early, I'll have to tell them something. I can't just tell them that, well, you pulled off a massive sale, so I let you go early."

"Fair enough," I replied.

"How's that cough of yours coming along? Any improvement?"

"Oh, I see. Actually," I replied, "cough, cough, splutter. I can't seem to shift it. It seems to come and go. Just when I think I've seen the back of it, bang it's back. In fact…"

"OK! OK!" replied Gerald. "Don't overdo it! Well, we can't have you bringing in all your germs taking us all down with you. This is an open-plan office, see. Best get yourself off home then boyo. But go see your GP first."

"Ah cheers Gerald. I really do appreciate your understanding on this. I'll head off now. See you bright and early tomorrow."

"You bloody won't. An illness of this severity? I don't want to see you back here until Monday. Now get yourself off home."

"Cheers Boss," I replied. "Cough, cough, sniff."

Half an hour later, I was back home holding a fully charged glass of Bin, reading a response to a particular email that I had sent a few days ago. *How did Dave know of this in advance? He told me about this in the morning, and this response was only sent an hour ago.*

Dear Alastair,

Many thanks for such a nice email. Honestly, you do flatter me! Let's put things into perspective though. I am a features writer in a regional newspaper! But thank you all the same. It isn't often that I receive compliments full stop though; never mind ones of a literary nature. So I'll take this all the same.

I hope you didn't feel too embarrassed when reading the article. That was certainly not my intention. What you did was very random indeed. It was also very much appreciated.

Now, in terms of your desire to get into journalism, I think I can help with this. But I am afraid that this is a take it or leave it deal. I'm sorry to be so blunt, but this is the only opportunity available right now. I take it that you have no journalistic qualifications? On that subject, I have a course in mind that you may find useful. The reality for you as it stands right now is that few papers will give you assignments with any real substance.

Right, on to the offer. There are assignments available that no one seems willing to tackle. This I understand. We have all earned the right at this point in our careers to give these things a wide berth. All of us here at one stage have had to start off doing such dross. The thing is it is worth it. It's actually character-building. The fact that we are all still here is a testament to this.

So, if you're willing to swallow your pride in the interest of progression, then I could meet you somewhere in town perhaps and then take it from there?

Let me know what you think Kev ☺

Thanks once again ☺

Suzi X

I felt numb. Of course I was going to meet her. I had to get out of what I was doing. It was sapping my spirit. *Surely, any journalistic assignment is better than this? That's it. It's decided. I'm doing this. What have I got to lose? What could possibly go wrong?*

Dear Suzi…

Chapter 29

It was 12.00 o'clock and I was meeting Suzi in Malmaison shortly. No time had been wasted in setting this up. I had responded to her email suggesting that we meet up the next day. Her swift response agreeing to this had filled me with confidence. I was holding my folder containing various songs, and a vastly reduced selection of mediocre poetry. I was apprehensive and excited in equal measure.

I approached Market Place and walked towards the obelisk. I had walked through this part of town on many occasions, and noticed this quirky granite structure with its lantern interned flames, wondering what it commemorated. It was perfect. Here was a man who loved his town so much, and with such great affection. This was the perfect homage. It was his eternal tribute to his fellow townsfolk, and a gift to all future generations. It read…

> Erected
> And lighted forever at the expense of Edward Simeon
> ESQ
> As a mark of affection to his native town AD 1804
> Lancelot Austwick ESQ Mayor

I found what I had just read highly moving. I wondered how a simple thank you expressed could do this. But it wasn't just expressed. It was carved into a metal plate.

Seriously, I thought. *How could anyone not be blown away by this?* I wondered if many people actually did take the time out to stop and ponder these words, and then ponder this man after reading these words.

I told Suzi that, as I had no idea what she looked like, she would need to be the one who made the initial approach. She seemed fine with this.

I walked past the main reception and on into the bar area. Its exposed brickwork contrasted perfectly with the soft airy furnishings befitting such a boutique-and slick establishment.

Apart from a rotund, sharply dressed barman, there was only one person in the bar. *This has to be her* I thought. I guessed from the original article that she must have been early thirties; the swickers76 bit gave it away. This lady sitting here engrossed in a glossy magazine had to be her. Journalists by default tend not to be late to appointments.

Sensing someone was close by, she looked up from her magazine. With her smoky mascara, pink lipstick and sallow complexion, she looked more interesting than classically stunning.

"Ah Kevin Keegan as I live and breathe!" she said. "How very lovely to finally meet you again! Please, have a seat."

I sat opposite her as she quickly filled an empty glass. The bubbles and froth rose up quicker than she could pour and swished all over the table.

"Oh, how clumsy of me," she said, as she removed a packet of paper hankies from her inside pocket. "I hope you like Prosecco. It's a massive favourite of mine. I can't get enough of it lately. They have it on special offer today."

"Ah don't worry. Here, let me help you. Please, let me help." She pulled out another bunch and placed them into my open palm. I quickly dabbed the puddle. Before long, all that was left was a film where the liquid had been.

"Special offer? Really? Wow, you really how to treat a bloke," I said jokingly.

"Well, I do aim to please," she replied, with a cheeky smile.

"So", she said, looking at my dog-eared tanned folder. "Is this what I think it is?"

"That all depends on what you think it is," I replied. "Yes, it is. Here before you today is a collection of my various pieces of work that I don't rate that highly, but Lynn, sorry Dave, seems to."

"Is this Dave a cross-dresser?"

"How do you mean?"

"Well you called him Lynn first."

I knew that I had really messed up. I'd need something quickly. I'd have to act now. And I'd have to sound confident doing it.

"Look," I replied. "Promise me that when you do meet Dave, and you will at some point, you must never tell him that I told you this, but yes, Dave is indeed a cross-dresser. He isn't gay or anything. Not that I'd have a problem with that. He just likes to dress up, in that way. He's not full time though. He said that in his own words, that that would be well weird."

"So, how often does he, errm, indulge these whims?"

"Not much. I'd say once every two weeks. He hangs out in clubs up in London."

"Well, what does he do in these clubs?"

"He says that he just sits around drinking, chatting and admiring how nicely the silk rests on his exposed thighs."

"Cool," she replied

"Well, it wouldn't be my sort of thing," I said, "but you know, to each his own. He's not harming anyone I suppose."

I knew that there was every chance Dave would find out about this, and when he did, serious words would be exchanged.

"As long as he's happy," she replied. "That's the main thing. That's all that counts really. Anyway, on to business. Right, I have an assignment for you, should you wish to accept it."

"But don't you want to read any of my work before hand?" I replied. "I've brought it especially."

"Not right now," she replied. "I would like to take it away and photocopy it though, if that's ok?"

"Sure," I replied.

"Look," she continued. "I'm sure it's top notch. It's just that time is of the essence. This article needs to be in as soon as. She's been promised an interview for two weeks now, but no one wants to go. This is where you come in. Do this well and you'll be offered more. Look, no one is expecting you to perform heroics. You seem to have a good command of the English language and that's all we need right now."

She removed a brown envelope from her inside pocket. I was intrigued. What was she just about to show me? She pulled out an A4 colour portrait of what was clearly a woman – a slightly freckled, generously proportioned woman, with a grey bushy woodcutter-type beard.

"Recognise her?" Suzi asked.

"Erm no. Not really," I replied.

"Look it isn't a trick question. You either recognise her or you don't."

"Sorry," I replied. "I don't."

"I don't suppose you would really. I take it by your slight, soft Celtic tones, that you aren't originally from here?"

"This is true. I'm not. I came here a little over a year ago. But I do feel a strong sense of being OF this town," I replied.

"Listen, that's all very good. But it also explains why you do not recognise, "The Bearded Lady of Winnersh"!"

"Well, as a friend of mine said recently, Reading isn't exactly London. I would have expected that I'd have seen her around at some point. I mean, I've seen and even spoken with Reading Elvis. I've seen Sir John Madejski, although that was in the Oracle and he was surrounded by the press, so I didn't really get to speak to him."

"Well, you won't have seen her – at least not bearded up. She hung up her brush a little over two years ago. The whole town was shocked. No one expected it. She made a bloody good living from her hormonal imbalance or genetic disorder if you prefer. And then one day, she decided that enough was enough, and off it all came."

"Perhaps, she had had enough of being typecast," I replied.

"Perhaps. But that was her livelihood. It was all she knew. These days she's struggling to make ends meet. She even has to resort to food banks occasionally."

"So, thanks for this riveting insight, Suzi; but where does my assignment come into all this?"

"This IS your assignment, Kev. As I said, she has been promised a full interview and we haven't delivered. I would like you to be the one to finally deliver this interview. She's waiting. So, are you up for this?"

If I could process a cockney wide boy from the 1970s who in the technical sense didn't actually exist, then surely an elderly woman who once had a beard and decided one day to shave it off, couldn't be that much of a challenge.

"Sure, Suzi, I'm up for this. I'll look forward to this more than significant challenge." I wasn't in truth, entirely convinced of this. But still, what could possibly go wrong?

Chapter 30

"Cross-dresser, yeah? Likes to hang out in clubs and enjoys the feel of silk against my exposed thighs? Are you sure mate? Are you fucking sure?"

It was 7.30 AM. Dave had woken me up early, again. This time it wasn't to test me, or to engage in general chit-chat. As expected, he had found out about my little faux pas with Suzi. He wasn't impressed.

"Look, I'll say it again Dave. I'm sorry man. I got myself into a hole and I had to somehow get myself out of it. This was the first thing that came into my head. I had to act quickly."

"Oh, so you thought you'd sacrifice me then. Fuck sake. I thought we was mates."

"Dave, we are mates. I messed up. I'm sorry. OK?"

"Spose," he replied. "Look I'm sorry too. It's just that I have a reputation to uphold. Know what I mean?"

"Well, yes and no. Yes, because, well, look at you. Look at you standing there looking like a football rock star."

His blue-green eyes formed a perfect crescent as a warm smile formed on his bronzed, chiselled features. He really did have a point. Imagine in the real world, the reputation of one so iconic being compromised. But this wasn't the real world. Still, I did feel bad.

"Look fella," I continued. "I am truly sorry. Given that only I can see you, it is unlikely that you two will ever meet, but I will set her straight. I'll come clean about Lynn, and that it was her who said it and not you, and that I panicked and said the first thing that popped into my head."

"No mate. You can't say that!" he replied. "You've got her on side now. Look, I appreciate the fact that you were willing to do this for me. Listen, let's just move on from this. It's alright, yeah?"

"Yes mate," I replied. "Cheers, I appreciate it."

"No problemo chap." He pulled the left sleeve of his football top up and checked his chunky silver watch. "Right then chap; places to be, faces to see. Catch up later yeah? I hope the interview with the now beardless one goes well."

"Cheers fella," I replied. "I hope so too". I shut my eyes then counted down from 10. 10, 9, 8, 7…

Four hours later, I was sat at a table in a quiet corner of the "Kebab and Calculator" pub, somewhere near

Wokingham. *What a strange name for a pub,* I thought. *Usually, when a pub is named the something and the something, there's some sort of correlation, but what possible correlation could there be between a kebab and a bloody calculator?*

The thought of my first foray into journalism filled me with excitement and a certain degree of foreboding. This was either going to go spectacularly well, or it was going to be a monumental balls-up. There was no grey area here. How could there be, really? My mini office – laptop, smartphone, and Dictaphone, were all ready and primed for action.

After roughly 10 minutes sat pondering possible failure or success, in she walked. She cut a forlorn, lost figure, and was considerably thinner than in the photograph Suzi had shown me. *Goodness* I thought. *A lot can change in some people, even in the space of just two years.* She made her way over.

I stood up and extended my hand. She shook it, forcing out a half smile through layers of her caked-on foundation-laid face.

"Please, here," I said, carefully filling her champagne flute with today's special offer Prosecco. "I hope you're ok with Prosecco? In my experience, Prosecco is a great leveller when you're unsure as to what the other person drinks. Also, it's on special offer," I continued.

"Special offer eh?" she replied. "Well, you really know how to treat a lady, don't you?"

"Especially a former bearded one!" I replied.

This response was met with a look of disapproval. *Shit.* I thought. *I've done it again, letting nerves dictate what comes out of my mouth.*

"Look," I continued. "I'm really sorry. I'm a bit of a tool sometimes. I get nervous and spout nonsense. Please accept my apologies. I meant no offence. Honestly."

"It's fine. It's fine", she replied. "I understand this is your first assignment?"

"It is."

"Nervous then?"

"You could say that."

"I don't blame you. I would be too, if my first assignment was to interview a freak show act."

"That's the thing though, you're not. I would never judge someone solely by their appearance. The day that I walk in your shoes, will be the day that I cast judgement upon you. Not that this will ever happen of course. Despite being late thirties, I still lack the ability to grow anything appropriating even a modest beard, and I look terrible in a dress. Haven't got the legs for it you see – too spindly."

This was met with a slight chuckle.

"OK then, shall we get started?" I continued.

"Let's," she replied.

"To start off, what's your actual name? People only know you as the Bearded Lady of Winnersh or the former Bearded Lady of Winnersh."

"Well, I was born, Patience, Janice, Johnson in 1927 in Portsmouth."

"No way!" I replied. "1927? No way! That would make you…"

"81," she replied.

"But seriously, and I hope you don't mind my saying this, I would have put you early to mid-fifties at the very latest."

She appeared taken aback. "Of course, I don't mind you saying that I look far younger than I actually am! It's a compliment. Apart from my family no one has ever paid me a compliment. Well actually, there was one other. But that was a long time ago. So thanks."

Once again, in the space of two days, I found myself being incredibly moved. Yesterday it was by something I had read, and today, it was upon hearing this. *What the fuck is it with society?* I thought. *Why does life have to be so fucking unforgiving?*

I couldn't contain myself any longer. I had to get away to compose myself. "Can you excuse me a second? Call of nature."

I hastily made my way from the table, clumsily knocking the heavy chair against her handbag.

"Sorry."

I reached the toilet cubicle just in time. Lines of salty streams rolled down my cheeks and onto my lips. Impatiently and angrily, I wiped them away. But more came until my ducts and emotion had been completely drained.

I dabbed my eyes quickly with tap water, impatiently trying to compose myself. I now felt ready to return.

"Errm," I said nervously. "Sorry about that. I don't know what came over me. First time nerves, I guess. Shall we pick up where we left off?"

"Let's," she replied. "And I know exactly what came over you. You're sensitive. That shows character. I respect character. I'm actually glad that they sent you, and not some up their own selves smart-arsed prick. It's clear to me that you're able to see beyond the hype and see the person inside, the real person."

I was lost for words for a moment. "Thanks Patience. May I call you Patience?"

"Of course you may. It makes a change from Beardy or Beardless. That's what most call me. I can tell you now that although I requested this interview, I too was nervous. You see, I need this interview for my own peace of mind. I expected them to send me some sensationalist-seeking know-it-all. Instead, they send me you; a genuine and caring soul. I have a strong hunch about this. It's going to go well."

Her hunch had proved very accurate indeed. The interview ended up morphing into an effortless and enjoyable free-flowing conversation. It was as if we were two old friends who had met up after a great many years, excitedly battling to get a word in. The Prosecco too had flowed with perhaps too much ease. Patience, it turns out, was far more versed in the world of Prosecco than I was.

Long after closing time, as she secured my taxi seatbelt into position, she smiled. "Thanks again." Thanks for actually listening to my story with such an open and caring mind, young man."

"You're most welcome," I replied. "It was a pleasure and a true honour to have met someone so honest and so decent."

"Oh yeah, and that question you asked about the connection between the kebab and calculator?"

"Oh yeah," I replied. "You mean, there's actually a connection between a kebab and a calculator?!"

"But of course there is! Well you see, Jimmy, the owner, once worked on the books representing a chain of kebab houses. One day, going through the accounts, he spotted, let's say, a few things that just didn't seem to add up. These were things that he couldn't accurately calculate. When he brought it to their attention, he was told firmly that he hadn't seen anything, and that it was in all their best interest if he amended his returns. He left shortly after that. He'd made his money. He told me that he'd always wanted to own his own pub. And now here we are, having just left "The Kebab and Calculator".

"Wow!" I replied, barely able to say more.

"Mrs taxi driver, make sure you get this nice young man back to Reading safely."

The driver nodded in affirmation.

"This man has important business in Reading tomorrow. He has a brilliant article to deliver!"

Chapter 31

~

I had emailed my interview with Patience over to Suzi an hour ago. I had yet to receive a reply. I wasn't worried. There was a lot to take in. I had come at this from what I would imagine from their perspective to be an unexpected angle. If they were expecting a sensationalised, tabloid-friendly, family-friendly, victim-assailing, neatly packaged piece of cheap titillation, then they were in for a huge disappointment. I was past caring if they delivered a favourable response or not. Worst-case scenario? I had met a truly dynamic, decent individual. This could only be enriching.

Thanks to Gerald's sense of camaraderie, I was into my third "sick" day. This couldn't have come at a better time, as Lynn's shift pattern meant that she too had a day off. I was meeting her today in the Crowne Plaza. I was going to finally tell her about Dave. No details would be spared. I felt now that the time was right. Besides, couples, especially those very much in love, shouldn't have secrets, and secrets between couples didn't come much bigger than Dave.

I had run this by Dave first. I was going to do this with or without his blessing, preferably with it. Fortunately, he was completely on board. In fact, he thought it was a great idea. He said that her acceptance or lack thereof, would be a barometer of the extent of how much value she placed upon our union. I have to say that I was surprised at the eloquence at which he had expressed this. He had then reverted to form when assuring me that he would be waiting close by in case things got well weird.

I turned out on to the Oxford Road with a slight feeling of foreboding. How would she take it? I still wasn't entirely convinced it was a good idea, despite Dave's reassurance and best wishes. I'd have to choose my words carefully and with skill. If I could engage with humility a person who had lived on the margins of society most of her life, then surely telling my loved one about a very dear friend shouldn't be too challenging.

It was a blustery sharp day. To many, this would be what they would lazily label a miserable day. I didn't see it that way. Every season has virtue. Although it seemed that the only season that we're meant to comment on favourably is summer. Not just an average summer's day, but a sweltering, stifling, humid almost overbearing heat. *Weather Fascists*, I mused.

OXFORD ROAD

The bombastic bulky yet elegant frontage of the Crowne Plaza came into view. I entered slowly and with a sense of apprehension. *It's never too late Al. You haven't said this yet. You don't need to. This could go really horribly wrong. Are you sure? I mean, are you really sure? Because, once this has been said, it can never be retrieved. I mean, does she really need to know this? Will she thank you for it? Who are you actually doing this for? It's really for you, isn't it?*

The ceiling-length windows down at the end of the main bar revealed a picture of great energy. Flocks of seagulls seemed to move as one strong unit of white, up and down and from side to side. I guessed that it may be feeding time. Perhaps some excited kids with their parents looking on were enthusiastically tearing off chunks of bread and throwing them randomly in Mother Thames. This activity seemed to mirror the erratic energy now shooting through me.

Quickly I scanned the place seeking out my Lynn. I couldn't see her at first. *Where are you?!* I thought.

"Oi Oi!" came a familiar and welcome voice. "Over 'ere!" I followed the ripples left by those dulcet tones, and there she was. She was sat among a small cluster of rouge-tinted chairs, to the side of the piano. She had chosen the area that afforded the best privacy such a place could offer. This suited me perfectly.

We had been together nearly five months now. The electricity that I felt jolt right through me whenever me met, didn't seem like abating any time soon. Lynn was blessed with effortless, subtle elegance. Even the way she sat, legs astride, shoulders pinned back and neck to the side, locking her gaze in on me, had the ability to take me off into a near hypnotic state of being.

"Goodness, love," I said. "You're early again. This is the second time in… well, it's the second time."

"I've turned over a new leaf," she replied. "Working in a position of responsibility as I do now with people under me, means that I have to be seen to set an example. Know what I mean?"

"Yes, I think I do," I replied. I wasn't sure what was happening here. Was she playing me? Or was she being serious.

"Anyway," she said. "Come 'ere you." She stood and very unexpectedly, deftly grabbed my crotch. "That'll teach you to choose a hotel to meet up in, instead of your bedroom."

"Well," I said, trying to compose myself, "I thought that given the sheer magnitude of what I intend to tell you, a place other than my bedroom seemed best."

"Fair enough," she replied. "Oh, I hope you don't mind, but they're running a special deal on Prosecco, and I thought that I'd get this one. The barman, not the fat one but that slim fit blond one, tells me that it's one of the best they've ever had in this place. Apparently it comes from the foothills of Tuscany and has got a nice apricot finish with subtle gooseberry tones. Here, let me fill you up."

She poured slowly and carefully as the level of liquid mirrored the level of bubbles. *Now that's classy,* I thought. *That's how it's done.*

I sat and took a sip from my perfectly poured libation. "OK, I'm just going to come out and say this. I've met someone."

"You fucking what?" she replied. "Ah, so that's why you said to meet here. That's why you couldn't tell me in bed. What's the matter? Afraid I'd cut your balls off? 'Cos I would you know."

"No," I replied. "It's not like that. I haven't met another woman, if that's what you're thinking."

"So, what are you telling me here? You've met a man? And you expect me to be happier with that? At least I could compete with a woman, but a bloke?"

"It isn't like that either. Yes, I have met a man, but he's not a lover. He's a friend."

"Give it time," she replied. "Give it time, yeah?"

"It isn't like that. I'm not hoping that it will develop into anything other than what it is. Please. You need to listen to me. This is serious. It's very serious in fact. But it's all good. OK?"

"OK, then. You have my full attention. Go on…"

"Right. You know that I have knocked drugs on the head? Yes?"

"Yes."

"Good. And you also know that, let's say, I have been having certain struggles of the mind?"

"Go on."

"Thanks," I replied, now feeling a lot more at ease. "Well, and I didn't want to burden you with this, but a cloud can suddenly come over me. There's no warning and there are no reasons. It just happens."

"Oh, OK," she replied. Her tone was now sounding softer and her facial expression now reflected her concern.

"Well, I read somewhere that if you name this cloud, then it somehow weakens its power. Its potency over time becomes a lot less. Anyway, I named my cloud. I named him… Jeremy."

"Why Jeremy? It doesn't really sound like a threatening powerful name. Not like Martin or Daniel or something like that. But Jeremy? Anyways, go on."

"Well, it seemed like the right name for the right occasion. Anyway, shortly after naming him, I was standing over by that tree seat past the clubhouse."

"What? The one that we had a picnic by?"

"Yes, that's the one. Well, I had called in sick. It was a Monday."

"Ali, I've told you about that. That looks well suspicious."

"I had to though. I had no choice."

"No choice? Why?"

"Well, Jeremy had decided to pay me a visit. I'm no use to anyone when he's around."

"OK. I'll let you off," she replied, with that mischievous cheeky smile.

This is going a lot better than I thought it would. Much better!

"Anyway, I was leant against the tree seat, eyes closed, sipping my coffee from a flask."

"What? Your very own special coffee?"

"The very one," I replied. "Then I heard someone speak. This person who I had never met before, was giving me his unsolicited opinion on what drinks he likes, and what drinks he doesn't. I thought he was just plain rude at first. Then he said something which told me that there was a lot more to it. That perhaps, all was not how it seemed."

"So what did he say?"

"OK. This is where it gets a tad strange, or as he says, well weird."

"Go on."

"Well, he said that his name was Dave and that he is here to kill Jeremy."

"What? How would he know about Jeremy?"

"Indeed. It gets better or considerably worse, depending on your viewpoint. He said that he was a figment of my imagination and that I have brought him in to kill Jeremy. The deal is, once he has done that, he'll be off."

"I don't know what to say, babes," she replied. "On one hand, I'm relieved to know that you're not shagging another bird. But I'm also a little bit, actually a lot worried, that you have an imaginary friend. Have you seen him much?"

"Actually yeah. I have. He turns up most mornings and wakes me up. He asks me all these really silly questions."

"Like what?"

"Well one was, if I was stuck in a locked room with my hands bound, and the only way that I could get out would be to eat a key out that was sitting in a bowl of slime, would I do it?"

"Oh yeah, that's from SAW," she replied. "I love that scene!"

"I've seen that too. But are you not concerned about my friend? I know in the technical sense he perhaps isn't real, but to me he feels real."

"Well Ali. Is him being around helping you? Do you feel Jeremy has shown up less since he's come on the scene?"

"Yes, definitely."

"Do you think that one day he will carry out his promise and kill this fucker? This inconsiderate fucker who makes your life unbearable?"

"Yes, I really believe that he will do this."

"Well then, I'm glad you've met this Dave bloke. I'd like to meet him one day. Although I know that it'll never be possible. Look, do you know the very first time we met? You was happy and laughing and joking?"

I gently nodded.

"Well, I knew that you had a Jeremy even then. OK. I didn't know him by that name. I don't even know how I could tell, but I could. Call it a woman's intuition. But I knew underneath all that joking and laughing, that you wasn't completely happy." "Look, Ali," she continued, trying to smile through moistened eyes, "I love you very much. I care about you. I'm glad you told me about Dave. I ain't always around, and I worry about you. So if you tell me that this Dave bloke has shown up to help out, then how could I possibly have a problem with that?"

Deeply moved, I leant in towards her and took her soft manicured hands in mine, gently caressing them.

All this worry, I thought. *And for what?*

"Right then", she said. "So, when are you taking me off to yours? To your bed?"

"Well. Seeing as though we're here, settled and comfortable, I thought that I'd see about staying. Up for it?"

"Why not?" How could I say no? As date nights go, and I know it wasn't just a date night, this seems the perfect ending! I'd love to stay here. Wow, you really do know to treat a girl."

"Well, I like to think I do," I replied. "Come 'ere you!"

Chapter 32

~

Today was the day of my article. I had chosen to buy the paper copy of the Chronicle, rather just read it online. The latter for me lacked substance. It seemed inappropriate to just scroll and click, when I could be literally holding the article. They said that as columns go, it was too long to put it on as one article. Articles tend to range from a thousand to sixteen hundred words they said. Mine far exceeded this. So, they had asked if I would be happy for them to serialise it. Of course I was happy. The important thing here for me was that they were willing to publish it at all. When I told Suzi this, her response was that I really should have more faith in my own ability – shit loads more in fact!

The bearded lady – but who is the real freak show?
By Alastair McLeish-Pidkin

I was after an assignment – a start if you like. In my mind, there wasn't an assignment that I wouldn't have been prepared to accept. As the old adage goes, if something comes too easy, then perhaps it isn't worth doing. Nothing could have prepared me though for the assignment that I was presented with. Would I accept this assignment? Of course I would! I didn't even give it a second thought.

So last Friday, I had the task, or as I was to find out soon, the pleasure, of meeting a certain Patience Janice Johnson. You might know her as "The Bearded, or now, Beardless Lady of Winnersh". Personally, I prefer Patience. But hey, that's just me.

The youngest of six siblings, Patience Janice Johnson was born to Melville Johnson, a draper, and Verity Johnson nee Harris, a washer woman, in Portsmouth in 1927. They were what would have been labelled at the time, members of the skilled working class. I suppose it would be somewhat fanciful to say that she led an entirely charmed life. They got by, and although not rich in the monetary sense, wanted for little, least of all love.

Patience's upbringing didn't differ from that of those around her. They all played out in the street. They played hopscotch, and with someone perching precariously on a rope, they took turns to swing each other around a lamppost. Sometimes the rope would snap and knees would be grazed, but that was fine. They knew the risks. Grazed knees seemed a more than acceptable price to pay if it meant that they could play "Lamp Rope". They even played "Knock,

knock ginger". If they were prepared to risk grazed knees, then surely a clip around the ear from mum or dad didn't seem like much, not that she ever received such a punishment. Violence in all its forms was an anathema to her devout Quaker parents. She, like all her siblings, was reared on a strict diet of tolerance, peace, respect, and vegetarianism. Seeking the light within all humanity was not only encouraged, but was expected. It's just a pity that others weren't so imbued with that same sense of spirit.

One day, the relative tranquillity that she took as a given was shaken. It started off with a small cluster of soft hair at the base of her chin. At first, she dismissed it as a consequence of puberty. Not much was known back then as to how puberty manifested itself on the faces of those afflicted. But it was largely believed that the sudden appearance of facial hair was something experienced solely by little men and not little ladies.

They didn't have face creams back then. So in a desperate attempt to remove this unwelcome fuzz, she would frantically scrub the base of her chin, using a wooden nail brush, caked in baking soda. This sadly never yielded the desired results. So still the hair kept coming. Before long, fuzz was to turn into sharp evasive bristles, until eventually by the age of nineteen she sported a beard that the most seasoned of sea dogs would have been proud of.

Her parents hadn't known what to do, and could offer few words of solace to ease her burden; and it was a burden. Most nights, she would wait until the house was still and then gently weep until spent of all energy and emotion. This went on for the next three years until one day she saw an ad that was to change her life – **The Circus is coming to town! Come along and see with your own eyes – Lions, Tigers, Elephants, these most powerful of beasts, dance, just for you. Come listen if you dare to the great SHOUTINI! And watch the bearded lady as she plays her enchanted violin. Coming soon to Southsea , 9th – 11th of November.** She showed me the surprisingly well-preserved add. She carries it around with her whereever she goes. I'm not sure why. I didn't think to ask.

Not wishing to lie to her parents, she had asked their permission to visit the circus. You see, her parents didn't approve of circuses. They didn't feel that it was right to watch animals stolen from the wild perform in order to satisfy mankind's warped sense of amusement. She agreed that they had a point, but went along anyway.

On the whole, it had been a bit of an anti-climax. She didn't know much about circuses, but even she could see that little was going according to plan. The elephants it seemed, hadn't read their terms of enslavement, and had steadfastly refused to mount the giant multi-coloured ball. This led to the frustrated Circus Master's excessive use of the whip which could have proved costly. Had it not been for the quick thinking of Valentio, the star acrobat, sweeping down from the rafters and whisking the Circus Master off to safety, he would have been trampled to death by four angry elephants. She said that they had tried to make out that it was all part of the act. She wasn't convinced. The clowns were the biggest let down. All they did was push cream pies in each other's faces and then run around the ring laughing. She didn't see the point in clowns. I tend to agree; and not all clowns wear makeup. The great SHOUTINI, well he was this small Argentinian man, dressed in an evening dinner suit – you know the one – long black jacket with penguin tails, top hap, and a white collarless shirt. She said that he stood in the middle of the ring, simply shouting out messages that had earlier been collected from members of the audience. But she also said that this was no ordinary shouting. It wasn't like the kind of shouting that one would hear around pub kicking out time, or when couples quarrelled. This was shouting of an entirely different kind. She described it as "operatic shouting," without the subtlety of opera. It was only when the bearded lady appeared that she began to take any real interest. For the first time in her life, she was seeing someone who looked just like her. Since the day that first cluster of fluff appeared where it had no right to appear, she had felt a type of loneliness that words alone couldn't do justice in fully explaining. Then this other "odd" person appeared. She was trying to play her violin. Initially few seemed interested in listening, preferring instead to inflict upon her, bellowing, snarling, sneering laughter. But still, she played on. Eventually, this toxicity gave way to silence, as they listened to what Patience described as the "most Heavenly piece of music that I had ever heard." She learned later that it was "Pavane" by Gabriel Fauré. She said that she had been moved to tears by such beautiful sounds, as had a great many of the audience. She had wondered who this talented and, despite having a beard, beautiful lady was. She would find out soon…

Please watch out for Alastair's second instalment of this riveting piece on one Reading's of finest! Coming sometime next week!

Also, do feel free to drop by online and leave your comments on this and any other article.

I sat back, lit my previously prepared rolled-up cigarette and exhaled slowly. I felt as if my brain was being flooded with all manner of positive chemicals and energy. I was now experiencing close to dangerously highly levels of pride and smugness. I had done it. Even though I had carried out this interview and recorded our conversation, part of me was finding it difficult to comprehend that I was capable of putting all this together like I had done. The other part of me was telling me not to be too surprised, as I always had this in me. I decided that for now, I would listen more to the latter.

Chapter 33

"Great article mate! I was hooked from the beginning. I was reading it thinking, how could Alastair have written this? I never knew you had it in you chap. Have you been doing a course in creative writing recently that you haven't told me about, or is this just a natural talent?"

"Ah, cheers Dave. It means a lot mate. I was very pleased overall. I have to say. You do flatter me! No, I haven't been on any creative writing courses lately!"

"You know what this means now though, don't you?"

"What? That I can write a bit; that I'm not too shabby."

"Not too shabby! Listen to him. Oh get you, Mr. Modest geezer! What this means is that you won't have to do this shitty little job for much longer."

"Dave, I appreciate your faith in me; but let's not get too carried away now. It's only my first article. You make it sound as if I've been shortlisted for a Pulitzer Prize. Do you know the lengths these guys have to go through to even get these articles written?"

"Not really. No. Don't really care as it goes."

"Well, I'll tell you anyway."

"If you must. Go on then. Let's have it."

"For a start, they risk their own lives. Some go deep behind enemy lines, posing as combatants. They are open to attack from both sides. Overhead, tomahawk missiles rain down all around, destroying everything they hit. If their cover is blown, well, then that's it. Game over. All I did was go for a few drinks with a woman who once had a beard and now doesn't, then write about it."

"Mate, you did a lot more than that. Can't you see? You allowed her to have a voice. You treated her with respect and with kindness. Others wouldn't have been so kind. They would have made it about the freak that she is, but really she ain't. Do you what I mean?"

"Not really, Dave. But go on."

"Cheers. Right. You're on the side-lines yeah? You're desperate to get on. The gaffer knows this, and well he ain't quite ignoring you, but he ain't looking you directly in the eye. He feels bad. He ain't gunna play you. Well, not unless his worst player, apart from you, is hacked down. And then it happens; inside left Barnesy gets chopped by Wilkins. Yeah? Barnsey is in absolute bits. He's rolling around, screaming in pain. The crowd are on their feet. They're sure Wilkins is off. But no! The ref pulls out a card. And it's only a yellow! It's the cup. There's a lot at stake. The gaffer looks over at you and gives you the nod. You're on. Don't get me wrong. You're shitting it. But you go on. Then you play a blinder – an absolute blinder. You jink nicely in past one player, bosh, you swing in past another, you give a third the slip, then bang! And the ball sails straight up into the top left hand corner. Poetry mate. Sheer poetry. The keeper never stood a chance. You then turn around to Wilkins, sticks him the finger, saying 'ave it!! Chelsea can't get on the M4 and back to London quick enough. No one gave us a chance that day. No one thought we could do it. But we did."

"Wow Dave. Don't get me wrong. It's a great story. But what on earth has that got to do with, well, anything?"

"Oh, do I have to spell it out?"

"Please."

"Well, the beardless one is the home team. Yeah?"

"Yeah."

The sub on the side-lines who no one really expects much from is you. Yeah?"

"Erm yeah, I suppose."

You get the chance. Not only do you play alright, but you play a blinder. You got that chance last week and took it, and you played a blinder. I knew you could do it, but I doubt anyone else thought you could. You said that she was only giving you interviews that no one wanted to do. She just wanted to tick it off a list, but she had no idea that you'd smash it. Do you know what I mean now, chap?"

"Actually, do you know what, Dave? I think I do. I really think I do you know."

I certainly got the gist of what he was trying to say. As back-handed compliments go, this had to rate among the best. Dave was using a lot of football analogies lately. I wasn't sure why. But as analogies go, they really were quite entertaining and abstractly informative.

"Right then," he said, glancing at his watch, "12.00 already. OK chap, time to fly. Places to be; faces to see."

I shut my eyes and counted down from 10…10, 9, 8, 7 …opened them, and he was gone. I didn't feel too inconvenienced at this unplanned visit. It was the weekend and at least this time, he'd let me have a decent enough lie-in.

I was meeting Mayfly shortly. He had told Kim that he had finally met "the man of the river" again. Kim, he said, was happy for him as he knew the story and the huge significance that it held for him. He also expressed surprise that in a place the size of Reading our paths hadn't crossed again before now. Not only was I meeting Mayfly though, I was meeting Kim and Fran. Not only was I meeting them, I was doing so by that bloody tent. When Kim heard that Mayfly and me had re-established contact, he had asked if we could come around to theirs for dinner and a general meet-up. Without consulting me, Mayfly had agreed and then informed me. I wasn't best pleased about not being asked. Had I been consulted beforehand, I may well have said no. To know that the tatty little cheap tent, the one in which I had tried to end it all in, now provided a home for others, was all I really needed to know. I got the significance. To labour this wasn't necessary. From a physiological perspective, I wasn't sure if returning to what I called "my crime scene," would have any positive effects on me. I really wished that he'd asked.

I approached Reading Bridge. I looked across the river and there it stood – the tent, that tent, that bloody tent. *Fuck!* I thought. *What am I doing? What was Mayfly thinking? Why would he want to bring me here? How on earth could he possibly think that doing this is a good thing for me? Is it a good thing for me? Is it a good thing for him?*

I suddenly felt a strong presence close by. It was Dave. What was he doing here? *He can't just show up in public! He said he'd never do this.*

"No doubt, you're thinking, why has he shown up now, in public? Yeah?"

"Well yeah? What are you doing Dave?"

"Look, I can feel your worry. I just wanted to tell you that it will all be fine. That's it really. I don't know why Mayfly agreed to this meet up by the tent. By that tent.

It's mental. But I'll be close by, waiting to jump in, if things start to get well weird."

"Cheers chap. I appreciate this. Only Dave, don't jump in, because if you do that, then I'll start talking to you and people will then witness a crazy person talking into mid-air. But do stay close by. Yes?"

Dave paused to consider this compromise. I stopped and waited.

"Do you know what," he replied. "That is almost perfik! So, I stay close by but don't show up; even if things get well weird."

"Especially if things get well weird, Dave. I tell you, the fact that I know you're close by will help greatly. It will seriously put my mind at rest. Right my friend, we'll need to leave it here if that's OK. I'm nearly there."

"Sure thing chap. But remember yeah, I'll be looking on. Yeah?"

"Cheers chap," I replied. "I really do appreciate this."

"Pleasure Sir," he replied.

I turned back and he was gone.

I continued on down the granite steps of Reading Bridge. Straight ahead, the tent came into view. It wasn't just a tent now. It was a home. They had extended the porch and a waist-high perimeter fence snaked around, marking out this nicely kept homestead. The turquoise tip had faded slightly into a soft grey. A sweet scent of burning foliage drifted up and around and down. A soft, yet commanding breeze conducted proceedings. And there they stood facing me, with a collective warm, inviting presence, Kim, Fran, and the ever so enigmatic Mayfly.

I hoped Dave would prove true to his word and stay close by. I had a strong feeling that things were just about to get weird; well weird in fact.

Chapter 34

I was pleased with myself. I had closed a huge deal. This had netted me a commission of around seven hundred quid. It seemed hugely ironic that when I finally, after years, had discovered an outlet that afforded me a huge degree of hope from occupational despair, I was enjoying my most successful period in a job I largely disliked. I couldn't quite work this one out. Anyway, this analysis was for another time. The second instalment of my interview with Patience had been published. Rather than as last time, hold a copy of the paper, I had gone online. This was at the advice of Dave. He had told me that there were some choice comments online that "was well worth a butchers". He had warned me against cheating and rushing straight to the comments section without reading the article first, as I'd miss out on the full experience. He also said that it's best practice after all to take a holistic approach to such things. His eloquence in this matter had disarmed me somewhat.

And there it was - the second instalment of my serialised article…

The bearded lady – but who is the real freak show?
By Alastair McLeish-Pidkin. "CLICK".

She said that not once even in childhood had she ever wished to run away and join the circus. She had never wanted to visit it when it came to town. The fact that her parents disapproved of them, could also have been a factor.

Visiting for the first time merely confirmed her overall boredom at the whole affair. Despite entering in through this giant tent with an open mind and a slight tinge of excitement, she just couldn't see merit in this spectacle. This was a view we both share. I too found circuses boring growing up. Now that most of them no longer have performing animals in them makes it all the more tedious. Don't get me wrong. I am a strong advocate of animal rights, and am of the firm belief that animals have no business appearing in such crude spectacles. But that is the one thing in my opinion that makes such days even slightly bearable. So when their presence was removed from the bill, that should have signalled the eventual demise of this genre. I mean, clowns pushing perfectly good pies into each other faces and then running off? Trying to make a quick get away in a car that fails to start? I mean, really? A short penguin-suited Argentinian man shouting out shopping lists? Seriously? Why? But a bearded lady bringing a violin to life, with such sad beauty? Now that's an experience well worth having! Especially if the person watching shouldn't really have a beard either.

She told me that she was fixated, hypnotised even. After the show, she made her way round the back of the main tent to seek out her doppelganger. When she finally did find her that was, as a very dear friend of mine might remark, when things got well weird.

Up until now, she said that she had ever only shown a tepid interest in boys and certainly wouldn't have viewed girls as anything other than friends, or in some cases, foes. This Goddess standing there in front of her however, was an entirely different sexual animal. With her neatly trimmed royal sandy beard, flawless complexion, and perfectly applied eyeliner and mascara, illustrating and framing these sea-blue eyes, she was beckoned inwards to her boudoir. It was actually a run down, untidy, unkempt, ramshackle trailer with peeling paint and a yellow-stained roof. But I prefer boudoir – it adds a certain mystique to the account. Don't you think? She then proceeded to give me a full rather graphic account of what transpired. As this is a family paper, it shouldn't be repeated really, I'll spare you the details. Besides, I don't think the editor would approve. The only downside, she said, apart from the squalor and the smell of must, was a really bad beard rash the next morning. She said it was itchy and stung quite a bit. The area around the beard was red and blotchy. She said that she hadn't known discomfort and irritation like it. Given that up until that night she had never kissed anyone with a beard – regardless of gender, this was hardly surprising. She didn't want to go home immediately the next morning, as her parents would have known exactly what she had been up to. Well, they wouldn't know in literal terms; like the discolouration around her beard being due to a night of passion with a fellow bearded lady. But they would have known that some kind of dalliance had occurred. The fact that she had stayed out all night would certainly have been a giveaway. Her reasons for staying away were more to hide her embarrassment, rather than out of consideration towards her parents. She said that her parents wouldn't have had a problem with who she was with, just so long as their precious daughter was happy. They weren't to be disappointed.

Deciding that she couldn't put off returning home indefinitely, she kissed Mariana, promising to return later that day, and set off for home. She knew that her parents wouldn't judge her. But the extent of their approval really did surprise her. She sat them down and told them that she had found someone very special indeed. After believing that no one else like her could possibly exist, she had in fact found her. She explained that she had never believed that the feelings she was experiencing were humanly possible, or could even exist. Her parents had responded along the lines that they were truly heartened, that their precious first-born had sought out the light in one so destined for her. They too said that they couldn't have countenanced the sheer brightness of the light, illuminating her being. They embraced and then they wept. It was after dinner that she completed the announcement. She said they paused to consider what they had just heard. Verity, her mother, said that they would miss her terribly of course, but that it was divinely ordained that wherever her light was she should follow it. The reaction of Melville, her father, she said, was tempered with a certain degree of bemusement, noting that "not in a million years" would he have believed that any of his daughters would run off to join the circus; never mind falling in love with one of its star attractions. Next stop – on the road and over the seas…

So, what will happen when two bearded ladies set sail together? Be sure to join us for the next instalment on Tuesday!

Dave was right. Some of these comments were indeed "choice". The keyboard warriors were out in force!

Comments …

Yawn fest! Can someone please poke me with A STICK! I'm falling asleep here!

The real voice

Mildly amusing, I suppose.

Oh please. What PC nonsense! It ticks all the "right on" boxes. A woman with a beard and a lesbian affair. I didn't see that one coming! Not!

Lady Googoo

Oh, the standard anti PC post, I see! I'm not racist, but…!

Another slow news day @readingchronicle, is it? Oh dear!

Adventurer

Mildly amusing. But the relevance is?

Oh boo hoo! She had such a difficult life. Poor diddum's. Listen people choise what lifes they gets. No one forsed her to go off with another woman. So what she had hair on her face. I know people what have had far worst things happen to them. I don't hear those complaining. I never new she was from Portsmouth. That would esplain a lot!

The wise one.

Now this is just plain nasty. It's also clear from the disjointed rambling of this ironically named "The Wise one", that even basic intelligence evades her. Fucking Luddite. Nasty AND thick! Nice!

It wasn't all one way though. As I scrolled further down, I could see that some seemed to have enjoyed the read.

Nicely done mate ☺ You show a great humanity in the way you write. It makes a refreshing change to read an article that isn't averse to delving beneath the surface, or in this case, the beard. Well done that man*!*

Cheesy Peas

Thanks Cheesy Peas ☺

Alastair, thank you for this article ☺ Apart from Patience once having a beard and now not, I had no idea of the journey she has been on. But then, how could I? I never asked her. Remember, we all have stories. I wish my own one was half an interesting as hers.

Daphn #demor

Indeed chap, who is the real freak show? Judging by some of the comments posted on here, I could mention one or two that would fit in perfectly to such a show. Ah bless them! Lovely article.

Tweedchap

I'm in tears as I type this. Honestly, what a very touching story! It's written with such care, respect, and humour too!

Tommy boy

Alastair, please get in touch via Chronicle's offices. I would have emailed you, but you haven't posted an address. I have left my contact details. Look, I really like this. Everyone needs to hear this story – Everyone! I think I can help. Well done! Please get in touch!!

Amandaprodo

Wow! A shaky start! Overall though, very positive. And now this! And who is this Amanda?

And then there was this…

Ali, I just want to tell you how very proud I am right now to call you my fella. I am proud of you anytime though. You see? I told you Madame Lynn knows best! X

LynnP@tesco.mangt.co.uk

For now though, I wouldn't dwell too much on this and who this Amanda person was. I shook my box of wine to check what was left inside. Its slush level suggested it to be a little under half full. *Definitely not half empty! Most definitely not half empty!*

Chapter 35

Daniel Witterington had not only emerged from the closet. He had then turned back, smashed it into little pieces, gathered these little pieces together, set fire to them, and then scattered the ash to the four corners of the planet. This man was now as far removed from the Whitters of old as he could possibly be. He was still a tart though. The only thing that had changed had been the objects of his lustful desires. His voice had softened too, and he now spoke with a slight lisp.

"So anyways, we went back to his yeah? His wife was away you see. I think she was visiting her mum or something. I didn't really care. We were here, ready for action, and I was ready for him. He wasn't just hung like a bull; he was hung like a prize bull and he was my prize bull. Anyway, do I need go on!?"

"You needn't," I replied. "I totally get the picture! Good for you fella. I'm really happy for you and your newly found honest identity."

"Ah thanks, hun. I'm really happy these days."

"So why then are you still here? Still here at Fastend? You hate this place."

"What and you love it?"

"Good point," I replied.

"I can't seem to get the type of job that I'm looking for. So I may as well stay until I do. Anyway, you're doing well. Your sales figures are through the roof… again. I'll be sending them upstairs a glowing report."

And that was it. In less than twenty minutes and with a decided lack of bullshit, another quarterly evaluation at Fastend Telefonic had been concluded.

"That's much appreciated Whitters. To say that this isn't exactly what I'd wish to do is a bit of an understatement to say the least, but I can't afford not to work. Cheers."

"Ah, don't mention it, sweetie. Laters, must pop. The Newbury lot are off on that nonsense team building thing. You know the place that you went to, "Great Providence Together Solutions". They asked me if I fancied coming along. I said why not?"

"Poor buggers," I replied. "I wonder if that Moustachioed Lothario is still there."

"I believe he is. Why do you think I'm going along? He's bloomin' gorge! Anyway, really need to go. Mwaa, Mwaa." He moved close, sending air kisses. He then glided daintily and with grace towards the door, pushed the handle down slowly, and as swiftly as he had entered proceedings, he was gone.

Taking every rather strange happening in my life into account right now, what had just happened had been very surreal.

I reached my desk in a state of mild bemusement. Whitters had been most entertaining without perhaps meaning to be. *This is all downhill from now,* I thought. I looked at my watch. *Shit! It's not even two!*

I stretched the headphones across my head and then pressed "Ready" on the handset. I was logged in. I was getting rather good at this. Dave said that I always had it in me, "as it goes." I just had to believe in myself. That's all. I tried telling him that I always did, and that confidence had never been an issue.

Anyway, who shall I call now? I thought as I scrolled down the spreadsheet.

James Adams – Aldermaston Ariel systems. I'd phoned him only last week. His secretary had said he was busy and to call back. *May as well...*

"Hello, welcome to Aldermaston Ariel Solutions; Berkshire's numero uno for the enquirer in you."

"Amanda, is that you?" I asked. I knew from the warm soft tones that it couldn't be anyone else.

"It's only Alastair," she replied. "The flying Scotsman of Fastend Telefonic, no less."

"The very one," I replied. "Is the main man in today? Or is he in some BORED meeting?" I asked, emphasising BORED.

"You never change, do you, Mr McLeish- Pudkin?" she chuckled.

"Well, why would I want to do that? It's part of my charm after all."

And it was. I enjoyed talking with Amanda, having the banter and engaging in laughter, but I had never met her and most likely never would. As much as I enjoyed the interaction, she was just a name – a name associated with another name. I was playing a role, and it was a role that I seemed to play with much skill.

"I'll put you through now, my flying Scotsman. He'll be glad you called actually."

"Really?"

"For sure. He's been singing your praises all week."

"For what though?"

"The article".

"What article?"

"Oh, don't go all modest now. THE article. The one that you wrote. The woman who used to have a beard but shaved it off. Why would she do that? Seems strange. Anyway, I'll put you through. Nice talking to you again. Speak soon."

"And you Amanda," I replied. "Yeah, speak soon. Always a pleasure."

"Well, if it isn't Alastair McLeish-Pidkin, the features writer of The Reading Chronicle!" It was James.

"Well, not quite," I replied. "But thanks all the same."

"But of course you fucking are mate! I knew you were a bit of a posh boy and used the odd unnecessary big word, but I had no idea that you could do this."

"Well," I replied. "I've read worse."

"I've read worse. Do me a favour. Anyway, did she say WHY she shaved off her fuzz?"

"From the pictures that I saw, it was a lot more than mere fuzz. It was a proper bush."

"We are still talking about her beard, aren't we?" he replied, in a rather crude attempt at humour. I wasn't impressed.

"Yes," I replied quite curtly. "Yes, we are still talking about her beard. She did say why she shaved it off, but you'll have to read about it in next weeks' instalment," I continued in a mellower tone. I wished that I hadn't been so curt towards him. He didn't mean anything nasty by that question. He was a good sort really. He just didn't have a filter, or if he did, had no idea how to use it. He was a bit of tool rather than a wanker. And if he was a wanker, then he was a harmless wanker, and at a stretch, perhaps even a nice wanker.

"So, no sneak preview for a mate then?" he replied. He wasn't a mate.

"Certainly not!" I replied.

"Oh, go on. You know you want to."

"I won't and I don't. It's like a very dear friend of mine remarked: you need to take a holistic approach to all this. Shortcuts can sometimes lesson the overall experience. Know what I mean?"

"Actually, I do. Now you put it like that."

"Really?"

"No. I think your friend sounds as if he was on the ol' wacky baccy when he told you that! Anyway, anyway, I've got a meeting in ten minutes, and I've got some bullshit bingo to prepare for my minions beforehand. So, on to business; I'm more than happy to sign off a repeat order. I'll email the PDF over tomorrow."

"Ah brilliant!" I replied. "Thank you."

"Pleasure. You've got a good product there. All the best. Hopefully catch up soon."

"Yes hopefully," I replied.

And that was it. I hadn't worked out the exact commission but it was in the region of £350. For the first time ever in my many years doing this job, exhilaration had surpassed tedium. I couldn't understand why or how this had happened. There was little point at all in trying to apply rational though. So I didn't.

Chapter 36

"All I'm saying mate is keep an open mind, yeah?"

"I always do," I replied.

"Ummm. Is that really true me old sweaty? I ain't convinced of that."

"OK, well perhaps not always, but I generally aim to."

"Look, I ain't saying that the Mayfly fella ain't a good bloke. He is. But he ain't the saint that people make him out to be."

"Sorry Dave, but I think you're going to have to spell it out for me. I'm not the best at second guessing. I never was."

"Don't I know," he replied. "Don't I know. Alright then. Telling people that they have it in them to make a difference to the lives of the less fortunate, by showing kindness, I don't have a problem with that. In fact, it's beautiful. It's really beautiful. But telling people that there's nothing after this - that there's no God? Do you think that's acceptable?"

"That's his belief. Is he not entitled to express his beliefs? This is Britain, not Saudi Arabia for goodness sake. If Christians and Muslims can stand up and preach, then why shouldn't an atheist do the same?"

"I'm not saying he can't. But go with me on this. Yeah?"

"Yeah."

"Right, you're an old dear. Yeah? Your name's Julie. Yeah? Nice name?"

"Yes," I replied. "I like it".

"Right, your joints hurt. You've just checked your bank and the tarts haven't paid your pension in. Yeah?"

"Urm yeah," I replied, not really knowing where he was going with this.

"Good. Good. Oh yeah and added to all this, it's raining. So you see a crowd of people outside M&S. They seem 'appy. So you goes over. You hear him say that we all have the power to help people, to lend a hand – to simply stop and talk to strangers. That it's all the little things in life that make life great. This makes you smile, 'cos you're lonely, and except for a cat, you're in this world alone. It gives you hope. If you can get through those crowds of fit birds standing in front of you, then you're going to speak to him. You're going to thank him for such powerful, kind, words. But then you hear him say that when you pop it, that's it. That there's no big bearded man in the sky with angels playing harps and singing, waiting to greet you. But more importantly, this means that you won't see Stan again, after all. You're gutted. So you turn and leave, tears streaming down your face. This time, you're walking quick, even though your joints ache. But you don't care. It's a price worth paying to get away quickly from this preacher man. You need to get back home to flossy."

"Flossy?"

"She's your cat. At least she loves you, and she's in the here and now. She'll never leave you. Well, at least not until her time comes and then she has no choice. You see, what Mayfly does in saying such things, is that he takes away hope from some people. I ain't saying that he don't say good things – he does. But does he really need to say the God thing?"

"I never really looked at it like that. I suppose."

"Few do," he replied. "Few do. Here's another thing. How does he know God don't exist? How does he know that this is it? That this is all we have? How does he know that there's no second half. That there never was? That your first tap – the one that let them in for the winner – was your only chance and you've blown it?"

"Well, he doesn't I suppose. I guess he can't."

"Exactly, all he has to go on is a hunch, no more, no less. So, if he don't know for sure which he can't possibly, then why spoil people's dreams? And if he is right and this is all there is, then you'll be dead. You'll be dead Julie, so it won't matter anyway, because you won't know. And why won't you know?"

"Because I'll be dead?"

"Because you'll be dead. So who is he to tell you that you won't see Stan? Who is he to tell you that you can't have that hope – that you ain't allowed to? What gives him the right to say all that?"

"Well, he doesn't I suppose. You're right. Why would he want to do such a thing really?"

Dave pulled up the sleeve of his Reading top and looked at his watch. It wasn't the chunky one that he usually wore. This was a slim line tanned leather strapped one, with a blue face.

"Ah, it's that time again. I need to do one. Places to be; faces to see. You know the drill. Catch up later. Yeah?"

"Sure Dave. Catch up later".

I shut my eyes and counted down from 10…10, 9, 8, 7…opened them and he was gone.

It was Saturday midday, and I was still lying in bed. I had enjoyed our paradoxical little chat. Dave was now such an integral part of my life that I struggled to imagine what it would be like if he suddenly left.

I was meeting Mayfly in what he told me, was "a very fine pub indeed". He said it was by the river. He thought it might also be a good idea to meet by the river, as he said that I seemed to like it there. I thought that was a curious thing to say.

It was a blustery, chilly day, as the rippled river bobbed the white plastic pier up and down and back and forth. The pier was built as an extra launching pad for the single and double coxes of the nearby boat club. Looking at it now, it was difficult to conceive that its purpose was anything other than a convenient stop-off platform for swans.

I wandered along the grass as it crunched with each step. I could feel a chill shoot through me. Its effect almost, but not quite as striking, as a bolt of lightning hitting a tree or perhaps even a reindeer. I couldn't have picked a colder day for my not-so-little jaunt. Well Mayfly had picked the day and I had agreed. But that was last week. Had we been able to peer into our non-existent magic ball, then perhaps we would have chosen a slightly less biting one. Anyway, it wasn't all bad; I was meeting a dear friend in a seemingly legendary pub, but for now, I had my specially fortified flask of coffee. I had slipped up somewhat in that I had forgotten to include the Haribo's in the mix.

I took a small sip. *Ummm, this isn't too bad actually.* I thought. *Perhaps it doesn't need to have that sharp edge that the tangs bring to it.* I took another slightly bigger sip and swilled it around my mouth. *Actually, I think I'm going to lose the tangs! I think I much prefer the smoother effect.*

The introduction of the tangs was an accident. Initially, I hadn't intended them to be a part of the mix. If Jacques hadn't dropped them in when I was mixing my first ever concoction, then they would never have made it in. But they had and when it came to the taste test, I decided to leave them in. I had never tried them with just the demerara sugar. Now that I had, the tangs had to go.

I was told that it wouldn't be possible to make it all the way to Pangbourne along the towpath as it lessened when it reached Tilehurst, to the extent that it couldn't be continued on foot. I was told that once I'd reached Tilehurst Station, then I'd need to walk over the footbridge and continue my journey up a hill, carefully, very carefully.

I reached the footbridge, continued walking, and then suddenly stopped. I felt that I had little choice. Something, a force perhaps, seemed to demand it. Looking back down along the tracks, I could almost see where Reading began and then as I looked across to the side from which I had travelled, where it all ended. The character to me of Reading was vast, yet its physicality modest. Peering across at the patchwork colours of fields, mixed in with the copses of pine trees and soft hills, I felt a connection stronger, far stronger than any place I had ever lived in. I now felt as woven into the fabric of this town and its hinterland as I could possibly be. I had always questioned providence. The very notion to me seemed irrational. But here, peering down the tracks, towards the gasometer, then back across to the fabric of lemon, hazel- and lime-coloured fields, I felt that perhaps, just perhaps, my scepticism of such irrationality was ill-founded. When I got off the train at Bracknell that time, in celebration, I had felt an intense draw, back towards my new home. I believed, despite my agnosticism, that that day had been ordained. Once again, I was feeling this. It was so beautifully overwhelming. I looked up and around. I couldn't see a single soul. It felt as if I was being directed to speak. I wasn't sure what to say. I wasn't sure why I was being directed so. I had no idea of the words I was being directed to speak. Then… **Seriously Reading! You know what? You know what Reading? I'm here! And I, Alastair McLeish-Pidkin of highly questionable moral character, feel privileged to be here! This is actually the beginning. It's just the beginning. Please let me stay here! Please never make it possible for me to ever have to leave. Reading, you make me a better person! I've learned things about myself that I would never have learned anywhere else. I have felt things here that I wouldn't have felt anywhere else. I have lived life here, more than I would ever have lived anywhere else. I am truly meant to be here. I will be here right 'till the end! Thank you Reading! Thank you so much! Yeeeesss!!!**

I suddenly felt a warm, subtle calm envelop me. It was as if a spirit was close by. A kind benevolent spirit, telling me that all will be well, and that there is no conceivable chance that I will ever have to leave this town. That I will in fact breathe my last here. I was overwhelmed, engulfed, enlivened. A sharp jolt of energy rushed through me, causing a sharp intake of breath. *Must steady myself. Need to steady myself. This is mental. Come on now. Calm down man.* I drew in a deep breath and then exhaled slowly, and within seconds, stillness had once again returned.

I reached the other side of Tilehurst Station. The contrast with the side of the station I had come from, really was quite striking. With a dearth of dwellings and rolling hills as far as the eye could see on one side, here stood lines and rows of Victorian red bricks.

I continued up a steep winding hill. There was no pavement and the road snaked. Why hadn't Mayfly warned me of this? It was unlikely that fate would be so cruel as to deliver a fatal or near fatal impact from an oncoming vehicle. Still, it was a real possibility. I continued on, cautiously aware and mindful. *Mustn't falter,* I thought. *Stay aware. All it takes is one hit. One hit. Don't fall now. You've come this far. You're nearly there.*

Eventually I reached the zenith, and with that a clear view along a straight line towards Pangbourne. Tired, yet with a good sense of achievement, I reached the Swan. Mayfly wasn't wrong. This place had a certain element of enchantment to it. I walked in through the low narrow wooden door. I stooped along and under the low

Tudor-beamed ceiling, and then out on to the wide expanse of the wooden decking. With great excitement, I peered out on to the majestically choppy, dear Mother Thames. I smiled and waved in celebration, as a double sculling skiff with three men dressed in boating jackets, one of which was holding a lively terrier, passed me by. *Where is Mayfly?* I wondered.

Suddenly I felt a tap on my shoulder. I turned around. It was Mayfly. "Hey dude! How was the journey? Did you enjoy your trip? What dia think of this place? Did I choose well?"

"I love it fella," I replied. "Really love it. I was confused earlier, when you said you chose this place because I like it by the river. I wasn't sure if you were playing with me."

"Dude, I would never play with you. Yes, I did choose this place because you do love the river. You wanted to go lights out by the river. This means that it holds a special place for you. You're still here right?"

"Yes, still here. I'm still here."

"And where are you?"

"I'm standing here by the river."

"And how do you feel standing here by the river?"

"I feel good. It feels right. It feels natural - like I'm meant to be here."

"Well my friend, that is because the river calls to you, and you answer."

"I never looked it like that," I replied. Actually, since meeting this man, I had begun to look at certain things differently; very differently in fact.

Chapter 37

~

"I've met Jeremy. We've had words."

It was Saturday, 10.35 AM, and Dave had woken me up. He said that he had some very important news for me – news that I might like.

"Really? What kind of words?"

"Well, put it this way. I've made things very clear to him. I've told him that he needs to stop all this; or else."

"So, you threatened him?"

"Not in so many words. But yeah, I threatened him. It was subtle though. It was subtle, but firm. Know what I mean?"

"Not quite. But go on."

"He wasn't easy to track down you know. I tried everywhere. I asked around. No one seemed to know. Then I got the tip off."

"Who was it? What did he say?"

"I can't remember. I think he said his name was Steve. But anyway, he told me that Jeremy was there. He said that he was waiting for me; that he was expecting me. So off I went."

"So, what's he like? My Jeremy."

"Ah mate, he's a bit of a saddo if I tells the truth. When I knew that he was close by, I was ready. Yeah? Tooled up and ready. I was going to do a job on him – a serious job. Know what I mean?"

"I think I do Dave."

"But when I did actually meet him, I felt a little bit sorry for him."

"But why? He's a dick. He makes my life fucking hell when he shows up like that, uninvited. I can't believe you're defending him."

"Mate, I ain't defending him. I agree, he is a dick; but he's got issues. Know what I mean?"

"Actually Dave, I don't. I don't at all. He's not the victim here, remember?"

"Of course I remember. Can you let me finish? It'll all make sense."

"Sure Dave. Sorry. Go on."

"Cheers. Anyway, there he is sitting alone. He cuts a very sad shadow. He's a mess mate."

"How? In what way?"

"For a start, he looks a mess. He's fat. His hair is scraggy, and he don't half pen!"

"Don't half pen?"

"Yeah, you know, pen and ink, stink. He stinks mate."

"Oh, I see."

"He's also got a stuttttttttteeer!"

"Nice one Dave. Haha!!"

"Yeah, I thought you'd like that! He had the shakes too."

"Seriously? He seems a right mess. You said that he was expecting you. What was his reaction when you showed up?"

"Yes mate. That's right. He was expecting me. Mentally I was tooled up. I was ready for this dick. I was going to let him 'ave it. But when I saw the state he was in, I decided to take a different approach. You see, even though you see the other team's weakness, it ain't always the right thing to go in for the kill straight away. Sometimes it's better to play the long game. Know what I mean?"

"Not really Dave. But go on."

"OK. So he asks me to sit down. He even pulls out a seat. So I did. He told me that he knew who I was and that this didn't need to get serious. I told him that it did need to get serious. But maybe we could avoid it getting proper naughty and that he'd need to listen to me."

"And did he?"

"Yeah, he did. I told him that what he was doing to a good man was really bang out, and that it would have to stop, all of it. He agreed that it was bang out and that he should really stop, and that it was well naughty. He said though that he can't really help himself sometimes. I told him that he'd need to, or else. He seemed to accept it."

"When did all this happen?"

"A few days ago. Has he been around lately?"

"He hasn't. But he only shows up every few weeks these days."

"Well, let me know if he does, yeah? You see, I warned him. I told him that I'd leave it for now. But if he does show up, then I WILL kill him. So let me know if he does yeah? I don't think he will though. He better not."

"Thanks Dave. I love you man."

"I love you too, Kevin Keegan! Did anyone ever tell you?"

"Actually yes," I replied. "Quite a few actually!"

"It don't really surprise me. You're the spit. I played against the real Kevin Keegan once. It was in the cup. We lost two nil. I played shit. He had a stormer. I haven't liked him since!"

"Well, that's going to do it," I replied. "Jealousy. It's a terrible thing! Only joking fella!"

"I know. I know. You tart!"

He pulled up his sleeve and looked at his watch. This was yet a different watch. It had a thin yellow plastic strap and a turquoise face with black hands.

"Right, it's that time again. Places to be; faces to see".

I closed my eyes, then counted down from 10…10, 9, 8, 7 …opened them and he was gone.

OXFORD ROAD

Where does he go? I wondered. *And what's with all these footballing analogies and anecdotes. This is all getting very strange indeed. In fact, this is well weird.*

Chapter 38

I was sat in front of my computer, about to read the final instalment of my piece on Patience. I felt proud. Looking at in now online, for some strange, illogical reason, it seemed to read better than when I was actually writing it. No doubt psychologists would have a perfectly rational explanation to this irrationality. Perhaps they would say that it's only possible to fully comprehend the extent of one's work, if one is gazing in from beyond, or some other such bullshit. Anyway, here I was, about to pour over the final instalment of…

The bearded lady – but who is the real freak show?
By Alastair McLeish-Pidkin

At first, Patience was a tad apprehensive at what she had signed up for. After all, she had agreed to bare her soul to audiences the world over, leaving her exposed and open to ridicule. Of course, she wasn't tied into it. But after agreeing in principal to join up, she felt duty-bound to at least give it a decent go. Besides, she had met, as she said, her light destined – her Mariana. It was Mariana who had helped put her mind at rest on such things. She told her to never forget that it is not them who is the freak show, but those who come to watch them. She was told to look upon this an as adventure – as the ultimate adventure. Whether she stayed for two weeks or two years, the experience would stay with her forever. She was to travel with them for four years.

So what would a bearded lady do for four years in order to earn her keep? What would her act consist of? Surely she wouldn't just stand in the circle aimlessly staring into space?

It was difficult for the Circus Master to come up with something at first. Yes it was true, people would be happy to just show up, look at her, point, and to laugh. But there had to be something else - some kind of act. She wasn't talented like Mariana was. Yes, it was true that the sheep who turned up, would do so anyway. All they'd really need was a woman with a beard. They were easily impressed. Lots of ideas had been passed back and forth, and dismissed, until they came up with the perfect plan – two bearded ladies for the price of one! Mariana would play; overhead Valentio would swing from the rafters, while Patience would dance. Although Patience hadn't received any formal dancing lessons up 'till then, she had watched a lot of footage of famous dancers. Fred Astaire was her favourite. She said his graceful, slick moves had always mesmerised her. So, when it came to her lessons, she was a natural. The footage of Mr Astaire had clearly resonated from her teenage years, right into her adulthood. So, the booming call from the ringmaster would go up, resonating up and around.

"Ladies and gentlemen! Please pray silence, for those ladies with the beards and the man from up on high – tonight. I give you Valentio, Mariana, and Patience – two bearded ladies, and the man in the sky!"

For six months, she travelled Europe and occasionally beyond, performing; and with each show, perfecting this act. Growing up, she could never have imagined that she would see so many different places, so many different cultures, and meet so many varied and dynamic characters. She said one of her fondest memories was the sun glistening on the terracotta roofs below, as the caravan snaked slowly and carefully down along the Amalfi coast towards Sorrento. Sorrento had added significance as it was where Mariana was from. She had met her parents, who had not only approved of their union, but embraced it. They had expressed what they termed "molto grandezza" at their daughter's joy.

Moscow she said was a cultural eye-opener. The circus was a staple of the Soviet Union. Its attendance was actively encouraged by the ruling elite. Its format of the common man being the main attraction – the star of the show – and the organisers playing the role of bit players, seemed to resonate strongly with their ideology. On the streets though, with queues of people snaking around corners seeking out enough bread for subsistence, the contradictions of this utopia were effortlessly exposed.

Still, with hindsight, it was clear to her that behind every perceived reality is a counter one. This was none more so, than when it came to the treatment of the animals. It was obvious to her that no self-respecting lions, tigers or elephants, would ever mount a beach ball out of choice. There had to be something at play that would cause them to dispense with natural instincts. One day, she found out what this was – the electric bolt. The circus was vast – divided up into different areas of talent and disciplines. Therefore, it was quite plausible that the acrobats weren't privy to the dark mind of The Clown. The Clown wasn't aware of the goings on of Valentio – and there were many goings on apparently. Valentio, in turn, although worldly wise, wasn't aware of the Circus Master's gambling addiction. And the bearded ladies weren't aware of how the animals were "trained". What Patience witnessed that day traumatised her and would form how she would view circuses forever.

She said that it was cruelty personified. There were five elephants all in a line, holding the tails of the one in front. They were swaying from side to side, traumatised, in great fear at what lay ahead if they didn't perform. In front of them was a ball. It was striped just like the colours of a beach ball. Only this had to be bigger and more durable than a beach ball, if it was to accommodate these colossuses. These once fearless, proud, colossuses, reduced to a subservient wall of grey; terrified at what may happen, if they refused to extend their foot towards this beach ball. This bloody beach ball, she said. Then the instrument of terror was revealed – the bolt. The trainer holding this sizzling, sparkling, long silver line of torment, seemed to be enjoying this warped power-trip. She said that she couldn't watch anymore; that there was no point. She knew what was coming, and so too did the elephants.

This was to be the last day of her circus experience. She had pleaded with Mariana to leave with her. Mariana couldn't; she had become institutionalised. They parted, each picking up the strains of their broken hearts. They were never to meet again.

For years, she carried the almost overwhelming burden of heartbreak around with her, drifting from country to country, from town to town, until one day arriving in Reading. She hadn't planned on settling here you understand. She was invited over by a friend for the weekend. She said that there was something about the place, about Reading, that drew her in, and made it impossible for her to ever leave. So how would she make a living? In Europe, she got by doing what she could – washing dishes in hotels, packing shelves. Basically, whatever she could get. It was only in Reading when pondering upon her future that Jackie her friend came up with an interesting suggestion. You see, Patience could read tarot cards. There were plenty people in Reading doing tarot card readings, but as far as Christine, Jackie's friend, knew, none who were female and bearded. In a saturated market, one needs an angle, and this was hers. And so, she became Madame Yollanda, the bearded lady of Winnersh.

She performed readings out of Jackie's front room for seven years. She liked being Madame Yollanda. She enjoyed being recognised wherever she went in the town. Word had got around quickly, shortly after her arrival, and within a short time, she had built a great many clients. She said that Reading loves its eccentrics – people who dare to be just that little bit different. But it wasn't just that. It was only when she stopped and chatted with strangers, that she realised that whilst the novelty of the beard was certainly a topic of conversation, she was in fact held in great affection. There were a few though who would openly ridicule her or rather attempt to, for even daring to be different. And it is this, dear readers, which brings me to the fruition of this title "The bearded lady – but who is the real freak show?"

So, last year, she shaved it off. No beard? How dare she? Why? How could she? I'll tell you why, shall I? Because she dared to dream! She dared to dream of becoming what most take for granted, and what some of us wish we weren't – normal. That's right. Plain, boring, and normal. I mean, why shouldn't she aspire to something most of us take for granted and wish that we weren't? Well, that's just what she did. You see, Patience is old; although you'd never guess this by looking at her. She's tired. She doesn't need the big paydays anymore. She's made her money. Madame Yollanda has served her well. These days, all she wants to do are boring normal things. Things like meeting friends for tea and cakes. Things like going on walks along the Thames. She simply traded in her celebrity for anonymity. So, the real freak show? Who is the real freak show? Certainly not Patience nor Mariana. No, this is dedicated to a small number of small-minded deluded folk, some of whom will be reading this. When did you become so delusional? When did your lives become so inadequate, that the only thing you have ever achieved in life is to approach a lady – and I tell you now, that is exactly what she is, a true lady – a class act, go up to her, point at her, and laugh? All because she had a beard? Seriously? Is that all you have in your life? I don't think they will keep this next bit in, but I live in hope. Right now, as I write this piece, I am laughing at you. Surely you know that if you were really that confident and happy with your lives, with your lot, then you wouldn't feel the need to attempt, and I must emphasise attempt, to put someone down. It isn't all doom and gloom though; there is lots of help out there these days; please avail of it. For the rest of you out there, Patience has asked me to convey this message: "Thank you good people of Reading. Thank you, for making me a part of this great town. I may have changed in a way. But I haven't gone away you know. I never will!"

Comments ...

Great work chap! This was such an enjoyable, yet at times rather sad journey. One thing it was all throughout though, it was really captivating. Nice one ☺

The Golden eagle

How very humbling, The Golden eagle. Cheers!

Boom! From the moment I started reading it all the way to the end, I was hooked! I'm happy to have shared in this, yet sad that it has all come to an end.

Sweet cheeks

You and me both, sweet cheeks

I love the powerful message that this whole article contains. You don't have to conform to some people's ideas of non-conformity!

Endeavour

Perfect irony, Endeavour! I like it – a lot!

Listen, sorry for last comment I posted. It weren't right. I should've thought about what I was going to say, instead it all come out the way it did. I can see now that Patience is much more than what we knew her to be. I'm glad that things worked out for her. I enjoyed finding out about her, and not just about the bird with the beard.

(Not so much) The wise one

Well, I wasn't expecting that! Serious kudos to this person. Goes to show that people can change I suppose.

I was suddenly struck with an almost overwhelming feeling of finality. This was it. My serialisation, my article, whatever it was, was over. At first, when presented with this assignment, I'd been excited at the prospect, yet unsure as to how to approach it. Looking at it now though, having read it, I was pleased that it had all seemed to have fallen nicely into place. I'd miss Patience though. Perhaps I'd see her again. After all, Reading isn't London.

Chapter 39

Patience had been in touch via my mobile. I had forgotten that we had exchanged numbers that night in the Kebab and Calculator. In fact, she had phoned sobbing, thanking me for my part in bringing her story to life. I was finding it difficult to comprehend the full extent of what it meant to her. She had done all the work really. All I had done was condense it all into readable form. We had arranged to meet next week in the same place. She was quite adamant that we meet, so she could thank me in person. She had insisted that apart from my train fare for the journey to Wokingham I leave my wallet at home. I was hoping that I may be able to spring a surprise of sorts upon her. I was meeting Amanda, one of the favourable posters on the article. Her offer to help in bringing Patience's story to a wider audience, seemed genuine and given her connection with a production company, a strong possibility.

She worked as a publicist for a company called "Inspire Media" – an Oxford-based production company. She also fulfilled the role of talent scout, sourcing out projects that could inspire the general public. She believed that Patience's story could greatly empower those who struggled with, as she put it, a leftfield identity. I was looking forward to seeing her and finding out exactly what she had in mind. She hadn't made it abundantly clear what angle she would take. Would she make a documentary? A short film perhaps? I really had no idea, and thought better about prying for now. I'd find out soon enough.

Jacques and Adri, due to their infinitely superior levels of maturity, continued to fulfil the role of responsible adults. They looked out for me on a daily basis. They cared, they worried, and they despaired, just like you'd expect any caring parents to do. Among one of the many, yet well-meaning lectures that I had endured was one on personal accountability. This time though, it had been a long day. I hadn't closed a particular deal that I should have easily nailed, and I hadn't had much sleep the night before.

I had just got back from work and was on my way up to my room to get wasted. With the door to the front room slightly ajar, Jacques had seen me start my ascent and felt that it was the right time to deliver a lecture. Usually it wouldn't have presented any significant issue to me. Like Ali on the ropes, I would soak up the punches until my assailant was spent of energy, and then simply leave. But not that time. My ring-craft that day had been rusty.

"Don't walk away while I'm talking to you," Jacques had demanded.

"I will! OK?" I had responded defiantly. "You know, sometimes you speak to me as if I'm a teenager. And you know what? I'm getting sick of it."

His response to this defiance had only underlined his domestically elevated status.

"Well, matey. If you start acting like an adult, then I'll start treating you like one."

That had been it for me. Defeated, yet still defiant, I had stomped all the way up these two stories of creaky wooden stairs and then slammed my bedroom door shut behind me. We laughed about it the next day over drinks in the front room.

Lynn had been very supportive of my coming out as a lunatic. She understood why Dave was important to me. If he was important to me, then it stood to reason that he was important to her too. She said that she would like to meet him one day, and that all three of us should go for drinks. I wasn't convinced that she in fact grasped the insanity of my reality.

I was meeting Amanda in the bar of the Forbury hotel soon. She told me that she claimed little in expenses generally, and that it was high time she ripped the absolute piss out of her expense account. In enlisting my help in achieving this, she had chosen well.

I turned out on to the Oxford Road. Once again after a long layoff, there was a niggling feeling of foreboding. Logically, there was no rationale to this. But then, there seldom was. It could only be Jeremy. Why after a long layoff of nearly three weeks, had he chosen to show up today of all days? When Dave told me that he had met him, and then described the pathetic figure that he cut, we both agreed that it may not be necessary to kill him after all. That the implied yet obvious threats might be enough to make him see reason. This was now clearly not the case. I was going to tell Dave to kill the bastard, the next time we met.

The sky was dusky and there was a sharpness in the air. Despite the presence of my own inner cloud, I was quite excited to be meeting Amanda. I didn't share Dave's absolutism that this one piece of journalism was the vehicle which could drive me away from having to sell phone systems. Still, at least he was a positive in my life, unlike that fucking low-life loser Jeremy. *And die you will, Jeremy*, I thought. *Dave will take care of you. Believe it!*

I reached Broad Street. Over by Woolworths stood Jason holding copies of the "Big Issue". *That's late*, I though. Apart from Sainsburys, there were no other shops open. And Sainsburys is down the other end. I went over to him.

"Hey Jason. How's it going? You're out late."

"Hi mate," he replied, extending his arm. "Well you know, suicide-Sunday."

"But it's Monday."

"I know but today has been strange. Usually Monday compensates. But not today. Not this Monday. I don't have much choice. I've gotta stay out for a bit. You know, see how things go. Where you off to? Anywhere nice?"

Given that Jason was stood here close to freezing, in what seemed like a desperate standoff with the elements, it didn't seem right to tell him that I was off to possibly the most expensive dwelling in Reading for free drinks.

"Ah nothing big really," I replied. "Just off to a mate's for a bit of a catch up."

"That's good mate. I like that. Friends are important. Have a good one yeah?"

"Cheers Sir," I replied, as I extended my hand.

I liked Jason. He was a decent sort. His gentle smile seemed to enliven his soft almond eyes, revealing a deep empathetic soul. He always seemed to find the time to chat, despite being at retail war with the rest of the "Big Issue" vendors up and along Broad Street. Each vendor had their own nuance and patter. The man outside Sainsburys would cry out, "Big Eeessue please!" His eyes would then probe the punted, hoping for a sympathetic glance back. Then there was the Jesus man sitting usually in Smelly Alley, selling and then reselling his single copy.

It wasn't always the issue he punted. His publications could range from anything like DIY manuals, to pamphlets on tourism or prints of Biblical verse. All enriched Broad Street and its surroundings, adding a touch of subterranean intrigue.

I reached Market Place and approached the Simeon Monument. *How handsome and striking is this?* I thought. *Fine Portland stone crafted to absolute perfection!* I turned around, scanning the square. It appeared deserted. *Strange*, I thought. *I know it isn't early doors, but it isn't exactly late either.*

I checked my phone. It was 7.40. I was meeting Amanda at 8. *I may as well wander over and get settled*, I thought.

"Not so fast. Not so fast," came a sinister sounding voice. I didn't like the sound of it at all. It was cackling and threatening.

I looked around. At first I couldn't see where this voice was coming from. Suddenly and quickly, a shadow-like image darted up across and around me, distorting and muddling my senses. I was struggling to breathe. Then, as quickly as this movement had started, it stopped abruptly and then I saw the cause of this rude interruption.

"Don't say you weren't expecting me," he said. "Did you honestly think that I'd let this slide? That I'd give up without a fight? So, WE decided to call in some muscle, did WE? Dave? I mean seriously? Couldn't you have come up with a better name? Jeremy. Now that's a good name. It has a certain resonance to it. It's a name that carries strength. It's a name that commands, neigh, DEMANDS respect. What did you hope to achieve? Did you honestly expect me to drift away? To fade out without even a whimper? Dave?"

I was palpitating, shivering with fear. This voice sounded sinister and depraved. It bordered on the demonic. I looked across and there he stood, striking a nefarious pose. This wasn't the pathetic, scruffy, bedraggled loser that Dave had described.

"Jeremy?! Is that you? Jeremy?"

"Who else do you think it could be?"

"But, but…"

"But, bbbbut! Ha ha. Listen to yourself. You're pathetic! Not so brave now, are we? Not so confident!"

This man, this embodiment of cynicism, was menacing. His teeth were yellow and stick-like. His lips curled up into a joker-like grin. He was wearing a straggly grey top hat and a torn pinstripe Edwardian-style long coat. As he got closer to me, so too did a pungent death-like odour. Quickly, I covered my nose.

Must do something. Have to do something, I thought. *What would Dave say to me? What would he do? I know one thing; he wouldn't be impressed with how I am right now. He'd be ashamed. In fact, he'd feel let down. He'd be disappointed that I didn't trust him; that I didn't have faith in him to get the job done. He'd say "Oi oi Ali! Get a grip my son!"*

This man standing in front of me, trying to steal my joy, was nothing. And as swiftly as the reserves of energy had drained from me, they returned, jolting me upright, priming me into action.

"Do you know what Jeremy? Do you know what? FUCK YOU!! Haha!"

He seemed startled by such a flagrant disregard for fear.

"What? You can't say that. Not to me. Do you know who I am? Don't you realise that I can cause you to stumble; to fall at any time?"

I moved slowly towards him, arms outstretched. "Perhaps in the past, Jezza," I replied mockingly. "But not anymore. I have Dave now. Yes Dave, with that soft, bland, weak name as you might say, but he's not weak or bland. Dave is more real to me now than you have ever fucking been, you soft, pathetic, sinister fucking cunt! I mean, look at you! You're the weak one. You're the loser. I had a chat with Dave after he tracked you down."

"I know you did."

"Yes, but of course you do," I replied, "the way he described you, you sounded pathetic, sympathetic even. I honestly felt sorry for you. According to Dave, you weren't all bad. That's why we decided to go easy on you, hoping that you'd take the warning and just stay away. But you couldn't, could you?"

"No, I couldn't," he replied. "This Dave of yours. He isn't all he seems, you know. I've known you most of your life. How long have you known him? A year? Two years?"

"That's none of your business," I replied with wrath. I was now incensed, and he knew it. "I'm ending this now," I continued. "I'm hoping to meet Dave tomorrow morning. You see, he wakes me early on school days. He said it's for my own benefit. Do you know what I'm going to tell him Jezza? Well?"

"Please don't call me that," he replied nervously. "You know I don't like it."

"I'll call you whatever the fuck I want, you sad fucking loser. OK?"

"Yes, OK. Look, I'm sorry. I know what you're going to tell him, but please don't. Look, I'm really sorry. I'll take the warning," he replied, tearfully.

"Too late, loser. I'm done here. You've had your warning. Tomorrow, I'm going to tell Dave to finish the job. To fucking kill you. I'm going to instruct him to get rid of you once and for all. Now fuck off. I've got a very important meeting in the Forbury. But then you know all this, don't you?"

"Look," he replied. "I'll go now. Maybe you're right. Maybe I've outstayed my welcome. It's probably best that I do go."

"Running scared, are we?"

"No. Just a bit disappointed. A bit sad actually. You know, I've only ever had your best interests at heart."

"How do make that out?"

"All I've ever done is alert you to danger. Is that such a bad thing?"

"It is when I'm finding it hard to function."

"Oh."

"Yes, oh indeed. Anyway, bye Jeremy. It's been emotional. Now fuck off. I'm going to turn away from you now, and when I turn back, I want you to be gone. OK?"

"OK."

I turned back and faced the Simeon Monument. "As a mark of appreciation to his native town". *How beautiful*, I thought. *Powerful. This will be here long after I've gone. This will be here forever.*

I turned back and once again I stood a solitary figure in Market place.

Right then, on to the Forbury. I've a highly important meet up to attend.

Chapter 40

It was 7.30 AM on Saturday. Deciding that I didn't need a customary weekend lie-in, Dave had decided to pay me a visit. It seemed he was here in an advisory capacity.

"Are you sure about this? Yeah? Completely sure? 'Cos this is gonna get proper naughty. Know what I mean? Proper naughty."

"Yes Dave. I'm completely sure. He needs to be taken out. You've tried reasoning with him, and that hasn't worked. Do you also know he presents different faces, to different people?"

"I don't follow mate."

"Well, when you met him, he was this apologetic loser – no self-esteem, scruffy – a no hoper, basically."

"Yeah, that's right. The pilchard."

"But when I last met him, he looked menacing. He looked sinister. He had yellow pins for teeth, pea-green, scarlet beady holes for eyes, and he was dressed like something from the Dickensian slums. He reminded me of an evil version of Fagin."

"Fuck! So, at first you was afraid?"

"Chap, I was petrified. I was literally shaking with fear. Then I realised something. And do you know what that something was?"

"Tell me."

"That I had you. That all I'd need to do would be to request his assassination."

"That's the spirit, and I'm at your service mate. But remember, when he's gone, that's it."

"Surely that's the whole point. I need him gone. He brings nothing positive to my life."

"What, not even the warnings?"

"He told you that too?"

"Yeah. He said that he don't mean to be naughty, but that his intentions are honourable."

"His intentions are honourable? Seriously?"

"Well, a certain amount of fear ain't such a bad thing. It alerts us to danger. Know what I mean?"

"Kind of. But you sound as if you're defending him now."

"I ain't. I ain't. He's a proper pilchard and he's gonna die. Yeah?"

"Yeah."

"Take the antelope yeah?"

"Yeah. OK."

"Right, the antelope in the wild, grazing on a sunny day on the savannah, yeah? He's with his mates yeah, having it, munching away without a care in the world. Then suddenly, out of nowhere, comes a pride of lions, salivating. They're hungry, and you're number one on their menu. You try to run but you can't. You're frozen to the spot. The warning has come too late. Bosh, before you know it, there's a pride of lions, covered in blood, your blood, feasting on your intestines."

"That's a rather grim, yet well put together cautionary tale Dave."

"I know. I quite like that. Maybe I could do journalism! Anyway, what I mean is that it's natural to be cautious and to be alerted to danger, but Jeremy goes too far."

"That's the point. I see the merits of your tale. In that if said antelope - me - had received his warning in time then he might have lived on."

"That's exactly what I'm saying. Have you seen how fast those things can bolt?! Most of the time, they're giving it large to the lions saying, "you want some? Yeah? C'mon then. Let's have it!" Knowing that the lions will never catch 'em. I would say that most of these antelopes, due to a combination of speed and an early warning system, live to a ripe old age, grandchildren antelopes – the lot."

"So what you're saying here is that fear is necessary. That it protects us?"

"That's exactly what I'm saying, but Jeremy's going overboard with it all. He's warning you when there's no threat to you. He's taking the piss mate. He's laughing at ya. And that my friend is why he has to die. I had the chance to do it, there and then, but he looked lost, broken, dejected. So, I thought I could reason with him. Didn't I get that one wrong? Sorry mate."

"Ah, don't worry chap. There's no shame in it. Jeremy's devious. He's fooled us both. In my time, I have met many odious, nasty individuals, but I can honestly say that I've never despised anyone as much as I do Jeremy. So yes Dave, please kill him, and don't spare the pain either. In fact, the more painful, the better."

"Right, right. I'll see what I can do, Kevin Keegan," he replied, cheekily.

He rolled up his sleeve and peered into his silver rather clunky watch.

"Nice watch, Dave."

"Ah cheers, fella. It's a Rolex. You like it?"

"I do Dave. It's very classy."

"Yeah, well, it ain't real Rolex. It's a copy. A mate of mine down the pub brought it back from Thailand. Apparently, they're master copiers over there."

"You'd never tell the difference. I certainly wouldn't have known it was a fake."

"Yeah, it's nice enough. Anyway, I've overrun a bit. Sorry but I need to go. You know, places to be, faces to see. Laters yeah?"

"Yeah, laters."

I shut my eyes and counted down from 10…10, 9, 8, 7 …opened them and he was gone.

Despite having had my weekend sleep pattern disrupted, I was glad Dave had shown up. Our little chat had helped. Meeting Jeremy in the flesh, so to speak, had really unnerved me. My meet up with Amanda had gone well, very well in fact. But all throughout, I couldn't escape from the terrifying demonic image of Jeremy. I hadn't let it spoil what had turned out to be both an enjoyable and useful meet up. I had taken a great many positives from it. Amanda, with my considerable help, had as she had planned to do, absolutely ripped the piss out of her expense account too! And we had done it in style!

Chapter 41

"Look, I know we spoke about this yesterday, and I agreed to take it on, but is that seriously all you have for me, Suzi? Forbury? Has no one's 101-year-old cat died? Or has, oh I don't know, a giant discovered that he has in fact got a family history of dwarfism?"

"Sorry, but that's all there is. You know the deal. You're still at apprenticeship stage. I know this sounds harsh, but the real journalists get the chunks and whatever falls from the table, that's yours. You knew this from the beginning. Besides, you'll be doing me a massive favour."

"How's that?"

"Well it saves me the job. No one else is prepared to review them, so it falls on me to do it, and I can't."

"And why is that, I wonder? Is it 'cos they're shit?"

"Partly, yes. But they're still managed, if you can call it that, by my ex. Things could get very awkward."

"Ah yes. The man whom I chased down London Street wielding a golf club. And you think he'll be happy when I show up? Oh, hello there. Remember me? No? Well, allow me to jog your memory!"

"Yeah, I can see your dilemma. But it was months ago. Surely he must have processed it all by now. Besides, they've been promised a more favourable review. They weren't impressed with my last one. You know the one I included with you and the golf club. You see, the lead singer, Daryl, is a nephew of the editor. I didn't know that at the time."

"Well, how did the bit about them being shit get past him then."

"He was off sunning himself in Benidorm at the time."

"This just gets better! So, you want me to go and review a band that everyone knows is a shit band. You then want me to come home, write my review of this shit band, and then lie to the good people of Reading, telling them, that actually, this shit band isn't in fact shit, after all?"

"Pretty much. Look, you're not yet up to the standard required to be a fully-fledged journalist. No offence."

"None taken."

"Yet. Based on your work so far, you're certainly not a million miles away. You'll think of something. Go for a happy medium. Just choose your superlatives wisely. You'll be fine. I can't wait to hear all about it. Listen, I have to go; a kebab van has lost its licence due to a spate of food poisonings. It's a terrible business. The people of Reading need to know about it. Catch up later, yeah?"

"Sure. Catch up later."

"Enjoy the gig! Ciao."

And that was it, phone conversation concluded – assignment number two. The gig was taking place in the Turtle. Adding to my apprehension was the fact that I hadn't been back there for nearly a year. Back then, I was beautifully embroiled in the perfect sensory experience. I'd have to be better behaved this time round; Lynn was joining me. I couldn't break my no-drugs-embargo when in her company, again. I wasn't entirely sure that she hadn't cottoned on that time when I took her to see "Dream Boys". Lynn, for all her urbane presence, wasn't always easy to read.

I was beginning to feel just a tad apprehensive at the thought of coming in to contact with James, the manager of Forbury and the ex-boyfriend of Suzi, given our initial introduction. *Does he even know that I've been the one sent to review them?* I wondered. *If not, then he's in for some surprise when I show up!*

As I had been asked to do this review yesterday, I had already arranged to meet Lynn and take her along. I was beginning to have mixed feelings about this. I had been off the stuff since Wonderwoman's that night. I was beginning to question my moralistic stance in abstaining. Actually, I wasn't. I just wanted to do gear, especially in this place. The party was self-contained, so no one would know. Doing gear with Pook and Steve, and especially in this place, seemed long overdue. In fact, it would be rude not to. *I love Lynn, but this isn't really the appropriate place for her. She wouldn't like it. I have to think of something. What do I say?*

I reached down from the bed for my phone. I had a message. To my surprise and joy, Lynn had saved me the job.

Text 1
Listen love, really sos to have to do this, but I won't be able to join you tonight. You see, my sis – bless her has shown up on my door in tears. That loser COCK! of a boyfriend of hers, has done it again – bigtime! She needs me to be there for her. I would bring her along, but I don't think she'd be good company. Catch up later. Luv Mdm Lynn ☺

Text 2
Meant to say, enjoy yourself tonight babes. I hope they're not too shit! Haha!! XX

Brilliant! I thought. *Now to procure said minerals…*

Within two hours, said minerals had been procured. I was now around Steve and Pookesh's new riverside apartment.

"Ah, this is brilliant! It's just like been reacquainted with a long-lost friend!" I exclaimed, with great enthusiasm, as a sudden rush of blood-flow massaged my nostrils.

"How long has it been now?" asked Pookesh.

"What? Off the minerals?"

"What else?" said Steve through the open door of the balcony – smoking was the only form of stimulant banned from their home.

"It must be close on two months now, give or take," I replied, feeling rather proud of myself.

"Two months?" replied Steve. "That's really impressive. What kind of recreational drug user are you? I can't imagine a weekend without minerals."

"For sure," said Pookesh. "It wouldn't really be a weekend would it? Without the minerals."

"This is true. This is sooo TRUE!!" replied Steve. "On mate!!" he exclaimed enthusiastically. "Come out Pud, Pook. You've got to see this. You've just got to see this! Look up at this beautiful sky of ours. Oh my God!! Come out. Come out. Quick! C'mon!"

We hurried out and stepped either side of Steve. We looked up. He was right. This sky was indeed beautiful. But it wasn't just beautiful; it was spectacular. It was stunning. It was sublime. It was glorious. Numerous colours blended in to form a deep, abstract effervescent pallet.

"Thank you, Zeus!" I exclaimed. "What a superb production. Thank you for today's display. Hey Pook, Steve," I said, trying to muffle my excitement. "Do you ever think, I don't know that certain days have been planned long before we were even born? Even before our parents were born."

"Eh no," replied a bemused Pookesh. "It don't really make a lot sense. I mean, how can the sky just plan things like that? Especially before we was even born."

"I like the idea," said Steve, sounding at least open to my theory. "Please explain."

"Right," I continued. "We're here, all three of us, yeah? Standing here on this balcony at this time, under this sky? Yeah? Well, what are the chances of that happening? All three of us together, at this time, standing on this balcony? What are the chances of that? Seriously? And this sky with all its array of different colours?"

"Wow!" said Pookesh. "I never really looked at it like that. You see, I've never been religious, but my parents are. You see Sikhs believe that the sky is made up of everyone who has left earth, and I mean everyone. Yeah?"

"Go on," enthused Steve.

"Well," continued Pookesh. "Well, when we pass. You see our soul has to go somewhere. So where does it go?"

"I don't know," I replied.

"It goes home," he replied. "Look, you see that sky, that beautiful sky," he said, pointing up. "It goes back up there. Back home. Everyone that I have ever known, Steve and anyone that you have ever known, Puds, who have left, are up there. They're looking down on us right now, man, and they're smiling. You see, because we know each other, all our people know each other. We, here, I Pookesh Rama, you Steven J Lindley, and you Alastair McLeish-Pidkin, tonight, have brought all our loved ones together, and this and Zeus, who isn't even real, is them thanking us for bringing them all together. On my days, Pudkin, you're right. THIS HAS BEEN PLANNED!!" he proclaimed loudly, his soul smiling through an outsized, glazed iris.

Pookesh was right. *I'm not too sure of the mechanics of it, but as long as friends, dear friends like us, are gathered together, then surely anywhere is home. Friends don't have to socialise incessantly or even on a regular basis to have this feeling of kinship. Seriously,* I thought, *thank you to all you people who have passed back up into this glorious sky of ours, thank you. Thank you so much for this sky. Thank you so much for my dear friends standing right here with me. Please let it always be like this. It can? Can't it?*

I checked my phone. For now, such ethereal analysis would have to wait. I had a band to review.

We meandered casually out on to Gun Street. The soaked granite of Reading Minster stood out like a mound, as down below people flowed ant-like, from door to door, from road to path, seeking out the perfect slot.

And there it was; my slot for tonight – The Purple Turtle – that citadel of bohemia. People in various modes of social uniform moved in through the off-lilac door frame, and just like a year ago, the throng was varied. Over by the corner of the bar stood a lady, the like of which I had never seen before, nor thought possible. With a lightly protruding jaw, perfectly sculpted cheekbones, she was as interesting as she was beautiful. She struck an elegant pose. She was dressed in a khaki shorts, a black cropped top, purple DMs, all punctuated with a crimson grin.

As psychoactive substances go, this had to be the best. The band weren't due on for another ten minutes. Meanwhile, the DJ was enriching us with great audio treats. The Pet Shop Boys were blasting out "Always on my mind". Usually I found the Pet Shop Boys lick anything but treats, but right now, as each note drifted through every pour of my being, I was hearing and seeing new insights into this Elvis Presley cover. These sublime sounds were framed in what I can only describe as the most radiant light show that I had ever witnessed. Hues of purple, yellow, crimson, primary, secondary colours bounced off the walls, all around the place, and then back to the DJ, illuminating this star of the decks.

Pook was at the bar, mesmerised, hypnotised, trapped in this wonderful moment, unable to avert his gaze away from this puppeteer's domain. I turned to Steve; he too was trapped in this splendid moment. I was finding it hard to conceive that, up until now, I had never been able to appreciate or indeed see, hear, or comprehend, the merits of such crafted brilliance as the Pet Shop Boys.

Collectively, our consumption of Mandy had been thus far three wraps. It was early still, and our supplies were more than plentiful. Further enrichment, should we need it, was only a phone call away.

My last indulgence with mistress Mandy had resulted in no sleep for roughly two days, during which time I had written a song and two poems, finished reading "War and Peace", and started a novel. If I was going to do this review due justice, then I would need to do it when I got back, whilst it was still fresh in my mind. To leave it, to delay it, would be to lessen its impact.

Panning all around the club, and seeing all those resplendent, animated different faces, of all different hues, I was suddenly struck with the absurdity of Mandy's lack of legal standing.

Oh, why does this stuff have to be illegal? How can something that brings people together in such perfect harmony be so wrong? Why ban something with such ethereal, powerful healing qualities? This is such a travesty. It's such a paradox. Who makes these rules anyway? Who gets to decide what I'm supposed to like?

Over by the stage, Forbury was setting up. The singer was standing by the assembled mic, glancing, moving from side to side. He seemed enriched with a magnetism that commanded respect and adulation, akin to the Alexandrian character he was portraying. He was framed in an aura of gentian blue. As if caught in a tractor beam, I could feel myself draw steadily closer and closer to him.

How could Suzi have got this so wrong? I thought. *How can something so powerful and captivating ever be described in the negative? Colours always reveal the truth. Darkness can't flow into light.* Before a single note had been struck, I knew that tonight was the night that negativity would cease. And out of darkness, light would flow. *It is never too late to do, or indeed say, what's right,* I thought. *It's never too late. I mean, how could it be?*

Chapter 42

"Look, Patience, don't get me wrong lady, I do appreciate your kindness. Honestly, I do. But all I did was write down what you told me. The credit should go to you. You're the one with the story. All I did was write it."

"All you did was write it?! Seriously? Can we stop with this false modesty? Please, young man? You took time. You listened to me. You empathised. Then off you went and crafted something really beautiful. Please, just learn to take a compliment. For goodness sake."

"OK then," I replied with a wry smile, conceding defeat on this matter.

Exactly a month to the day we met, I was back in "The Kebab and Calculator" with Patience, about to deliver some exciting news.

"So, what's this exciting news you want to get off your chest?" she asked. "I'm all ears."

"OK, and before I tell you, it's entirely up to you if you want to do this. If you don't, I will understand. Honestly."

"Well, just tell me. Please? Let me be the judge of that. Yes?"

"Alright then," I replied. "Well, I don't know if you remember some of the comments people posted on the article."

"Every single one," she replied.

"Seriously?"

"Seriously. There's something else you're about to find out about me; I've got a photographic memory."

"Seriously?"

"Yes. Absolutely. How else could I have given you such a detailed account of my life?"

"True." I replied.

"Yes, I remember those comments," she continued. "Most were really positive; others were written by complete morons."

"I like it Patience. But let's face it, you're biased."

"Listen here young man," she replied sternly. "This has nothing to do with bias. I try to be gentle in my approach and dispense my words with kindness. But if I didn't like it, trust me, you'd know. Continue."

"OK," I replied. "Understood. Well, do you remember someone who posted a comment on the article, called Amanda?"

"I do."

"Do you remember what she said?"

"Yes, it was along the lines of everybody needing to hear this story, and she could help?"

"That's it," I replied. "Well, I hope you don't mind, but I met her."

"Why would I mind?"

"Because in hindsight, I really should have brought you along. Sorry about that."

"No, no, not at all," she replied. "You had to see what it was all about before telling me. I understand that."

"Oh, that's good," I replied. "Well, it turns out that this Amanda, as well as being stunningly beautiful, works for a production company."

"And?"

"Well, her job is to look out for stories of interest. Stories that can be turned into film - television ones mainly. She has been involved in some short movie films."

"Wow!" she exclaimed. "That's quite big."

"It is. Well, y'all ready for this?"

"I'm ready."

"Sure? Y'all ready?"

"Just tell me, young man!" she exclaimed. "Please!"

"OK then. Well Amanda tells me that she was incredibly moved by your story. She said that such fortitude and strength are an example to us all, and…"

"Oh, will you just get to the point?"

"OK, OK! In short, she would like to, obviously with your permission, make a film about your life story."

Patience looked pensive, as if caught completely unawares.

"So, they want to make a film about me? Hmm, I don't know what to think."

"Well as I said, you don't have to do it, obviously. I just thought I'd tell you. Anyway, we polished that one off fast didn't we?" I said, shaking the olive-green bottle of Prosecco. "I'll be back in a tick. I'll leave you to take all this in."

I arrived back holding the bucket containing our third bottle of Prosecco. Patience was smiling. She took a sharp breath.

"I'm in. I want to do this. I want my story to be told."

"Are you sure you want this?" I replied. "Because once it's on film, that's it. It can't be taken back."

"I'm completely sure," she replied. "I think it'll be a really good thing."

"I'm glad you think so. Here's the thing too; she said that she'll give you full creative control in this. She wants you to be involved."

"What does this mean exactly? Full creative control?"

"It means exactly what it says, Patience. It means that nothing gets approved unless approved by you."

"That's very kind of her. I don't know much about the film industry, but I can't imagine that this is common practice."

"It isn't," I replied. "She told me as much. But she insists upon it. She's even going to get a contract drawn up to this effect."

"This is serious then," she replied. "So, what happens next?"

"Well, she's asked that we set up a meeting in their offices, as soon as possible. She's very keen. She doesn't want to piss about, as she said."

"I like her style!" replied Patience. "She sounds like my kind of person – passionate, determined, wants to get things done."

"Well, that's how she came across to me too. She does have a lighter side too. She has a thing for pandas."

"Really? That's a bit random. Why pandas?"

"Well, she said it's because panda rhymes with Amanda."

"Oh right! That would make sense."

"She had a small one attached to her purse."

"What? A small panda? That's a bit cruel, isn't it?"

"Well, it wasn't a real panda. It was made of plastic. It was quite cute really."

"Oh, that's good. I can't abide animal cruelty."

"Neither can I. It's wrong, very wrong."

"OK then," she said. "C'mon, pour. I've told you before young man it's rude to keep a lady waiting!"

Young man! I thought. *If only! If only!*

Chapter 43

It was 10 AM - a civilised hour for a weekend morning, when Dave had decided to pay me a visit.

"So, how did it go with Patience the other day?"

"It went well, Dave. She's up for this. Seriously!"

"Mate! That is quality! I'm proud of you. I love you chap."

"Cheers chap. Loves you more."

"Oh stop it, you!" he replied.

"Never, Dave, you're the best."

"'Spose I am, as it goes. So she's going to do this! Mate, don't take this the wrong way, yeah?"

"Oh goodness, this sounds ominous."

"What?"

"Ominous, as in doomy – as if you're about to deliver a serious blow. Anyway, never mind. Carry on."

"Doomy?! Is that even a word?!"

"Not sure actually. It just came into my head."

"What are you like, eh?! Anyway, before I showed up, before you cried out for my help, you was in a right mess.

Don't get me wrong, you're still in a mess, only not as much of a mess as you were. You know what I mean?"

"Umm, I do actually. I'm not quite out of the woods though, but I can see the light."

"So, I'm a positive influence then?"

"Dave, of course you are! Do you even need to ask?"

"Alright then. I appreciate that. So then, why did you do Mandy? Am I not good enough for you? Just me? By myself?"

"Mate. You'll always be more important to me than Mandy. I just fancied revisiting her. It had been a while."

"Look, don't get me wrong. I do understand – the rush – the excitement. I get it. It's amazing at the time. But it don't last. Trust me. I know what I'm talking about."

"What? You've met Mandy too?"

"No mate, she weren't around in my day. We had different flavours then. Know what I mean?"

"Kind of. Anyway, it's done now. It was nice though. I couldn't have done the review that I did, had I not had her assistance."

"Perhaps not. But have you checked your sent items, since you sent it in?"

"Actually I haven't. There's no need. I was happy with it at the time. I can't see how that could have changed."

"Mate, you weren't in your right mind. Well, as much as you can be."

"I don't get it. I don't understand."

"Mate, it's simple. Mandy, she makes you feel good. She makes you feel great, even better than you're feeling. Actually, much better than you're feeling. Know what I mean?"

"No."

"Fuck sake, Pud. Do I need to spell it out for ya? Mate, I love ya. But you're doing my nut in right now! Know what I mean?"

"Actually, yes. I do chap. Sorry fella, I never meant to. I'm not quite right."

"True. You ain't. But you know what?"

"No."

"You will be. I tell you what. I fucking tell you what? You will be though mate. And you know why I'll do this? That I'll make sure you'll be right?"

"I don't know why. Why?"

"My job is to help you, and I like to do a good job. Yeah?"

"Yeah."

"You met Mandy again. Look, I'm not against you too getting a hook up from time to time. But can you tell me the next time you intend on hooking up?"

"Sure."

"The reason being, my posh Jock friend, is that I weren't able to visit you for days after. Did you not think that was bit strange, that something was amiss perhaps?"

"Actually, come to think of it, I did wonder why you hadn't been around sooner."

"Well, that's because I was trying to get through, but couldn't. The channels were blocked. You see, if I have advanced warning, I would've said, right, Pudd's off post for a bit. Best visit others."

"How can you visit others? I made you for me, not for others."

An uneasy, slightly irritated look came over Dave.

"Look. I'll tell you all one day. I promise. But for now, you've got to trust me. Yeah?"

"Fair enough Dave. Agreed."

"You see Pud, you've played the first half. And do you know what? You've done better than I expected you'd do. But you've still got a second half to play. So, I need you to be in optimum shape mate. Optimum. Yeah?"

"Sure chap. I understand completely. Optimum shape. Can I ask you a question?"

"Sure. Fire ahead."

"I like football. I like rugby too, but football has always been my favourite. I actually come from a rugby tradition. You see, my uncles, grandfathers, they all played it, but my dad preferred football. He taught me how to play a bit. He was a master of the instep. He showed that skill to me."

"Ah yeah, the instep. I've lost count of the amount of times I've used it. It served me well over my time there. But where are you going with this, mate?"

"Well, I noticed lately that you're coming out with a lot of footballing analogies. Is there a reason for this? Not that I mind."

Dave, looking pensive, paused to consider my question.

"Well, there is a reason for this, yes, a big reason. I will tell you, but not yet. I don't think you're ready to know just yet. I'll tell you when I feel that you're ready. Is that alright?"

"Sure Dave. That's alright."

Dave pulled up the sleeve of his football shirt and glanced at his watch. This time he was wearing his chunky silver one.

"Good. Right then, treacle. Places to be, faces to see."

"Sure Dave. I can't imagine that I'll be visiting Mandy anytime soon. But I promise, the next time I do, I'll let you know."

Dave smiled. "What are you like, you tart?! You take it easy yeah? Be lucky!"

"Cheers. And you."

I shut my eyes and began counting down... 10, 9, 8, 7 ... opened them and he was gone.

As psychotic episodes go, this one had to rate as the best. I had now passed the stage of merely passing the time of day with myself. Now I had moved into the area of self-admonishment. This whole Dave thing had become strange, very strange in fact.

Chapter 44

I wasn't best pleased with Gerald right now. In fact, I was very pissed off with him. I had decided though to keep my annoyance under wraps, at least for now.

Fastend were on the cusp of their biggest deal ever – a contract with the Royal Berkshire Hospital. This place home to roughly five thousand employees, and sadly a great many inmates, represented a deal that would increase their portfolio considerably. I was being sent to close this deal.

Gerald had couched this in very complimentary terms, saying that they needed their best man on the job, and that this best man was me. This compliment was paradoxical. Yes, on one hand, they genuinely viewed me as the best that there was. On the other hand, though, this wasn't my area. I was repeat business. This was new business. No amount of money could dull the absolute ballache that I knew lay ahead of me, in having to schmooze people in suits for two hours, or however long this was going to take. And what if I failed? This whole thing could cost me my job. And then what?

Dave had visited earlier to wish me luck, and to also tell me to stop being so negative. He said that a negative mind-set benefited no one. I had to concede that he had a point. And now here I was, standing outside, facing the Bath-stone Doric-pillared frontage of the Royal Berkshire Hospital. This place had an essence all of its own. Yes, I was stood outside the entrance to a hospital. But this wasn't like any other hospital that I had ever visited. Not that I had visited many. These Doric Bath-stone columns which had in part succumbed to the onslaught of time, displayed an ethereal majesty. I was mesmerised and awestruck. I tried to move but couldn't. I was rooted to the spot, unable to avert my gaze downwards from the portico, under which read ROYAL BERKSHIRE HOSPITAL. Suddenly, I heard a voice. It was a soft, gentle tone.

"Are you lost?" came this voice.

I tried to look down, but my gaze upwards seemed fixed. I paused to consider her question.

"Umm, you know, some days I am," I replied. "But most days, not really. Before, it was practically every day. I didn't know if I was coming or going. But I would say, by and large, most things have been processed. You'd kind of hope that would be the case really. I mean it's been at least a year now."

"Erm, but are you lost right now I mean?"

Suddenly my neck muscles loosened, allowing me to direct my gaze downwards, and there she stood - an image of foxy, sassy elegance. She had the poise and presence of a young Chaka Khan, only taller.

"My name's Lola," she continued. "We can't keep standing here. We'll get hit. I almost did last week. Luckily I am in the right place if I did! Come on. Move up the steps. I'll follow."

I did as advised, and then stepped in through the tall oak doors. Straight ahead of me was a wide marble staircase, framed with copper banisters. Its broadness and grandiose design reminded me of the staircase of the ill-fated Titanic. Thankfully, the screechy strains of Celine Dion were nowhere to be heard.

There was a strange but not earie sense of familiarity about Lola. I could have sworn I'd met her before. I wondered if she was a person of the sight. I had heard about such people before. But I never thought that I'd actually meet one of them. I turned to face her.

"Hi Lola. I'm Alastair. Can I ask you a question?"

"Sure."

"OK. Now this is, as a dear friend of mine would probably say, going to sound well weird. But please, no offence is intended. OK?"

"Sure," she replied. "Anyway, I don't offend easily."

"OK. Good. Are you? Shit this is going to sound very, very weird. Are you? Well, are you a person of the sight?"

"I don't think that's a weird question at all. It depends on what you mean?"

"Well," I replied rather awkwardly. "It's just that you asked me if I was lost."

"That's because I knew. I'm good at spotting the signs. I spot lost people every day. I've been here two years now, and I must have directed hundreds back on to the paths that they need to be on."

"I knew it!" I replied, with great enthusiasm. "I just knew it!"

She smiled. Her warm broad beam revealed a bright inner radiance to match her outward elegance. I now knew for certain that she was truly a person of the sight. There was no question of it.

"Come on," she said. "Let's go for a coffee. I know this great little League of Friends place. There are other places dotted about the site, but the money this place generates stays here. The coffee's great too!"

"I like that," I replied. "You can keep your Costas and your Starbucks. Give me a pub anytime. But if it can't be a pub, then a good local coffee shop is a great substitute!"

As we snaked around the main corridor and on towards the League of Friends coffee house, we were approached by someone who looked vaguely familiar to me. *Wait a minute! This can't be!* I thought. *What is Marie Fredriksson from Roxette doing at the Royal Berks?! That is mental! It can't be. Am I losing my mind? Again?*

"Hiya Kaye", said Lola as "Marie" passed us. It wasn't Marie.

Lola smiled. "I know what you're thinking. What is the lead singer of a Swedish rock group doing wandering the corridors of a Berkshire hospital?"

"Well yeah," I replied. "Something like that."

"She gets this all the time," replied Lola. "I keep telling her that she should get on the books of one of those lookalikey agencies. She'd clean up. She just laughs it off!"

"Perhaps she doesn't want to be typecast," I replied. "I'm getting this feeling that…urm, is she a person of the sight too?"

"She is, yeah. I think it's her tenth anniversary soon actually."

"Ten years!?" I exclaimed. "She must have such a great well-developed insight by now."

"Well," replied Lola. "She certainly knows her way around."

After a short leisurely stroll, we had reached the airy greenhouse-type style of this League of Friends coffee place.

"Take a seat," she said. "I'll get these. What would you like?"

"Can I have an espresso please?" I replied.

"Double?"

"If that's alright."

"Sure it is. I don't how you can drink that stuff though. Not that I've ever done it, but it must be like drinking tar."

"I haven't tried tar myself," I replied, "but if it tastes like espresso, then I may just give it a go!"

She smiled and took her place in the small queue.

A person of the sight, I thought. *I've finally met a person of the sight. I can't wait to tell Dave! Although he probably already knows.*

A short while later, Lola returned with a small china cup and placed it down slowly in front of me.

I looked longingly into this half-filled cup of black gold.

I took a small sip. "Ah, perfection can sometimes come in the smallest of vessels, don't you think? Thank you, by the way, that's very good of you."

"You're welcome," she replied, "Yes, I suppose it does."

A sporty-looking twenty-something lady with a nose ring and purple hair placed a substantially larger cup down by Lola. "There you are, a large soya latte. Enjoy."

"Thanks, Holly," replied Lola.

"I don't know how you can drink that," I said jokingly. "Not that I'd know what it's like, but it must be like drinking snow."

Lola smiled in response, clasping her hands around her mug. She brought it to her mouth and took a decent swallow.

"I've actually tried snow," she replied, "and it's nothing like a latte."

"You've tried snow?!" I gasped. "When was this?"

"I was a kid growing up in South London. That year, I can't remember when exactly, witnessed the heaviest snow fall, at least that I remembered. It was great! All the schools were closed! Anyway, we were in the local park pelting each other with snowballs. I caught one of these snowballs and bit into it."

"What did it taste like?"

"Well, it tasted, it tasted like water, because that's what snow is, water, only frozen."

"This isn't always the case," I replied.

"How do you mean?"

"Well, you have heard of yellow snow I presume?"

"Oh yeah, yellow snow," she replied. "Yuwww! Luckily, this particular piece of snow contained no yellow. But I didn't risk it again. Sometimes it can be just a faint spot of yellow and you might not be able to detect it. No, once was enough for me. I've got to ask you this," she continued. "And I hope you don't mind, but what takes you here? I hope that it's nothing tricky, if you know what I mean."

I smiled. "What a kind thing to say. Potentially, it could be tricky, but not in the way you mean. No, there's no sick relative, and I haven't been experiencing any physical discomfort."

"That's good to hear. So, what takes you to this town within a town?"

"Town within a town. I like that. I suppose it is. Well, it's business related. I'm here to close a deal."

"Wow! That sounds exciting. What kind of deal would this be then?"

"A phone deal."

"Oh, cool."

"If you say so! What it is, is that there's going to be a massive overhaul of the hospital phone system. All the groundwork has been done and I've been sent to get a certain Mr Tom Dale to dot the I's and cross the T's."

"Who? Tom Dale?"

"That's him. Yeah. Do you know him?"

"Yes, I do. Good luck on tracking him down. He's not an easy man to catch! I'll take you down there if you like, just in case you get lost."

"The company would be nice, but I know where I'm going."

"You do?"

"Oh yeah, I always do research on the area I'm going to, in case I get lost and that results in my being late. I'm a bit anal like that."

"So, you're not lost?"

"No, not in the geographical sense anyway! I like to think that I've got a good sense of direction."

"I could sense that actually," she replied.

"But of course you can," I replied. "You are a person of the sight. I never thought I'd get to meet one of you. This really is such a privilege!"

Lola smiled.

"So, tell me Lola, how long have you been a person of the sight?"

"Well, I suppose I've been close by for the last five years. It's only been the last two that I've been truly a person of the site."

"Well, I hope that you'll always be a person of the sight."

"That's the plan anyway," she replied.

"I can't see that changing, Lola. Once a person of the sight, always a person of the sight."

"Well Alastair, I have to agree. I've met a few people who have tried to break away from the site, but most are happy to stay."

"Always stay, Lola. Always."

"I will. I promise."

"That's good," I replied. "Now, off to get that all important signature."

"Pleasure to meet you, young man. Actually, has anyone ever told you?"

"Yes," I laughed. "Just a few though. Just a few!"

"You know, have YOU ever considered one of those lookalikey agencies?"

"I hadn't before today, Lola. But maybe. I dunno. Who knows? What's the worst that can happen? Take care, person of the sight. I'm sure our paths will cross again."

"Oh, I'm sure they will," she replied. "You take care too."

And that was it. I smiled and turned in the direction towards switchboard, about to close the biggest deal Fastend Telefonic had ever closed. *No pressure then* I thought. *Here we go.*

Chapter 45

It was Saturday. Two weeks to the day that I had reviewed Forbury on that hazy night in the Purple Turtle. My review was now online. I was sat around my computer with Jacques and Adri, about to pour over my handy work.

Reading it now, I was undecided if submitting my review whilst I was "in the moment" had been a wise choice. Or perhaps it may have been prudent to have waited a bit.

The article…

The Chronicle's Alastair McLeish-Pidkin went along to see local band "Forbury" perform at the legendary venue, The Purple Turtle. This is his rather insightful review of not just the band, but it seems an overall experience of an interesting night out!

Assignment number two was coming! I was beside myself with anticipation and excitement! What was up next? Surely I had proved myself now. Hadn't I displayed the merits necessary to hold my own in the world of journalism? Well apparently, I'm not quite there yet! Being new to this whole world, I'm still at the stage of being offered crumbs from the journalistic table. But hey, that's fine. We've all got to do our different apprenticeships. Assignment number 2, should I wish to accept it, was to do a review of local band Forbury. I was excited! You see, I'm a big fan of live music. Too few venues put on live music these days. It's dying out fast. Before long, the only available outlet remaining will be karaoke. Personally, I blame The X Factor for empowering the deluded and untalented.

The evening started off well. I hadn't been out with two of my very dear friends Pookesh Rama and Steven J Lindley for a good few months. So, deciding that a meet up was long overdue, I texted them. Before long, I was enjoying some naughty pre-gig treats around their newly acquired riverside apartment. All the omens seemed in place for the perfect evening. The first of these omens was a truly spectacular, celestial display. The sky seemed awash with every colour available to the supreme architect. I felt as if I was looking up admiring a Turner masterpiece. Pookesh told us that the reason for this display was that the coming together of the three of us, at this time and at this place, had brought all our relatives that had passed on, together. This Heavenly display was them thanking us and also to say hi. This made great sense to me.

So, with this celestial treat resonating and inhabiting us, we took a leisurely stroll in the direction of Reading Minster. The second of these favourable omens was the Minster itself. You see, earlier, there had been a light fall of rain. The ensuing dampness combined with a low sun produced the perfect illumination. This evening was now framed for the perfect night in music worship!

As soon as we approached the Turtle, I could tell that we were in for an all-round epic experience! Once inside, I was transported off into a subterranean, magical world. It seemed as if a whole cross section of urbanity had descended upon this particular part of Reading tonight. There were hippies with rainbow colours weaved into their locks. There were trendies, stylishly attired in designer gear. There were denim and leather-clad rockers head-banging away, regardless of the musical genre being pumped out by the beaming, super pumped-up master of the decks. Then, there was Forbury. Before even a note was struck, I had a good feeling about these guys and this optimism wasn't to be dashed.

Daryl, the lead singer in black leather trousers, ivory white t-shirt and Alice band, which kept his flowing black mane from his eyes, strode the stage as if he owned it. His sheer presence commanded audience attention. Various colours just seemed to beam out from his person, holding those who stood watching, listening in awe, in some sort of hypnotic trance. I had read somewhere,

OXFORD ROAD

I think it was on Wikipedia, that mystics, they may be Buddhist, say that everyone on this planet has inner colours. But that only the very enlightened have the sight required to be able to see these colours. The interesting thing here was that I was only able to see Daryl's inner colours. The fact that I could even see one person's colours, showed that I had at least possibly attained some form of enlightenment. Perhaps this was the beginning of my own personal journey towards full enlightenment. I'll keep you posted on this, readers. They kicked off proceedings with the Doors, "Break on through" – a personal favourite of mine. This seemed appropriate, given Daryl's uncanny resemblance to the late, great Jim Morrison. It felt as if the great man himself was projecting his energy through this doppelganger. Perhaps he too, just like our dead relatives earlier in the sky, was dropping by to say, "hi, I haven't completely gone away you know!" At least that's what I hoped. The rest of the band completed this awesome musical experience. Perhaps their colours were projected in sublime sounds which couldn't be seen, unlike Daryl's, which could be.

Swept up in the whole sense of occasion, one song seemed to drift off in to the next and so on. Eventually it became impossible to differentiate between them. Perhaps, this was meant to be – that fate had deemed this so.

I have been to see many big acts. I've seen Feeder and The Foo Fighters in Glastonbury; Paul Weller in the

Marquee club; ABC, Yazoo, and Howard Jones at Rewind; but I can honestly say right here, right now, that none of these experiences come close to what I witnessed tonight. I felt privileged to be alive, on this day, on this hour, and in this place. If there is any justice, not just on this planet, but in this universe, undiscovered universes, and all dimensions, then this band is destined for great things. The best thing in all this? They're a local band. They are a Reading band! And all this comes from me, a Scotsman, but OF Reading.

One love and much respect – Ali ☺ X

Comments…5

Mate! WTF?!

The troubadour

Hmm. Thank you for such a great review and overall account of a great night out! I loved your description of the sky as you saw it. I wasn't aware that the colours that night were created by your passed-on loved ones. As for the band review, I shall definitely be looking out for these chaps! Great review.

The Jester

Mate! Was we at the same gig? If so, I saw them too and thought they was s**t! Be lucky!

TheRandomOne

Wow, looks like you really did "break on through to the other side"! I wonder what these pre-gig treats you talk of are! These "treats" seem to have done the trick!

Naked Princess

Cheers for the review fella! Very much appreciated! Hopefully this will lead to more gigs – preferably paid ones!

Daryl of Forbury

I looked across to Jacques and Adri. This whole experience it seemed had rendered them mute.

"Well," I enquired. "What do you think?"

They faced each other and then me. "Well," said Adri. "It's a very original type of review, I must say."

"Yes," I replied. "But did you enjoy it?"

"Well," she replied. "It was certainly entertaining."

"Not too many laboured images then?"

"Not at all," replied Jacques. "You need to look at this way. You're new to this. It's only your second article. Your second article. And I will say this, you're still finding your feet man. But can I be really honest?"

This sounds ominous, I thought.

"I preferred the other one. It seemed written at a more relaxed, slower place. I get it, you got back, you were pumped up and wanted to get it down. But, perhaps, the next time, you should sleep on it and then write it. Now, that would be some treat!"

I had to concede that my good friend and surrogate Reading-based father had a point.

Oh dear, I thought. *Act in haste, pay at leisure. My only question now is, did Suzi like it?*

Chapter 46

~

It was late. I was tired. I'd been up all day talking to Dave. It was mainly Dave talking, with me listening. He did let me get some words in, though. Not many, but a few. Still, I was grateful for this.

It wasn't late in the conventional sense. To me though it was late. I hadn't slept for 8 hours. My mind was racing and was refusing to listen to the pleas of my body. There was only one thing for it – get out there.

Dave had set me a task. This task was, he said, to have a "proper blinding day", and to tell him all about it when he showed up tomorrow. I had asked him if there was anything specific that he had in mind for me. He said that there was, but it wasn't for him to say. I really had no idea what he meant by this.

Twenty minutes later and after a much-needed rejuvenating shower, I was feeling as Dave might say, a lot more vital. I wasn't sure if he knew my plans. Given that he was a part of me, I suspected that he at least knew the basics.

I was meeting Lola today – that kind-spirited lady that I had met earlier in the week when closing that big hospital phone deal. Dave had said to say hello. He said that he was impressed at what he had seen, describing her as "proper tasty".

It seems he'd been hovering around all throughout. It was fortunate for me that he hadn't made himself visible during this time. Had that happened, then at the very least, I would have felt obliged to introduce him to her. To not do so, well, that would have been rude.

Half an hour later, I reached Broad Street. It was buzzing. It wasn't just alive; it was living. It was breathing. It was inhaling and exhaling the energy and buzz created by the various diverse people pounding its concrete channels. Shouts from the vendors went up, trying to draw in the throngs to their seemingly tantalising deals. "Hair weaves, for a fiver! Two hair-weaves for seven!" You know you want to!" There was the harlequin-trousered balloon bender, crafting all manner of colours and sizes into a great many shape of animal and plant. He had sausage dogs. He had antelopes. He had bunnies. He had palm trees.

Suddenly, a most glorious sound resonated, lifting itself high above the crowds and these speculative friendly punts of hope. I looked around to see if I could locate its source. Where was this euphoric crescendo emanating from? Who was producing it?

OXFORD ROAD

Then I saw it. It was a man, a guitar, an amp, and two peddles. He was standing over near Woolworths. Close enough to make an impact this end of Broad Street, yet keeping a respectful enough distance from Jason, so as not to disrupt his "issue" sales.

The song the man was playing wasn't one that I knew in the literal sense, yet I felt connected with it.

"You go east. I go west".

"We live for today, then take care of the rest".

"We've got life for today".

"You've got magic all the time".

I was mesmerised. Every word and every syllable in these words were seeping in through my pours and whooshing through my bloodstream. And his voice! It was unique. It was impossible to define. A sign in front of his guitar case read simply, "Just Tom". The word "just" to me seemed to suggest ordinary, average, regular. I admired the man's modesty, but this sign was at best, a very poor representation of this man's talents, and at worst a travesty.

He continued.

"You've got time on your side

You need to get out and hide"

His words, his voice, and his presence were having a profound effect on my levels of consciousness. I couldn't move. I didn't want to move. What was the point in even trying? For now, right here, if there were such a thing as fate, then I was meant to be here. I was meant to have come in to contact with this person. This man had a look of a young James Spader, and the charisma of a seasoned, confident Grant Nicholas from Feeder. Suddenly the streetscape fell silent and the people moved into one entity. I was now part of a creeping salamander as it engulfed all around, sucking up buildings, stalls, and a rather milky sky.

What am I meant to do now? I thought. As if directed by some sort of magnetic field, I felt my neck being drawn in the direction of the ground, and there, close to my feet, was that red kite, again. I wasn't sure if anyone else could see him or her. I was just curious. My curiosity, however, couldn't bring me to ask anyone standing with me, if they could see this fine little creature too. *What if they can't see him?* I thought. *Where does that leave me then? Marked out as a loon tune. Do not approach this man!*

"Hey Kitey chap! How's it going fella?" I whispered.

I suddenly felt a tap on my shoulder. I looked around. It was Lola. She was accompanied by a sporty-looking, thirty-something man.

I looked down quickly, to see that my kite friend was no longer there. *Thank goodness*, I thought. Not that I didn't enjoy our little meet ups but because I wasn't quite ready to introduce others to this deeper level of insanity.

"Hey Alastair," she said, as she smiled broadly. "I was just passing, on my way to BOBS to meet up as arranged and saw you standing here, worlds away. He's pretty good, isn't he?" she said, pointing at this musical maestro.

"He's amazing!" I replied. "Totally amazing."

"There's nothing "just" about him either. The word "just" suggests ordinary or just about passable. There's certainly nothing ordinary about him. In fact, I would say that his modesty is very extraordinary."

"That's one way, to look at it," I replied. "So," I continued, "shall we head?"

"Sure," she replied. "Oh, forgive my rudeness, this is my friend Stueie. And guess what? He's a person of the site too".

"Really?!" I exclaimed.

"That's right. Yeah. I'm putting up scaffolding outside Benyon ward at the minute."

"Ah that's brilliant! Another person of the sight too! Amazing!

"I suppose you could say that," he replied. "I never really thought of it that way before. But yeah, I must be. Person of the site! I like that!"

"Oh wow," I replied. "You people are like busses! I have waited years to meet a person of the sight, and in one week, I meet two! It's a great pleasure to meet you, Stueie!" I extended my arm towards him. His grip was firm and reassuring. "My name's Alastair. But then, I expect you already know this."

"I do actually. Yeah. Pleasure to meet you too."

Before long, we had reached the broad expanse of the riverside, "Back of Beyond" pub, known affectionately among Readingites as BOBS.

Looking around, there seemed a good mix of ages in this atmospherically lit, drinking and food emporium.

"I'll get the first round in," said Lola enthusiastically. "What would you like to drink? What am I talking about? I know what we all drink."

"But of course you do," I replied jokingly. "Let's go down the end and get a riverside table. It's nice and tranquil just watching those lights sparkle off the river."

"Sounds good to me," agreed Stueie.

We took a table by a window. I looked out as the various colours from the apartments across from us bounced off the Kennet, producing a kaleidoscope of calm and tranquillity.

I couldn't help noticing Stueie's watch. I hadn't seen one like it. Even Dave's varied designs of timepiece couldn't come close to this watch. It seemed to have hypnotic qualities. I felt myself drawn in, unable to look away. *What's happening to me now?* I thought. *It's a watch. It's just a watch.*

"Ah!" exclaimed Stueie, nodding. "Another one drawn in by the power of the watch."

"What?" I replied. "There are others?"

"Of course there are mate. You're not the first to be seduced by its charms. It's a Hugo Boss number actually. I like other designers. I like Gucci, although he's a bit overrated, and sometimes, I like a bit of Ralph Loren. I sometimes, but very rarely, will try a Lagerfeld. The blokes a bit of a tosser really. You see him on that screen trying to be the centre of attention, giving it the BIG I AM. And what's with him wearing shades indoors? I think that's what makes him a tosser more than anything."

This made me laugh. "I've always thought that too. I see people being interviewed indoors wearing shades and I'm thinking, why? Why are you doing that?"

"I'm glad it's not just me! But yeah Alastair, I like different designers, but it always seems to come back to Boss. Do you know what I mean?"

"I do actually. It makes complete sense. It's OK to try other designers. But if these designers are complete tossers, then it makes sense to stay true to one who isn't. I don't really know much about designers, but I'll be keeping an eye out for this bloke Boss, from now on."

"Good stuff chap. I always tell people; you can't go wrong with a bit of Boss!"

Lola returned with a silver tray and three large bulb-shaped glasses.

"Look, I know these aren't our usual drinks, but I thought that I'd like to take us on journey of sorts."

"I'm not sure I understand," I replied.

"We're gonna drink gin tonight. Did you know that you can now get gin from all over the world these days? And you know what they say about travel?"

"What? That it costs a lot?" laughed Stueie.

"Well, there is that," she replied. "But more importantly, it broadens the mind. First stop, India! Cheers!"

"Nice one," said Stueie. "I've always fancied a trip to India!"

"Me too," I chimed in enthusiastically. "Me too!"

Contentedly, I relaxed back into my bumpy, yet comfy seat. Dave had set me the curious task of having a blinding day today. I was looking forward to telling him all about it when he showed up tomorrow; although he'd probably already know. He'd still let me tell him all about it. He placed a high importance upon our conversations. It was yet another thing I liked about him.

Not only had I borne witness to a musical treat of Heavenly proportions, Kitey had paid me a visit, and I had met another person of the sight.

Two in the same week, I thought. *What are the chances of that?*

I wouldn't dwell too much on the minutiae for now. *Live in the now*, I thought, as once again, I felt my gaze drawn helplessly towards a magic watch.

Chapter 47

~

"So, you preferred his watch then?"

"I never said that."

"Course you did. It's fine though. It don't really bother me as it goes."

"Well, it clearly does. But shouldn't. Shit. I wish I hadn't said anything now."

"Nah mate, don't worry about it. I'll be alright."

"I feel really bad now. But all I really said was that his watch was really nice. I never said it was nicer than yours."

"Whatever. Just forget about it. I'm bored with this now."

"But Dave. C'mon chap!"

"Well, I don't know. My watches are very personal to me. I feel affronted. Know what I mean?"

"I do Dave. But I never said anything unkind about your watches. You know I really like them. They're varied, well-designed, and interesting. I like them. I really do."

"Well, I don't know."

"C'mon Dave. Seriously now."

"Well."

"Look Dave. Whatever I said to offend you, I'm sorry. OK?"

"Well."

There followed a short pause, as Dave cupped his chin in his hand, and then looked up pensively to consider my conciliatory words. He then smiled and pointed at me.

"Your face, mate! Priceless! Of course I know that you didn't mean anything by what you said. Sorry mate, I couldn't resist, but you're such an easy target. You have to admit."

"I suppose so. You do have a point. My dad was forever telling me off for being so naïve growing up. He used to say that what is charming in childhood, doesn't always translate well into adulthood."

"Very wise man, your dad. I wish I'd met him."

"Perhaps you will," I replied. "One day. Actually, that's daft. How would that be possible?"

"Never say never, Ali. Never say never."

He pulled up a sleeve of his retro Reading FC top and looked into his turquoise watch face.

"Wow Dave. Lovely watch. Spectacular! It's certainly the most stylish watch that I have ever seen. That's for sure."

"Nice try Ali. Nice try! Haha! Right, it's that time again. You know the drill. Places to be, faces to see. Laters, yeah?"

"Sure Dave. Catch up later."

I shut my eyes and counted down from 10…10, 9, 8, 7 …opened them and he was gone.

It was early afternoon on Sunday. I was sitting on the side of my bed. This was at Dave's insistence. He had told me that lying in bed beyond a certain time wasn't good for my posture, and that it was best that I sit up back straight whilst I was talking to him. He also said that it's a bit rude to be lying in bed while he was standing. He said that by lying in bed when he was around, I wasn't paying him my full attention and that I missed out that way.

The whole reason for him visiting today, I thought, was to ask me about my fulfilling the task he had set me of having a blinding day. I had told him of the angelic sounds of the busker and the profound effect that it had had on me. I had mentioned Kitey yet again showing up in public. But it was when I got to the part of Stueie and the watch that the whole mood of the conversation suddenly changed. I know he said that it was a joke and that I had been easy to wind up. But I wasn't convinced. Perhaps there was something that he wasn't telling me.

Gerald had texted earlier asking that we meet up today. He had some "awesome news" that he wanted to tell me in person. He also said that he had a favour to ask – a big favour. I was intrigued. I had suggested that we meet in the Rose. He had suggested the Nags. In the end we had compromised on the Fisherman's Cottage along the canal.

It seemed the perfect compromise. It was close to his Eldon Square residence, and it was a particular favourite of mine.

A magical sense of seasonal smells lingered in the fresh, crisp air. The sky was a soft watery blue. As I approached Blake's Lock, a spray from the foam created by the confluence of the gap and the drop enlivened my face. The ammonia permeating in through my nose journeyed through my bloodstream. Spring had sprung. Daffodils randomly presented themselves as the seasonal treat, alongside the perpetual tufts of grass and weeds marking out the boundaries of the torn riverside fence.

What can this big favour possibly be? I wondered, as I approached the resplendent bay windows of the tavern. Gerald was sitting over by the pool table. He seemed deep in thought. I gently patted him on the back. He turned around and looked up.

"Hey Pudds! Great to see you mate. Sorry, I was miles away. I've lots to process. Typical management, they wait until 5 on a Friday, just as I'm getting ready to leave, to lay this on me!"

"Gerald, no apologies my friend. I'm forever drifting off into many different worlds!"

"Oh, yes. I remember now. Golf clubs, dingy nightclubs!"

"Golf club actually. And the "After Dark" isn't so dingy. I'd describe it as subterranean. It's got a feel of bohemia about it."

"I've never been. You must take me sometime."

"Erm, OK. Sure."

A slightly uneasy pause followed.

"So," I continued, as I pulled out one the wonky stools. "I'm intrigued. What is this awesome news that you've been dying to tell me? The news that couldn't wait 'till we see each other in work tomorrow?"

"Well, who said I need an excuse to hang out with my best bud?"

"True," I said as the significance of the words "best" and "bud" sunk in. *How far have we come? I thought. It's not that long ago that I actually despised this man. Now here we are, sharing a nice bottle of Prosecco. And what is this Prosecco thing? It seems to be a bit of a fixture all of a sudden.*

"I hope you don't mind," he continued, "but they seem to be doing a bit of run on special offers on this stuff. I thought I'd better get in before it's all gone, see."

"I see, see. That makes a lot of sense. It's just that I'm wondering if Reading has been recently flooded with a consignment of the stuff! There seems to be special offers on it everywhere. Anyway, no, of course I don't mind. It's a fine drop, this Prosecco stuff."

"Ah, I knew you'd be fine with it," he replied warmly. "Here, I'll be mum," he said as he poured me a generous serving. "Now yes, this news. Well, you know Tom Dale agreed in principal to the contract, pending a financial survey."

"Yeah, he signed an exclusivity deal, meaning that if feasible, then he will sign it off officially."

"That's right. Well here, my flying Scotsman," he continued excitedly, as he reached into his inside blazer pocket, "and here it is, all signed off officially." He handed me the document.

"Now take a look at this and let it all sink in my friend. I'm off for a waz or perhaps more. Well done again, bud."

"Yeah, cheers for that," I replied, and there it was, cast in ink, one of my greatest ever achievements. Suddenly, I was engulfed with a striking sense of pride. The fact that this was achieved in a business that I had little belief in made this achievement all the more remarkable.

Fuck sake Pud, I thought. *Allow yourself a little smile for goodness sake. You've bloody earned it!*

"Turns out I only needed a waz after all," said Gerald, as he came back from the toilet. "Because of this great achievement of yours, my worth in the company has soared."

"In what way?"

"Well, they've only offered me Assistant Regional Manager."

"Brilliant! Actually, is that Assistant Regional Manager or Assistant TO the Regional Manager?"

"Very funny, Pud!" laughed Gerald. "No, it's the real deal. They've offered me the Assistant Regional Manager's job."

"What will this mean?"

"In terms of what?"

"Well, will you still be based here in Reading? They won't be expecting you to move to Newbury, will they? It's just that I've grown rather fond of you over these past few months."

"And I you, Sir. And I you," he replied. "No, I'll be staying here in Reading. In fact, I'll be staying at my desk. I'm happy there, see."

"I do see," I replied.

"Indeed. They did ask though if I would move up with "them upstairs". I said no way I'm sitting with that lot. I'm more than happy with my desk, partially closed off with three dividers. Oh, and a cracking view of Alesandra!"

"Chap, I don't blame you for not wanting to move in that case! I wouldn't. I'm glad you're staying."

"Ah cheers, Pud. Yeah me too. Also, the news doesn't end there."

"Really? What else?"

"Well, there's the small manner of your commission. OK, I might have set this up, but you went in and closed it, see. Bob said that he was very impressed with you in the way you carried yourself. He said that you were confident, yet highly personable."

Personable, I thought. *That's like something you'd see on a CV.*

"So, you want to see how much you made then?"

"Definitely!" I exclaimed.

"Are you sure now?"

"Gerald, just bloody tell me chap! Don't keep me in suspenders!"

"OK, OK. I won't tell you. But I will show you." He handed me what appeared to be a folded cheque. "Look, I know this is old school, but I really wanted to hand you a cheque. A bank transfer doesn't have the same feel, does it? It lacks the excitement and sense of occasion, don't you think?"

"Sure. Sure. I do." I unfolded this slim piece of pigmented paper, and there it was, the sum total of my day's toil at the Royal Berkshire Hospital.

"Please pay the bearer of this cheque, Mr Alastair McLeish-Pidkin, the sum of five thousand and twenty-three pounds and fifty-three pence."

I paused to let it all sink in.

"I knew this was going to be a lot," I exclaimed. "But I certainly didn't expect this. Wow!"

"Pretty good, eh?" replied Gerald. "You see. It mightn't be the premier league or Top of The Pops, but it isn't all bad in the broad world of telecoms. Is it now?"

"Looking at this beautiful sliver of unremarkable parchment right now, Gerald, I'm very inclined to agree with you. Very inclined. As a man once proclaimed, "it's good to talk"."

"It certainly is. Keeping people connected. I mean, that can only be a good thing. Can't it, fella?"

"I completely agree, Sir. Completely."

"Oh, and on the subject of keeping people connected. Camila and me, well, we've set a date."

"Ah mate. I'm so so happy for you. For you both. Camila's lovely. You both are." I leant forward and embraced Gerald. This was a seminal moment. Here was someone whom I had shown utter disdain to. This was a man whom I had endeavoured to belittle in front of others. And all because I disliked what I thought he was about. Briefly, I cast my mind back to those shameful days, and flipped a firm judgemental middle finger up at that smug sneering little shit that I was back then.

Gerald patted my back and we sat back. "Ah cheers, Pud. That means a lot."

"So, when is the big day then? When do you plan on making dishonest people out of each other?"

"Dishonest people, Pud! I like that. Well, we thought we'd do this in the summer. So, we've chosen July. The 18th, to be precise."

"That's brilliant!" I replied. "It doesn't give you much time though."

"No, it doesn't give US much time."

"Of course," I replied. "I mean it doesn't give you and Camila much time."

"No, Puds. That's not what I meant. It doesn't give us, as in you and me, much time."

"I don't understand."

"Well, stag dos take a lot of planning. And I don't want to be short-changed either. I want the works. Class As, strippers, bungee jumping, the lot!"

"Are you asking me along on the stag, Gerald? Sure, I'd love to come."

"You're not just coming on it, matey. You're organising the bloody thing. I mean that's what best men do isn't it? Or am I missing something?"

"What? You're asking me to be YOUR best man?"

"Of course I am. So, will you mate? Will you do me the honour or organising my last days of freedom then?"

"I don't know what to say."

"Well you could start by saying yes."

"Oh mate. Of course I will. Oh my goodness chap, I'd be honoured to. Fucking honoured! Ah just a second chap. I got a bit of grit in my eye earlier. I thought I'd worked it out. Won't be long."

Overall, I would have to say that today had been rather strange. It had started that way, carried on in the same vein, and now this. In order not to add to the strange nature of the day, I felt that it would be best to work out whatever it was that was filling up my eyes, for both our sakes.

Chapter 48

"That's brilliant, mate. I'm happy for you, really happy. You two have certainly been on some journey. So, where ya planning on having it?"

"Well, it's not for a while yet. But I was thinking of a couple of places. Prague sounds good, but then, so too does Amsterdam. He hasn't set me an easy task."

"How do you mean?"

"Well, he wants strippers, but he also wants bungee jumping. Strippers could be sorted easily and so too could bungee jumping but not in the same place. If we had longer, a week perhaps, then we could do both, but we've only got a weekend."

"Well, it looks like he's going to have to choose – bungee jumping or strippers. He's got to choose strippers, really. I know I would."

"Really? You do surprise me Dave."

"Well, that's me fella, always full of surprises. Right, then," he said as he pulled up a sleeve, revealing yet another stylish timepiece. This time it was a hexadecimal silver head with slim brown leather straps.

"New watch, Dave?"

"Kinda. It's about two weeks old. Got it from Phil down the pub. He got back from Thailand last Saturday. Anyway chap, sorry to have to cut our little soiree a tad short. There's somewhere I really need to be. You know…"

"I know mate – places to be, faces to see. Catch you later."

"Sure thing geeze. Laters, yeah?"

I closed my eyes and counted down from 10…10, 9, 8, 7, …opened them and he was gone.

Of all the many visits, this was by far the shortest. I wondered why?

I was meeting Mayfly soon. I hadn't been to see him preach for a few weeks. I'd missed it all. The crowds, the excitement, the buzz, the whole atmosphere was really something special and dynamic. It was like being at a ROCK CONCERT.

I turned out onto the Oxford Road. I felt a buzz of excitement in the early evening air. As I passed by the "Music Man" shop, I couldn't help overhearing something of a domestic. Actually, I wasn't overhearing it; it was being imposed upon me. Not just on me, but it seemed anyone within a two-mile radius who wasn't hard of hearing, or even if there were some audio-challenged close by, would struggle not to hear at least the general gist of the proceedings.

She proclaimed.

"So yeah, what if I stay out all night? It don't mean I'm shagging someone else."

To which he replied.

"He ain't just someone else though, is he? He's my bruvva, and what I want to know is what was you doing all night with my bruvva. Yeah?"

"What do you think we was doing?"

"Well you tell me then."

"We was playing Monopoly. Happy?"

Suddenly the flow of exchanges seemed to take on a more relaxed nature as the man paused to ponder her explanation.

As the tone lowered and people began to resume whatever important journeys they had been on, I stopped and leant in towards the source of their dialogue. I was now trespassing.

"You was playing Monopoly?"

"Yes babes, Monopoly."

"That would make sense actually. I bought that for him only last month. He said that he always wanted a set. That he's always been a fan. Can't see the fuss myself though. They ain't called "bored" games for nothing though."

"Haha! I like that babes. That's one of the many things I like about you. Your sense of humour. That and your huge cock!"

"Ah fanks Babe!"

And that was it. Domestic concluded.

I continued on and reached the top of Broad Street. Jason was stood over by his usual pitch, punting the "Big Issue".

"Ladies, gents, get your 'Big Issue'. Today's featured article, WEALTHY BUSINESSMAN FINDS TIGER'S TOOTH IN HIS LASANGE!"

This is worth the price for that article alone, I thought. *Cross-contamination in food processing is serious business.*

"So, how's it going then, Jason? Sales going well today?"

"Not so bad, Ali. Which is always a good thing. What with tomorrow being suicide Sunday."

"That's what I don't understand though, Jason. The crowds on Sunday don't seem that different to Saturdays."

"I know," he replied. "Tell me about it. Maybe they're in shitty moods 'cos they know they've got work the next day."

"Actually, I never thought of that," I replied. "That would seem to make a lot of sense. Miserable bastards! Look, I know I don't usually take it, but would you mind if I took my copy this time? It's just that I'm intrigued by today's headline. I mean, a tiger's tooth in a lasagne? What's all that about?"

"Mate, that's no problem at all. I don't blame you. I've read this article. It's messed up. You'll like it."

"Cheers chap," I replied, as I tucked the rolled paper under my arm. I continued down through the crowds of those meandering leisurely down along this thoroughfare.

I reached the assembled crowds outside M&S. There was a collective buzz of anticipation. The stage was set.

Enter the people. Enter the man! He was on. I'd missed this.

"People. People." He paused slightly. "There may be a God."

A collective hum of disbelief went up. He continued.

"Something happened to me today. Something happened to challenge my disbelief in belief. Something profound. Something really quite profound. But you know what? Do you know what though? IT DOESN'T MATTER! It doesn't matter if there is a God or if there isn't. The message is still the same. That doesn't change. Be decent to each other. Care for each other. You don't need to know someone to show kindness to them. In fact, it's better if you don't know them. Because you know what? Do you know what? Kindness to strangers? Yeah? It's the purest form of kindness that there is."

This wasn't going well for him. There was now a steady trickle of people leaving. They had clearly heard enough. What was he saying that there may be a God? Why had he suddenly become agnostic. This performance was so far off point. I felt for him. I approached him slowly. By now there were only a handful of people left. I wasn't even sure if those left had come to see him or were simply sat around passing time.

He looked despondent.

"Hey Puds. This has been a bit of a wash out. Time to call it a day."

"What, for good? Don't let one day's poor performance cloud all the good ones."

"Cheers for that, Pud. Just what I wanted to hear," he replied sharply.

"Sorry chap. That sounded wrong. I just meant believe in yourself. We all have off days. I certainly have my fair share of them," I replied, trying to lighten the tone. "What happened anyway?"

"Look, I'll tell you later," he replied. He sounded quite awkward. "Meet me in the Forbury, yeah? I just need to clear up. I've got a box of wine and some nibbles. Although I could do with something far stronger than wine and nibbles right now, I tell you,"

"Let's just stick with the "vino collapseso" for now though yeah?" I replied. "I'll see you over there shortly."

"See you over there chap," he replied. "I'll be fine. Yeah, we all have off days I suppose."

"Yes, we do. I know I do. Lots in fact. And it's not a case of you'll BE fine. You ARE fine. In fact, you're great. You're Mayfly!"

He smiled in appreciation, but I could tell it was a forced smile. Still, I appreciated the gesture all the same.

As I sauntered along towards Market Place, I wondered if he would be fine. I wasn't convinced by this face of acceptance that he was showing me. I wondered what could have been so profound to have shaken his strong sense of disbelief to the core.

Chapter 49

"So, are we on the same page then, Alastair?"

"Well, we were. But I'm not sure if we still are. I don't think that I can ever be on the same page as anyone who says "the same page". I hate that corporate speak. I thought you did too."

"I do. I do. I'm only winding you up see. Honestly!"

"What are you like, Gerald?" I replied in a more light-hearted tone. "But are you sure you want them to play? I was wasted when I wrote that review. For all I know they could have been shit."

"I truly doubt that. Yes, you may well have been wasted when you wrote it, but quite often, real opinions come to the fore when wasted, see. There are less inhibitions. If you honestly thought that they were shit, then you would have said they were shit. See?"

"Humm, yes I do see," I replied, nodding to him in affirmation. "OK, that's the band sorted. But what about the venue for the stag. Amsterdam or Prague?"

"I mean Alastair, c'mon mate. Do you honestly think there's even a contest there? Prague's all very well if you're after a cultural experience. But if you're after real action. You know what I mean by real action, yes? Then it's gotta be Amsterdam. I know as the best man you get to choose, but please say it's Amsterdam. Please Pud?"

It was Monday. Gerald had called me into his office for a quick catch-up.

"OK.OK. Amsterdam it is. So, you're happy to go with strippers rather than bungee jumping?"

"Just a bit! Bungee jumping would be nice, mind. But if it's a choice between that and strippers, then it's no contest, really."

"I agree. Well. That's good. It certainly makes my life a lot easier. Amsterdam is huge. It doesn't have many green spaces close by. Actually, how about this for a mad idea, Gerald?"

"Go on."

"Well, and I can't believe that I didn't think of this before. But there's no rule that states you must do it all in one go."

"I'm not with you."

"Well, how about this? We do bungee jumping here in Reading or close by and do the main stag in Amsterdam?"

Gerald was suddenly enveloped with a look of extreme excitement.

"Seriously, Pud. You must know this, but I want to kiss you right now."

"No, you don't."

"Of course I don't. It's just a figure of speech, see, meaning that I love this suggestion. You're the man."

"Oh, you do flatter me. Cheers. I'm not sure about the class A's though. Don't know the terrain."

"Fair enough. Can't have it all, I suppose."

Gerald pulled the sleeve of his starched effervescent shirt up slightly and peered into his cherry-faced watch.

"Ten past twelve. Crikey! Well, I suppose we better get on with some work."

"Goodness is it really that time Gerald? Time flies I guess when you're passing the time of day with good friends."

"Ah cheers, Pud. Same as. Best crack on, chap."

"Indeed" I replied.

I returned to my desk and pulled the headphones across my head. Mayfly's fragile state of mind was causing me great concern. When speaking to him yesterday about his profound moment, what he told me didn't seem to make a great deal of sense. He just said that he'd seen a ghost. He wouldn't go into much detail beyond that. I told him that most people at some point in their lives will see a ghost or, most likely, ghosts. His reaction was that he wasn't speaking metaphorically but literally, in that he had seen or at least he thought he had seen an actual ghost, as in someone who was once alive but had since become deceased. Not only that, but this ghost wasn't your average ghost, rather the ghost of someone "really famous". When I asked him who this famous person was, he said that there was no point in telling me as not being from Reading I wouldn't know him. So, at least I knew the gender of this ghost – it was a "him". And not being from Reading? He was right of course, but the cheek! He went on to tell me that having seen a ghost challenged fundamentally what he was all about. If what he had seen was an actual ghost and not just some result of poor diet resulting in malnutrition delusion, then his fundamental belief in disbelief was now shaken to the core. The ramifications were far-reaching indeed. If what he had seen was indeed a ghost, then this surely rendered his belief that we all drift off into nothingness, redundant. Granted this non-theistic stance didn't comprise his whole sermon, but it was a central tenet. He had decided that until he was certain beyond doubt that he had seen a ghost, then he would downplay his belief in disbelief. I had countered with the suggestion that perhaps he should drop it completely and instead focus solely on the humanitarian message of which he was a great exponent. There was absolutely no point in preaching something that he didn't fully disbelieve in. He agreed.

The money from the hospital sale had now cleared in my account. I now boasted a bank balance far healthier than that of my mind.

Who do I call now? I thought. Although the fruits of my effortless labour were now becoming obvious, my motivation levels seemed to be lagging far behind.

I scrolled down the spreadsheet. It wasn't even a spreadsheet that I had composed myself. Phil in accounts had set it up as she was concerned that sifting through endless reams of paper didn't exactly look professional. She had a point. This was far easier and far less of a ball-ache too.

I continued to scroll down… until… ah *"Signs of the Times" Woodley. I wonder how Drake is? I haven't spoken to him for a while. Must be a good five months now.* I dialled.

"Hello. Signs of the Times – no sign too big, no sign too small. Fine displays, one and all. How can I help you?"

"Drake, is that you?"

"Alastair?" he replied enthusiastically. "Is that you? My crazy Scotchman!"

He doesn't know the half of it, I mused.

"So, I'm made of Whisky now, am I?"

"Oh, you know what I mean. How ya didlin'? I haven't heard from you for a while?"

"Ah, ya know. Staying out of trouble or at least trying to. How are things in the world of signs?"

"Well, if you're asking if I'm going to renew this month then, I'm afraid the answer's going to have to be no."

"That was the original reason for the call, but I wasn't going to come to it this soon in."

"I know. I know. It's just that my mind is all over the place right now. So I find myself coming straight to the point quickly now. Sorry."

"Chap, no apologies necessary. What's up? Business not so good then?"

"It's worse than that."

"Worse? How?"

"As in, I've called in the receivers. I've had little choice. I can't compete with the big boys anymore. They can produce what we do, on a much bigger and cheaper scale. Although being mass produced, it lacks the obvious craftsmanship that Stan has. Stan injects such passion into his work that I'm sure each sign he leaves behind contains a part of his soul. You don't get that with robots."

"True, you don't. I'm really sorry to hear that fella. So what next?"

"I don't know mate. I can't think straight right now. I haven't even told the workforce."

"What you haven't told Stan?"

"No, I haven't."

"Ah, poor Stan the man. But what can you do? It's a business, not a charity."

"Well, it's not even a business now. Oh shit, Alastair, I've got to go. I've just seen Stan's Nissan pull up. Now is as good a time as ever to break the news. Listen, I just want to say quickly, thanks for the lovely phones. I know we've only had two, but they were dear to me. Very dear in fact. Listen, I better go before; I make a complete tool of myself."

And that was it. Phone call concluded, swiftly.

I really felt for Drake. If he had carried on for much longer, then that would have been it. He'd done the right thing though in ending our conversation when he did. Otherwise, things could have got well weird, as a very dear imaginary friend of mine might remark.

Chapter 50

~

"Ah, a familiar and most welcome smell of Reading!" I said, as a sweet skunky scent in the air hit my nostrils. "I don't even smoke the stuff myself, but I've always loved the smell. It's a gift that keeps on giving."

"It's true dude," replied Mayfly. "It's practically a daily occurrence for me. It's a bit like London in that they say, you're never more than 10 feet away from a rat."

"I've heard that too. It's a scary thought."

"It's eerie," he replied. "Reading's a bit like that when it comes to weed. It seems you're never more than 10 feet away from someone who's just enjoyed a cheeky toke."

We strolled on leisurely past the war memorial and in through the silver gateway of Forbury Gardens. I pointed over to the lawn close to the lion.

"Shall we pitch up there?" I asked.

"Cool," he replied. "That sounds like a plan."

We stepped over the low-perimeter boundary fence; I set the wicker basket down and laid the woollen tartan blanket out.

There was a soft hum of nearby traffic and the chimes of birdsong hung in the fresh spring air.

"Right," I said, as I filled our Sainsbury's procured plastic glasses with some lively Prosecco.

"So how have you really been this past week?"

He smiled. There was a palpable look of contentment etched across his bronzed, slightly lined face.

"I'm back in the room!" he exclaimed. "I've worked it all out. It couldn't have possibly been a ghost. You know that I haven't been eating regular meals. Don't you?"

"Yes," I replied. "You said you do it because it clears out the body and cleanses the mind."

"That's right," he replied. "But it's also to help me get closer to people who don't have much sustenance in their lives. Be that food, family, friends. You see, sustenance comes in many forms."

"This is true," I replied. "It's a noble thing that you do."

"Thanks. It is, yeah. But it's also a bit daft."

"Why?"

"Well, if you saw a man limping, and it turns out the reason he limps is that one of his legs is shorter than the other, would you chop off part of your leg, just cos you wanted to empathise with him?"

"Err no! "I replied.

"Well, it's the same thing here with my fasting. I don't need to fast in order to experience what it's like to be hungry just so I can empathise with those who are hungry. I was playing the hero. It's what I do, and it was harming me. Goodness knows the damage that I have done to both my mind and my body over these past few weeks."

"I hate to say this," I replied. "But I did warn you of the possible dangers and pitfalls."

"Nah it's fine," he replied. "I should have listened to you. Besides, as I said, there was no point, and you were right. One of the dangers of long periods of fasting is that you may become delusional and see things that perhaps aren't actually there."

"It makes sense," I replied. "It's about a lack of oxygen to the brain, yeah?"

"Yes! That's exactly it, and that's what I reckon happened. There are no such things as ghosts! I'm not going to change a philosophy that I believe passionately in, because I think I saw something that I didn't actually see. Now that would be daft."

"But you definitely saw something."

"I don't deny this. But instead of just jumping to the conclusion that what I had seen had to be a ghost, I should have been more measured."

"Well, there's never any harm in taking a calm approach."

"I wish I had done. Coming out and saying that there may be a God at the start of my sermon was a bad move. A really bad move. The knock-on effects of this on my reputation as possibly Reading's leading atheist could be massive."

"Well, only time will tell," I replied, attempting damage limitation.

"I don't think we'll have to wait that long," he replied. "You saw them walk away."

"I did. But there could have been any reason why they walked off like that. They may have made arrangements to meet others, or perhaps, they needed to do a bit of shopping. I mean it was near five and a lot of the shops in the Oracle might have been closing by then. It could be anything."

"It's unlikely though. All going off to catch the shops before they close or to meet someone? All at the same time? Very unlikely actually."

"Yeah, I guess you're right," I conceded. What I don't understand is why did you jump to the conclusion that it was a ghost and not some random bloke who looked like this famous person."

"Trust me. This was no random bloke. This was someone famous who died a good while back. He wasn't just famous; he was loved by this town. He was also a real character. A proper geezer he was. This is why I jumped to the conclusion of it being a ghost. What I saw was an exact likeness of this legend caused by an insufficient supply of oxygen to my brain brought on by fasting."

"It's got to be that," I replied unconvinced. "But who is it that you thought you saw?"

"Ah you wouldn't know. You're not from Reading."

"No, but I am OF Reading."

It's not the same. Trust me, unless you're from here, then you won't know him. More importantly, we don't mention his name."

"Why is that?"

"It's tradition. It's not written down in law, but it's understood."

"That's weird, but why?"

"Well, his name is just too big. It's said that to say it can bring bad luck. It's a bit like Shakespearean actors never say "Macbeth"; instead they say "The Scottish Play".

"But that doesn't make any sense."

"It does," he replied rather vehemently. "It makes perfect sense."

"OK. OK. Fair enough. I won't pry any further. Actually, what do Readingites say then if you can't say his name?"

"The Geezer. We just say, The Geezer. My dad took us to see him play a few times. He was amazing. He could really make that ball talk, I tell you. He was something else. He wasn't just a player on the pitch either. Legend had it that he would go down the Spread for pre-match drinks, have a proper skinful, and then go on to win man of the match!"

"The Geezer sounds like a legend," I replied enthusiastically. "They don't make them like that anymore. A true George Best."

"Nah, he was better than Besty. He just didn't get to showcase himself like Besty did. He needed a bigger stage I suppose. It's often remarked that he was the best footballer that never was."

"You know that statement makes complete sense and none in equal measure."

"I know," he replied.

"Anyway, now Mr. Rock Star atheist preacher, what do we do to fix this reputation of yours?"

"I think the only way is to get back on to that saddle of fine oratory," he replied jokingly.

"That's the spirit," I replied. "Actually, sorry. Shouldn't really say that after all of this."

"Shouldn't say what?"

"Spirit. It's too soon after that experience with the ghost that didn't it turns out actually ever happen."

"Nah, it's fine. I knew exactly what you meant. You meant spirit as in gumption as in character. I tell you what though; this whole experience has been very surreal, very weird in fact."

"I have to agree with you there, Sir. This has indeed been very weird. But you'll be back to your preaching best before long. That's a given."

This was a lie. Not even a half-baked lie. The truth was, try as I might, I really couldn't see him turning this all around, at least not anytime soon. I really hoped that I was wrong, really hoped. He needed this. He needed to be Mayfly.

Chapter 51

I hadn't seen Dave lately. In fact, he hadn't visited in nearly a week. This was very much out of character. At the beginning, I felt his visits to be intrusive but that was back then. I now looked forward to them. I enjoyed very much our little catch-ups. Perhaps he was off looking for Jeremy to have a word. This would make sense as I hadn't felt Jeremy's eerie presence for quite some time now.

I was meeting Greg later. Apart from a few brief visits on his way back to his two up two down near Bracknell, we hadn't really had much of a proper catch-up. He said that he had some news and wanted to tell me in person, rather than over the phone. I was intrigued.

This whole day I decided was on me. Dangerously high levels of commission earned were causing me a great restlessness. I had told him to seek out a little white-washed boutique hotel near the station called Malmaison. As a fellow Prosecco fan, I told him that it boasted quite possibly the finest selection of these bubbles, at least that I had come across. I also said that they couldn't be beaten on price comparatively, although I did say that he needn't concern himself with this detail, as I was paying.

Was he going to tell me that he had been offered a ridiculously lucrative new contract? Or that he had traded in his classic 1987 Sierra in for a more current bland model? I hoped the latter wasn't the case. Even though I had never driven it, I loved that car. It was after all the chariot in which I had reached Reading on the cold lonely bleak winter evening.

I reached the top of Broad Street. There was a cacophony of sound, as the various street vendors, buskers, and Jason, the Big Issue vendor, punted for business. Crowds of weekend strollers casually browsed the varied and colourful stalls and groups of friends stood chatting all under a slightly hazy blue, spring sky.

The buzz of this lively main thoroughfare never failed to ignite and enliven me. Today though it seemed elevated even from these usual high levels. I couldn't quite decipher what was different about today, but it felt unique. I was doing this again. Doing what I did best, overanalysing, overthinking. Stop this now, I said to myself. What would Dave say? He'd tell you to 'ave a word with yourself. That's what he'd say, and he'd be right.

I continued along and on to the mini auditorium. There was no Mayfly this week. He'd decided to jump on the train to Wokingham. He'd said that he needed to get away for a bit. He wasn't quite ready to jump back on to the preaching saddle just yet. Interestingly, he'd been reprimanded by both Rev Vigland Hythe and Hasim Abdul for saying the God thing. This did seem a bit strange given that both were very much in the God business, albeit coming at it from different angles. They had told him that people were confused enough as it was and that telling them that there may be a God only added to this.

In Mayfly's usual space stood a worthy replacement. It was that busker that I had seen at the other end of the street a few weeks ago. It was "Just Tom". He was playing an old childhood favourite of mine, Foreigner's "I Want to Know What Love Is". I stood there mesmerised. The clarity and crispness of his voice matched the precision of his musicianship as he strummed and picked with an effortless glide. I suddenly had a thought. *Maybe he can play at Gerald's wedding? It makes sense.* I still wasn't convinced that I hadn't imagined and embellished Forbury's musical prowess. *I mean what if Suzi's right and they are shit? Where will that leave me? This could put me in a very tricky and potentially mortifying position indeed. Even if I did get it right and they were indeed prolific, is their material wedding-friendly? This man here could be the perfect solution. From the limited time I have had to gauge his stuff, he seems to strike the perfect balance between covers that everyone knows - real crowd pleasers - and original material. I'll ask him after this song ends.*

And so on, he continued. "In my life, there's been heartache and pain. Oh I don't know, if I can face it again…" There was a decent crowd all standing there mesmerised. I mean they had to be. How could they not be? It ended to rapturous applause. I expected that he was used to this kind of response and just took it all for granted, all in his stride.

I approached him. "Hi there. I really enjoyed that. You've got some set of lungs on you. How do reach those notes? Oh sorry, I'm Alastair. And your name is…?"

"It's Tom. Just Tom. What's the matter? Can't you read?" he replied jokingly.

"But of course it is," I replied, "duh! How silly of me! Listen, I don't want to take up too much of your time so I'll come straight to the point. Can I book you for a wedding?"

"Well, I haven't done a wedding before. Actually, I tell a lie. I did one about fifteen years ago. I seem to remember it was a Greek and Irish wedding. But it wasn't a full slot. There were a few acts including the obligatory Irish traditional session and some bloke smashing plates in time to the Bazooki. It was a bit mad."

"Do you reckon you'd have enough covers for an hour's set? There'll be another band playing, too. They're called "Forbury"."

"What? After Forbury Gardens?"

"I believe so."

"Any good?"

"Well, opinion seems to differ greatly on that one. So, would you be up for it?"

"It depends when it is?"

"It's in July. The 18th to be precise."

"Sure. I can travel back for that. I'll add the cost of the travel and any expenses that I pick up along the way, you know, food, a few pints and the like, on to my fee. I think I'll fly out this time. No need to worry about the expense if someone else is paying! You OK with that, chap?"

"Er yeah, sure, that'll be fine. Really great that you'll be able to make it. And where will you be travelling back from?"

"Amsterdam,"

"Oh, are you Dutch?"

"Duh, Irish. Can you not tell?!"

"Oh but of course!" I replied sheepishly. "What am I like?! So, how do I get in touch with you?"

"Here. Have one of these." He handed me a business card.

"Cheers fella." I slipped it into my inside pocket.

"Pleasure. Catch up soon. Just in case you forget my name again my friend, it's written on the card in big letters. "JUST TOM". I hope this helps!"

"I can't see that happening again!" I replied. "Cheers."

I continued on. I had a good feeling about this "Just Tom" person and his sharp caustic wit.

I reached Malmaison. I checked my phone. It was 4.20. I was 10 minutes early. *I wonder what special offers they have on bubbles today?* I thought.

I entered the bar area. Greg had beaten me to it.

"Here," he said. "Have a glass of this loveliness." He handed me a glass.

"But chap. I said that this is all on me. How much do I owe you?"

Rather impatiently, I yanked my wallet from my coat.

"Mate. Put it away. This is on me. Listen, I have big news – very big. This is all going to require a lot more than one bottle. You can pick the rest up. Yeah?"

"OK. This seems fair," I replied. I pulled out a chair and sat opposite him. I took a sip from my glass. "Oh, nice. Really nice. These bubbles are charming."

"They're not bad, are they?" he replied. "Splendid in fact."

"Indeed," I replied. "Splendid bubbles. So good to see you, chap." Our hands joined and I gently gripped his arm with my right hand. "I've missed you, man. So, what is this huge news that you can only really tell me in person?"

"You didn't waste any time!" he responded smiling.

"True but when you told me that you had big news and could really only tell me in person when we met in 5 days, I could think of little else. So, I've actually waited quite a bit before coming to it."

"Yeah, I suppose. I did set off a bit of an incendiary device. Actually, I have two big bits of big news to decant."

"Two bits? Crikey. Best start with the first then."

"That makes sense," he replied. "Well, do you remember someone called Ruth? From back in Uni days?"

"Oh yeah, the one from Bedford. Is that right? Is that her?"

"The very one."

"And she looked a bit like Halle Berry, from what I can remember."

"But she's not black!"

"Neither is Halle Berry though," I replied. "She's mixed."

"True. But she still doesn't look like Halle Berry. I've always thought that she looked a lot like Sigourney Weaver though."

"Actually, she does, come to think of it – a young version. Circa Alien."

"That's spot on. But if you think she looks like Halle Berry, then how could you think she looks like Sigourney Weaver too? They look nothing alike."

"Oh, I don't know. They have similar eyes – both big and brown – a truly attractive trait."

"Anyway," he continued. "One day a little over a month ago, I see a friend request on Facebook. It's only her! Of course, I accepted this request, without hesitation.

The next minute, she's messaging me asking if we could meet up."

"That's great."

"It gets better though. I invited her round mine. I said that I would cook dinner. She seemed impressed. Anyway, she came around and ended up staying for the next three days. Well, you can imagine the rest!"

"You lucky bastard!" I replied. "You shagged Halle Fucking Berry!"

"Sigourney Weaver!" he replied adamantly". Anyway, in between, well, you know, we discussed a lot of things. In particular, how we felt about each other. I've been into her for years, and all this time she was into me too. I had no idea. She seemed to have a preference for short blokes back then. Not now though!"

"Clearly not," I replied. "I'm made up for you, as a certain Liverpudlian friend of ours from back in the day might say."

"It gets better."

"How's that even possible?" I replied.

"Look, I know you're going to think I've lost the plot, but I asked her if she'd be interested in moving to Ireland with me, and she said yes!"

"Well, you have mentioned from time to time that you'd like to go back one day, most likely to retire, but that's not for about forty years. Well, there's nothing like a bit of forward planning I suppose."

"Well, that's the other thing I was going to tell you about. I've been applying for a lot of jobs over there in the last few months. I've managed to land a really decent contract, and the best thing is the office is near mum's place. Which will be handy for when Ruth gets a couple of kiddies under her belt."

"I don't know what to say," I replied. "You seem to have this all nicely planned out." My brain was struggling to process, never mind make sense of all this sudden rush of electrical signals.

"The interview was about a couple of months ago over in Belfast. They offered me the job, there and then. I'm still buzzing from it. To think this time in five weeks I'll be on my way to Heathrow. Then en route to Belfast…"

With a broad smile, he took the bottle from the bucket and began shaking it.

"Not much of a noise is it in there Pudders, old bean? Come on chap. No slacking now! We've got some serious celebrations to continue. Your round I believe."

"You're not wrong there, chap. I'm really delighted for you. Wow! A double whammy. You're leaving the country and you're taking a potential future wife with you. This indeed calls for continuation of said serious celebrations."

Greg was a dear friend. Who wouldn't be happy for a mate who had realised a dream of his, and who was soon to be embarking upon the next important chapter of his life? But this was also the very reason for a striking sense of unhappiness that I was feeling right now. As one chapter in his life opened onto a new page, a chapter in mine closed. I'd miss him, the big man.

Great, I thought. *Another paradox in my life. Another fucking paradox.*

Chapter 52

It was now over a month since Dave had visited. I wondered if I had done something to offend him. I hoped not. Since coming into my life, he had been a rather potent force for good. In fact, it all seemed to coincide with a marked uplift in my mood, and good fortune now seemed in great abundance. As well as the friendship aspect, my fear now was that if he had decided to move on, then a relapse to misfortune was a decided possibility.

Amanda from the production company had told me that funding for Patience's biopic had been finally agreed upon and would soon be in place. She had asked if all three of us could meet up today in Reading, to discuss possible plans. Patience couldn't make it as she was in Portsmouth visiting a cousin. I suggested to her that we wait until all three of us were available. She was quick to dismiss this, citing a delay could lead to the cancellation of the project. I thought this sounded just a little overcautious on her part, but when I put myself in her mind-set, I could understand where this came from. I doubt if she ever expected that her astonishing life story would be brought into public view. It would be a travesty if it all was suddenly brought to an abrupt halt.

We had arranged to meet once again in the lobby of the Forbury hotel. Like the last time, Amanda told me that she had a mission to put a serious dent in her never diminishing expense account. She said that she had tried on numerous occasions to do it serious damage, but try as she might, she didn't seem to have much success. She noted that the last time we met up and she had given me the remit to assist her in this, I had performed heroically. She expected more of the same from me today.

I was approaching this blindly. I had no idea of the approach Amanda was going to take. I could never have envisaged, when sitting down with Patience to discuss her life story for publication in a local newspaper, that it would lead to her biopic. There was a lot at stake here. Whatever approach we took, we'd have to get this right. Exactly right. I approached the Simeon Monument and stood in respectful silence. I had read this inscription numerous amount of times, but each time I read it, I felt a deep stirring of consciousness.

Forbury Gardens was a buzz of different sounds each one an important ingredient in this springtime cacophony.

I meandered slowly up the marble steps of the Forbury hotel, with a heightened sense of anticipation. Ahead in the lobby was Amanda, head buried in a magazine. I walked over.

"Hi Amanda!" I exclaimed. "Really good to see you."

"Oh hey!" she replied. "It's only Kev. Kevin bloody Keegan!" It seemed everyone was calling me that now. I wasn't sure if it was because she had read the article, or she genuinely thought I resembled that most iconic of centre forwards.

"Come, let's go in," she continued, pointing towards the hotel bar. "We've a lot to discuss. I followed her over to what I liked to call "a Blue Peter table" - one that had been prepared earlier. *How well prepared is this!?* I thought. I could almost feel this slightly oft cream table, upon which rested a silver champagne bucket, creak and moan under my heightened expectations.

"I'm sorry," she said, "but I've taken the liberty of kicking off proceedings with a bottle of the finest bubbles they have."

"Here, can I have a look?" I replied.

"Sure."

I carefully and gently pulled the neck slowly through the ice and there it was inscribed over a coat of arms… "Maison Fondée en 1843".

"I can't believe it," I exclaimed. "Krug! You do know how expensive that is? Well, of course you do. You did buy it!"

"I don't care about the expense. My expense account seems limitless these days. I couldn't kill it if I tried, and I have tried. Anyway, this isn't about how much this cost in the monetary sense, but the value of what it is commemorating."

She took both glasses from the table, and with great precision slowly began to fill them. I had never seen bubbles poured with such precision. Usually governed by the laws of Newtonian Physics, some collateral loss of bubbles would be expected, but not here.

We sat down into the soft furnishings of our oblong table.

"To Patience!" she cried.

"Yes," I replied. "To Patience!"

"So, Amanda. What's the plan?"

"To get a bit tiddly, I suppose, and please, call me Panda. All my friends do."

"Why do they call you that? Do you have a thing for pandas?"

"Yes, I do actually. They're cute. But you wouldn't want to mess with them. That's a bit like me. But that's not why they call me Panda."

"So why do they then?"

"It's because Amanda rhymes with Panda, and I just happen to like pandas."

"That's as good a reason as any," I replied. "So, Panda, what's the plan?"

"Well, as you know the funding for this is in place, at least to a certain extent."

"A certain extent?"

"Yes, it's all about that old chestnut of time is money. We have enough in place for roughly a year of filming. If it runs over that, then things could get tricky. Very tricky in fact. So where we can, we need to keep costs down as much as possible."

"So, how can we do that?"

"Well, this is where you come in."

"I'm happy to help. So where do I come into this? How can I help?"

"Well, the overall plan is to open up auditions to the general public on a deal basis."

"A deal basis? What kind of deal would this be?"

"We sell it as a community event. People love that kind of stuff. You know, engendering a sense of community. It's relevant these days more than ever, what with the advent of social media but lack of social cohesion."

"I'm loving this. So, I'm guessing here that we will ask them to lend their services for free?"

"Yes, exactly. Well, initially anyhow, with a promise that if and when it takes off in a big way, which I really believe it will, then we pay them. But we can also sell it as a way that they can play their part, in fact very big part, in not just paying homage to a local legend, but getting the name of Reading out there again to a wider audience."

"That is such a brilliant idea!" I exclaimed.

"I thought you'd like it," she replied, as she rested her glass gently back on the table. "So, it's like this, we set up a piece on Southeast Today. All three of us will be there. It'll be a live interview, so dress well and prepare well."

"Dress well, sure, but prepare well? How do I do that? What do I do to prepare?"

"You mentally prepare yourself for being on live television in front of a million plus viewers."

"I can see what you mean. It's exciting yet daunting."

"Yes, it can be daunting. But all you need to tell yourself is that you'll be with two friends and a person that you don't know, asking us questions about Patience."

"That's a great way of looking at it," I replied. "So, when will you be looking to set up this interview then?"

"That process has already started."

"Really? So, when is the interview?"

"It hasn't been finalised yet. Our people are speaking to their people to find the best time and the best angle to approach it from, but I reckon about a month."

"Oh, that's good. It gives us time to prepare."

"Indeed. And that's really important. Suits from Channel 4 will be watching it, so we will need to nail this interview. If we don't, then I can see them withdrawing their funding."

"What? They would do that even after we say live on air that Channel 4 are funding this?"

"Part-funding it. But sure. These television types are a funny breed you know. If they sense even a hint of a glitch, then the project could be history."

"No pressure then!" I replied jokingly.

"Oh, none at all, well, not a lot, as a certain magician might say."

"I never really rated him as a magician," I replied. "I think he's still living off his success from the 1980s if you ask me."

"That's a bit harsh, Ali."

"Harsh but true, Panda. Sorry."

"Ah, he's a national treasure. He's up there with Emu, David Attenborough, and The Queen."

"What? As in Emu and Rod Hull?"

"Yeah, the very one."

"But Emu's a puppet!"

"And your point is?"

"Well, you can't really go putting Emu and The Queen in the same sentence! It isn't right."

"Oh, I'm sure Emu won't mind. The Queen is very popular too you know!"

"She certainly is. Definitely worthy to stand alongside Emu, if he was still around, that is."

I paused to consider the significance of such a development. To think that a little over four months ago, I had walked in to a bizarrely named pub to interview a seemingly outlandish soul, we were now talking about a film. I could feel myself suddenly engulfed with a strong sense of pride. I wouldn't allow myself to dwell on it, though. Yes, I was involved and had played a not-so-insignificant role in all of this, but none of this could have been possible had it not been for one of the kindest and noblest of souls that I had ever met. This wasn't about me; it was about Miss Patience, Janice Johnson of Portsmouth and now of Reading, and all those like her who found themselves pushed to the margins of a society that they had once trusted. If I was to allow myself any semblance of pride, then it would be to have played my supporting role, to have done my bit. I had put something back into a pot that I had over the years helped drain.

"Here's to Patience!" I said, raising my glass.

"To Patience," she replied as our glasses gently clinked. "To Patience!"

Chapter 53

"Are you really sure, chap? You'll need to be. 'Cos if she says yes, then there's no going back."

"I'm not really sure what you mean. No going back?"

"What I mean is that if she says yes, then that's great, see. But what if a little bit down the line, you decide for whatever reason that you've been a bit hasty? Once you've asked that question, you can't backtrack."

It was late afternoon, and I was in Gerald's "office" canvasing some marital advice. His lack of enthusiasm had disarmed me.

"Mate, I thought you'd be happy for me. I didn't expect you to be so cautious, especially given your own upcoming nuptials."

"Chap, I am happy for you, see. But yes, I am cautious. You don't exactly have, and this is by your own admission, a good track record when it comes to this sort of thing. You said that marriage didn't suit your indifferent character, that you even found it stifling."

"Well. People can change, can't they?"

"Well, have you?"

"No. Not really, I suppose."

"Well then. You can see my dilemma here, can't you?"

"Putting it like that, I guess I can. You're supposed to be bigging me up though."

"Mate, don't get me wrong. I want to big you up, see. I really do. I'd love to say, hey Alastair McLeish-Pidkin, friend, colleague, all together top bloke, I'm delighted for you. You should definitely go for it. But I can't."

"Why?"

"Well, you know why. You told me that although you once loved Tanya, you couldn't handle living with her."

"It wasn't just her. That would have been the same for anyone I loved."

"Fuck me Ali! You don't believe in making things easy, do you?" he sighed.

"It's not intentional. It's just how I am, who I am even."

"But if you said that you couldn't handle living with Tanya and in general, anyone, then what makes you think that you could live with Lynn?"

"Who said anything about living with her? I know I couldn't do that.

"I don't follow?"

"It's simple, really. Who said that married people have to live together?"

"Lots of people actually Ali. It's a given."

"Generally, yes. I agree, and that was the one thing that was stopping me from asking a woman on whose ground I worship, from throwing her lot in with a man with a hyphenated surname."

"So, what changed? Why now?"

"I read an article."

"Any good?"

"It was great. That's not the point though."

"So what is?"

"It was the message contained in the article."

"And this message was?"

"Actually, there were two messages – longevity and compromise."

"Go on."

"Well, it centred around a couple. They were very much in love. Both had failed marriages behind them."

"I'm loving this already. Please, carry on."

"Yah, it's nice, isn't it? Anyway, she wanted to pop the question."

"I like it!" replied Gerald overenthusiastically. Fortunately, most people had decided to take advantage of the warmth and were having lunch alfresco in the nearby Beefeater. "That's the woman popping the question! Finally!"

"Indeed, my friend," I replied. "Indeed! Anyway, there was a slight problem with this plan. She loved how things were. They both had their own places. They both in large part led separate lives, meeting only a few times a week. But when they did meet, it was explosive – bloody explosive – and I mean in a good way."

"So, why would they want to risk that? Why fix something if it isn't broken?"

"Well, they were both equally loved up. But she wanted to take his name. She didn't like her own. I can't remember what it was actually."

"Well, it must have been boring then, if you can't remember it."

"Indeed. Anyway, it turns out that he was Italian, well not really Italian, but of Italian heritage."

"Which actually, Alastair, would make him Italian. But go on."

"Really? He's from Bromley. I didn't know that there was a Bromley in Italy".

Gerald forced a smile. "Go on, you tart! So what happened?" He held his phone up. "They'll be back soon."

"They won't actually." I replied. "It's sunny and they're in a pub garden."

"True."

"Them upstairs are away on some pointless conference. This leaves you in charge, Gerald."

"True."

"They prefer your more trusting and laissez-faire-style type of management practice. They're also quite fond of you."

"Seriously?" he replied. "Well, go on. You can't just say that and stop. You can't open the gates like that and then close them again quickly."

"Good analogy, Sir!" I responded with enthusiasm. "I like it. It's commonly agreed that since we've had you as a bridge, the atmosphere has mellowed in a big way. We used to hate having to report to some twat upstairs. There's a different buzz about the place now. Even me, I don't hate what I do, nearly as much as I used to. That's down to you. You see, because there's a more relaxed, more trusting buzz about now, people just get on with things."

"Actually, I have noticed that myself, see. So my hands-off approach is working then."

"It is my friend, big time! That's why when they come back, they'll crack on and get things done. A good atmosphere fosters good practice. They feel relaxed about you in that you're not clock-watching. They know that you trust them not to take the piss, and they won't. Well not much anyway! Only joking. Anyway, oh yeah, so she popped the question? And what did he say?"

"Yes, he said yes. But there was a proviso."

"And this was?"

"That they'd retain their singular living arrangements. It turns out that all this time together, she never knew that they were singing from the same hymn sheet."

"Don't say that."

"What?"

"Singing from the same hymn sheet. You hate that cheesy management speak."

"I do. Sorry!"

"So what happened? Are they still together?"

"Yeah. She's been going by the name of Sandra Macari-Ricci for over ten years now. Amazing isn't it?"

"That's brilliant!" he replied. "So, that's your plan then? Singular living arrangements for you two? So, that's what you're going to suggest to Lynn, then?"

"Exactly. So what do you think? She too doesn't want to change our living arrangements. She said she loves me but wouldn't ever want to live with me."

"In that case," he replied, "I like it. I really bloody like it. You know, that could just work. So, what's the plan? When are you going to give this marriage pitch?"

"I don't know yet, a week, two maybe."

"Well, be sure to keep me posted. Won't you?"

"You'll be the first to know, my friend. Actually, the second. I think Dave will know before anyone else does actually. But you will definitely be the first person, I tell."

"Who's this Dave chap? Actually Pud, never mind. But do let me know as soon as you know. Promise?"

"Promise."

"Good stuff chap," he replied as he extended his arm. "Right then, let's crack on and look as if we're doing some work before that lovely lot get back."

"Good stuff my friend," I replied. "Look, and I know that I've said this before, but I'd like to say it again. I'm sorry."

"For what mate?"

"You know, for the way I behaved towards you in the past – those snidey comments, excluding you from things. I still feel ashamed, very ashamed."

I wish I hadn't said this. There was no need. Yes, it was an honourable gesture, but it really wasn't necessary. I could feel myself filling up. I had to get away.

"Mate," he replied, "I appreciate the sentiment, I really do. But listen, you're a top bloke and someone whom I regard as a dear friend. We all make mistakes. It's whether we learn from them. And you have. Now, and I do mean this politely, but please piss off before you start me off too."

"None taken!" I jokingly replied. As I made my way towards my communal desk, I wondered if I had learned from my mistakes further back, and if I so, would Lynn have the vision to see that I could really start afresh after all.

Chapter 54

～

It was Saturday night. I was in BOBS with Stueie. He was gently twisting the black straps of his ever so stylish Hugo Boss timepiece. He looked up at me.

"Mate, do you know one of the best things that can lift the mood?"

"I don't know. An overly generous intake of alcohol mixed in with a liberal pinch of Mandy sometimes does the trick for me. But I have to say that it's only a short-term fix as the comedown the next day is a massive pay back."

"Well, I wouldn't really know about that. But you don't want short term. You need soul food."

"Soul food?"

"Yes my friend, food to enrich the soul. We all need it."

"So how do I come by this soul food? Surely I'd need to be a person of the sight, just like you are."

"That's the beauty of it. You don't need to be. This kind of soul food is accessible to all."

"Really? So, I don't need to be a person of the sight?"
"Mate. You don't!"
"So, how do I find this soul food?"
"By helping others. You find this by helping others."
"What kind of help do I need to give?"
"It comes in many forms".
"What forms are these?"
"It's the little things. The everyday things. Smiling at strangers. Holding the door open for others.

Helping people who are lost find their way back. Providing nourishment. Feeding people."

"Feeding people? I like that. It's a powerful metaphor."
"It can be, yeah. But I mean it literally."
"What? As in, actually feeding people?"
"Yes, as in actually feeding people. I do this every few weeks. I'm going off to do it now. Up for it?"
"Sure. Where are we going?"
"Market Place first, and then we'll do a sweep of Broad Street and finish around the Butts."
"But what are we doing?"
"I told you mate. Feeding people. We're going off to offer solace to those who need it. We're going off to feed the homeless!"
"Wow! I love this. What a great thing to do."
"Well, you know. It needs to be done mate. We'll swing by mine, yeah, and pick up the sandwiches. I've

made two big holdalls full of them. Well it wasn't just me. Aidan pitched in."

"Aidan? Is he a person of the sight too?"

"I've never really stopped to consider if he is. But yes mate. I suppose he is."

"Wow. Another person of the sight! That's three of you in the space of a month. Amazing!"

"Well, we're out there Ali. One thing though, yeah?"

"Sure."

"No one knows that I do this. I'd like it to stay that way. OK? I don't even think Aidan knows. All he does is help me make a mountain of sandwiches. No questions asked."

"I'd say there's a good chance he knows though, Stueie. If I was asked to help someone knock up a mound of sandwiches every so often, I'd wonder why?"

"I suppose. Maybe, he does have an idea. But he never asks. Anyway, you'll keep this between us though, yeah?"

"Sure, I won't tell anyone, but why? Why wouldn't you want people to know that you do good? This needs recognition."

"That's the whole point though. It doesn't. I just want to help others. It's that simple. I don't need recognition or even want it. I just want to make a difference. Yeah? So then, up for it?"

"Yeah. Let's do this."

"Good stuff. Seriously mate. You'll get a lot out of this. I won't lie though; this is going to enrich us for sure, but it's going to be tough, too. When you feel yourself filling up, and trust me mate, you will, move away from them. They can't see you lose it in front of them. Their lives are tough enough as it is, without them seeing that."

Ten minutes later, after picking up the sandwiches and drinks, we were handing them out to the needy in Market Place. I was stood opposite the obelisk. It was too dark to read the inscription but I'm sure wherever he was, Mr. Simeon would have a warm glow of approval, as we tended to the needy of a town he held so dear. Among this group was a middle-aged fluffy lemon-bearded man with a battered sailor's cap.

"It never needed to come to this," he bemoaned. "I was only a month behind on my rent. A month I tell you. It weren't my fault they let me go. They said I was good, but that I weren't the same after falling off the ladder. So they had to let me go. They said that they had no choice. I was the best brickie in Reading. Well at least in the top five."

"Some people, eh?" I responded with a sympathetic tone. "They've just got no sense of fair play. To let you go just like that? You gave them what was it? Four years of your life?"

"It was four and half actually."

"Four and a half years and that's your reward. Thrown on the scrap heap. Erm sorry, what was it you wanted again?"

"I'll have the egg and cress, thanks. I'm a veggie you see."

I rummaged around in the holdall, scanning the contents until…

"Ah, here we go. Egg and cress. And not forgetting the water. Is sparkling Ok? The shop was out of still."

"Well, it's going have to be then, isn't it?" he responded with a mischievous grin.

"Pleasure talking to you, chap," I said, as I moved on to the next person.

I looked over towards Stueie. He was bent slightly towards an elderly lady. She was sobbing and had her head buried into his shoulder. He was patting her gently on her back. It would never have dawned on me to do what we were doing right now. Stueie was right. There's such a great reward in tending to those in need.

This is great I thought. *A bit sad, but great all the same.*

After furnishing the needy there, we were now approaching the market area opposite Reading Minster.

"Most of 'em tend to congregate around here when the market's shut. Don't know why," explained Stueie, pointing over towards a cluster of empty stalls where a group of five had gathered together. They seemed happy to see us.

"Hey there," said Stueie. "How are we all doing?"

"Oh, am I glad to see you!" exclaimed a rather weary-looking man of indeterminable age. *Being exposed to the outside elements must make it difficult to gauge people's ages*, I thought. He could have been anywhere between 20 and 40. I guessed he was closer to 20, judging by his clear tonal pitch.

"Yeah, sorry fella, we overran a little bit over up in Market Place," replied Stueie. "Old Carol's lost her cat, AGAIN!"

"Oh no," replied another in the group. "That's the third time this year."

"I know," replied Stueie. "Bless her. Of course, we all know that she lost old Mowser five years ago when he left this world. Poor old dear has to keep reliving this over and over as if it's happened for the first time."

"The truth is, she never got over it first time round," responded an elderly man wearing a slightly weathered tweed jacket. "She was never the same after that."

I looked at Stueie. He nodded gently. "I'll be back shortly," I said. "Just need to make a quick call."

"Mate," he replied smiling, "get yourself off home. I'll text you tomorrow. Thanks for your help tonight. Bless you."

"Pleasure" I replied, extending my arm. "It's been an honour. Catch up tomorrow then."

"Oh, before you go, can I have a word?" he asked.

"Sure" I replied.

"Hang on a sec, lad", he said, pointing to the group. "I'll be back in a mo. Just need to have a quick word with my friend Ali here. Dig in," he said pointing at his hold-all, which was resting against one of the stalls. You'll find the usual sandwiches and drinks in there. I've only got water this week. Sorry."

He turned to me gently grabbing a shoulder. "You see this watch?" he said, proudly tapping its face. "It's nice, isn't it?"

"It's a thing of beauty," I replied. "A thing of beauty. That's for sure."

"Cheers, it is. It's really precious to me. As I said earlier, I'm a big fan of Boss. Always have been. Most of my stuff is Boss actually. T-shirt, jeans, jacket and of course my baseball cap. I don't even like baseball, but I like the caps. Anyway, I didn't even know that the bloke makes watches too! That's nearly as mental as fucking Nestlé making pies!"

I really had no idea where he was going with this. I didn't care though. I was just enjoying the moment. Nothing else seemed important right now.

He continued.

"So I said to myself, I promised myself that I'd get one of these Hugo Boss timepieces. This is one of my most precious possessions. But I tell you what, Alastair mate. It means fuckall in comparison to you being right. I've sensed it. I can feel it. I can see it."

"But of course you can. You're a person…"

"…of the sight, yeah. I am. I haven't known you that long, have I?"

"No."

"But I feel as if we've known each other for a lot longer. Here…"

Slowly he undid the dark straps of his precious timepiece.

"Here, try this on," he said, fastening it around my wide left wrist. It just about fitted.

"Take a good look at it. Nice, isn't it?"

"Nice doesn't even come close," I replied. "It's stunning."

"Well," he replied, "it's yours now. Yeah?"

"What?!" I exclaimed. "But I don't understand!"

"Well, it really is quite simple. Shit, how do I put this?"

"Put what?"

"Your moods change, don't they? One minute, you're up, and then the next, you're down. And I mean, really, really down."

"How do you know this?" I exclaimed. "Oh yeah, sorry. You have the vision."

"I have, mate. As I said, we've not known each other long, but I care about you. I care about your safety. I care about that more than I care about my watch, and my watch is my prime possession. So, please do something for me, yeah?"

"Sure," I replied, "name it".

"Keep this watch. Yeah?"

"But…" I exclaimed.

"No buts please. Keep this watch, and whenever you're in one those low moods of yours, look at it. Look at the face of this stylish Boss timepiece and remember, Stueie needs me to be alright. Stueie needs me to be alright. Say it."

"Stueie needs me to be alright."

"Good. I want you to always know this, and I want you to know that you only have to call me. That's why I have given you this watch, to remind you of this."

I didn't know what to say. I tried to say something, but I couldn't find the words. Right now, no amount of words and no perfectly organised flow of output seemed adequate or indeed appropriate as a response to this, the purest of gestures.

"Catch up tomorrow, my friend," he said, as he patted me gently on the back.

He turned to the group who seemed preoccupied, as they rummaged in the holdall like a screech of crazed seagulls on a pier, for the most favourable sustenance.

"Right then, you lovely lot," he said as he picked up what was left of my holdall. "There's enough for everyone. More's on the way."

Head bowed slightly, I meandered slowly away towards the Oxford Road. His prediction that I would fill up was sadly accurate. They couldn't see me like this. Their lives, it would appear, were indeed tough, tough enough.

Chapter 55

It was a balmy Friday evening in Palmer Park, and Amanda and I were engaged with BBC Berkshire in a much-anticipated interview about a former bearded lady. Sadly, Patience couldn't make it, citing an extreme bout of indigestion. I wasn't convinced, and if it was indigestion, then what had caused it? Stress can do strange things to a person.

Meanwhile, back in the studio…

"Apart from our much-loved Reading Elvis, another character well known on the streets of Reading is Patience Janice Johnson. No doubt many of you will know her by another name, The Bearded Lady of Winnersh, and in recent years, The Beardless One.

Mariza Calliante takes up the story…back to Palmer Park…"

"Thanks, Charlotte. Patience Janice Johnson's story is a powerful one. It contains all the elements usually associated with a Hollywood-style epic. It has intrigue, it has conflict, it has romance, it has adventure, but most importantly, this story contains an important message, never accept your lot if you aren't happy. This is the ultimate in triumph over adversity, and now her story is set to be turned into a film.

I'm joined here in a sunny Palmer Park by Alastair McLeish-Pidkin and Amanda Erskine.

Alastair, turning to you first. How did this all happen?"

"Well," I replied, "I guess it all started off with a golf club."

"A golf club?!" exclaimed Mariza.

"Yah, I continued "one morning after what must have been a full on weekend, I woke up clutching a golf club. I had no idea how I came to be lying beside such a thing. I don't even like golf. I don't really see the point. Hitting a tiny white ball across a field? I mean, what's all that about?"

I looked over at Panda; she was smirking. I think she enjoyed my irreverent opening.

"To cut a long story short, I found out how I had come by this golf club, through an article I read on the Chronicle's website. This led me at the suggestion of Lynn, my dear and stunning partner, to contact Suzi, the article's author, asking if she would help me somehow to get into journalism. You see, although I've written a few articles for the Chronicle now, I'm not actually a qualified journalist. So we met in Malmaison, enjoyed some pretty delightful Prosecco, and it was then that she offered me my first assignment – to interview a woman who had a beard and one day decided to shave it off."

"So," replied Mariza, "what was your initial thought?"

"Well," I continued, "I thought she was joking at first. But then she showed me the before and after photos. It was then that I sat up and took serious notice. So off I went to interview this now beardless lady of Winnersh, and it was a day that will rest fondly with me, till, well, you know until when. Within a few seconds of meeting her, I was talking with Patience Janice Johnson and not some circus act. I felt that it was important to look beyond the obvious and bring her story, her actual story, to the people, rather than give people what they believed they wanted to read. I like to think that I achieved that."

"You certainly have!" enthused Mariza. "Thank you, Alastair. Turning now to you, Amanda Erskine. Amanda…"

"Please," replied Amanda, "Panda".

Mariza nodded.

"So, Panda, how did you get involved in this remarkable story?"

"Again, just like Alastair, I too enjoy my leisure time, probably more than perhaps I should. I got back in after a full-on night out, celebrating a friend's 40th. Usually after a good night out, I like to unwind by going online.

You know the usual – YouTubing, Facebook, the usual time-wasting, yet fun sites."

"Yes, I know what that's like!" replied Mariza.

"But for some reason, I felt compelled to have a bit of a read before calling it a night. So, I started trawling through various sites looking for interesting articles to read – articles that I could really get stuck into. Do you know what I mean?"

A smiling Mariza nodded.

"Eventually after cutting through a lot of dross, I came across an article whose title stopped me in my tracks. It was entitled 'The bearded lady – but who is the real freak show?' That was me, gone, lost in a brilliant, captivating read. The next morning, I showed this article to the MD. As if picking up on my exact thoughts, he made the suggestion that we should look into getting this up and running as a film project. I then through the Chronicle's website got in touch with Alastair and Patience and here we are now."

"That's great. And were you expecting such an enthusiastic response from your boss?"

"Well, it was more in hope rather than expectation if I'm honest!" she replied. "So, we put some funding in place and set up a meeting with Channel 4. They saw real potential in this and have agreed to put up the rest of the funding."

"This is all very exciting. So, what happens next?"

"Well, now we need to get some actors. Alastair here suggested that we throw auditions open to the public."

This was typical of Panda, deflecting credit away from herself.

"So, how do any budding or indeed seasoned actors get in touch?"

"Well, if they visit our website www.enlivenproductions.com/Lady_Patience, this will give them a breakdown of the main characters. If they feel that they can bring anything to these roles, then we would like to see them at the auditions."

"And when do these auditions take place?"

"They take place at Christchurch Meadows, Caversham, on the 16th of May. Auditions start at 3, but anyone interested should aim to get there for around 2."

"You're doing this alfresco then?"

"Kind of. It is open air, but the actual auditions will take place in a marquee. We really want this to be a big community event, so too does Patience. Obviously, the auditions will take centre stage, but there will also be peripheral events like face painting, jugglers, clowns, music, you know that sort of thing."

"Clowns!?" I exclaimed. "I didn't know this. Does Patience know? She doesn't have great memories of clowns, you know."

"She suggested it!" laughed Panda.

"You forgot to mention the hog roast and something for the veggies."

"Oh yeah, that too!" replied Panda. "Once the auditions are over, there will be music from local band Forbury."

"Forbury?" Replied Mariza. "I like that name. Any good?"

I looked nervously over at Panda.

"Yeah," she replied, "they really are good. Very good in fact."

Mariza turned and faced the camera. "So, there we have it. Watch this space. Thank you Alastair McLeish-Pidkin and Amanda Panda Erskine. Back to the studio and Charlotte… and… cut."

"I really enjoyed the chat guys!" exclaimed Mariza, extending an arm towards Panda and then me.

"Likewise," replied Panda, "we really appreciate this opportunity. You know, her story does need to be brought to as many people as possible."

She was right. This story needed to be heard and now seen. It really was about time society began to revaluate what it deemed to be important. This wasn't just about a beard. It wasn't just about a woman who had one and then decided that she no longer wanted one. This was about someone refusing any longer to continue to play a role that certain sections of society had deemed she should fulfil. The beard was just as much a metaphor for independence, as it had been an unkempt big bunch of yellow facial candyfloss. At least that's how Patience' one had looked. She was right to shave it off. It never suited her.

Chapter 56

~

There was a hum of anticipation around Broad Street, as Mayfly stepped up with a confident swagger on to the mini-stage outside M&S. Rev Vigland Hythe had just concluded a spell-binding set, which had the crowd in joyous rapture. All throughout, she had paced the stage like she owned it. Up until now, I had never really viewed the tambourine as an instrument, at least not in the same vain as I viewed a guitar, a piano, or an oboe. But today, she had made this asymmetrical collection of zills positively sing. Banging and shaking as she evangelised the Risen Lord, The Lamb of God, and The Prince of Peace, the crowd had swooned, swayed, and gasped, as their eyes followed her, trying to keep up with her frenetic pace. Mayfly had a very tough act to follow. If he was feeling this, it certainly wasn't showing.

It had been a struggle getting him back to where he was today. His lack of disbelief had taken a severe knock after his supposed apparition. For him to continue to even exist as Mayfly, it was essential that his disbelief was restored. He needed to be Mayfly, as returning to his life pre-Mayfly could prove fatal. I had felt compelled to do all I could in order to ensure that this never happened. I had gone around to his modest, compact, but bijou riverside flat, armed with books by Daniel Dennett, Sam Harris, Christopher Hitchens, and Richard Dawkins – the four horsemen of New Atheism. It was particularly irksome having to refer to Hitchens and his smug sneering self-righteousness. Dawkins, by comparison, seemed humble and understated. All throughout though, my uncertainty around the tenets of disbelief had remained largely intact.

With fists clenched and a beam to match the girth of Broad Street, he began.

"People! Friends! Be blessed!!

His whole demeanour seemed to have changed. He was now more Freddy Mercury than Jim Morrison. Enthusiastic screams emanated from this sizable and varied crowd. It seemed that I was far from alone in being highly buoyed to see him back where he needed to be, where he belonged. He continued…

"Whatever your beliefs in our origins and what has led to us being assembled here together, today, in fellowship, it doesn't matter. It isn't important. We are here. That's all that matters. Let's celebrate now, and let us celebrate each other right here! Remember this,

tomorrow isn't promised. So, live in the now. Sorry for the long delay in getting back here! Did you miss me?"

"Yessss!" came a warm, loud, collective response.

"Thank you! That's good to know. Really good to know. My confidence took a hit. My last gig was disjointed. After that I felt lost. But a very dear friend of mine came along and he told me that he believed in me. I was lost and he helped me find myself. I tell you, this man read some words to me uttered from a man he has no faith in. I could see his pain. I could feel his strain, yet he did this for me. Some of you standing here today will say that God heard my call, and that God brought this man to help me, to be my salvation. And you know what? That's OK. Others here will say that it happened for a reason, that fate brought us together. That's fine too. Others still will say that there ARE accidents and that this man happened to be in the wrong place at the right time, and that is fine also.

What I say here today is that different people standing here have views that will differ from the person standing next to them, and I tell you, that doesn't matter. Do you know what matters? Do you know what unites us here? I'll tell you, shall I?"

A loud, collective "Yes" rose up in response.

"We are all in this life together. We all feel. Yes. We all need. We all laugh. We all cry. We all love. We all die, and that's OK too. Some of you call it a life force.

Some of you call it a natural instinct. Others among you here will call it the workings of God, and all this is good. All this is real if it brings us all here together. All here today, and all here to help. So, I say this – help your fellow man in times of need. Laugh and cry and sing and dance and celebrate our time here. Celebrate the air in your lungs! Celebrate the majesty of our sun. Celebrate our lives. Celebrate the fine screeching wind, as its voice carries far and wide, around and through the trees, heralding the soon to come message of calm."

The assembled crowd were now in raptures of elation. The chants went up. "Mayfly! Mayfly! Mayfly!"

A clearly moved Mr. Mayfly stepped slowly to centre stage. His earlier exhilaration, it now appeared, had seemed to have drained his output. I suddenly felt helpless. I wanted to offer solace to this dear, damaged, vulnerable friend of mine. With his voice beginning to flounder, he continued.

"You know something people? I've been thinking a lot lately. I've been thinking a lot about a dear friend. A dear friend, who passed some time back. There isn't a minute in an hour, and an hour in a day, that I don't ache at this profound loss. I truly wish sometimes that I had the belief that many of you standing here, hold dear, that we once again will get to meet absent friends, even if it's just to tell them we love them dearly. To thank them for setting us apart. But you know what? My friend is still here. If I can feel Ben in my heart and in that strange unexplained energy that shoots through my being, then he is always close by. But why wait till then? Till we can feel them, but not see them? **Love! Love! And then love them again and never stop loving them! Never stop expressing your love for them while they are still standing here! Tell your friends that you have set them apart in the purest of forms. That you have ordained them as dear, precious, family members! People! Be grateful, be kind, and be blessed! Thank you!"**

And that was it. Mr Mayfly's comeback gig, concluded perfectly. I had been to see a great many varied live performances before. But never before had I witnessed such fine oratory delivered with such an electric charisma than I had today. This rated even higher than Tony Hadley's spell binding performance of "Gold" at Rewind, in which he conducted the audience like the supreme puppet master. This was even more engaging than Freddy Mercury at Wembley in 1986. If Mayfly had any doubts in his own ability to engage his brethren after witnessing our tambourine-wielding Rev Hythe, then he needn't have worried. The fly was back!

Chapter 57

"But why? I don't understand!" I exclaimed.

"Because I don't really believe that you want to Ali," replied Lynn. "Well for a start, it ain't even a real ring. It's plastic and it's from Argos."

"You're missing the point," I replied. "It's about the symbolism the ring represents."

"What? Plastic symbolism? If that's the tone you intend to set for our marriage, then it's not looking too great, is it? Look, don't get me wrong. I appreciate the gesture, I really do. But I don't think either of us are ready. But that don't mean that we won't be, one day."

"Really?!" I exclaimed. "So there is a chance then? That one day you might say yes?"

"There's every chance, Ali. I tell you what. Ask me this time next year, yeah?"

"I will," I replied smiling. "Definitely!"

It was a clear, fresh, crisp day as we relaxed on a bench looking out onto Mother Thames. A gentle breeze moved like fingers through the tufts of grass, parting all in its flow. A couple of moored skiffs nearby bobbed gently, caressing slightly the overhanging blades of grass. I had felt it appropriate to choose a place dear to me to propose the ultimate question, to my ultimate companion.

Curiously enough, I didn't feel disappointed. Her rejection hadn't seemed to dampen what was a glorious Saturday afternoon.

"Also," she continued, "if we do this one day, then I don't want any of that living separately bollox. It ain't right. It ain't natural. What? Married and living in separate gaffs? What's that all about?"

"But didn't you say that you love me, but will never want to live with me?"

"Yeah, but that was nearly five weeks ago, Ali. A lot can change in that time. Anyway, marriage is different."

"Well then, this is about giving our marriage the best possible chance of success. Think about it. I read recently that one in every three marriages in the UK ends in divorce. One in every three!"

"Are you sure? That does seem a bit high. Where did you read that? You don't read newspapers. You said that they're all full of propaganda."

"They are. It's true."

"So where did you read this FACT then?"

"I read it online. You always get the truth online. It was a link on a friend's Facebook profile. I couldn't believe it. One in three?!"

"Well, I don't believe it."

"Believe it. It's true. Now think about this. How many of those former couples do you reckon lived together, in percentage terms?"

"Ali, that's a crazy question."

"Indulge me".

"OK, then. Oh, I don't know, sixty percent? Seventy?"

"Keep going," I responded.

"What, higher than seventy?!"

"Yep, higher than seventy. Much higher."

"Oh, just tell me will you?" she replied impatiently.

"OK. I will. The actual figure is ninety-three percent. That just leaves seven percent who lived separately. What does that tell you my gorgeous, stunningly fit, former prostitute girlfriend?"

"Oh, I don't know," she laughed, "my posh Scottish former married person. What does it tell you?"

"Well, it tells me that if couples retain their singular living arrangements, then they're over twelve times more likely to stay married than if they cohabited."

"Interesting statistics there Ali, but my stance remains the same. If we do this one day, then we live together. No compromise. Agreed?"

I paused to consider. "Agreed, Lynn," I replied. "You know, I had built up today with so much hope, with so much expectation. Well, it was more hope than expectation. We haven't been together that long really, but we've both been on a journey together. I never want this journey to end. But I feel, but I feel... I can't really put it into words, but it's fine that you said no today."

"Well, you certainly know how to flatter a lady, don't you?!" she replied with a wry smile.

"Oh, you know, I didn't mean it like that, babe, I love you. You know this."

"I do babes," she replied, reassuringly. "When you approached me that night, all that while ago on the corner of Zinzan Street and the Ocki Road, I thought what's Kevin Keegan doing, walking along here looking for a piece of naughty skirt? But then you got closer, and you know what I saw?"

"Probably just another horny punter, no doubt."

"No. Well, yeah actually. Yeah, I did see that. But I saw something else too. I saw your eyes. I didn't just see them, but I looked straight into them, and I saw someone lost. I saw a lost soul. You had a kindness about you. You see, Ali, I'd had a shit night – a really bad shift. I'd been laughed at. I'd been spat at, and a group of birds had threatened to send me to the Royal Berks."

"Really?!" I exclaimed, angered and sad that anyone could even consider harming my Lynn – my beautiful, kind-hearted companion. *Why are some people such terrible cunts?* I wondered.

"For real," she replied, "and then, and then you came along a few minutes later. I was thinking of calling it a night after that lot threatened me like that. Yeah, and then you came along, looking lost, like a lost lust-fuelled Kevin Keegan!"

"Lost, lust-fuelled Kevin Keegan! You really do have such a wonderful way with words Lynn. What superb alliteration!" I replied, laughing.

"Aw fanks babes," she replied, in more familiar syntax. "Well, that night, I saw someone of a playful nature, yet incredibly shy. I wanted to take you off to my place and never let you leave."

"I think that's what's called kidnapping," I replied. "The law tends to take a dim view of such things. How would you have done it? Chloroform perhaps? I hear that's quite effective for such purposes," I replied mischievously.

"Oh, what are you like Ali? You see, that's what you were like that night, joking and laughing, but with a serious side too. Do you know Ali, I read somewhere, online too I think it was, that broken people often use humour to mask a pain deep inside."

I paused to consider such a profound analysis.

"Umm, I think it was a combination of both back then," I replied. "That playful side that you saw that night, is the real me, but I found myself overdoing the old comedy routine, to mask a deeply broken soul, if I'm entirely honest. I really don't know what it was."

"Your marriage ending won't have helped, babes," she replied with a warm tone, cupping my hands in hers.

"That could have played a part," I replied. "But I was over it at that point. I had practically processed it all. No, it was something else that I couldn't quite work out, but that's all gone now. I, I seemed to have reached, well, I know this is going to sound well weird, as a dear friend of mine might remark, but I feel **still** inside now. I've been getting close to reaching stillness for quite some time now, but now I feel as if I'm there."

That's great Ali," she replied. "I knew you'd get there one day. "I'm proud of you, really proud," she said, with her soul shining through red misty eyes. "I knew you'd get there. I just knew it."

"Oh, my love! My sweet Lynn. You really do mean the world to me," I replied smiling. I suddenly felt a jolt of energy shoot through me. "Oh, my goodness!" I exclaimed. "There it is again!"

"There's what again?" she replied, sounding concerned. "Babes don't do this. I'm worried now."

"Oh, my love, there's nothing to worry about. Trust me. This is beautiful."

"But what is beautiful? What is this?"

"I don't know what it is", I exclaimed. "But it's been happening a lot lately. I feel a sudden jolt of energy rush through me, and it's as if a light switch flicks, illuminating me. It's been happening a lot lately."

"Ah," she replied, "I think I know what this is. When this happens, do you feel as if a friend is close by, supporting you?"

"That's exactly how it feels. Wow! Just when I think that you can't surprise me with your insightful logic, boom, you do it again! That is exactly how I feel. In fact, I'm feeling it right now!"

"I'm really delighted for you, Ali. People wait in silence, and in hope, a lifetime, and never feel what you're experiencing right now. This is quality, real quality."

"How do you know this though? You're not a person of the sight. Actually, are you?"

"No, I'm not!" she replied with a chuckle. "But that bird that you met at the hospital, Layla is it?"

"Lola," I replied.

"Yes Lola. And the bloke, Steven?"

"It's Stueie."

"Sorry, Stueie. And then what about that kind couple you told me about in Guildford, that you met on that misty night? You was walking through town, head down, and lost. You said that they just appeared out of the mist. That they introduced themselves, smiled, and said all will be well, then just continued on."

"Ah yes, Diana and Peter. Well remembered. That moment was both profound and really beautiful, in equal measure."

"Well, I really believe, all of these people were sent to you. They probably don't know that they were. But trust me babes, they were. You see, people come into our lives for a reason. They come into our lives at a particular time, to help us on our journey. To help guide us to where we need to be. Just like all those months ago, on that cold lonely night, when I'd lost all hope. And look at me now!"

"You don't think I'm a person of the sight, do you?"

"Do me a favour Ali!" she replied, aghast.

"Cheers" I replied.

"Oh Ali, I didn't mean it like that. Few are chosen for that role. It isn't always easy. But it don't mean that you don't have great qualities, cos trust me, you do. You're way stronger than you think."

"Really?"

"Yeah, for real! If it weren't for you that day, then I'd probably still be knocking out hand jobs at the back of Reilly's for a tenner. But instead, I'm now Assistant Manager at the biggest Tesco in Reading. And all this because you told me that you believed in me. No one has ever believed in me. But it took you, a stranger, to come into my life, telling me that I was worth something. You should be proud of yourself, Ali, really proud. Now come on, I don't know about you, but I could do with some serious attention. I know that I've said no, but can we still go to that room in the Plaza?"

"I suppose," I replied sheepishly, "it is paid for after all. There's no point in wasting it."

"Is the correct answer!" she replied. "Now come on Kevin Keegan. You know what I want," she continued, "let's make the most of this plush, conveniently located nearby, 5-star riverside hotel."

"It's 4-star actually," I replied jokingly.

"4-star?!" she exclaimed. "Well, I hope when you pop the question this time next year, that you'll get us a proper 5-star. Cos I'm worth it! Or don't you think I am? Do you know the Forbury hotel?"

"You know I know it! And yes, you are worth it!!" I exclaimed enthusiastically."

"I'm only, playing with you!" she replied with a wink. "But you will ask me again though, won't you?"

"Of course I will. So on the 9th of May 2010, on this very bench, at this very time, I will look into those deep hazel, almond-shaped eyes of yours and ask you to be my more than significant other."

As we stood to walk in this soft spring breeze and on towards our pre-marital home for tonight, I wondered what series of not-so-random events had deigned that this flawed angel, walking with me, was even here at all. One thing was certain though, stillness had finally arrived…

Chapter 58

So, the day had come. The stage, or rather the marquee, was set. People of different hues, ages, statures and shape mingled and milled about. The date was Saturday, the 16th of May 2009. I could sense the warm presence of a friend close by.

Patience was sat over by the entrance, her silver head buried deep into a script, learning her lines. I had a feeling that these lines had a curious familiarity about them. She wasn't auditioning for her own part. This was for the benefit of the auditionees, so as not to lose their place. I pulled the folded A4 page from my satchel which contained the running order of today's events that Panda had prepared. I still couldn't believe that this was actually happening.

09:00: Caterers and bar staff to arrive to set up bar/kitchen

10:00: Fire eaters and jugglers to assemble outside the east porch to begin preparation

11:00: Forbury to set up on the smaller backstage towards the North Portico. Once set up, then to leave the stage promptly

14:00: Auditionees to take their seats in the cordoned-off VIP area close to the main stage

15:00: Patience Janis Johnson (Protagonist), Amanda Erskine (Royal Production Company), Mike Bowers (Channel 4), Alastair McLeish-Pidkin (Journalist) to take to the mini stage within the VIP area, and behind auditionees seats, to wait, then sit in judgement

18:00: Conclusion of auditions

18:00–19:30: Meet, greet, and mingle with auditionees, friends, and/or relatives

19:30: Forbury to do soundcheck, then straight into set. Set not to exceed 30 minutes. No encore unless in the unlikeliest of scenarios, the audience calls for one

20:00: Conclusion of proceedings. Then on to the Crowne Plaza for unnecessary extra-alcoholic beverages. Person or persons who find this elusive second wind that everyone keeps telling me about, to point me in its general direction!

Love Panda

The caterers were busy preparing their banquet. Our arranging of the hog roast had been ill-judged, given Patience's now strict interpretation of veganism. She said that she didn't care what other people put into their bodies, that it was their own business. But she didn't want her good name to be associated with the slaughter of a baby pig.

The plan to entertain the crowds with clowns too had to go. She said that she always thought clowns were daft and pointless, and their mere presence was enough to drive her mental. It was hard enough getting her to agree to the jugglers and fire eaters. She thought that the story itself should be more than enough to convey that part of her journey, without the need for tacky peripherals.

Forbury were over towards the top, setting up on the backstage. To Suzi's relief, there was to be no awkward reunion with her ex. They were now managed by a young music producer, steadily making a name for himself on the live events circuit. Rodney had them on a "no money no commission" deal. Apart from today's gig, he had yet to secure them a paid one. I had it on good authority from Karl the bass player, that all this was soon to change, due to his tireless work promoting them. If there was any justice in the world, he said, then it was only a matter of time before the name Forbury was known in places as far away as Ascot. I told him that I admired such ambition, and that there was never too high a bar to set in the pursuit of success.

The hog roast and clowns were losses that I was happy to bear, especially the hog roast. The more I thought about it, the idea of eating a baby pig wasn't just bizarre, but bordered on the macabre. The one thing though that

I did hope would be well-received, was a surprise that we had planned for Patience. At first, I wasn't entirely convinced of the merits of this idea put to me by Panda. Forty years is a long time to not be in someone's life that you were once an essential part of. How would she feel? How would she react? My suggestion was that if we were going to do this, then perhaps it would be best to canvass Patience's opinion on the matter, but Panda was convinced that the element of surprise would add greatly to the whole sense of occasion – a bit like "This Is Your Life" for circus performers.

With Channel 4's more than ample monetary resources, they had managed to track Mariana down. A few years after the split with Patience, she had returned to the small southern Italian village of her childhood and stayed there. There was no ill-feeling towards Patience, only a mild regret that lingered for a short time after they split. Her regret was that she hadn't left the circus and run off to Wales with Patience, which is what Patience had suggested at the time. Mariana too had dispensed with the beard, only she had done so immediately after quitting the circus. Judging from Patience's description of her during the interview, she hadn't appeared to succumb to the ravages of time – just like Patience. The source at Channel 4 had described her as tall, olive-skinned, and despite her actual age of 78, of the appearance of someone in their mid-fifties – just like Patience. Panda had texted me last night to tell me that Mariana's 18.50 flight from Naples had touched down safely at Heathrow. She was due here in the evening, with the auditions concluded, and Forbury about to take to the stage.

I began to reflect upon the series of not-so-random events that had brought me to where I now was today. I was especially mindful of that night. That long dark, turbulent night, a reliable Ford Sierra and a very patient friend. Standing alone on the Oxford Road the following morning, trying to process it all, it was inconceivable to imagine that I would prevail, never mind, play a part in an important event such as this. That lonely day by the river now seemed like a lifetime ago. Placing myself momentarily back then, and casting an eye upon events, it was if I was remembering an account of someone else's inner turmoil. I felt a strong empathy towards this broken person that I once was, yet I felt despair and resentment towards him too. Was it really that bad? Was there really no point in even trying to prevail? Was that deep gorge of despair that he was peering down into, really so endless? But I couldn't really sit in absolute judgement over him. He had prevailed and so too, had I.

I peered into my ever so stylish Hugo Boss timepiece. It was 12.30. As the auditions weren't due to begin for another few hours, I decided that a riverside walk would provide the perfect tonic to fuel today's events. I passed by Patience quietly, reluctant to disturb her strong focus.

OXFORD ROAD

Illuminated by a watery golden-sun, I stepped out into a fresh gentle energising breeze. Over to the top of the marquee, an angst-ridden scarlet waist-coated juggler was struggling with hand-to-eye coordination, as the three skittles he was trying to direct upwards seemed intent on disobeying him. I could feel both his pain and his justified displeasure, at such blatant dissent.

I continued on past the empty tennis courts. I wondered why they were empty. Usually, on a Saturday, a day of liberty, a rest-bite from servitude, they would be chock-full of future Wimbledon aces.

I looked across at the tent which for one night had housed both my despair and my shame. Fran and Kim had certainly turned it from a sheet of temporary housing into a welcoming homestead. The low wooden perimeter fence was adorned with multi-coloured flowers of different varieties. A couple of yellow waist-height wooden windmills by their mini porch swayed and rasped in the refreshing, gentle breeze. The acrid and sweet smell of burning foliage drifting up from the embers of a small, smouldering wigwam-shaped fire, further enhanced this picture of tranquillity. That they could turn what had started out life as a gilded death chamber, into a cosy symbol of life, was both ironic and very heartening. Still, they were welcome to it – every last stitch. I had a different tent now. A far bigger tent. A tent that contained optimism and hope.

Turning away from past failings, I continued on in the direction of Caversham Bridge. I couldn't really complain. It would be the ultimate disrespect to the supreme architect. The sweet chimes of birdsong hung in the air, as stillness continued to fortify me. No harm could possibly come to me again. And no dark shadows could dim this newly found inner light.

I crossed up on to Caversham Bridge and down by the Crowne Plaza. As I passed by the tea boat, to both my ultimate surprise and joy, that kind couple on that otherwise dark day were there. I wondered if they were still as it appeared that day, ultimately and supremely, the most important people to each other. I wondered if they still set each other apart from even the purest and most beautiful treasures available to humanity. Judging by the way they held each other in such a gentle passionate gaze, it was clear that they did.

I nodded gently, as I ambled on past the boathouse. Across the river, three men in a boat far too small to house them and a dog trudged laboriously along. Two of them wheezed and heaved under the instruction of the steering-less coxswain.

I could almost hear the oars groan, as the two boater-jacketed burly men turned and dragged, as this overloaded vessel defiantly crawled along this most majestic of watercourses. With great enthusiasm, I gestured to them, urging them onwards.

"Chin chin, old bean!" exclaimed the director of proceedings, also adorned in a stylish boater. "Best of British what what!?"

"Indeed!" I responded. "Best of British to you all! Not forgetting the dog! What's his name?"

"Monty," he replied, as the dog seemed to give an affirming yelp. "He's a fox terrier, don't you know?"

"Well, best wishes to you all then, including old Monty!"

Invigorated from this lively, surreal encounter, I continued on, and there it was, over by a small grove of trees, my tree seat. Nature had indeed crafted the perfect throne. I meandered slowly over towards it. The timing couldn't have been better. Wearily and laboriously, I dragged my feet in its general direction and sat. I leant forward, resting my head in my hands.

"Well, you've certainly earned your rest mate. You've been going non-stop. Slow down chap!" came a more than familiar voice.

I un-cupped my hands and looked up, and there he was, the intrepid voyager Dave!

"Mate!" I exclaimed. "Where have you been man? I've missed you! Great to see you!"

"Great to see you too fella. Well you know…"

"I know, you've been off in places, seeing some faces."

"Well yeah, there is that. But I've got some news that I think you'll be happy to hear".

"Go on my friend," I replied. "You have my undivided attention Sir."

"Undivided attention Sir," he replied jokingly. "You tart! What are you like eh?"

"I'm not sure I know, Dave. You will let me know if you ever find out though, won't you?"

"No need, chap. I think we both know! Anyway, tell me, have you seen much of Jeremy lately?"

"Actually, no, I haven't. In fact, it's been nearly a couple of months, almost as long as it's been since I've seen you. What an amazing coincidence that is!"

"It's no coincidence, mate. You remember when we first met, right here at this very spot? Remember what we talked about?"

"Yes!" I replied. "I seem to remember wondering, who does this chap think he is? Coming up to me and invading my space? But then you introduced yourself and explained who you were, and why you were here. As soon as I knew this, I warmed to you."

"Ah, mate, stop!" he replied. "You'll set me off."

"Sorry Dave."

"It's alright geeze. It's alright. Anyway, so you remember what I said I was here to do?"

"Yeah, you said that you were here to kill Jeremy."

"Correct! That I was here to kill Jeremy. And guess what?"

"No!" I exclaimed. "Are you telling me that you've done it? That you've killed Jeremy?"

With his arms folded, he nodded. "In one! That's exactly what I'm telling you. I've done the deed mate. I've killed him. I have killed Jeremy."

"Wow! You've actually done it! That's amazing! So, erm, how did you do it? Actually, don't tell me. I don't need to know."

"Trust me, mate. You don't. You should have heard him, slagging you off, he was. Pudkin this, Pudkin that. Loser this. Loser that. He weren't that sad character that I first met. No, he looked exactly as you described him – yellow teeth, torn long pin-striped jacket. And fuck did he pen?"

"Pen?"

"Oh, wake up Ali! Pen and ink, stink? It's cockney rhyming slang. I've already told you this before. What are you like eh?!"

"Oh, I must have forgotten then ," I replied smugly. "Besides slang was discouraged around the dinner table when I was growing up!"

"Really?" he exclaimed.

"Your face," I replied jokingly. "I had you there."

"No, you didn't," he replied. "Anyway, I don't care as it goes."

"Actually, Dave. You do care. But it's fine. Listen, sorry man. Please continue. So, what happened when you met again?"

"Well," he replied, sounding rather confused. "I killed him."

"No. I mean in the run up to killing him."

"Oh yeah, well, he's giving it all large, asking me if I want some. And I'm going, listen mate, you don't need to make this any harder than it needs to be. Then he's going, well, I'd like to see you try, then I'm going, look mate you know it's going to 'appen one way or another. So why not make this easy for both of us. I'm meeting up with the guys down the pub. It's Champions League night. I haven't been home for a shower yet. Of course, he don't know that my sort don't need to shower, but I say it anyways. It just adds to the overall feel. Know what I mean?"

"Yes," I replied, "I believe I do actually."

"Good. Well, he's going, I'm going to stay and fight, you don't scare me, come on then!"

"So I did. And I ain't gonna lie mate. It was messy but it was quick."

"So, he felt no pain then?"

"Oh yeah, he did feel pain. I've never heard a man scream like that before, wailing like a proper banshee he was. But it was over in seconds."

"When did this all happen?"

"It was six weeks ago Friday."

"Well", I gasped, "that would have been around the last time I felt his presence."

"Well, that would add up, wouldn't it?"

"That would exactly add up. That is amazing. So he's not coming back then?"

"Well, seeing as though I've killed him, I would be inclined to say no. He won't be. You won't be seeing him again. That's for sure. And it is this my friend, which brings me to the tricky bit."

"What tricky bit? Don't do this to me, Dave. You know I don't like surprises."

"Well, put it this way. Where there's a beginning, there's an end. Nothing lasts for ever."

"I get this, Dave. I understand all of that. But what's that got to do with here? With now?"

"Mate," he replied, "you're more like Jeremy than you think."

"I'm nothing like Jeremy," I replied angrily. "How can you say that?"

"I don't mean it in that way, I'm sorry, chap. You're a decent bloke as it goes."

"Thanks mate."

"You're welcome chap. What I mean is that, like Jeremy, you don't believe in making things easy for yourself, do you?"

"Actually Dave, you're spot on. I don't. I wish I did. But again, what's all this got to do with today? With us being here? In this place?"

"It's got a lot as it goes. Remember what I said that I was going to do when I killed Jeremy? And you seemed happy with the arrangement at the time."

And suddenly I did remember. It was all becoming very clear. Right now, looking at him, gently stripping away my mask of denial, I felt enveloped with a profound sense of loss. Of course I knew why he had shown up, on this day, at this time, here by this seat. This was where we had first met, and it was now where we would be parting. It seemed appropriate. Dave was classy like that. He had come to say goodbye. I was trying to hold it all in. To try and fight back what I knew was likely to be far more than a trickle, and then I remembered something Dave had asked me to promise him. He had put this request higher than he had ever put anything to me. Yes, he didn't approve of the drugs. Yes, he said that I needed to show Lynn the respect that both us knew she deserves. Yes, he didn't approve of my tendency to pronounce finite judgement upon others. But the one thing that he made me promise him was to always be true to myself. I couldn't let him down. Not now. Especially given that this was most likely the last time that we would ever meet.

I had to allow myself to yield to my emotions. I owed him this at least. Didn't I? Who was I now of all times, to try to adopt a dignified stance? I had done well enough without it so far. So why change now? Especially now? Making no attempt whatsoever to conceal my loss, I threw any remaining dignity to the ground and pleaded with him.

"Can you not just stay around, chap? I'm not ready to see you walk away forever."

"But mate. I can't. You knew the deal from day one. I kill Jeremy and I leave."

"Well, fuck the deal then, Dave. I never signed anything."

"Ali mate, that's a bit strong. Get a grip. Please. You're better than this. Anyway, even if I wanted to stay, it's not down to me."

"Sorry Dave. It's just that my life has changed for the best since you showed up."

"It's very nice of you to say, Ali, but now that Jeremy's gone, it's impossible for me to stay."

"Well, oh I don't know, can't you just go back on the decision to kill him? Because although I hate him and he troubles me greatly, I'd rather have him around, if it meant that you were around too."

"I can't un-kill Jeremy. How do you suggest that I do that?"

"Oh, I don't know. Can you not travel back in time or something?"

"What?"

"You know, back in time just before you killed him, but not actually kill him. Warm him or something."

"I tried that. It didn't work. Remember? He had to die. There was no other way."

"But what if I don't want you to go?"

"Mate, that decision ain't down to us. That is decided by a power far higher than us two."

"But that's not true. You quite clearly told me that day, the day we met, that you were a figment of my imagination."

"Mate," he sighed, "I told you what I felt that you needed to hear at the time."

"So, you're not a figment of my imagination then?"

"Perhaps yes. Perhaps no. Sorry. I can't be any clearer. It's against the rules. Just trust me, yeah? Have I ever let you down?"

"Oh, don't be sorry. You don't make the rules. I know that. Can you at least tell me if Dave is even your real name?"

"Do you think Dave is my real name?"

"Well," I replied, "yeah, I do. I mean, I don't know you as anyone else. So yes, I believe that Dave is your real name."

"Then, as far as you are concerned my friend, I am Dave. You see, I go by different names to different faces in different places."

"So when you were looking at those different colourful and stylish timepieces, saying, you know, places to be, faces to see, you were going off to aid others in similar predicaments to my own?"

"Very nicely put. Yeah. That's what I was doing. You see, there's a lot of broken people out there."

"And Mayfly? Did he see you too?"

"Well, Mayfly's a funny one as it goes. He thinks he knows it all, that he's convinced about what he calls his disbelief."

"Well, not anymore!" I laughed. "That's well and truly broken now! Well, at least it was, back then."

"I know," he replied, "I was watching his sermon that day shortly after in Broad Street, wondering if I'd done the right thing."

"Well, he isn't so bad now. He's back sounding just like Mayfly again. He's dropped the whole Dawkins thing which isn't a bad thing actually. He just focuses now on the human aspect. He's still not convinced in belief though. I would say that he's once again firmly of the belief in disbelief. I would say it's about sixty–forty in favour of disbelief or, at a stretch, possibly sixty-five-thirty-five. He needs this. He needs to be Mayfly. He can't go back to being Giles Kingston. It would be too much."

"Well, I'll make sure that that never happens, Ali. He'll find out anyway, one day. You all will. Listen," he continued, his voice breaking, "it's that time again, you know…"

"I know," I replied. "Places to be, faces to see, but before you go, Dave, can I ask you something?"

"Anything mate," he replied smiling, "anything for you, treacle!"

"I really enjoyed your football anecdotes. You really know how to put someone in the picture. The one you told me of Wilkins and Chelsea I particularly enjoyed. I could imagine myself standing right there amongst the faithful in Elm Park, shouting Reading on. On the subject of football and Reading football in particular, Mayfly mentioned that he had seen the ghost of a Reading football legend, so famous in fact, that people couldn't even say his real name, instead they called him The Geezer. That wouldn't be you by any chance would it? The Geezer?"

He paused as if trying to formulate an appropriate response. "Well," he replied with a wry smile. "Like I said, I am many different things to many different people. If in some folks eyes I was a legendary, gifted, rock star footballer, with film star looks who never got to play on the big stage and who expired well before his natural, then who am I to disagree?!"

This was the perfect response. It was cheeky, yet charming, which absolutely summed up the essence of this man. Whatever his name to others, he would always be Dave to me. It was becoming increasingly difficult now to stop my emotions from breaching my stubborn defences of pride. I was just about holding on.

C'mon chap. You don't have long now. Hold it together, man. You must. This could well end up being the last time that you'll ever see this legend. You can't let him remember you like this. You can't go out like this.

Suddenly I felt still again. It was as if someone close by - a friend perhaps - was telling me to place my trust in whoever this person or force was, and to believe that although a profoundly sad moment was at play here, all will be well.

He checked his watch and stepped forward. "Mate, it is that time. I'm really sorry, but I've already delayed it, and she needs me. She's not in a good way, you see." He extended his arm. It was luminous and without a definable physical form. I appreciated the gesture.

"Listen," he said, "promise me one thing, yeah?"

"Anything," I replied, "name it."

"Never give up again! Yeah? Never! Look how far you've come fella. Look what you've achieved. It's mental! Sorry, I shouldn't say mental. But you know what I mean. You were on your knees, then you stood up, and you stayed up. And you know what? You'll always be standing. I don't think you'll ever know the positive vibes that you've brought into people's lives. Mayfly can say what he wants, but you know what Ali? There's no such thing as chance. People pop up in the lives of others because it's been planned in advance. OK, it don't always work out for the best, but that's just the way it is sometimes, and now here we are. I've done what I said I was going do. I've killed Jeremy. And you? You're off to a much better and more powerful tent than the one you first pitched up, back at Reading Bridge. And you've got a watch – finally!

So, yeah, it's sad to be going away from ya, but also, today is a big celebration. You've done it mate. You have prevailed. Right, I really do 'ave to piss off. This one thinks she's no use to anyone. If I'm any later, then God knows what she'll do. These low self-esteem cases really are tricky. At least that's not something that I could ever accuse you of! Anyway, you know by now…"

"I know Dave, faces, places. But can I just ask you one final question?"

"Oh, go on then. Fuck sake! What are you like?!"

"You once said "never" about seeing each other again once you've left. Is it really that final? Is that it now? I'll never see you again?"

"I didn't mean to say "never". Yeah, sorry 'bout that. It just kinda slipped out. Never is a long time. Who knows? But the thing is, Ali, I only appear to them who need me. So if I do pop up again unannounced, it'll mean that you're unwell again. Is that what you want? Cos that's what'll 'appen! Ali, it's been emotional. I'll miss you. But I really need to piss off now. Be lucky, son!"

"I know Dave. It's been emotional indeed. Thank you so much for everything. I mean that. I'll miss you too chap. Take care."

I shut my eyes and began counting down from 10…10, 9, 8, 7 … I opened them, and that was it. As seamlessly as he had entered and brought a great sense of charm into my life, he was gone.

OXFORD ROAD

As I turned back in the direction of my new more powerful tent, I wondered if I would see Dave again, one day. I really hoped that I would. After all, everybody needs a Dave. Don't we? I know I do. That's for sure.

FIN

Printed in Great Britain
by Amazon